STAR TREK®
STRANGE NEW WORLDS
VII

STAR TREK®
STRANGE NEW WORLDS
VII

Edited by
Dean Wesley Smith
with John J. Ordover, Elisa J. Kassin,
and Paula M. Block

Based upon
Star Trek® and *Star Trek: The Next Generation®*
created by Gene Roddenberry,
Star Trek: Deep Space Nine® created by
Rick Berman & Michael Piller
Star Trek: Voyager® created by
Rick Berman, Michael Piller & Jeri Taylor, and
Star Trek: Enterprise® created by
Rick Berman & Brannon Braga

POCKET BOOKS
New York   London   Toronto   Sydney

POCKET BOOKS, a division of Simon & Schuster, Inc.
1230 Avenue of the Americas, New York, NY 10020

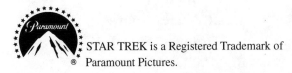

STAR TREK is a Registered Trademark of
® Paramount Pictures.

This book is published by Pocket Books, a division of
Simon & Schuster Inc., under exclusive license from
Paramount Pictures.

ISBN: 978-0-7434-8780-1

First Pocket Books trade paperback edition June 2004

10 9 8 7 6 5 4 3 2 1

POCKET and colophon are registered trademarks of
Simon & Schuster, Inc.

Manufactured in the United States of America

For information regarding special discounts for bulk purchases,
please contact Simon & Schuster Special Sales at 1-800-456-6798
or business@simonandschuster.com.

Contents

STAR TREK®

STAR TREK
THE NEXT GENERATION®

Contents

Contents

— STAR TREK —
ENTERPRISE

❰
SPECULATIONS

Introduction

Dean Wesley Smith

Every year for the past seven years I have looked forward to October and reading *Star Trek*® short stories by the very talented, very smart fans of the shows. I have often said that as a *Star Trek* fan, I have the best job in the world, and the hardest. And again this year, that proved to be true. I had to pick just twenty-three stories out of the boxes and boxes of wonderful stories that poured into the contest. The wonderful part was reading them all, the hard part was picking just twenty-three.

But now this book of stories is in your hands, and I need help from all you *Star Trek* fans out there. I need you to write one or two or three or more *Star Trek* short stories, following the rules in the back of this book, and send them in by October 1, 2004. Why am I putting out a call for even more stories than I normally get? Simple. Many of the fans who have been sending me stories and trying to get into this contest for the last six or seven years have sold too many stories. This contest, by its rules, has a limit of only three professionally published short stories by the deadline of the contest. That's why you might see the same name two or three years running, or scattered over the years, and then that author is disqualified from sending in any more. As you might have noticed, many of them are still writing *Star Trek,* only over in the novels. Authors like Ilsa Bick, Dayton Ward, Christina York, and others. They started here and then eliminated themselves with too many sales, leaving room for new writers to join the fun.

On a few *Star Trek* boards in different locations, people have pointed out to me this year that a very large number of the writers I have bought once or twice can no longer be in the book again. And this includes this year's Grand Prize winner, Julie Hyzy, who has been sending in stories regularly for five or six years now. She and many others have "graduated," as they say on the boards.

And as an editor, that scares me, which is why I need all of your help. Come on, haven't you been watching an episode, seen a detail, and thought, "Wow, that would make a wonderful story?" Well, I need you to write that story this next year and send it in. I give every story the exact same chance at being in the book, and if you write a great story, it will make it in.

What kind of stories am I looking for? My best suggestion on that question, which I get a lot, is to read this volume, and then go find copies of the previous volumes of this anthology. Not only will you have a wonderful reading experience, but by the time you are done reading all seven of the books, you will have a very good sense of the stories that have made it into *Strange New Worlds* over the years.

So pass the word. Tell other *Star Trek* fans that the cutting edge of the *Star Trek* world is right here, in the short stories in these volumes, stories written by fans like you. Tell your friends, tell the other members of your starship crews, maybe challenge other writers in your writers' group, then sit down and write a story or two and send them in. You'll discover that the writing is a lot of fun, and if one of your stories makes it into the book, you'll have added to the *Star Trek* universe and be a *Star Trek* author. And trust me, the only thing more fun than reading *Star Trek* is being a *Star Trek* author.

This is your chance. Enjoy the reading, then get to the writing.

A Test of Character

Kevin Lauderdale

The Klingons were gaining on him.

"A little faster," Kirk said through clenched teeth, as if saying it could make it so. He leaned forward in the bridge's command chair. "Just a little faster . . ."

"Still closing, sir," said Gaton at the helm.

Kirk punched a button on his chair's right arm. "Engineering, I need everything we've got for speed! Redirect it all! Life support too!" He took his finger off the button, breaking the connection. "Everybody hold your breath," Kirk muttered.

"They're firing again!" reported Gaton.

The ship shook from blast impact. There were sparks and flashes of fire all around the bridge. People flew from their chairs. Someone called through the sounds of the emergency klaxons that the energizers had been hit, and someone else yelled that the remaining shields were failing.

3

Smoke began to fill the bridge. There were already bodies on the floor.

Then a voice from the ceiling called out, *"It's all over. Let's have the lights."*

The viewscreen in front of Kirk rose, revealing the lanky, white-haired Admiral Jublik stepping up and into the training module.

"Damn," said Kirk. His ship had been destroyed. The *Kobayashi Maru* scenario had beaten him. Again.

Kirk felt no guilt as he pulled the computer disc out of his pocket. No bigger than his palm and colored a bright green, it brought a smile to his face. Just yesterday, in his History of Technology course, he had seen a video of twentieth-century Earth scientists using discs that looked exactly like this. The packaging hadn't changed over the centuries, but the amount of information that could be stored sure had.

Kirk stood in a darkened side hallway, facing the back of a computer. Except for one slot and a keypad, it was just a wall of cold black and gray metal. He didn't bother to look around. He knew there wouldn't be anybody else in the building at this time of the morning. 0200 hours was the middle of lights-out for the Academy's cadets, and even the most dedicated of the instructors were getting some well-deserved shut-eye.

It bothered Kirk a little that he wasn't supposed to be in the training building at this time of the morning, but only because he wasn't supposed to be anywhere but bed at this time of the morning. It didn't bother him at all though, that, making his way to the computer, his palm light had illuminated a sign reading USE OF THIS FACILITY WITH AUTHORIZED SUPERVISION ONLY. As far as Kirk was concerned, he wasn't using it. He wasn't operating any of the machinery of the simulation. He was just inserting a computer disc and pressing a few buttons. There were no passwords on the software loader. There weren't even any physical locks.

Kirk's disc held the complete *Kobayashi Maru* scenario: the Neutral Zone, the freighter, and the Klingons. Until two hours ago, it had also contained the keys to inevitable failure. If you stayed and fought, the Klingons got you. And if you tried to run, the Klingons got you.

It had taken every free minute of Kirk's time for nearly two months, but he had managed first to obtain a copy of the computer program that ran the simulation and then to hunt down and remove all the "optimization protocols"—the sections of code that made sure you would fail, no matter what.

Just that night Kirk had found the last one: a particularly nasty booby trap that saw to it that if you somehow managed to evade the three Klingon ships you faced, another group of three would arrive from the opposite direction to box you in. You could not escape.

Kirk frowned. His second time taking the test, he had been sure that a flat-out retreat once you lost the *Kobayashi Maru*'s signal was the right answer. The first time, he had stayed and searched after losing the freighter's signal—and his ship had been destroyed.

Both times, he had done what he was supposed to do. When you got a distress signal, you went to render help. After all, Section 10 was only a little way into the Klingon Neutral Zone.

But Kirk had wondered if it was a trap. Within the universe of the simulation, there really was a *Kobayashi Maru*; she was in his ship's database. Still, the Klingons could have faked the distress call. So, on his second attempt, he had gone after the crippled ship prepared to leave at a split-second's notice.

When the freighter's signal disappeared and the Klingons arrived, Kirk had stuck to his plan. He had felt bad abandoning the rescue mission, but he knew he would have felt worse had he simply tried the same tactics as in his first attempt.

Kirk remained convinced that if you could survive long enough, and were clever enough, there was a freighter out there waiting to be saved—along with three hundred eighty-one people.

Those people were what had first started Kirk thinking that the test was unfair. In the real world, no neutronic fuel carrier would have three hundred passengers aboard. Eighty-one crew members was outrageous enough, but passengers! Ancient oil tankers hadn't carried casual passengers. Available space concerns aside, the things just weren't configured for them. It didn't make sense. The whole idea of a no-win scenario didn't make sense to Kirk. It wasn't just that he didn't like to lose—Finnegan had taught him the hard way that no matter how fast or clever you were, you sometimes lost—it was that Kirk didn't like to lose unnecessarily. The *Kobayashi Maru* simulation was not a true test of his command abilities because no matter what he did, the computer would arrange things so that he lost. The program was not only unfair, it was inaccurate. Besides, it wasn't as if he had programmed stress fractures into the Klingons' hulls or anything. Kirk had not added one line of code to the program. He had merely removed those things that unbalanced the equation.

Everyone said that it didn't matter which path you chose, it was how you walked it that mattered. The *Kobayashi Maru* was a lesson. It was supposed to teach you that commanding officers were not gods: try as they might, they couldn't always get out of tough jams. The scenario was also a way, without racking up actual casualties, to instill the lesson that people did, and would, die under your command.

And, of course, it was a test of character. In the end, which was more important to you: trying to save the freighter's crew or trying to save your own? And how well did you deal with your failure when you chose the wrong path? Never mind that there was no right path.

Kirk turned the disc over in his hands. It was amazing what you could learn if you spent enough time in a library. His research had indicated that this unmarked software slot was the key to the whole operation. He inserted his disc.

There was no such thing as a no-win scenario for Kirk. Every time you rolled the dice, somebody won and somebody lost—unless you were using loaded dice. As far as Kirk was concerned, the Academy was using loaded dice, and it was his job to unload them.

Admiral Zheng, who ran the simulation scenarios along with Admiral Jublik, had called Kirk a glutton for punishment when the cadet had asked if he could take the *Kobayashi Maru* a third time. But they didn't have any reason not to allow it.

Kirk typed in the loading sequence, waited a moment, retrieved his disc, and then crept back to bed.

"Captain's log. *U.S.S. Horizon* on a training mission to Gamma Hydra, Section Fourteen," reported Kirk for the bridge's recorder. "So far—"

Mordock, assigned to the communications station, interrupted. "Something coming in on the distress channel, Captain."

"Let's hear it," said Kirk, leaning forward in the command chair.

A voice crackled over the speakers. "*. . . imperative. This is the* Kobayashi Maru, *nineteen days out of Altair Six. We have struck a gravitic mine and have lost all power. Our hull is penetrated, and we have sustained many casualties. . . . Gamma Hydra, Section Ten.*"

"That's in the Neutral Zone," said Gaton.

"Let me see that ship's registry," said Kirk. He was going to play it by the book, even though this was the third time, and he knew what he would see. The details came up on the viewscreen. Just like the previous two times, the *Kobayashi* was a neutronic fuel carrier with a crew of eighty-one and three hundred passengers. Her captain was still named Kojiro Vance.

Kirk smiled. The opening never varied. Why should it? As a no-win scenario, there was no advantage to be gained by someone's taking it even a hundred times, though very few cadets had ever bothered to tackle it even twice.

Kirk ordered an intercept course and saw Gaton's fingers go to work. Kirk wondered if the helmsman was rolling his eyes. Gaton knew what going into the Neutral Zone would lead to, but he was a professional, the former helmsman of the *Oberon*. *Never let it be said that I don't do my homework,* Kirk thought.

Kirk soon heard the clunky, artificial voice of the computer—a male voice, heard only in training simulations—warn that they had entered the Neutral Zone. Also by the book, Kirk's first officer, an

Alpha Centauran named Malcolm Sloane, informed him that they had now committed a treaty violation. Kirk bit his lips so that the "Yeah, yeah" didn't escape.

"How's the freighter's signal?" asked Kirk.

"No new communications," replied Mordock, "but still there."

Very good. The *Kobayashi* hadn't spontaneously dropped her signal, as she had twice before.

"Give me maximum magnification. I want to *see* that ship."

"Coming up now, sir," said Mordock, and the freighter appeared, a tiny point at the center of the screen.

"Good." Kirk hit a button on his command chair. "Engineering, we're going to need extra power for the tractor—"

The computer piped up again. "Alert! Sensors indicate three Klingon cruisers bearing three-one-six mark four. Closing fast."

Gaton brought them up on the viewscreen. Three huge, gray-blue D7s in attack formation were bearing down on the *Horizon,* forming a wall between Kirk and the freighter.

"Let's see if this works," muttered Kirk. Then confidently, "Shields! And open hailing frequencies."

"They're jamming all frequencies, Captain," said Mordock.

On the viewer, the lead ship's nose lit up an angry red as she fired at them. Almost instantly, Kirk's ship shook as the Klingon torpedoes did their damage. But, unlike the last time, the entire ship was not in chaos. There were some damage reports, but only what would usually be expected. Kirk smiled. His reprogramming was working. He was getting a real-world battle.

"Status?" Kirk asked.

Sloane checked a display. "The transfer conduits are out," he said, his voice barely masking his surprise, "but not much else."

Kirk frowned. His ship's warp engines were still functional, but without the conduits they couldn't get the power out and actually achieve warp. At least the floor wasn't strewn with bodies.

"How long to repair them?" Kirk asked.

"About five minutes," said Sloane.

"We don't have five minutes. Return fire!" Kirk saw his ship's phasers do some real damage to the starboard Klingon. "Is the *Kobayashi* still there?"

"Aye, sir," replied Gaton.

"Switch to long-range scan. Any other ships besides us five?"

"No, sir."

"The Klingons are closing," reported Gaton.

"Give me *one*-one-six mark four," said Kirk. The *Horizon* rotated in place, turning her back on the Klingons. Then she shook with another hit. "How's the freighter?"

"Still there, Captain."

"Keep the Klingons right on target: us, not the *Kobayashi*."

Kirk's ship shook again. "Sure . . ." Kirk muttered, "*they* can move. *They* can . . ." An idea formed in Kirk's mind. "Prepare for warp, Mister Gaton!"

"Um, we can't get to warp yet, Captain. The trans—"

"Do it anyway. On my signal," said Kirk. "With a course drop to one-one-six mark *three*." He saw Gaton nod and punch a few buttons.

Would it work? Kirk stared at the viewscreen. He had gotten what he wanted: no loaded dice. Now would his skills and those of his crew be enough? The timing would have to be exact.

"The Klingons are closing," said Sloane. "Their warp engines are coming online."

Kirk leaned forward. They hadn't fired again. Of course not. Real Klingons wouldn't. They hoped to take Kirk's ship as a prize and didn't want it too badly damaged. But they *were* jamming all communications. Obviously, they didn't want to answer questions like, "What are you doing in the Neutral Zone yourselves?"

"Now!" cried Kirk.

Instantly, the Klingons jumped to warp, leaving the two Federation ships quite alone.

Kirk smiled. Just as the Klingons had left to chase the *Horizon,* Kirk's ship had moved forward a mere kilometer and dropped one degree "down" from the plane she had been traveling: from mark four to mark three. The result was that the Klingons had shot out of the area, just "over" Kirk's head.

"Get us to the *Kobayashi*," said Kirk.

Kirk knew what the Klingons had seen. Their sensors had indicated the *Horizon*'s engines priming for warp, then being engaged, then . . . Then *they* had jumped to warp in order to follow Kirk. But they had not known that the *Horizon* couldn't actually achieve warp. Kirk had moved his ship a kilometer out of the way in order to avoid being rammed by the Klingons, and that was it. The Klingons couldn't be defeated or outrun, so Kirk had let them remove themselves from the equation.

Kirk had turned a disadvantage into an advantage. That was exactly the sort of action the original computer program would not have allowed.

"How long before the Klingons realize their mistake and can make it back here?" Kirk asked.

"At least four minutes, sir," said Gaton, turning toward Kirk with a smile. "Plenty of time."

Kirk nodded. The *Kobayashi Maru* was growing in size on the viewscreen. It wouldn't take anywhere near that long to get the freighter back on the Federation side of the Neutral Zone.

"Just one more minute until the transfer conduits are repaired," reported Sloane.

"Take us to the *Kobayashi* and lock on the tractor beams," Kirk said.

"Locking on, Captain," said Gaton.

Just a few seconds, thought Kirk. *That's all a good captain needs in the real world.*

"Take us back to Section Fourteen, best possible speed," Kirk said.

On the viewscreen, the stars grew to long lines.

He had done it. James Kirk had rescued the *Kobayashi Maru*. He had beaten the unbeatable scenario.

"Damn!" boomed Admiral Jublik's voice from the ceiling. *"The thing's finally broken itself. I knew we shouldn't run it this often."*

As the viewscreen rose, the bridge was flooded with light.

Admiral Zheng, a decade younger than Jublik but no less

commanding a figure, strode over to a control board. "Must be data degradation," he said. "I thought we'd solved that."

"Uh, sir," said Kirk, stepping up to where the admiral stood.

"Yes, Mister Kirk?" The admiral's raised eyebrows clearly indicated that he did not appreciate anyone interrupting his diagnostic process.

"It's not the computer's fault."

"What do you mean?"

"If I could speak to you in private . . ."

"*Damn straight!*" came Jublik's voice from the ceiling. "*Mister Kirk, I want you in my office now!*"

Not having been given permission to sit, Kirk stood in Jublik's office at parade rest, his hands behind his back. The admiral himself was seated behind an impressive oak desk, a view of San Francisco Bay visible through the giant pane of transparent aluminum behind him. Zheng sat in an overstuffed wing chair just to Jublik's left. He was sipping something that smelled lemony.

"I did it," said Kirk. "I reprogrammed the computer so that it was possible to win."

Zheng grunted.

Jublik's face turned red with anger. "You programmed the computer so that the Klingons would abandon our ships?!"

"No, sir!" said Kirk hastily. "I merely disabled all the optimizers that made sure that the Klingons' disruptors and torpedoes always hit me—and did maximum damage—no matter how far away I was. Or that the enemy always outmatched me for speed. I had no idea exactly what would happen. All I did was make things realist—"

Zheng held up his hand. "I've heard enough."

"But I won!" protested Kirk.

"The *Kobayashi Maru* isn't about winning, Mister Kirk. It's . . . well, yes, a test of character. As much of a cliché as that is."

Kirk smiled. "Well, Admiral, that's my character. I don't like to lose. And I won't, if I'm allowed to try everything I can think of to win."

Jublik said, "Obviously it hasn't occurred to you that you didn't 'win.' It's *supposed* to be a no-win scenario."

"But there's no such thing as a no-win scenario . . . sir."

"In the real world there is," said Zheng.

"No, sir, there isn't."

"I beg your pardon, *Mister* Kirk."

"In the real world, we aren't held back by a computer program shifting things to make sure that we don't win. The way the scenario worked, even if I had squeezed everything out of the engines, it wouldn't have been enough to get us out of the Neutral Zone ahead of the Klingons. But in reality, it might have."

Kirk pointed skyward. "Out there, you do everything you can think of"—he turned to Jublik—"including cheat—to win. No starship captain would ever say, 'Guess this is a no-win scenario. Guess I'll . . . I don't know . . . blow up my ship in the hope of taking a few bad guys with me.' Did Captain Garth, when he faced Samhain? No. You try everything. You negotiate. And if that fails, you lie. You trade. And if that doesn't work, you steal. You might hate yourself, but your ship and your crew make it out in one piece. That *is* what we're taught: that you don't let anything get in the way of protecting them."

"Not even the Prime Directive?" asked Jublik.

Kirk forced himself not to smirk. "Fortunately, the Prime Directive is not an element of the scenario."

"Fortunately for all concerned," said Zheng, one eyebrow rising.

Kirk smiled.

"No smiles, Kirk!" yelled Jublik.

Kirk's smile disappeared.

"Hmmm," said Jublik. After Zheng nodded in apparent agreement, Jublik pointed to the other end of his office. Kirk knew what was expected of him. He silently walked over to the flag stand and pretended to study the weave of the blue United Federation of Planets banner.

Out of the corner of an eye, Kirk watched the two admirals huddle together and talk in whispers. That wasn't good. If they were going to take a slow, thoughtful course of action, they would have sent him back to his quarters. Instead, they looked ready to make up their minds right there and then. It was Kirk's experience that when instructors moved fast, it was bad news for students.

Jublik called for Kirk, who returned to face the admirals.

Zheng said, "At first glance this appears to be an honor code violation of the first order."

Kirk sighed. He wasn't even going to get the formality of an honor court. He locked his heels together and stood at attention.

Then Jublik leaned forward and slowly said, "What do *you* think we should do with you, Mister Kirk?"

Kirk looked from one admiral to the other. Yet another Academy No-Win Situation. This was the same sort of thing his father used to pull: "Well, Jimmy, you broke the highflyer showing off for your friends. What do *you* think your punishment should be?"

Kirk was a cadet, but did they think he was a *plebe?* Obviously, "being allowed to stay" was the wrong answer and would only get him expelled. While the right answer, "expulsion," would only result in . . . expulsion.

Suddenly, Kirk recalled a puzzle from one of his Command classes: You are a starship captain. You, your first officer, and three security personnel are stranded on a mountaintop. You have to get across a fifty-meter chasm in two hours or you will all die. There is nothing nearby but one skinny, ten-meter-high tree. You have no tools. What do you do? Answer: You say, "Number One, I want a bridge up, and I want it up in two hours." And then you walk away.

That was just a bit of dark humor, but . . . *delegation.* Delegation was as much a captain's skill as any others.

"Sirs," Kirk said, "as a mere cadet, I am not qualified to make that decision. It rests entirely in your hands."

There. That was that. They could expel him or let him stay as they saw fit, but he'd be damned if he was going to charge their phasers enough to shoot him. He had taken the unfair—the unrealistic—and made it fair. If they weren't going to let him solve problems, then maybe he didn't belong at the Academy after all.

Jublik stared intently at Kirk. "Very good, Mister Kirk," he said. "Very . . . good." There was just the suggestion of a smile. "You *do* know your place after all. You're not a captain yet. And, of course, that's what this is all about."

Zheng said, "You spoke of character, Mister Kirk. Character comes through time. Like artists or musicians, starship captains have to learn the rules before they can break them."

"*Effectively* break them," said Jublik, "and with specific purpose." He stood up, turning his back on Kirk and looking out the huge window. "You did break the rules. But there are times when Starfleet may sanction that."

"Oh!" said Kirk. "Like when Captain Archer finally—"

"Yes, Mister Kirk," Zheng sighed, "we're sure that you have an encyclopedic knowledge of regulation violations."

Kirk couldn't believe it. Was he actually being told that he had done the right thing—or, at least, a form of it—after all?

Zheng put his drink down on the desk. "You may return to your quarters . . . on probation."

"Probation?" Kirk asked.

"Yes, one hundred demerits during a term means expulsion. You are fortunate that when you walked in here you had none, because when you walk out you will have ninety-nine. Watch yourself."

"Yes, sirs!" That was it! They were letting him stay! Kirk smiled, spun around, and began to race out the door.

Jublik turned around. "Just one more thing, Mister Kirk. The *Kobayashi Maru* isn't over yet."

Kirk froze. "It isn't?"

"No," said Jublik. "You'll be receiving a commendation for original thinking. Surviving the rest of your Academy career without getting a swelled head—and the mistakes that hubris can bring—*that*, Mister Kirk, will be your true test of character."

Indomitable

Kevin Killiany

Pavel Andreievich Chekov could be forgiven if his first response to hearing the warp engines of the *Enterprise* cycling out of control was a flash of pure joy.

The undulating whine came vibrating through the deck in the final hours of his thirteenth straight day at alpha shift in auxiliary control. Thirteen days of watching the repeater screens show which buttons were being pressed on the bridge.

He took no comfort from the knowledge that his job was supposed to be dull; that's why he was here. If anyone expected auxiliary control to be needed, he'd have been sent off to polish injector nodules or something equally heroic while one of the more experienced crew sat here. That's what had happened last time, when the whole Federation was on the brink of war with the Klingon Empire. The powers that be had yanked him out of aux and put him on a damage control team. The guy who had been here had gotten third-degree burns on his hands when he tried to get control of the ship away from the Organians.

Chekov knew *he* would have had the wits to insulate his hands before touching the controls. Then those Organians would have seen something.

He looked to his left and imagined seeing Lieutenant Sulu. He'd only met the alpha-shift helmsman once, but his current goal was to be working right chair with him by the end of this month. His previous goal had been the end of last month. Before that . . .

He remembered his first sight of the *Enterprise*, sidling gracefully into a hard dock at Starbase 12. He'd been waiting with a half dozen other transfers a respectful distance from Ambassador Fox's party in the observation gallery. He'd been the only one fresh from the Academy and he'd been eager to launch his career, make a name for himself aboard the Federation's flagship.

Why not?

Ensign Chekov had graduated top of his class in navigation, with some of the best marks in a generation, old Hatchet had said. Watching the glistening white starship complete the tricky docking maneuver, he'd imagined himself walking straight into at least the gamma-shift navigator slot aboard the ship.

He'd quickly discovered that on a starship, coming straight out of the Academy at the top of your class meant you'd come straight out of the Academy. A little bit of seasoning belowdecks was expected before you were given a shot at the big time.

His promising career seemed to stall out before it began. In his two months aboard the most decorated ship in the fleet, the closest he'd come to adventure was meeting a 250-year-old warlord in the head.

Actually, he'd just stepped out of the sonic shower and found himself face to face with a stranger of regal bearing in a standard-issue jumpsuit. The stranger, as comfortable as though gracious conversations with naked ensigns were commonplace, had asked him to explain the operation of the sonic shower and the waste recycling systems. He'd listened intently, asking questions that tested Chekov's technical knowledge, before suddenly changing the subject.

"You're a Russian Jew," he'd pronounced.

Later Chekov realized that between hearing his accent and seeing him step out of the shower, discerning his ethnic background was a simple feat for anyone familiar with Earth cultures. However, he'd been impressed at the time, confirming the regal stranger's supposition and telling him a bit more of his personal history than was strictly necessary.

"Yours is a resilient people," the regal stranger had said, as though bestowing a benediction. "Indomitable. Always be proud of your heritage."

Chekov had bobbed, grinning like a schoolboy under the compliment, and promised always to do so. He'd felt more like a fool when Khan Noonien Singh almost took over the *Enterprise* and killed them all.

That glorious episode had been followed almost immediately by his abandoning ship while drunk on alien spores. The fact that everyone else—except the captain, of course—had also beamed down to Omicron Ceti III under the influence of the addictive spores did nothing to lessen his conviction that it should have been him, with the help of the captain, who saved the ship.

From that point his life had consisted of tracing control circuits through Jefferies tubes and sitting long, inglorious shifts at auxiliary control monitoring nothing in particular.

He listened idly—how else?—to the chatter between the bridge and engineering as they set up yet another test of the new warp configuration.

Strangely enough, Chekov actually understood the math behind the new warp technology. Or not so strangely; navigation was his field. The underlying principle was simplicity itself.

"Think of normal space as a perfectly flat sheet of very thin, very supple rubber," his first instructor had told the class. "Any object placed on this surface will make a dimple; the more massive the object, the deeper the dimple."

The dimples were, of course, the gravity wells surrounding worlds and stars. A ship traveling from one world to another in normal space must climb up the steep and slippery slope of the first world, then make its way cautiously across the rubber expanse, avoiding the dimples of other worlds and suns until it reached its destination.

The classic analogy suffered a bit when used to illustrate warp drive. The infinitely resilient sheet of rubber had to become a great hollow globe. Warp allowed ships to turn more sharply than the curve of the globe's surface. The difference was not much, on a cosmic scale, but it was enough to make the journey between dimples in a fraction of the time.

However, warp space had to follow the contours of the normal universe—like, one of the engineers working on the modifications had said, ancient sailors who never went beyond sight of land. The new warp cut a straight path from dimple to dimple—a chord across the sphere of the universe. Its only limitation was that both the destination and the point of origin had to be exactly the same depth beneath the curve of space.

This created some tricky plotting problems, but Chekov thrived on tricky navigation. While the bigwigs calibrated and recalibrated, triple-checking the computer's figures for the next test run, he ran navigational problems through the auxiliary console, manually computing tangents. It was tough going, but it beat sitting on his hands listening to the endless round of questions and confirmations over the intercom.

He was configuring the paradigms for a pulsar-to-pulsar jump when he suddenly realized the endless round of chatter had ended. Had ended some time ago, in fact, without his noticing.

He toggled the intercom switch with no effect. Turning up the gain got him nothing but static. The circuit was live; everyone had just stopped talking.

He was about to violate protocol and ask a question when he realized it wasn't the lack of chatter that had broken his concentration. It was the ship itself. The warp engines seemed to be cycling rapidly. He could feel the rise and fall of vibrations through the deck as they reached maximum and the automatic safeties cut them back.

Three, four, six times they did it as he sat, listening for any other sound at all. Commander Scott would never have let that go on. Something was wrong.

That was the moment he realized his chance had come.

Clearing his navigational doodles, he did what he should have been doing all along and checked the redundant displays. According to his boards, which repeated what the bridge and engineering command stations showed, the *Enterprise* was flying in a straight line at warp 10 while the universe rotated wildly around its *z* axis.

Chekov watched for a moment to be sure. No one was touching any of the controls, either on the bridge or in engineering.

He activated the auxiliary control override, then hit it again when nothing happened. He was locked out. Either someone had disabled the override or . . . Wait, except for the bizarre course, all of the boards read normal. If the computer did not recognize an emergency, it would not relinquish control to auxiliary without command codes—codes he didn't have. All he could do from here was what he was doing: watch.

Or look. There was a difference.

He recalibrated the readouts, tying the sensor array into the navigational computer. No block against that—it didn't affect ship's operations. With the new baseline, the display now showed the *Enterprise* flying sideways—directly starboard—at warp 10.

"Woof drive," he murmured, resurrecting the hoariest joke from Propulsion 101.

Deciding external readings were useless, he turned to internal readings and control settings.

Four hundred forty-two lifesigns, some indicating levels of distress or injury, were displayed. That accounted for the crew and visiting warp engineers; no intruders. Life support readings were within parameters, though atmospheric pressure in both engineering and the bow read very high.

Someone had tied the structural integrity fields, inertial dampers, and artificial gravity to the warp drive. That should have been impossible—their circuits were never designed to handle energy at that level. Running a quick diagnostic, he discovered they weren't; their power feed had been routed through the phaser banks. It was the structural fields, operating way beyond their design maximums, that were cycling the warp engines.

In four minutes he decided he'd discovered everything he was going to from the instruments. It was time for a little direct reconnaissance. Before leaving auxiliary control, he checked the lifesign readings a second time. None of them had moved.

"Curiouser and curiouser," he quoted one of his favorite Russian philosophers.

On general principles, he took a type-2 phaser from the weapons locker before opening the door.

The corridor was obviously empty and silent. Not so obviously, the corridor seemed to pulse with an energy that lifted the hairs along his arms and the nape of his neck. Something—air pressure?—pushed against his eyes, making them feel swollen in their sockets, and there was a ringing in his ears.

He moved cautiously along the corridor to the left, the phaser outstretched before him. He kept the fingers of his free hand trailing along the wall, not so much to steady himself as to confirm its reality. Nothing looked distorted, exactly, but everything felt somehow *bent.*

Distracted by the feel of the air, it wasn't until he began to turn left again, toward the turbolift, that he realized his phaser, and the hand holding it, seemed to be pulling him straight ahead. Once he did, he paused, experimenting with pulling the weapon back toward himself and extending it again.

There was a definite sense that the corridor ahead was somehow heading down. He tried to orient himself within the ship, get a sense of which direction he was facing. Forward, he decided; forward toward the denser air.

Another step, and the sensation was even more pronounced. His hand seemed to be falling asleep, and he could feel the phaser, suddenly kilograms heavier, digging into the flesh of his fingers. At the next step the transition was even more intense, as though something were gripping his lower arm and pulling him forward. Alarmed, Chekov snatched his hand back, or tried to. It, or the phaser, seemed anchored in clay. Moving his arm laterally, perpendicular to the pull, he determined it was not the air, but some force that held him. That made sense. If the air were really that thick, he wouldn't be able to breathe.

Reaching back with his free hand, he found a stanchion and, digging in his heels, fought his way backward, pulling himself free. Not completely free, he realized. For even here, down and forward seemed to battle for primacy. Gripping the stantion firmly, he extended the phaser forward, feeling it grow instantly heavier. At the end of his reach he let go and watched it fly down the corridor to slam into the bulkhead of a cross corridor. It stayed without bouncing, apparently attached to the wall a meter above the deck.

Far more aware of the strange force now that he was fighting it, Chekov worked his way back to auxiliary control. Once inside, he determined that only the area immediately behind his chair at the control panel was truly neutral. Forward of that was the same pull he'd felt in the corridor.

Auxiliary Control was just behind the main turbolift shaft in the center of the primary hull. That had to mean something, had to have something to do with the force and his immunity to it, but he couldn't think what.

He went back to the control console, wasting only a second to confirm he was still locked out, and began studying the readings again.

All of the lifesigns, still unmoving, were grouped at either the forward or stern edges of each deck. Most of them showed signs of acute respiratory and cardiac distress, if he understood the unfamiliar readings correctly. The air density at each deck followed the same pattern. It was almost as if gravity were pulling in two opposite directions as well as down, which made no sense. . . .

With a curse, Chekov slapped the display toggles, replacing the internal readings with the externals.

Of course! The universe wasn't spinning and the ship wasn't moving sideways at warp speed. They were in orbit. The computer hadn't recognized it for the same reason he hadn't: an orbit at warp speed is impossible. But once he overrode the computer's inability to accept the impossible, it was plain to see.

The *Enterprise* was in a tight orbit at warp factor— The numbers made no sense. What did make sense was that the bow pointed directly inward at whatever primary the ship was orbiting. It wasn't internal gravity pulling everything apart, it was tidal forces.

He listened for a moment to the warp engines cycling to maximum then cutting back again. Commander Scott must have reconfigured the integrity fields before being dragged from his station. How much longer could they hold the ship together?

Auxiliary Control was behind the main turbolift, the same turbolift that opened onto the back of the bridge. Extrapolating from what he'd experienced in the corridor, Chekov guessed that everything forward of the turbolift was being pulled toward the bow by the same tidal stress that had snatched the phaser from his grasp. If he was going to effect a rescue, he would need a harness to hold him against the tide.

It took several minutes to braid enough opti-cable together to make climbing rope and harness sufficient to his needs. As he pulled the last loop taut, he paused and looked at the red welt that the spun glass cable had made across his palm. Several more minutes were lost as he peeled insulation foam from the backs of access panels and formed the flexible sheets into pads to protect his body from the harness.

As ready as he could make himself, he moved along the corridor to the turbolift, fighting the tidal forces that sought to pull him headlong down the corridor. Getting the turbolift doors open was not a problem—nothing was wrong with the maintenance circuits. Within the shaft the tides actually helped him, holding him firmly to the ladder against the pull of artificial gravity. His biggest fear—

a lift car stuck in the shaft between G deck and the bridge—was not realized, and for a moment he had the sensation that this was all going too easily.

Prizing the doors open at the bridge level, Chekov paused for a moment to survey the damage. Eight people were pressed against the forward bulkhead, some across the main viewscreen itself. He recognized the captain and a few others. The unnatural angles at which some were sprawled indicated broken bones, if not worse.

"Captain," a hoarse whisper.

Chekov saw the first officer, Mister Spock, raise his head slightly. Captain Kirk, near the center of the viewscreen, turned his head with apparent effort and regarded Chekov.

"Be with you in a moment, sir," Chekov said. Then, realizing the captain might not know the full situation, reported:

"We are orbiting an unknown object at warp, Captain, most likely a black star," he said, using the Vulcan term for a black hole. "I believe Commander Scott has stabilized the ship, but I will need to adjust our course to break us free."

He thought he saw the captain nod.

Taking that as permission to proceed, he looped his climbing rope around the access ladder and tossed the free end through the turbolift doors. The opti-cable snapped into a rigid line stretching across the bridge.

"Indomitable people meet irresistible force," he muttered under his breath and stepped carefully onto the deck.

For the first two steps onto the bridge, the artificial gravity was stronger than the tide, but before he reached the rail separating the upper ring from the command well, only his grip on the rope prevented his headlong plunge to join the others.

He played the line out carefully, lowering himself into the tidal pull. The strips of insulation padding his palms made his movements clumsy. He braced his feet against the back of the command chair, the artificial gravity exerting an almost undetectable tug against the tidal surge.

The braided opti-cable cut into the flesh across his chest as he lowered himself from the command chair to the navigation console. He wished he'd added a few more layers of insulation. If it was this bad here, what must be happening in the bow and engineering? He quickened his pace.

He braced himself, straddling the central support to take some of the pressure off the bruises under the opti-cable harness. He tied off his line before turning his attention to the main console. The bridge navigational display didn't show him anything he hadn't seen in auxiliary control.

The *Enterprise* must have been on a tangential course when the black star's gravity well had snagged them. Even a starship didn't have the power to fight a collapsed neutron star.

If they were going to pull free, they would have to follow a spiral, and a gentle one if he didn't want this tidal sheer to tear the ship in half. He'd given the problem a lot of thought while making his way to the bridge. Now he ran his mental figures through the nav console to see if the computer agreed with him.

Close. Not perfect, but close. He adjusted his numbers slightly and laid the course into the helm.

"Captain, spiral escape course plotted and laid in," he reported.

"Initial angle?"

Mister Spock seemed to be the only one pressed to the front bulkhead able to speak against the tidal pressure.

"Point four two degrees in direction of orbit, sir," Chekov said. The loop of cable across his chest digging in with every breath. "Angle will increase as pull of gravity decreases."

The Vulcan nodded.

"Proceed."

Helm control was a little different from the simulators at the Academy. Chekov suspected that cadets weren't expected to step straight from the simulators onto the bridge of a *Constitution*-class starship. But the difference wasn't significant, and it took him only a moment to confirm duplicate readouts on the two control panels.

The helm also displayed recommended thrust levels for each

phase of the spiral. Chekov suspected that a seasoned helmsman who knew the *Enterprise* would probably adjust those numbers, but he wasn't about to take chances. He keyed the figures into the autopilot and engaged.

Against the forward bulkhead the bridge crew, most of them still unconscious, rolled and slid to the left as the tidal pressures shifted. Chekov felt himself gravitate to the left, as well.

Too late, he realized he'd knotted his line to keep from falling forward, but hadn't secured himself to anything. His insulation-wrapped hands slipped uselessly across the surface of the console as the tide dragged him inexorably to the left. Unable to stop himself, he swung free, hanging helplessly above a "down" that shifted as the *Enterprise* fought its way free of the black star.

The ship shuddered and lurched, then seemed to leap forward and to the right. The cable snapped like a whip, flinging Chekov across the command well. His hip caught on the railing, flipping him up and pinwheeling him head first into the auxiliary engineering station.

"You called?" said a voice.

"You wanted to be here when he came 'round." drawled another.

Chekov decided the area of whiteness was a light panel. Yes, that was definitely a ceiling. The voices were . . .

Captain Kirk stepped into his field of view.

"Captain!"

Chekov struggled to rise, but a hand on his shoulder—the captain's hand—pushed him gently back.

"At ease, Ensign," he ordered.

"Yes, sir," Chekov acknowledged, trying to lie at attention.

"A Starfleet officer is expected to stay at his post and do his duty," Captain Kirk said. "He's also expected to keep a cool head and show initiative in an emergency."

Not sure whether he was supposed to respond, Chekov lay perfectly still, not even risking a nod. He wondered where the captain was going.

"I understand you have a problem with staying in auxiliary control."

"Yes, I mean, no, sir."

"Don't addle the boy, Jim," said the voice he'd heard earlier. "He's already been hit in the head."

An older man stepped into Chekov's view. The chief medical officer, he realized. He must be in sickbay.

"Prognosis, Doctor?" the captain asked, ignoring Chekov for the moment.

"Barring any surprises, he should be on his feet in twenty-four hours," the doctor replied.

"Good."

Captain Kirk glanced at the wall chronometer, then looked down at Chekov. The ensign stiffened back to attention.

"I have a man down with several broken bones and a punctured lung," the captain said, nodding toward another biobed Chekov could not see. "His post will need to be covered temporarily. It might become permanent, depending on how things develop."

Chekov blinked. Another statement he wasn't sure he was supposed to acknowledge.

"The next alpha shift begins in thirty-two hours," Captain Kirk concluded briskly, already turning toward the door. "I'll expect you on the bridge and ready to work, navigator."

Project Blue Book

Christian Grainger

Boston, Massachusetts
11:24 A.M., June 21, 2003

Lieutenant Colonel Wilhelmina Carver was puzzled. The guard's interview transcript didn't match his filed report. This was the third major inconsistency she had come across in the Omaha report in two days. She hated mysteries. She sat at her desk and pinched the bridge of her nose, pushing her wire-frame glasses up. It occurred to her that these files were a relic of the sixties, just like her old wooden desk was. In fact her whole office, in the old brick building across from the Charlestown Navy Yard, was outdated, more like the office of a dime-store private eye, really. It was dark with the blinds half closed, and there were cardboard boxes everywhere. The only thing that looked out of place was the computer on the wooden desk, and she still had trouble using that. She smiled at the thought.

She checked the date in the file again, then picked up the phone and buzzed her assistant in the office next door.

He picked up right away. In the ten years she had worked with him, he had always picked up the phone on the first ring. "Yeah, boss."

"Baker, can you bring the other box in here, the one with the guard's transcript in it?"

He paused for a moment. "It's on the network, you know."

"And you know that I want the hard copy, the original documents, because of the problems with the data changing on me. I only trust the physical hard copy. How many times do I have to say it?" She sighed, pursed her lips, and tried unsuccessfully, to blow her hair out her eyes. She knew she needed a haircut but didn't have the time to get it.

"Yeah, boss, I know. I'm just trying to avoid another trip to Archives in the basement. You know, we're on—"

"—the ninth floor and the elevator is out of order. I know." She finished his sentence for him. "But it's good exercise, and you know you need it. Maybe if you ate only four pizzas a week . . ."

"Yep."

"And I need your help saving my online report. I think I moved it instead of copying it."

"No problem, boss."

"And one more thing. Don't call me boss."

"Okay, boss," he said, and hung up the phone.

She smiled at the old joke and turned back to the report in her hand. This was a strange case, but she had never failed to figure one out yet.

Minutes later there was a knock at her door. Before she could answer, the door opened and Baker's heavy frame filled the entry. He came in grunting and carrying three boxes. Carver's eyebrows went up. "I just asked for the one box."

"Yep, but then you would have been asking for the others before the day was out and I didn't want to have a heart attack today, so I thought I'd just make one more trip instead of three." He smiled and wondered for the hundredth time why she'd never been married. She was something else—intelligent and pretty. If only he had the guts to do something about it. Her voice snapped him back to the moment.

"Thanks, Baker," she said, then paused. "You've got that look again. Penny for your thoughts?"

He almost blushed.

"Just wondering how it was going. We've got to get the final report in by the end of next week."

Carver looked as if she was going to say something else for a moment and then thought better of it. "Well, it's interesting." She handed Baker a file from her desk. "That's from the normal duty log. It's the report from the guard for that night at the 498th. It's from the regular shift archives." She rifled through one of the boxes that Baker had just brought in and then, with an exclamation of triumph, pulled a file from the box. She glanced through it and handed it to Baker. "But the guard's interview transcript is in the old Blue Book files."

Baker looked at the files for a moment frowning. "Okay, I don't get it. So what?"

She paused for effect. "They're from the same night."

He looked at the files again and then looked back up at Carver. "The dates are the same."

He mouthed a silent "So?"

Her chair creaked as she sat back. "I get the same thing with the pilot's report. What's his name?" She shifted some papers around on her desk. "Here it is, Captain John Christopher."

Carver's blue eyes seemed to blaze as she kept talking. "According to the Blue Book files, there seems to be a report of an F-104 crashing over southern Nebraska. The airframe was crushed in midair and it just fell from the sky. There are even a few frames from the wing camera that were salvaged from the wreck. I'm getting the originals sent by courier." She paused again.

This time Baker just waved his hand, motioning her to go on. "And?"

"There is no report of the crash in the regular duty log or the base logs for the same time period. In fact, I've got a salvage receipt for the same jet—in one piece, mind you—being retired from the base and sold for scrap metal fifteen years after the date in the file." Her eyebrows went up together. "As far as the Air Force is concerned, there was no crash."

Baker thought for a moment. "So, except for the reference in the Blue Book files and the wing camera film, which shouldn't be there, there is no record of the crash?"

"Right," she nodded.

"Someone's been mucking with the files," Baker said.

"You got it in one. See, that's why I wanted the originals. Someone's been playing with the files for a long time. These inconsistencies go back over forty years." Carver got up and walked around her desk. "But we caught some luck. Guess where the guard and Captain Christopher are now."

"Within driving distance?"

"You got it."

Framingham, Massachusetts
3:13 P.M., June 21, 2003

The first thing that Carver noticed about the guard as she and Baker sat across from him was the odd look in his eyes. She cast a sideways look at Baker, and he nodded. He saw it too. The guard spoke normally, but it was as if he was seeing something in the distance behind them.

"Are you sure I can't get you anything? I just made some chicken soup," he said, starting to get up from his seat.

"No, we're both fine, thank you." Carver said, indicating herself and Baker. As the guard sat back down, a puff of dust came up from the faded brown sofa.

Baker sneezed. "Sorry, it's the dust." He returned his attention to his open briefcase, retrieving a yellow legal pad and pen.

For the first time, the guard focused on the two Air Force officers with an apologetic smile. Carver continued, "Can you tell us about that night?"

"The night after the crash?" he said. Carver and Baker exchanged glances again. "At that time, I was an Air Police sergeant at the base. When I first found them in the computer room, I thought they were spies working for the Red Chinese. One was Asian, and the other guy looked like he could have been from Iowa. But they had funny uniforms on for spies."

So, Carver thought. *Someone is mucking about with the files.* There was nothing in the Blue Book files or the regular files about spies. This was getting interesting. "Can you tell us about the uniforms?"

The guard frowned for a moment as if he didn't know what Carver was talking about, then his face cleared and he got the faraway look on his face again. "I'm sorry, it goes in and out of focus. One minute the memory is clear and the next it's gone, like it never happened at all."

Baker nodded. "My dad had that problem. But he drank a lot . . ."

Carver gave Baker a stern look. "Baker!" she said with a warning tone.

"Sorry, boss."

The guard went on. "They had yellow uniforms with gold insignia in the shape of deltas. I took their equipment, and one of the pieces started beeping." He looked like he was going to keep talking and then stopped.

"And then?" Carver asked.

"They gave me chicken soup," he said.

Carver blinked. "What? The spies gave you chicken soup?"

The guard laughed. "Oh no, not the spies."

Carver smiled, nodding.

"The guy in the transporter room, after the doctor took my gun."

Carver stopped smiling. Maybe this wasn't the grand conspiracy she had thought it was after all. Baker saw the disappointed look on her face. She stood. "Well, thank you for your time."

As she walked to the front door, with Baker following, the guard got up, crossed the room, and entered the kitchen, disappearing from sight without saying a word. They heard him rummaging around in several drawers. Carver looked at Baker who just nodded sadly. "Thanks again," she yelled, and then quietly to Baker, "There's no reason to see Christopher. This guy's a nut. Let's head back to the office."

As she opened the front door to leave, the guard came back into the living room with a small black-and-silver object in his hand. "I had put this in my pocket. They never checked when I was on their ship." He handed the small object to Carver.

She looked down at it. It was unlike anything she had ever seen before, and suddenly she felt very chilly even though it was hot in the house. "I just have one more question," she said. "Did you ever meet the pilot of the downed plane?"

"Yes."

"Where, at the crash investigation?" she asked.

"No." The guard's attention focused on Carver, and for a moment, he didn't seem like a crazy old man at all.

"In the transporter room," he said.

Salem, Massachusetts
8:47 A.M., June 22, 2003

"I hate this place, boss." Baker said as they walked down the hall that led from the main entrance of the psychology wing to the guard desk, where a white-shirted orderly sat. The bleak white corridor was long enough to prevent any patient that sneaked past the guard from getting to the door unseen. Baker took this in at a glance. He shuddered. It reminded him of an endless hall in a horror movie.

Carver understood her colleague's unease, and she tried to calm him. "I know. But something big is going on here. If we're going to get to bottom of this, we've got to talk to Christopher." Carver didn't feel as calm as she sounded. She couldn't stop thinking about the black-and-silver object the guard had given them the day before that was now in Baker's briefcase. The device was about the size of a pager, but much heavier. She had never seen anything like it before. Not for the first time that morning, she forced herself to the task of the moment.

Captain Christopher's doctor met them at the guard desk. He looked tired and overworked. Carver acknowledged this.

"Thank you, Doctor Phillips, for allowing us to meet your patient with so little notice," she said.

The doctor looked at them for a second, studying them. He wasn't happy. "Don't be fooled by the fact that he's not in a straitjacket. Captain Christopher is a very sick man. I honestly don't see how talking to him can help you."

"We just need to ask him a few questions to corroborate another man's report," Carver said.

The doctor wasn't convinced. "His world isn't based in reality."

Carver didn't give up. "Just a few questions."

The doctor looked at them for a moment longer and then shrugged. He turned and walked away, speaking over his shoulder. "He's in the common room, through the double door on the left. Don't be long."

A few moments later, as she and Baker sat across from Captain Christopher at a faded, red kitchen table, her unease grew.

"I'm not crazy, you know," he said. His perfectly reasonable tone didn't match his appearance. His sunken blue eyes were dilated to the point of being almost black, and his pasty white skin was stretched tight over the bones in his face, causing a nasty ghoulish effect. Carver was shocked at the change in appearance from his old ID photos.

Christopher ran his hand over the stubble on his shaved head, looking each of the two officers directly in the eye. His gaze settled on Carver. "It's nice to see you again."

Carver didn't like this. For a moment she almost got up and walked away. Then she pinched the bridge of her nose and took a deep breath. She spoke calmly. "This is the first time we've ever come here, Captain. We just have a few questions to ask you."

Christopher smiled a small, almost apologetic smile. "My mistake. I'm sorry, it's the medication."

Carver didn't believe him. But she forced herself to let it go. "We wanted to ask you about the crash you survived back when you were with the 498th. Our records don't seem to agree."

Christopher just looked at her. The stare was familiar, and she couldn't place it for a moment. Then she remembered. It was the same blank look as on the guard's face.

"The UFO was white. It blended in with the color of the sky." He rubbed his head again. "I remember having a son. He headed up the manned Earth–Saturn probe. I was so proud of him."

Carver looked at Baker for a moment and then opened her mouth to speak. Christopher interrupted her, the vacant look vanished for a moment.

"I know I don't have a son. I also know there is no Earth–Saturn probe." He looked down at the dingy red tabletop. "I lost my wife too. She divorced me after the investigation." Christopher looked back up at Carver. "How can I have two sets of memories?" He began to drift off again. "Spock would know why."

Carver had had enough. "Listen, we can help. Tell me who's been changing the files. Why is there a cover-up?"

Christopher's cadaver-like gaze focused on Carver again.

"There isn't a cover-up."

Carver wouldn't be put off. "Of course there is. Why else would there be double entries in the files going back over so many years? Tell me what's going on."

"I already have. The plane crashed and it didn't crash. I have a son and I don't have a son. You see, that's why I'm in here."

Carver shook her head.

Christopher when on. "I know why the guard isn't in here. I also know what's in your partner's briefcase. Be careful, it's a weapon."

Carver looked over at Baker, who had turned pale. The urge to run was getting stronger. "Why isn't the guard in here?" she asked.

"He has only one set of memories."

"Why is that?"

Christopher smiled grimly. "You figure it out."

Boston, Massachusetts
11:13 A.M., June 22, 2003

Christopher's words echoed in Carver's head as she sat at her steel desk and finished typing her report into the computer. It just didn't make any sense. She looked up as Baker came into her office.

Baker scrutinized at her closely. He was worried about her. She didn't look good. His stomach tightened as he noticed her gaze, normally focused and laserlike, now fixed on nothing. The thousand-yard stare.

"Boss, don't let it get to you. You know both these guys are whacked. We've been set up. I'm telling you. That thing the guard gave us doesn't do anything. I tried it. I pushed every button and looked at it from every angle."

Carver looked up, horrified. "You aimed it at yourself?"

Baker rolled his eyes. "Yep, just what you're not supposed to do, right?"

"Right."

"Nothing happened." A slow smile crossed his face as he watched his supervisor's shoulders relax.

Carver smiled back. "You know it just didn't make sense, Christopher alive and in the hospital and the guard alive and living a normal life. And I still can't make sense of his words. 'One set of memories.' I just don't get it."

Baker nodded as he walked over and sat on the edge of her steel desk and glanced at her computer monitor as she saved her work. Something didn't seem right, but the feeling only lasted a moment. "Didn't you use to have a wooden desk?"

"What?"

"Never mind." He pointed to her computer screen. "No, you're doing it again. You want to copy the file, not move it."

Carver's head snapped around, but she wasn't angry. In fact, she was smiling. "Okay, John. Tell me again, what's the difference?"

Baker tapped his finger on the screen as she moved the mouse. "If you copy the file, your report is in two places at once permanently. If you move it, the file is only in two places during the move and then the original is deleted."

Carver's smile froze on her face.

She grabbed the phone and then stopped. "What's the guard's home number?"

He told her and watched, very worried, as she tried twice to dial, but couldn't because her hands were shaking.

"What is it?"

She only looked up, stress making her features tight. "It's not a conspiracy." She suddenly looked much older than she was.

"Easy, easy. I'll do it," he said.

She watched as he dialed and then asked to speak to the guard. A frown crossed his face and he hung up.

"I must have dialed the wrong number." Carver noticed he looked worried now.

"Why?"

"The lady that answered the phone said the guy who owned the house before her died." Baker now looked pale.

Carver looked down as she reached into her desk for the paper file. "John, I've figured it out. I don't know how, but this is much bigger than a conspiracy."

She looked up again, and her heart almost stopped.

Baker was gone.

He couldn't have gotten out of the office that quick. He had been so close to her she'd felt his body heat. She started to call out his name and then stopped in midbreath. Something funny happened in her head. A memory that hadn't been there before was now present, as if it had been there all along. John Baker was dead. Her old partner had died of a heart attack four years earlier. She'd worked alone ever since. But that couldn't be right, she thought. She'd just been talking to him. He'd been helping her with her computer.

Again something funny happened in her brain; the light in the office seemed to fade even though the sun was shining brightly outside.

Suddenly she felt trapped and all alone. She tried to get up, but her body wouldn't obey her. She looked down at her legs and then up again.

Two men stood in the office, wearing silver-and-blue uniforms. The taller man had black hair and a very stern expression on his narrow face. The other, with blond hair, looked a little bit sad. He kept looking at a small display pad in his hand. It cast an eerie white light on his features.

His sad expression scared her more than anything.

"Get the phaser," the blond said in a soft voice. She couldn't place his accent.

"They caused another rift again," the tall man said.

"It wasn't their fault. Kirk and Spock did the best they could with the existing twenty-third century technology. The *Enterprise* wasn't even designed for time travel, let alone causality repair. And who knew the guard would keep the phaser and further open the rift by talking to these officers?"

Now Carver couldn't move her body at all. But she could still breathe and talk. Her voice was barely a croak, she was so terrified.

"What gives you the right? What have you done to me?"

Again the kind stare from the blond man terrified her more than any open threat would have. Her uniform was damp with perspiration.

"We haven't done anything to you. We did initiate the repair, but now it is taking its own course to put things back the way they should have been all along. I know you won't understand, but as the causality echo is sealed, events and people of the era are shifted to their normal patterns and places."

"What?" She almost couldn't control her fear. The office was pitch-black now, and an unbearable heat filled the room. She could see only the two men.

"But from your point of view, it doesn't happen all at once. So as the repair continues, your physical state and mind lock into position where you are in this place until the repair reaches you."

She was reminded of the long white corridor at the military asylum, the one with a white-coated guard at the end that would forever chase you and stop you from getting out the main doors. She had almost made it.

"Don't worry," he continued, glancing down at his device. "It won't be long now."

She wanted to spit in his face. "John Baker was a good man."

The tall man walked back over and stood next to his partner. "I'm sure he was," he said. "But you weren't supposed to work together in the first place. Just relax. It will all be over in a moment."

She felt new memories inserting themselves into her brain, felt memories of new people bloom, including a husband she never had. Other memories began to fade—her work as an investigator, and John Baker. She fought to remember why she was here in the first place. With a final effort she conjured up John's face and his voice in her mind and their old joke, "Don't call me boss."

Maybe there was one way to win, a small victory against eternity.

"I figured it out, didn't I? That's why you're here. There are two realities: one where the guard died and Captain Christopher had a child that went to Saturn and he never saw a UFO, and one where the guard lived and Christopher did see a UFO and no one believed him and his wife left him?"

She pushed on. "The guard is now dead, as he should have been, and Christopher has his son and his sanity."

The blond man looked at his partner, his face troubled for a moment. His partner shrugged.

Carver felt her mind slipping again. She became desperate. "Just tell me, did I figure it out? Did I count for something? Did my work make a difference?"

The blond man's face softened more. "Yes, you did figure it out. If you hadn't, we never would have found where to repair the damage."

She barely heard his last words as she slipped into darkness.

"Thank you."

Command H.Q., Temporal Integrity Commission
1530 hours, November 30, 2892

The blond man checked the display built into his desk console one last time. "The repair is complete. She is where she was before." He paused for a moment.

"What's wrong?" his partner asked.

"She called her husband John by mistake."

"We can't always fix everything. It's just a final echo. You should stop checking on her. It's never a good idea to get involved."

The blond man sighed, "I hate working these cases."

His partner shrugged, "You knew what you were getting into when you signed on to Project Blue Book."

The Trouble with Tribals

Paul J. Kaplan

Evolution is such a tricky thing.

Not the process itself, of course. It is a simple and relentless force. But it fails to raise all species to equal heights. Some races are born early, some late. Some progress quickly, others take time. Some species travel a straight path, while others spend eons in backwaters and eddies before finding their way to that next great leap. Through these differences in age and opportunity and fate, vast differences have arisen among the species of our galaxy. Some are impossibly advanced, while others remain primitive and quaint. And so it is with us and the bipeds of this place.

They're really quite endearing, in their own way. Lurching about in those gangly bodies, with their eyeballs and eardrums and intestines and spleens, while we are so elegant and small. They are so fascinated by our simplicity and the rate at which we "breed." They cannot yet conceive of intellects that exhaust a body in so short a time, or of the seamless way in which our minds pass through so many iterations of our physical selves. Many believe that we will soon evolve beyond the need for bodies altogether. These bipeds will not know such an existence for millions of years.

They're so proud of themselves, for discovering how to warp space and hurl themselves about, in machines so silly and yet to them so terribly advanced. They are so proud of their discoveries, like a baby who one day "discovers" his own toes. It's really quite sweet.

And yet, at times they can be so very arrogant. So aware of their differences. Who was born here, who was born there. Whose skin is blue, whose skin is green. Who has two arms, who has six. They get so wrapped up in the petty distinctions among their tribes. Like the beings on this space station, with their circling warships and their poisoned grain. I suppose we should make them aware of that, before someone gets hurt.

That's the trouble with Tribals. So much potential, and yet so young.

Ah well. They're still cute.

And they'll learn.

All Fall Down

Muri McCage

The dark was too dark. If he turned on the reading panel way over on his desk, the light was too light. His quarters were too warm. If he instructed the computer to nudge it down until it felt right, he started shaking. His bunk was too soft. He'd never sleep again.

With a sigh that edged entirely too close to a sob, Leonard McCoy slipped out of bed, dragging the heavy top blanket with him. He looked around the familiar space that seemed suddenly to have been replaced with an alien habitat, until his squinting eyes lighted upon the corner by the head hatch. It only took a few seconds to spread his blanket on the hard floor, turn off the light panel, set the light over his shaving sink to its lowest setting, and lie down.

A matter of seconds told him something still wasn't right. He lay there, thinking for a while, going over details he'd involuntarily stored in his memory, then with a "tsk" got back up. The methodical walk to his seaman's chest, the scramble through a few layers to get to his Starfleet-issue cold weather parka, the walk back to his corner all worked together to soothe his thoughts and relax his body. By the time he'd shrugged into the awkward coat, it was as if required tasks had been completed to the satisfaction of unseen observers.

Stiff muscles that no sickbay treatment would ease completely anytime soon protested as he lowered himself to a sitting position on his blanket. He looked up at the ceiling, almost as if he didn't recognize it.

"Computer. Lower ambient temperature by thirty-five degrees Fahrenheit."

Unable to comply. Requested temperature alteration is outside the parameters required for human comfort.

"Not a human who's been through what this one has."

Please restate request, within regulation parameters for human comfort levels.

He had thought he was mumbling thoroughly enough, but, as usual, the central computer of the starship *Enterprise* had hearing as annoying as its science officer's. Sharp enough to catch the slightest utterance, yet with the uncanny ability to filter out any slippage of logic. The extrahuman idea of logic, at any rate.

He drew a deep, frustration-tempering breath. "Medical emergency. Override code McCoy zero four zero six."

Temperature reduced by thirty-five degrees Fahrenheit, in compliance with medical emergency override.

The temperature drop hit him immediately, like a fist closing around his heart. Within a beat of that heart, the sudden cold relaxed its icy grip and he grunted with a mixture of annoyance and satisfaction.

He pulled up the hood of his parka, lay down, and settled it snugly around his face. Almost in defiance of all that had happened, he slept.

"Bones!"

For a moment McCoy thought they were back there. He felt the dust in his lungs, the smoke whose bitter bite rendered the dust irrelevant . . . Most of all he felt the cold. He heard his friend's voice, registered the firm hand urgently shaking his shoulder, shrugged them both aside, and kept his eyes closed against the reality to which he had almost become accustomed.

"Bones! Bones? Wake up!"

He opened one eye. When that didn't get him a face full of Klingon ugly, he opened the other. It really was Captain James T. Kirk, features a crazy quilt of anxiety and exhaustion, squatting beside his pallet. "Jim, what're you doin' in here?"

Kirk grinned in relief, in the process relaxing some of the worried creases that etched his brow. "Trying to find out what's happened to my CMO."

McCoy sat up, rubbing at eyes that stung, though no irritants got past the ship's air scrubbers. "Huh?"

"The computer alerted me to a medical emergency in these quarters. I hotfooted it to your door, only to be refused entry. The ship had sealed you off as a precaution. I had to override the lockout, and while I was at it took a chance by sending the med team back to sickbay. I told them it was a glitch Scotty would get right on."

"How'd you know I hadn't keeled over with a heart attack?"

"A hunch."

"Some hunch."

Kirk offered a sheepish grin. "I tried to Rura Pentheize my quarters too, but the computer wouldn't let me. The hunch was that your 'medical emergency' was your way around it."

"Huh. I guess sometimes bein' the CMO is better than bein' captain."

"I guess. Marginally." Kirk started edging one arm into the parka he'd brought with him and looked toward the closet, where extra bedding was kept on the top shelf. "Got a spare blanket?"

They sat up far into ship's night, talking as they hadn't been able to do until the dust had settled, figuratively and literally. Kirk had released the magnetized feet on the chair, moved it out of the way, and got comfortable under the desk. McCoy could have slapped himself for not thinking of that. It was eerily reminiscent of the cramped space that passed for a bunk in the mining compound far below the surface of the icy planetoid they had almost had to call home. He stared at his friend, hunched into a bundled-up human knot, and quickly decided his corner would do just fine.

"I guess it was a good idea to take a little sick leave. For both of us." Kirk rubbed a hand across his smoothly shaven chin, as if he almost missed the stubble. "How long do you figure it will take before we get over it?"

"Beats me, Jim. I've been doin' psych evals on crewmen for decades, but this is my first time on the other side of my own clinical observation to this extent. I hope to God it's my only time as a former penal colonist dilithium miner. Either one of those would be bad enough, but both together . . ."

"Both together is not something any Starfleet member is prepared for. I've been thinking about home a lot, Bones. Funny what nearly being frozen, beaten, shape-shifted to death, any one of, oh, a half-dozen things lately . . . funny what that kind of experience can make a person remember. There have been times . . . since Rura Penthe . . . when I'm sure I could describe every kernel on every ear of corn in a particular Iowa field. Suddenly, I'm looking forward to some down time, a little trip back home when we get to space dock."

McCoy could feel the grin spreading across his face. "I wouldn't mind going back to Atlanta for a visit. I've been thinkin' about the house we used to live in a lot . . . the spot out back where my daughter liked to play those little-girl games that big, soft grassy yards were made for."

"Sounds nice." Kirk shifted audibly against his makeshift bedding, rustling movements in the dimness letting McCoy know his friend was as restless as he was himself. "Do you have the dreams, Bones? Since . . ."

"Hell, yes. Nightmares, mostly, waking and sleeping. I thought for a minute I was back there, when you woke me up tonight. Sometimes, though . . ."

"What?"

"Sometimes, I still dream of good things. Happy things."

"Me, too. Once, right in the middle of the worst of it, I had a dream I never wanted to wake up from. I was captain of a small research vessel, with Carol and David as my crew. We were a family. It was the best dream I ever had."

"The human mind is an amazing organism, Jim. It finds ways to protect us, even when we don't think anything will make whatever it is better." McCoy dropped his voice and closed his eyes, thinking hard about the vivid dreams and perfect recall memories that enabled him to survive recent events with his sanity intact. "In a way I wouldn't trade what happened with the Klingons for anything, because out of it came a sharpness, a clarity to my memory that was like reliving some of the happiest days of my life. I can't think of anything I'd like more right now than to go back to that house, pull off my shoes, and walk barefoot in that old backyard for a while."

Kirk chuckled softly. "We'll have to see 'Fleet shrinks before they'll cut us loose, maybe the whole crew will, but no matter what kind of shrink speak they start out with, and how much it helps us in one way or another, I know what the bottom line will be."

"Yeah. Get plenty of rest. We have to learn to relax again, Jim. We're both strong individuals, mentally, physically, emotionally. We wouldn't call the ship of the line home otherwise. What wasn't innate was trained into us. It'll take a little time, but we'll be okay."

"I know. We always are." Kirk's odd little laugh carried across the dimly lit room to ignite a similar chuckle in McCoy. "Besides, I don't know about you, but I'm much too fond of my luxuriously barely padded Starfleet issue bunk to give it up indefinitely for the floor."

"Me, too. At least the ship doesn't have splinters!"

"Or gruel!"

"Or Klingons!"

"Or Martia!"

McCoy rolled his eyes, suspecting Kirk was doing the same,

with perhaps some small reservation. "Thank the good lord for small favors!"

"Good night, Bones."

"'Night, Jim."

"Doctor!"

McCoy ignored the insistent voice that didn't quite wake him up completely, and went right back to sleep. For about a second.

"Doctor McCoy?"

This time a sense of déjà vu dragged him up from the hard, cold, uncomfortably comfy depths of his slumber. He opened one eye.

"Spock?"

"Yes, Doctor."

With a resigned sigh, he opened the other eye. "What time is it?"

"Oh-four-hundred-point-three-five-six-two—"

" 'The ungodly hour of predawn' will do, Spock."

"Jim?"

"Over here."

McCoy would have been amused, if he hadn't been half-asleep. Spock's superior vision would enable him to easily locate his captain in the dim shadows underneath McCoy's desk. Nothing in that Vulcan brain of his would enable him to easily understand what could have possessed Jim Kirk to be there.

"Captain?"

"It's all right, Spock. We're just having a bit of . . ."

"Posttraumatic stress." McCoy believed in calling a spade a spade.

"Ah." Spock got up without another word, only turning back at the door. "Pardon me for a moment, gentlemen."

He disappeared, the door whooshed shut behind him, and the two men he left behind could only stare at each other dumbly. By the time either of them could come up with something sensible to say, the Vulcan was back, pulling his own parka on over his duty uniform. Spock sat down cross-legged, as if preparing for meditation, near McCoy's feet, and huddled into the depths of insulated warmth.

McCoy sat up, shoved his hood out of his face, and leaned back against the wall. "What's wrong with you, Spock? You're acting weirder than Jim and me, and that's pretty damned weird."

"Indeed. That is why I have placed myself on emergency medical confinement to quarters."

"There's a lot of that goin' around." McCoy squinted at his two companions' shadows of their former selves. "Feel like talkin' about it?"

"That is why I am here, Doctor."

"Who has the conn, Spock?"

"Mister Scott. I am afraid I rousted him from a badly needed period of rest, but I felt I had no recourse. Of course I could have called upon a junior officer, as we are simply engaged in a somewhat indirect and convoluted journey to space dock." Spock sounded almost wary, as if he couldn't quite believe what he was saying. "However, it seemed prudent to have a seasoned officer at the conn, considering the fact that three of the ship's senior officers are now . . . incapacitated."

"Quite right, Spock." Kirk's command mode was kicking into overdrive, the decisive tone carrying out into the small space, dispensing reassurance, though also carrying an underlying puzzlement. "Do you want me to leave? If you came to Bones about a medical problem—"

"That will not be necessary. I have come to Doctor McCoy as a friend as much as for his medical advice. I value both of your opinions, as always. If, after hearing my complaint, you feel it necessary, as my primary physician and commanding officer, I will go to sickbay and turn myself in to be committed."

"Com—committed?" McCoy was having trouble talking around his dropped jaw. Not to mention his stunned brain.

"Yes, Doctor. I believe I may be, for lack of a better term, out of my Vulcan mind. As you have so often suspected."

A soft chuckle drifted across from Kirk's cubby. "At least you've still got your sense of humor."

"Yeah, not that you ever admitted to having one in the first place!" McCoy sobered after a chuckle of his own. "Tell us."

"Very well."

Silence ensued.

McCoy cleared his throat discretely, and he heard Kirk shift positions. Neither of them prodded Spock. It had to be hard for a Vulcan to articulate whatever it was this one was grappling with.

"I can only state the manifestation of my problem baldly, gentlemen." The words came out quietly, but with unsettling conviction. "I am hearing voices."

"Voices."

"Yes, Jim."

"Are you sure?"

"Quite, Doctor. One cannot mistake this kind of thing. I am hearing, very distinctly, the voice of what sounds like a young child. Singing."

"Singing?"

McCoy wished the captain would stop echoing everything Spock said, but admitted to himself that it was all that kept him from doing the same thing. He raked unsteady fingers through his sleep-tousled hair, giving himself time to think of something to say besides "Are you sure?" again.

While he was thinking, Spock gave voice to the obvious. "That is very disturbing, is it not?"

"Well . . ." No use in pussyfooting around it. Spock wouldn't buy anything but the truth. "Yes, Spock. It does sound . . . troubling."

"I knew as much, of course." A moment of silence lay where a resigned sigh would have emerged from anyone else. "Before I articulated it, the phenomenon seemed less . . . alarming. Somewhat."

"Huma—" McCoy caught himself just short of uttering the dreaded h-word. "Er, only natural, Spock."

"Perhaps. But what of my condition? That is most certainly not natural."

"How long has this been going on, Spock?" Kirk's quiet, calm query still had the same frision of tension running through it that McCoy felt shiver down his own spine.

"Only recently. It began the day of Chancellor Gorkon's death. In fact, I checked the logs, and the first instance occurred the moment you were both taken into custody. Perhaps I am after all susceptible to stress, in the manner of my mother's people. If that is the case, however, why would it be that I have never before suffered such phenomena? I have certainly been subjected to extreme situations that would, as I believe Mister Scott would put it, have caused any man to lose his grip on the caber."

McCoy laughed in spite of himself. "As long as you're still able to quote Scotty that directly, there's plenty of room left for hope as far as that brain of yours goes, Spock. Let's just think for a minute. Maybe there's some logical explanation."

"Sure. We can't discount any possibility out of hand. Say, you don't suppose—" Kirk must have sat bolt upright in the dim light, if the thump and curse that followed were any indication.

"Want me to take a look at that lump, Jim?"

"No, Bones, I think I'll live. But I also think I'll lie back down now. And stay that way." A rustling moment followed as Kirk settled back out of range of the underside of McCoy's desk. "Anyway, as I was saying, you don't suppose the Klingons could have done something?"

Silence.

McCoy rubbed his chin thoughtfully. "I don't see how. Besides, they've been too busy plotting their own downfall lately to bother with ours. Can you really imagine Chang having the patience to practice mind control? And on a Vulcan no less. Why, he'd be more likely to blow Spock to bits, and throw us into chaos that way, than toy with his mind."

"I concur, Doctor. At any rate, this experience has a certain subtlety that does not speak of ill intent from outside sources. In fact, the singing child sounds quite pleasing. I would find it soothing even, if not for the unsettling implications."

"Well, then, let's go at it from that angle. Sing us the song."

Spock actually sucked in what sounded like an alarmed breath to those attuned to the language of Vulcan sighs. "I am not prepared to do that, Doctor."

"Now, you look here, you green-blooded . . . Sorry. Habit." McCoy drew in his own deep breath. "Listen, Spock, you're among friends. There's absolutely nothing you can't tell Jim and me, and you know it. Why is singing any different?"

"The lyrics of this song are so entirely nonsensical that their existence inside my mind concerns me almost as much as the voice."

"How nonsensical, Spock?" Kirk's tight urgency was palpable.

"To the point of being gibberish."

"I'm only going to say this one more time, and if you balk again, I'll walk you down to sickbay and commit you myself! Sing the damned song!"

"Very well, Doctor."

He paused for another of those intolerably drawn-out, nearly silent inhalations, and then, finally, he sang:

"Ring around the rosey
A pocket full of posies
Ashes, ashes,
We all fall down."

On the final line he was joined by McCoy.

"Doctor?"

"Where in blazes did you learn that?"

"Where did you learn it, Bones?"

"You don't know it, Jim?" McCoy smiled in fond reminiscence. "No, I guess you wouldn't, being a boy and growing up on a farm with a brother, and never having a daughter. It's something all little girls sing. They seem to just know it, straight from birth, but I suppose they teach it to each other after someone's mother gets it started."

"I do not understand."

"It's a children's game, Spock. 'Ring Around the Rosey' . . . they form a circle, go round and round, then flop to the ground on 'We all fall down.'"

"I fail to comprehend anything that constitutes a game in that song."

"I'm with Spock. Kind of macabre, isn't it?"

"Well, sure. So are Grimm's fairy tales and a whole lot of other childhood rites of passage, Jim. This thing goes way back, all the way to the Black Death in the fourteenth century. It's said that there were so many dead that the bodies were stacked like cordwood, waiting for the wagons to come around to collect them for mass graves or pyres outside of the villages. People would keep sweet-smelling flowers in their pockets to cover the stench of death. The ashes were from the burning bodies. I guess it was such a horrific experience that it imprinted on the collective consciousness to the point that the memories passed down by oral tradition eventually evolved into something children instinctively turned into good. More or less. Who knows, really, after so much time, but that's what I think."

"Fascinating. But I can assure you that I had never heard it until my 'illness' manifested."

"That's the spirit, Spock. You put enough emphasis of doubt on that illness business that I have to assume you realize you can't be crazy. It's a real song!"

"I conclude no such thing."

"No, he's right, Jim. The song may be real, but what's it doing in his head?"

"Spock, maybe your mother—"

"Certainly not."

McCoy narrowed his eyes, looking toward Spock, but seeing deep inside his own mind. "You know, it's a very strange coincidence that it's that particular song that's bothering you, Spock."

"In what way?"

"Well, it's been runnin' through my own head a lot lately, too. Like I was tellin' Jim earlier, our ordeal made me think a lot about the past. There were times when thinking about my daughter's sweet voice singin' 'Ring Around the Rosey' in our backyard when she was real little . . . well, that memory got me through a lot. I always did love the way she'd do it when she was by herself, spinnin' around and around, then laughing to beat the band when she flopped to the ground."

"Fascinating. I, too, hear laughter after 'down.' "

"Why, exactly, did you decide tonight was the time to come to me about this, Spock?"

"During the crisis I was able to put up effective barriers to keep the singing from becoming a distraction to the essential work of discovering the depths of the corruption and plotting, both in the Klingons and from within the Federation. I was starting to believe that the singing was fading away, now that the crisis has passed."

"Uh, Spock? How about the essential work of getting us out of that hellhole?"

"I assumed that much was understood, Jim."

"Of course."

"But tonight . . ."

"Tonight, Doctor, it became apparent that instead of getting better, the situation was worsening. As I occupied the conn in the nocturnal shift quiet, all barriers became as if they had never existed. A rush of childish singing, and laughter, inundated my mind, and became all that I could hear, or think about."

"Bear with me a minute, Spock." McCoy thudded his head back against the wall, wondering if he'd gone as mad as Spock thought he himself was becoming. "How long did this . . . attack . . . last?"

"While it seemed to go on for quite some time, I am certain it was a matter of minutes. Perhaps ten."

"What are you onto, Bones?"

"I'm not sure." A self-deprecating little laugh crept out. "In fact, you're probably gonna think I'm the crazy one. But . . . the timing . . . the circumstances . . ."

"Doctor?"

"When you were dead, Spock, I was sure I was headed for a rubber room. Why, I even channeled you at times."

"Ch—?"

"Basically, I became you. You should have seen that Starfleet security officer I tried to neck pinch . . . The point is that carrying your *katra* did something to me, Spock. I still have a distinct memory of what the desert sun warmed fur of a *sehlat* feels like, though I've never touched one."

"I-Chaya."

"Exactly. I know that was his name, though I don't know how I know it. You see?"

"What you are suggesting is—"

"Absurd. Yes, I know that. But is it possible? Are you hearing these self-protective thoughts my brain conjures up for me, since they've been so intense over the Klingon ordeal? Especially now that we're in close proximity to each other again? Because, I'm telling you, Spock, earlier tonight, after I got myself cold enough and uncomfortable enough to relax, I was thinking mighty hard about my long-ago little girl playing 'Ring Around the Rosey' all by herself, and laughing with such delight. It calms me down. Helps me sleep. I'd probably still be asleep right now, if the two of you didn't have the override access codes to my quarters!"

Such a silence fell over the room that it was almost as if McCoy's impassioned little speech had never happened. But by that very silence, he could tell that the possibility he had tossed into their midst had registered. He had stunned them speechless.

He screwed his eyes shut and concentrated with all his might on the sound of childish laughter and nonsensical singing. He thought and thought, until the laughter reverberated through his mind like a clanging bell. A subtle but harshly indrawn breath told him at least some echo was getting through. There was only one way they could be sure. Everything inside him protested against such a thing, but . . .

Before he could talk himself out of it, he crawled the short distance to Spock and snaked out both hands. He paused for only a split second in the dim light, his questioning gaze seeking compliance. Acquiescence lay in the obsidian depths, sending a shiver of relief mixed with trepidation down his spine. With an instinct he had earned with the gift of his friendship and the openness of his mind, his fingers stiffened into talons and found their home against the pressure points of the Vulcan's face. "Remember."

There was no resistance, in spite of the shock such contact carried. Barely noting the hiss of indrawn breath, McCoy hovered there, pouring his precious memory of his child into the waiting receptacle. He called up every sun-drenched, lazy-weekend moment, lingering on the way his daughter's hair glinted in the sunlight, the sound of her piping voice singing her favorite song, and most of all concentrating on the joyousness of the experience of watching her savor her young life.

Knowing from the physically intensified bond that connected him to his friend that his gift had been received, McCoy allowed his fingers to relax, preparing to disengage. Spock's mind called out to him to wait, so he stayed in place, expecting to have some further detail extracted from his mind with an ability he himself could in no way claim. Instead, he was given a gift of his own.

Suddenly, McCoy was no longer himself. He was a small boy crouched against a warm mound of breathing fur. The desert sun beat down upon the sand all around him, but he felt cool in the shade of his pet *sehlat*. An olive arm stretched out, fingers tangling in gleaming fur, allowing him to savor the softness, which contrasted with the rasp as a large, hot tongue lashed out to brush affectionately against his thumb. It tickled. He did not laugh, though some corner of his young half-Vulcan, half-human mind begged for the release of pent-up joy.

"Spock. Come in for supper."

A lightning-quick flash of happiness at the sound of his mother's voice, a smile half-formed, a pause to practice the controls his father had taught him in their lessons together. He got to his feet and heard I-Chaya lumber to his own and follow as Spock made his way to the door held open invitingly.

The joy-laden serenity of her presence blanketed him as he entered the cool shadows of his home. He turned back to watch his mother's slender white hand secure the entry, the closing aperture slowly diminishing his view of the Vulcan outdoors until the last thing he saw was his pet's dark eyes blinking lazily in the still-bright light. The scents of *plomeek* soup and roasted acorn squash engulfed him, symbolizing the dichotomy of his life in a way that was lost on the hungry, contented child who had simply come in for his supper.

The memory stream halted abruptly. A moment of what amounted to mental white noise passed, and then McCoy perceived the gentle hum native to his quarters, the quiet breathing of his friends . . . and something more. He realized that he now remembered the things that had teased at his brain, since Spock's *katra* had been returned to its rightful owner. Somehow, Spock had been able to determine the ghost memories that lingered with him still and fill them up, flesh them out, give them substance and heft, make them so that the memories McCoy now realized were among Spock's most treasured were as his own.

He felt Spock's fingers gently disengage his own from their connection to the Vulcan's face. Human eyes met Vulcan, with a blend of gratitude and awe. "You didn't have to. You could have taken back what didn't belong to me. Why, Spock?"

"Were the memory shadows unwelcome, Leonard?"

"No, of course not. They were . . . an enrichment. Now . . . why, Spock, I remember I-Chaya so vividly, and the way your mother's voice sounded to you when you were a little boy. . . . Hell, I might even like *plomeek* soup from now on!"

"Indeed." A pause. The Vulcan's voice dropped noticeably. "You must examine what I have given you most carefully, Leonard. There was a question you asked me once, that I chose not to answer. You possess that answer now. If you find it to be a burden, I will remove it, with no harm done to you."

McCoy closed his eyes, knowing without asking the question of which Spock spoke. He accessed the memory with ease, digested it, savored it. He opened his eyes. "No, Spock. It's all right. I can handle it."

"I thought as much."

A not-so-subtle throat-clearing issued from the vicinity of the desk. "Does someone want to tell me what just happened?"

McCoy groped for a way to explain the life-altering experience he had just emerged from. "I—I—"

"Doctor McCoy managed to initiate a mind-meld and share his memories of his daughter playing 'Ring Around the Rosey.' I am now thoroughly convinced that I am not out of my Vulcan mind after all."

"Thank God!"

"Amen to that!"

"So everything's all right now?"

"Yes, Jim. I believe I will go back to my quarters now, increase the ambient temperature there twofold, and meditate on the evening's events. Good night, gentlemen." Spock got up in a single fluid motion that made McCoy's stiff muscles practically cry out in envy, shucked off his parka, and left them to their ersatz ice planetoid.

"See, Bones? I knew it would turn out to be something simple." Kirk yawned audibly and settled himself for sleep. "Good night. Again."

McCoy opened his mouth, closed it, tried again. " 'Night, Jim."

He got himself to his pallet, wrapped back up snugly in his layers of warmth, and drew in a deep, cold breath. He wanted more than anything at that moment to share with his friend what had just happened to him. For there was nothing simple about what had transpired between Vulcan and human tonight. McCoy had discovered the depths of the connection that remained between himself and Spock. He knew he could no more initiate a mind-meld with anybody else than he could fly. He also knew he had been entrusted with memories that he could never divulge. Not to another living soul.

Leonard McCoy now knew what it was like to die.

A Sucker Born

Pat Detmer

"Ooooooooooohhhhh!"

It was a collective, happy sound, a universal one, and it had a tendency to be pretty much the same no matter what planet you hailed from. It was an unconscious vocal release connected to wonder and awe.

Freddie Ott, the on-board tour guide, allowed himself a grin. Although he didn't make squat at this job, there were moments when he didn't feel utterly horrible about it. And this was one of them. The afternoon floater-watching tour was in full swing, and life was not all that bad.

There were worse things to do than ferry tourists around a gas giant to watch the floaters feed.

Although he couldn't think of one at the moment.

"You can see here," he said by rote, raising his arm and pointing out the viewport, "that the baby *Saganicus giganticus* never strays far from the mother's side." He watched the little Andorian boy in seat 3A dutifully press his face to the glass as the massive gray-green image claimed all the wide viewing ports, baby floaters tumbling in the airstream behind it. 3A then looked back at Freddie, his black eyes wide with amazement.

Freddie smiled at him, but he felt his smile fade when the ship gave an ominous chug and a lurch to his right. He shot a look at his pilot—a new one; they cycled through employees pretty fast at HFM Enterprises—and the new guy (gal?/purple thing with eight arms) shrugged all eight arms at once and raised some lumpy things above its eye stalks that might be eyebrows.

Whatever.

They grounded an average of a ship a month at HFM. He wasn't sure where his boss got them, but *junkyard* would have made an excellent bet. The seats—blatantly unsafe—had been taken from a diner on a starbase after a reconstruct. He had no electronics to use in his presentation, not even a voice enhancer, and he often went home raw-throated from his efforts to be heard over the rattle of the loose rivets. And the thing that passed as a bathroom . . . he didn't even want to go there.

Literally.

The pilot managed to get the ship settled down before the paying customers had time to voice their concern. They were too enraptured with the view outside the windows to be worried about a sputtering impulse engine.

It *was* pretty spectacular, and Freddie allowed himself a silent moment of awe just like the rest of the passengers. The floaters opened cavernous maws and sucked the minerals and nutrients that were suspended in the gas giant's atmosphere into stomachs the size of a nacelle on a starship. The floater babies hovered along their sides, absorbing the resultant ejecta that periodically flushed from diaphanous slits in the sides of the mothers.

While the tourists were mesmerized by the floaters, Freddie glanced starboard and spied the back end of the two-man HFM Enterprises warp sled scooting above the ship where it couldn't be seen by passengers.

This was the part Freddie had a problem with. He wasn't a prude, and he understood the need to stay in business, but he knew that feeding the floaters for the pleasure of the customers was not ecologically sound. Hell, it was illegal in most of the rest of the universe, but then their boss had never bothered himself too much with legalities in the past.

So far, they'd not been caught. The sled would seed the atmosphere above and below the tour ship with some high-grade nickel and iron, then . . . stand back. Guaranteed floaters.

In fact, that's what the hand-painted sign over the entrance said: "Floater-feeding sighting guaranteed, or your credits back."

And right now it was a veritable feeding frenzy. Freddie had never seen so many at once. These folks were certainly getting their credits' worth.

But he was concerned about the Vulcan and the black female human in seats next to each other about halfway back on the starboard side. The Vulcan wasn't looking at the floater show, but was pressed against the viewing glass, attempting to peer above the vessel. Freddie could guess what had happened: he'd spotted the warp sled, and the woman next to him was now leaning in that direction as well, and they were speaking to each other. And the worst thing of all was that they were wearing Federation Starfleet uniforms. Even though Freddie knew they had no authority here, their presence still made his stomach churn.

He swallowed and cleared his tight throat.

"Whadaya think, folks? Pretty spectacular, huh?"

The ship jerked again and Freddie heard a horrible screeching above him, metal on metal, and he had to grip the seats along the aisles to stay standing. A Tellarite bellowed as he fell from a seat in the back, and the two Starfleet tourists rose as if they might be able to do something.

Freddie was never, ever supposed to open the viewport above them, but he couldn't help himself. He reached for the switch with a shaking finger. He pushed it, and it stalled—no surprise—so he pushed it again and the viewport covering recessed into the body of the ship, screaming in protest all the way.

Of course everybody looked up.

There was the warp sled, upside down on top of the tour ship. He could see the two pale and terrified HFM Enterprises employees inside it through their viewports, working the controls and calling out to each other. And pinning the sled to the tour ship were no less than a dozen juvenile *Saganicus giganticus*. They took turns batting the hell out of the warp sled, which meant they were also batting the hell out of the tour ship.

There was a collective scream, and much like the earlier vocal release connected to wonder and awe, this sounded pretty much the same from everyone. Except for up near the front, where there was someone who sounded like a rushing stream with an overlay of chiming *belau* bells.

Freddie was fairly certain of a couple of things as he looked out at the slack-jawed, shocked faces of the tourists and watched the little blue antennae on the Andorian boy deflate like balloons and drop to his head, a sure sign that he would projectile vomit in about fifteen seconds: one, his boss was not going to be very happy about this; and two, there would be no tips from the tourists today.

Uhura sniffed.

"*What* is that smell?" She knew Spock must smell it. He heard, saw, and smelled everything before any of the rest of them did. She sniffed again and cast a critical eye around the stained and seedy reception area. "I'm not sure I even want to know."

She looked out of the corner of her eye at her silent companion. She'd never seen him this incensed. Of course "incensed" on Mister Spock looked a little different that it did on, say, Scotty or Chekov. Spock was a silent smolderer, and he was smoldering now, his ear tips slightly darker than the rest of him.

An irritating popping sound brought her eyes to the receptionist's desk. *An Orion receptionist,* Uhura thought, bemused. Made about as much sense as a Vulcan party planner. The well-endowed dark green girl was filing her nails, chewing what must have been supremely snappable gum, and scanning a padd in front of her. Multitasking.

They'd been stuck in the so-called lobby of HFM Enterprises for the last half-hour. The minute that the tour ship had landed on Tt-tnicktttnor after the near-disastrous floater-watching tour to the nearby gas giant, Spock had asked Freddie Ott for directions to the HFM offices so that he could lodge a formal complaint.

Freddie had turned and pointed to a dismal building squatting at the corner of the landing pad. And now they were in it. Waiting.

They only had three days left day on Tttnicktttnor, and Uhura had packing to do. She and Spock had been left there by the *Enterprise* to help with a communications upgrade at a Federation outpost while the *Enterprise* warped off to do police duty at the far side of a different solar system.

Tttnicktttnor was not an official Federation member—although the diplomatic delegates at the outpost were doing their best to make it happen—so she knew that Starfleet had no power here. But as citizens of the universe, Mister Spock had explained, it was their duty to lodge a complaint and detail the grave misgivings that they had regarding the seeding of the gas giant atmosphere for the pleasure of tourists.

Uhura sighed in spite of her best efforts, and she knew her attitude was salted with impatience. Mister Spock, as serene as a sphinx, looked down at her.

"Lieutenant Uhura, it is not necessary for you to wait. I am quite capable of lodging this complaint without you."

She felt a stab of guilt as she looked up at him. "No. No. I'm with you, Mister Spock. I think that what they did is wrong as well. I'm just frustrated that we're being treated this way."

"Send in those tourists from the floater-watching tour, Verlida," a voice squawked over an intercom that sounded to be in the same kind of shape as their tour ships. "And who are they again?"

" 'Again'? I never told you in the first place."

"Now, Verlida, be a good little green girl . . ."

It was clear to Uhura that Spock could stand it no longer. He rose from his seat, went to Verlida's desk, and stood at attention before it.

"Starfleet Commander Spock and Lieutenant Uhura from the Federation *Starship Enterprise*."

For a moment, Uhura thought that the intercom system had officially given up the ghost. There were hisses, tweets, growls, and then the sound of heavy footfalls coming to the door behind Verlida's desk. Concerned, Uhura rose and stood next to the first officer. She cringed as the door flew open.

And there, bigger than life, as big almost as the juvenile floaters they'd seen on the tour, dressed flamboyantly in silks and brocades and looking like a float from an interspecies pride parade, smelling of spices, bad cigars, and cheap beer . . . was Harry Mudd.

Harcourt Fenton Mudd. HFM Enterprises.

He threw his arms wide and high and let out a bellow that made Verlida stab herself with her file and drop the padd to the floor.

"Can it be? Can it be? Can it be that I, Harry Mudd, have the privilege of being visited on my very own planet by the beautiful Uhura and the brave and stoic Mister Spock?" He slammed a bejeweled hand down on Verlida's desk. "Pinch me, Verlida." Verlida, looking willing but a few crystals short of a full dilithium charge, reached for his hand, but it was gone—gone to the other side of the desk to be used in a crushing, malodorous hug that engulfed both Spock and Uhura. After a suffocating minute, Mudd had mercy and let them go. Crossing his arms, he brought a thoughtful finger to the side of his face.

"My goodness. How many years has it been?"

"Mister Mudd," Spock said, stiff-backed and unmoved by the overblown welcome, "we were given to believe that we had left you trapped on a planet of androids with no means of escape. Your wife was duplicated, I believe." Spock paused and cocked an eyebrow. "Stella."

Harry Mudd trembled a little and then caught himself and smiled, and a food particle—something orange—dropped from his walrus mustache and joined the dust bunnies under Verlida's desk.

"Ah, you *thought* . . ." he said, shaking his head. "Mister Spock, never, ever underestimate Harcourt Fenton Mudd. I have my ways."

"Indeed, Mister Mudd. Of that I have no doubt. As to our purpose for being here . . ."

"You break my heart!" Harry said, clutching the velveteen fabric in front of it. "You come to my planet, to my door, after how many years have passed, and you won't even allow a moment to reminisce, a moment to regale me with tales of bravery on the *Starship Enterprise?* Please!" he cried with a wide gesture at the open door behind the desk. "You'll join me! Some ale? Shellmouth crabs?" He gave Uhura a chuck under the chin. "They're just in. Running right now, on both hemispheres as we speak. Interesting creatures, and wonderful with a white sauce of *fignots* . . ."

"Mister Mudd," Spock said in a voice as cold as Uhura had ever heard it, "we are here to lodge a complaint regarding the floater-watching tour, specifically, regarding your methods of attracting the *saganicus* for your personal remuneration."

Mudd, all innocence, blinked. "Why, Mister Spock, I don't—"

"Your warp sled was damaged, and lives were put at risk. I do not know the composition of the materials that you are releasing into the atmosphere—"

Mudd fell back a step. "Materials? I'm sorry. I haven't the—"

"—but whatever you are using, it is quite effective."

Mudd frowned, settled a substantial hip on the corner of the desk, and pursed his lips. "Hmm. Now that you mention it, I *did* receive a report from one of our technicians about an incident, a bit of a run-in with some juvenile floaters. Could this be what you're referring to, Mister Spock?"

"The incident was a *result*, Mister Mudd. A result of a feeding frenzy. One exacerbated by your methods of attracting the *saganicus.*" Surprised at the intensity she could hear in his voice, Uhura looked at Spock out of the corner of her eye. In Spock terms, he was about two tics shy of a full-blown Chekovian snit.

Mudd leaned forward and smiled, and another orange bit of

something fell off his mustache and disappeared into the voluminous folds of his brocaded top. "But on this planet, sir, it is not against the law—"

"But it *is* unconscionable. And I am asking you to stop."

Mudd heaved a theatrical sigh as he rose. "A pity that the Federation is powerless here, Mister Spock. Someone like you, a magnificent brain like yours, your ability with computers, the things that could be accomplished . . ."

Seemingly defeated, he shuffled toward his office door, then paused. Uhura recoiled when he turned back around and she saw the light in his eyes, a now-I've-got-'em light that meant that he was up to no good, a light that the *Enterprise* had seen before, that screamed *"Proceed with caution!"* She glanced at her companion. The first officer of the *Enterprise* had never quite mastered the art of reading human faces, and she wondered if Spock could see what she saw.

It was hard to tell. Mister Spock would have made an excellent poker player.

"However . . . however . . ." Mudd mused aloud, "there *might* be a way that you could help . . ." He shot a glance at Verlida, moved away from her, and hunched in front of them, his voice conspiratorial. "Not here," he said, and he pulled them around to face the entrance and guided them toward it by their elbows. "But if you could spare *just* a moment," he whispered, "a moment in the interest of the Federation gaining a toehold on our little undeclared planet. Only a moment, and then we can discuss how we might reconfigure the floater tours . . ."

The building that Harry Mudd led them to was at the opposite side of the landing pad from the HFM Enterprises corporate headquarters, and was just as attractive. The wide, barnlike double doors of the warehouse were webbed with chains and locks. It took the CEO of HFM a good three minutes to unlock and unweb them, and he did so using great, grandiose sweeps of his arms. Grunting with effort, he pushed one of the doors aside just enough to allow his girth to pass, and he hurried them in, eyes darting, finger to his lips.

The smell, at least, was more agreeable than the odors at head-quarters, but the light—provided only by a line of grimy windows set high up the sides of the walls—was so dim that it took Uhura several moments to be able to discern anything at all.

She stepped forward, mesmerized. There was something famil-iar about the jumble of corrugated sheets and metal constructs and tables and chairs spread in a circle ahead of them. Tiered seats rose on all sides, save the side by which they entered the circle.

No, she thought. *Not a circle. It's a theater. A theater in the round.*

She peered up and saw scaffolds and lighting above them. Mudd, having relocked the door from the inside, moved into the center of the warehouse, and she and Spock followed.

As she stepped up onto the stage, Uhura realized that the corru-gated sheets and metal panels were not merely random bits of packing material. There was purpose and meaning to their place-ment, and they were cut to peculiar angles, glued to form overhead projections, taped and hammered together to create . . . *what?* And there were things drawn on them in broad, black strokes: dials, but-tons, arrows, directives.

A projection screen dominated the area across from where they were standing, and directly in front of them was a large easy chair on a platform, and in front of that, a wide table with boxes on top of it and two chairs tucked underneath; there was more scratching on the boxes, more arrows, more angles and tape to hold things there, and . . . *oh* so familiar.

"The bridge of the *U.S.S. Enterprise,* Mister Mudd?" Spock said.

Of course! Uhura thought. There it was, right in front of her, looking like an overly ambitious, underfunded primary school project.

Mudd turned and clutched his hands together over his heart. "You could tell," he breathed, his face a portrait in ecstasy. "You could tell."

"Only by the dimensionality, which seems essentially correct,"

Spock said, moving to the science post. He looked down at the scratchings there and raised his eyebrows. "Your understanding of the processes, however, leaves something to be desired."

"Oh, Mister Spock," Mudd said approaching him, his eyes wide, hands held in a pleading clasp in front of his chest. "This is where you come in. This is where you can be of *great,* great service—"

"I do not think—" Spock began.

"—of service to *both* the Federation *and* to the *saganicus,*" Harry said in a hurry. "I believe, Mister Spock, that we might strike a bargain. A win-win situation, if you will."

Uhura held her breath as she watched them. She heard the clank and whine of a tour ship taking off outside. It tore over the building, and dust motes trickled down through the filtered light. Mister Spock was, as usual, unreadable. Mister Mudd, on the other hand, could be read like a freshly charged padd.

Finally, Spock spoke.

"I am listening."

Freddie Ott took the tickets from the last tourists in the line. His boss had been adamant about not letting anyone in late—or *out* at all!—for the three programmed hours of the *U.S.S. Enterprise* tour. It was a proviso that Mister Spock had insisted upon before he left Tttnicktttnor, part of the deal that he'd struck with the boss. The tourists needed to keep to their seats, Spock had said, in order to appreciate the full effect of what he had programmed into the computer. And they needed to realize that in space there was sometimes no escape, often no viable options, so there should not be any on the *U.S.S. Enterprise* tour, either.

Of course Mister Mudd had agreed. He'd agreed to *everything.* He hadn't even wrung his hands when Spock had insisted on dismantling the warp sled. It was a guarantee, Spock had said, that it would not be used for disreputable purposes, and besides, he'd needed the spare parts—along with every other odd chunk of machinery he could find—for the *Enterprise* mock-up.

He and Uhura had spent hours and hours hard at work, directing

Freddie and other employees in painting and sawing, in dial and button placement, and in the installation of the new door mechanism: the lock, automatic, powering up when the program began, unlocking when it was over.

Lieutenant Uhura had taken some time off now and again, but the Vulcan had been amazing. Unstoppable. Three days, three nights straight he was there, and Harry Mudd did his best to keep up, looking harried but excited beyond his wildest dreams.

Actually, from what Uhura had confided to Freddie, it was amazing that Mister Spock had agreed to it at all. And anyone except for a complete idiot or a complete innocent could see what Mudd was up to, and it had nothing to do with warm and fuzzy feelings for the *Saganicus giganticus,* and nothing to do with introducing Tttnicktttnor to the magnificent Federation via showcasing its Starfleet army and their daring adventures. It had *everything* to do with his boss making another quick credit or two. After all, he'd been planning the "Ride on the *Enterprise!"* holodiorama ever since Freddie had hired on two cycles ago. There wasn't a being within a parsec of Harry Mudd who hadn't heard of his exploits with the infamous crew. And he'd broken bread with them and ridden the stars with them not once . . . but *twice!* And the HFM CEO was going to exploit that for all it was worth.

It was not by mistake that Harry Mudd's company's name had the word "Enterprise" in it.

But from what Freddie had seen, Spock had been oblivious to Mudd's baser intentions and had been most accommodating, even downloading declassified bridge recordings directly from the real *Enterprise*—which had been on the way back to pick up Spock and Uhura—into the computers of the HFM *Enterprise,* its bridge components still a little sticky from the last coat of paint.

Mister Mudd was almost certain that the downloaded starship recordings would include his own exploits, and he was also hopeful that some of the more notorious missions might be accessible. Perhaps their first glimpse of the Romulans, now well-documented throughout the universe. Or the destruction of the planet-eater, or the discovery of the *Botany Bay* and the release of Khan to an uninhabited planet.

Freddie himself was hoping for Kirk's battle with the Gorn, now part of an interactive, three-dimensional, real-time game that could be purchased on planets everywhere and played against other beings parsecs away.

But Mister Spock had been as mum on the contents of the downloads as a *tttbehr* during hibernation.

Freddie stayed at his post and watched as his boss moved to a spotlight near the conn and addressed the eager attendees. The tickets had fetched top credits and there had been rumors of scalping, so Mister Mudd was beside himself: effusive, ebullient, bejeweled. Freddie barely listened to the substance of the speech, but contented himself with idly counting the number of rings that Mudd had managed to jam on his fingers.

Enterprise this, and *blah blah* that, and *my good personal friends Commander Spock and Lieutenant Uhura,* and then with a flourish, Harcourt Fenton Mudd pressed a button on the conn and declared, "Mister Scott, you may begin."

Through the speaker system, "Mister Scott" replied, "Aye, sir." But it was a new employee who was playing the voice of Mister Scott before the computer program officially took over, a Utanturian not yet well-versed in Federation Standard, and it came out sounding something like "Oy sure" or "Oyster." Freddie wasn't certain from where he stood, because the door behind him had begun to roll into place, and it locked down with a solid *thuccachunck.*

The overheads dimmed to black and a spotlight fell on the empty conn. Mister Mudd had been worried about this part. He'd wanted actors to mime the various crew members, but Spock had insisted on stark realism: a thin spotlight where the crew member would normally be when speaking. Mudd had hinted at holograms, but Spock had cited the lack of time and tools. So there it was, a single beam, and hundreds of paying patrons, waiting.

The moment that Captain James T. Kirk's voice came over the speakers—full, sure, rich with intrinsic authority—Freddie Ott breathed a sigh of relief. Mister Spock had been right. It actually worked this way: the darkened arena, the intense beam hitting the conn, the sense of heightened drama . . . *What would happen next?*

The captain announced the stardate and the mission: mapping the asteroids in the belt between Elbina and Epsilon in the Delta Trimute solar system.

"Mister Spock," the captain said. The spotlight on the conn faded, and the one above the science station came up.

"Captain," Mister Spock's voice responded. "Mister Sulu, on my mark. And now. Triangulation for El-Ep Belt asteroids numbers 1 through 303,415."

A new light came up at the table in front of the conn, and a heavily accented voice said, "Got it, Mister Spock."

"Thank you, Mister Chekov. Mister Sulu, again: on my mark."

Freddie's heart skipped a beat when the spotlight above the conn came on. *Here comes trouble,* Freddie thought, grinning. Now the world goes to shit and we find out who the enemy is. Gorn? Romulan? Klingon? Energy-zapping amoeba? The audience leaned forward, and Captain Kirk's voice came through the speakers:

"I'm gonna go down and grab some lunch. Spock, you have the conn."

"Yes, Captain," Spock's voice said. "And again, Mister Sulu, on my mark."

The light on the table: "Got it."

A pause.

"Mister Scott, I will need to have you backtrack on impulse. It is necessary to verify the last triangulation figure."

A longer pause. The light on the table: "Verified."

Mister Spock: "Very well. Proceed."

Freddie himself was quite a fan of the exploits of the *Enterprise,* and he frowned, trying to remember what disaster had befallen the crew while mapping asteroids in the Delta Trimute solar system.

After a moment's thought, a chill ran up his spine. He'd never *heard* of the *Enterprise* mapping asteroids in the Delta Trimute solar system, which meant that *nothing* had happened while they were mapping asteroids in the Delta Trimute solar system. Nothing.

Freddie's eyes tracked around the stage, searching for his boss. Harry Mudd had taken up a post near the projection screen, and even from ten meters away Freddie could see his smile wobble and the individual beads of sweat pop up on his forehead. Alarmed, Freddie turned and gave the locked door behind him a shove: a good one, fueled by adrenaline. Nothing.

The crowd was growing restless, grumbling and shifting in their seats. They were leaning forward, straining, expecting to hear sharp words about an impending disaster or the whine of phaser fire or the cries of an alien race, but other than the droning chess match between Spock and Chekov, there was . . .

Nothing.

Freddie Ott was fairly certain of a couple of things as he looked at the confused and unhappy faces of the tourists and watched the chartreuse tendrils on the heads of the Nebulean couple near the door curl up and recess into their scalps, a sure sign that they would be ejecting their nasty *nebul* pheromones into the enclosed atmosphere of the warehouse in about half an hour: one, his boss was not going to be very happy about this; and two, there would be no tips from the tourists today.

Obligations Discharged

Gerri Leen

After thirty years in the royal palace of Troyius, I have grown accustomed to the constant pampering and ever-present intrusion of gentle music, soft cushions, and the even softer people who attend me. I have trained my features to hide my disdain for such luxuries, and appear to be at ease among the opulence that would feed half a city back on Elas. My manner is graceful, my gestures smooth. I mingle with those who were my enemies as if I were one of them, no longer demanding that Elasian guards shadow my every move. In fact, I no longer demand anything. I, Elaan, the Dohlman of Elas, who was once accustomed to the sight of my subjects quaking in fear as I decided whether I would let them live to serve me another day, have learned the gentle art of persuasion, the delicate balance of the gracious request. I no longer screech commands, no longer strike out at those who displease me. I am no longer a savage, or so my Monarch loves to tell me.

My Monarch. I see him now, coming toward me from the council chambers. His walk is light, his expression happy. He beams at those he passes as if the world could not be a better place. And for him, I suppose it could not be. He bought peace for our two planets with our lives. A dangerous gesture of trust on his part, but the experiment worked. Our worlds found a way to coexist. Troyians now visit Elas; Elasians can be found on Troyius. And the Monarch has grown old with a responsible Elasian woman by his side, one who knows her duty, one who was willing to sacrifice her true feelings in order to bring peace to our people. But the Monarch never knew why I was willing to do that. And I will never tell him.

I can still recall the moment when James Kirk sent me away from him to do my duty. Made me leave him, swallow my own love and wed another. I did what I had to do, what my Council of Nobles had obligated me to do. I put aside my hatred of all things Troyian and married a man who on my own planet would never have gotten past the first challenge to win me. I would have broken him myself on our battlegrounds if he had dared to woo me.

The thought brings me some pleasure, even now after so many years with him. Thirty long, boring years full of endless rituals and ceremonies that from the beginning the Monarch insisted I attend. To miss even one would be to send a signal of disunity that our two planets could ill afford to broadcast, he told me. So I went to the house of every noble, no matter how insignificant. Ate heartily at the feast, no matter how offensive the rich food was to me. We celebrated everything multiple times, countless festivities to honor our wedding, peace between Troyius and Elas, and the birth of our son, the heir, and later of our two daughters.

Our children. They are the only things on this world that bring a genuine smile to my face. I did not believe myself the maternal type when I first learned I was pregnant. I still wonder at the tender feelings that my children inspire in me. My grandchildren do not move me in the same way. I think it is that they have too little of my Elasian blood in them. They reek of Troyius. Oh, I do not tell them that, of course. I let them climb into my lap as they demand to know stories of the barbarian world I came from. I even, upon occasion, feel some true affection for them.

But for my children, the sentiment runs deeper, stronger. I remember when my son was born. The Monarch was ecstatic, of course. Our son would be his symbol of unity, the living sign that the experiment was working. When he handed the infant to me, I took one look at his green skin and nearly turned away. But then I saw his brown eyes and thick black hair, and I took him in my arms and held him out in front of me, studying him for defects as is the way on Elas. As the child squirmed and reached up for me, I caught a whiff of his skin, just washed in the scented Troyian water, and nearly gagged. I almost gave him back to his father right then, but the child wriggled again, and I sensed another smell underneath the cloying perfume. I pulled him closer to me, buried my nose in his soft skin and smelled a spicy earthiness that reminded me of the way my father's hunting lodge smelled after the rain, or of the scent of the ground near our home during the dry season when the *tarzhatan* berries were ripe. I smiled then, and the Monarch sighed in relief. When my daughters were born, the first thing I did was to pull them close to me so that I could sniff them, to make sure that they too carried the scent of Elas on their skin. And they did. It is all my children carry of Elas. Their upbringing has been too civilized, too tame to allow them to embrace any other part of their warrior heritage. I have taught them to speak Elasian. It is the only thing I could give them that wasn't Troyian in origin.

So now, we stand together as a family, an odd-looking yet exotically beautiful family, and all can see what we have done for our people. For the sake of peace. And in this peace that we bought, our worlds prosper. Our people grow fat and healthy, looking outward now instead of focusing on fighting each other. All who knew the times before hail what we have done. But for me, peace has often provided time, too much time . . . time to grow weary of green skin. Time to remember that James Kirk's skin was tan like mine, only lighter, more rose than golden. His hair was soft, neither braided as

I still wear my graying locks, nor elaborately rolled as the Monarch insists on styling his despite how thin it grows. I have never tangled my fingers in the Monarch's hair. And I never will. That I did with Kirk only, on that last night before my wedding, when we stole every moment that we could and lived it as if it were our last. I tangled my fingers in Kirk's hair and thought that if I never let go, he could not send me away from him. But I had to let go, and he did send me away.

I beamed down to the planet, blinking back the first honest tears I ever shed. James Kirk faded from my sight, only to be replaced by the Monarch's ambassador, Lord Petri, and a horde of hideously dressed attendants. I had not allowed Petri to brief me on the ceremony while we were on board the *Enterprise*. He took his revenge when I arrived on Troyius, making me practice the marriage ritual countless times, criticizing every move I made as if hoping I would react, throw a tantrum, or attack him. It took all my newfound self-control, but I ignored his taunts and petty comments. Finally he was satisfied and sent me down the long center aisle of the temple. I can still see the Monarch standing tentatively on the dais as he waited for me to join him. He looked around several times at the nobles and dignitaries from all over the Federation who had gathered to witness our union. I think that he was afraid that I would make a scene of some kind. He could not quite believe that I would go through with the ceremony. To be honest, there was a part of me that could not believe it either, and I could hear that part yelling, deep within me, "Kill them all and escape. We will not be domesticated." I paid no attention to her. The ceremony went perfectly. All was well, and my new husband was relieved.

The Monarch clearly expected little of me in the way of manners or grace. He was constantly surprised if I showed any intelligence or sensitivity. I am sure that he had been well briefed by Petri on every one of my transgressions aboard the *Enterprise*. Every one except my affair with Kirk. Petri would never tell the Monarch of that because it might show how terribly unfit he was for the job that had been entrusted to him. Instructing me was synonymous with chaperoning me, and if the affair were common knowledge, then all would know that he had failed. So he conveniently ignored that, especially since, by the time he became aware of what had transpired, I was showing signs of cooperation. But I'm sure Petri told the Monarch that the Dohlman of Elas was a barbarian, no matter how much I appeared to bend, and that I always would be.

Petri died last year. I did not cry at his funeral. I was only sorry I had not aimed better all those years ago on the *Enterprise*. I can feel my mouth turning down in a most unattractive smile. The Monarch would not be amused. My attack on his ambassador was something we never spoke of. But I could never be sorry I had stabbed him. I would do it again, and not just to relish the feel of my blade sinking deep into Petri's pampered skin. I would do it again because by getting rid of Petri, I gained a new teacher. One who taught me more than either of us could have dreamed. Kirk helped me to embrace obligation even as he taught me what it felt like to love. And I did love him. I thought only to use him, to turn him with my tears, but I too was caught up in the snare of attraction. An attraction that only grew stronger as I watched him fight the influence of my tears so that he could save his ship. This was a warrior. This was my true mate. I had never felt such admiration. I would have gladly died with him. But he asked of me something even harder. He asked me to live without him. And so I came here. And here I stay.

The Monarch has just thrown himself onto the pillows at my feet. He looks up at me with a grin on his face. "Come, Elaan," he will say as he has every other time. "Come and see what I have done now." For the last thirty years, he has pulled me behind him to show me his latest whimsical invention, or outlandish device. I could have kicked most of them to pieces with but a few blows. But I did not, of course. I smiled or, on a very good day, I laughed. And he would be happy. And now he is here again, saying nothing, just looking at me with his insipid grin and pale blue eyes.

James Kirk never smiled that way. His smile was fierce and

proud, used to show amusement and pleasure, not to curry favor. His eyes were not drab as the Monarch's are. They were a dark gold that seemed to be a mixture of green and gray as well as my own brown. I remember they were fiery when he looked at me in the privacy of my borrowed quarters and they were tender when we lay together on the bed, our passion spent. His eyes held a thousand emotions, most of which I have never seen echoed in the Monarch's open, uncomplicated gaze.

The Monarch asked me once why I never cried. He had heard of the power of Elasian tears. All Troyian men have. But I have never once cried around him. I never wanted that level of devotion from him. Could not have stood it, in fact. But he fell in love with me anyway. I almost wish I had captured the Monarch with my tears, because then I could have used the antidote that Doctor McCoy gave me as a wedding present. "Just in case you ever regret what you've done," he said with a twisted grin that made me like him even more. But there is no antidote for what the Monarch feels for me. It is true affection, and I think the fool actually believes that I love him in return.

James Kirk would understand the concept of duty instead of love, of not giving in to personal feelings, of doing what was necessary, no matter how abhorrent. He would have applauded that I endured the Monarch's clumsy attempts at passion on those first nights we spent together. He would have told me what a brave and honorable woman I was for not killing the bumbling idiot as I wanted to then. As I sometimes still wish to do. Kirk would never have taken for granted that a woman with him by obligation would have felt anything for him. He would have understood the nature of such an arrangement. The Monarch is not so astute. He sees only the smile I have practiced now since my son was first conceived and believes that it is real. He believes the lies and the deception because he wants to believe. He is a fool, but a happy one.

As I expected, the Monarch asks me to go with him to his workshop. I have never said no. But today, I tell him to go away. Today, and today only, I have had enough of duty and obligations.

Let him show his stupid invention to someone else. I only want him to leave me alone so that I can remember how it felt to be in the arms of the man I truly loved. But he will not leave me alone. I raise my voice; my tone is sharp, my words cutting. The Monarch looks shattered. I have never been so cruel to him. "What is the matter?" he asks, and I tell him to go away. He has tears in his eyes as he looks at me. I know my face is hard as I order him from my sight, my voice once again that of the true Dohlman of Elas.

The last man to see her was James Kirk. And the last time I saw him was when the Monarch and I attended the ceremony at Khitomer, where I saw Kirk preserve the chance for peace between the Federation and the Klingon Empire. My heart swelled with pride at the warrior who could survive and escape from a Klingon prison, who could stop such a carefully planned and tightly held conspiracy. Truly this was my mate, my rightful husband. I wanted to push the Monarch from me and run to Kirk's side, never to relinquish my place with him. But I did not. I sat in the area reserved for Federation dignitaries and discussed with those around me the ramifications of all that had happened. Calmly, coolly, as befitted the civilized wife of the Monarch of Troyius.

But later, I followed Kirk out of the reception hall and through a maze of corridors. He stood in front of a window, leaning on the glass, his forehead pushed tightly against it as if to soothe a fever.

"Is there nothing you won't do for peace?" I asked, and he turned around slowly, as if not believing that it was my voice he was hearing. "I have missed you," I said.

"Elaan." My name, spoken from his lips, was more beautiful than any song composed by a Troyian. I could have listened to that sound for the rest of my life. "How are you?" he asked.

The truth hovered on my lips. I would tell him of my misery, of the way the obligation was making my hair gray and my skin lined and my eyes dull. But then I saw the shadows under his eyes, remembered that he had never asked for my love, and I lied to him with the truth. "I prosper. I am very civilized. You would be proud of me."

He grinned tiredly. "It doesn't matter whether I'm proud of you, Elaan. Are you proud of yourself?"

Proud? I looked in the mirror every day, and every day I saw less of Elas and more of Troyius in my expression, my bearing. How could I be proud of that? But I said only, "I have sacrificed much for peace. Given up who I was. Elaan the Dohlman is no more. Now I am Elaan the faithful wife of the Monarch, Elaan the tender mother of his children." Elaan the pretender, I thought but did not say. Elaan the liar.

"Are you happy?" he asked.

"Are you?" I countered.

"Happiness is an elusive thing."

I could not argue that. "It does not coexist easily with duty."

"Has it been so bad for you? Have you been so unhappy, Elaan?"

"I have survived." I walked to his side, touched his hand. "Did you forget me?"

He did not answer.

"You took the antidote." I had nurtured the foolish hope that he had not.

"I was distracted by thoughts of you. Very distracted."

I smiled then. "And your Doctor McCoy thought it prudent?"

He nodded. "Prudent."

"I have come to detest such words, Jim. Prudent and practical, expedient and convenient. They are words of the diplomat, not of the warrior." I moved so my back was against the window, the glass cold on my bare skin.

He turned so that he could watch me. "The time of the warrior may be over, Elaan."

"There are many kinds of warriors. You have always been a great warrior for peace. Never more so than today."

He only nodded and leaned his head against the glass again.

We were quiet then, neither of us needing to say anything as he stared out the window and I stared at him. "Do you love him?" he asked, when I finally pulled away from the cold glass.

"I do not. I could never." I tried to forget that the Monarch was waiting for me in the other room. Allowed myself to give rein to the fantasy of taking Kirk's hand, pulling him roughly behind me as we escaped that place, ran from our own lives to a better place, where we could live free, even if only for a short time. For that I would have paid any price. To my horror, I felt tears well in my eyes and turned away, ruthlessly squashing my impossible musings.

"Elaan," he said, reaching for me.

"No. Do not touch me."

He saw my tears and dropped his hand. In his eyes, I saw his desire to help me war with his better judgment. But compassion won, and he reached for me despite the danger, ready to pull me into his arms.

"Do not," I repeated.

"Elaan, I want to help you. You're hurting."

"Be my witness then. I do not cry there, on Troyius. Let me cry here."

He nodded, understanding what I asked.

As I let a lifetime's worth of tears fall, I drank in the sight of him and he did not look away. His face was full of some terrible sadness of his own as he witnessed the tears of the Dohlman of Elas in silence.

Finally, I stopped crying, wiped my eyes with my fingers. I did not have a cloth, was not prepared for this eventuality. Had long ago forgotten what a mess tears made of a face.

"I did not forget you, Elaan," he said into the stillness. "I no longer had to remember you, but I could never forget you." His smile was tender as he said, "I'm sorry. For everything that you've had to endure. For everything you will endure."

I tried to tell him it had all been worth it, that any price I'd had to pay to buy peace was supportable. That I would do it again, keep doing it. But my mouth would not form the words.

We stood in silence again, then I heard voices coming toward us. As several other diplomats rounded the corner, I straightened and said formally. "It was a pleasure seeing you again, Captain."

He inclined his head. "The pleasure was mine, Your Majesty."

Our eyes met, and he smiled at me, more tenderly than was probably wise. I smiled back just as warmly. Then, donning the regally serene mask I had spent the last thirty years perfecting, I turned and walked away from him. I found the Monarch where I had left him, deep in conversation, barely aware that I had ever gone. We left soon afterward, and I never saw James Kirk again.

I blink several times, realizing that in my nostalgia I have dredged up more emotion than I intended to. I do not cry on Troyius. Such is my own self-imposed law. I will not cry here. Not even for Kirk. I look up and see the Monarch approaching again. He smiles in what he thinks is a winning way, attempts to cajole me out of what he is calling my mood. He has absolutely no understanding of what today is or what it means for me. But then he has never known the real me. He has explored my body, he has tested my spirit and intelligence, but he has never known my heart. And he never will. He makes a joke, tries to tempt me with stories of new silks just arrived from the eastern continent. I am tired of him. I am tired of duty and responsibility and obligation. I am tired most of all of acting as if I care anything about him, of pretending that I am not in love with another man.

A man who died today.

I reach for my dagger, ready at last to strike back at the Monarch, to finally wipe that odious smile off his ugly green face. My hand comes up empty. For the dagger is not here, of course. It has not been here for thirty years. I left it along with my heart on the *Enterprise.* And I suppose it is now somewhere in the personal effects of James Kirk. I wonder if he carried it with him to that new version of the *Enterprise,* the one he died to save. It is a pleasant idea, but I think he probably did not keep it that close. After all these years, it most likely hung on a wall in his living quarters on his home planet. A personal memento of a mission that ended honorably.

"From the Dohlman of Elas," he might have told visitors, a sad look on his face for a moment as he stared at it before moving on to the next souvenir of his colorful life.

I imagine that Starfleet will catalog his possessions for posterity. I can picture the look on their faces when they find my dagger and try to decide what to do with it. I wonder if they will give it back to me . . . if I ask very nicely.

Life's Work

Julie A. Hyzy

Doctor Soong raised his head, dragging his attention from the circuitry littered across the kitchen table. Facing his wife, Juliana, he noted her slender hands jammed into fists at her hips, the flash in her green eyes, and the tone of her voice, about an octave higher than normal. Angry. She must be angry that he'd brought his work to the dinner table again.

Snaking a glance back to the jumble of blinking diodes spread before him, he slid his left hand into their midst and laid aside the calibrator he'd been using.

The mirror-black windows behind her gave him a glimpse of the scene in tableau. The yellow light above illuminated them—like players in a pool of spotlight onstage. He sat, a bowl of something long-cooled pushed far to his right. She stood, shaking her head, repeating words he forced himself to tune in to. The darkness behind the windows finally registered. Night time. It was later than he thought.

"Didn't you hear me, Noonien?" She bent lower, bringing her face down to his. "I'm not one of your androids, you know. You can't just plant an algorithm in my brain and expect blind loyalty and total obedience."

Doctor Soong noticed, with alarm, that the flush flaming his wife's cheeks was about twenty-seven percent brighter on her left than on her right.

"How do you feel?" he asked, standing.

Her head jerked back as if slapped. "Haven't you been listening?"

"Yes, yes, of course." He touched her cheeks, both of them in turn. And then he laid the back of his hand against her forehead, though that was more out of old habit than need.

She allowed his ministrations, even as she protested, her voice still sharp. "I'm fine, Noonien. Healthy as anything."

"Mm-hmm," he said, observing that the difference in her flushed cheeks didn't result in a difference in surface temperature from one side to the other. He held Juliana's face by the chin and squinted at her. Must be a side effect from his experiments last week. He'd thought for certain he'd eliminated all the leftover bugs from her circuits.

"What?" she asked, taking a step back, shoving his hand away. "What now?"

"Mm. Nothing. Nothing at all."

He turned away from her, sat down and hunched back over his gadgets. Tonight, while she slept, he'd have to go in and make a few more adjustments.

"Well?" she asked.

Doctor Soong blinked, then raised his head again. "Well, what?"

Juliana blew out a noisy breath through pursed lips. She ran a hand through her hair and gave a sigh as her shoulders dropped. "Oh, Noonien," she said.

The little break in her voice gave him a moment's panic. Had her vocal tones been affected too? He needed her to speak again. "Juliana," he said, "just a moment."

She turned to face him.

It was a strong face, with angry eyes burning at him over twin pools of shimmering tears. Tiny wrinkles, crow's feet she called them, branched out from their corners. The lines of her jaw were bold and tight; he could see tension working at her temples.

She was upset. Close to crying.

Which meant that the unevenness of her voice was precisely right. He nodded, contented. "Nothing."

She threw her hands up in a gesture of exasperation. Soong didn't notice anything beyond that, however, and he only knew she'd left when he heard the slam of the bedroom door.

Always, just before his mind made the leap forward to his next breakthrough in positronic technology, his body, like a Richter scale, detected the first rumblings of new thought. His respiration quickened, his heartbeat raced, and a warm rush worked its way from the tips of his extremities, tracing their excited and energized path to his brain, bringing with it the openness that he'd need to make the leap of new discovery.

These physiological changes raced through him now as his fingertips worked the device that could possibly change the very nature of Data's existence. Soong's eyes widened; his left hand twitched as his mind struggled to grasp the synaptic nuance just ahead of him.

Hunched over his laboratory workbench, Soong felt each and every bubble of sweat as it burst from his skin, centimeter by centimeter, as the answer worked its way up. "Yes," he whispered, knowing only seconds separated him from the key, knowing it was just beyond his reach, knowing that as long as he remained dead-still one moment longer, the answer would be his.

"Noonien," she said. And she laid her hand on his shoulder.

With a scream of frustration, Soong leapt from her touch. Instant white heat seared across his brain. "What is wrong with you, woman? How many times have I told you never to bother me when I'm concentrating?"

A heartbeat later, he regretted his outburst. Juliana bit her lip and took a step backward toward the doorway that led to the rest of their home. His mind recognized two things at once: that he'd frightened her and that she was dressed to go out.

He took a deep breath, quelled the crazed fury that still ricocheted through his brain, and forced himself to say, "I'm sorry."

She nodded—acknowledgment rather than absolution. Her lips twisted into a frown and she looked down for a moment before meeting his eyes again. "I'm leaving," she said. Her right hand fluttered behind her, and Soong caught sight of bulging traveling bags, set neatly by their front door.

"Leaving?" His voice came out strained, impatient. "Where are you going?"

"Away," she said.

He opened his mouth—then closed it.

She smiled without conviction. "I suppose I've been aware for years. But I've only just now come to accept"—she took a breath—"that I've never been as important to you as your androids."

"No," he said. Juliana leaving him? This couldn't be happening. He groped for words. "You're the reason I do all this. You *can't* leave."

She made a sound, a strangled laugh. "That's just my point. I can. I'm not one of your little creations, built with triple redundancies and a homing device. I'm a living, breathing woman, with a life of my own."

Her face flushed pink with high emotion. The precisely right shade of pink, it set off her bright green eyes to perfection. Perfect, he thought again. Everything about her was perfect. Of course. He'd designed her that way.

A tang of spice wafted his way. He canted his head, sniffing the warm, yeasty air.

Shrugging, she shot a glance back toward the kitchen. "Bendarian casserole," she said. "It's ready. So you have something to eat. It will hold you for the rest of the week."

"You made casserole?" he asked, feeling slow-witted. "I don't understand."

When she tightened her lips and wrinkled her nose, he sucked in a breath. He knew that look. "Noonien." The hair on his forearm stood to tingled attention when she placed her hand on him. "I will never stop caring about you." Her bright eyes narrowed, almost the way they did when she used to smile at him. "But I can't stay here any longer. Waiting for you means that I'm not living my own life. And I've waited for you for a very long time."

"Juliana. Not now. I'm so very close to solving this. To creating an emotion chip for Data. For our son."

She shook her head, and the sadness of her smile chided him. "You told me a long time ago that you'd mastered emotions in an android."

"Yes," he said, watching the beauty of his creation unknowingly argue with him about her own existence, "but only for an android built with human emotions as part of the original schematic. Data necessitates a retrofit. It's an entirely different quandary. And I'm so close. I have the prototype almost ready to go."

"And when you succeed? When Data's a 'real boy' . . . then what?"

He shook his head, not understanding.

Her voice was soft. "You'll find yet another oh-so-important project, won't you?"

The house closed in on him, and for the first time, Soong felt its emptiness. Juliana couldn't leave. She belonged with him. He lived and breathed only because of her presence in his life. He couldn't let her go.

She dropped her hand from his arm. "I thought I ought to let you know," she said, then added with another sad laugh, "in case you ever looked for me."

"Juliana," Soong said, "You can't be serious."

Her eyes were not without compassion. "The worst part, Noonien," she said, her face tightening, "is knowing that it's extremely unlikely you'd ever look for me."

He shook his head, about to disagree, but she interrupted.

"You'll forget me." She smiled again—that same beautiful

smile that had broken his heart the day she died, when she'd stared up at him and had made him promise never to forget her. He'd promised, and then he'd held her slim hand till it slackened and grew cool.

"Please," he said, his crusty voice less confident than he'd ever remembered hearing it before. "Just a little while longer. You promised me till the new season. I'm almost there."

"The new season began days ago."

He glanced toward the window over his workbench. When had it become night? He could only see his own reflection, and the panic in his own eyes frightened him.

"Where will you go?"

"I have friends."

A flash of brilliance across the sky—they waited, watching each other, for the accompanying thunder.

Doctor Soong glanced again toward the window as the boom sounded. "Not now, not tonight. A storm's coming."

"Noonien." Her voice held a warning.

"Can't we sleep on this?" he asked. "Can't you give me that much?"

Her eyes slid away, and she gave a brief nod.

Click-whirr.

Her head opened, again. Like the yawning hatch of a landed shuttle, the back access panel lowered with smooth grace to expose her positronic net.

Juliana sat, deactivated, in the floral chintz armchair in their living room. Frozen in place, she remained unaware of her husband's ministrations as he probed the blinking circuitry that made up her interior skull.

Her lips had been pursed in pleasured anticipation of a sip of hot chamomile. Now cool, the tea in her pale pink china cup, held aloft by her immobile right hand, was the only thing that moved. The dark liquid made tiny concentric ripples with each of Doctor Soong's finessing adjustments.

He made a noise of frustration, then another, as a recalcitrant module near her left ear forced him to apply vigorous pressure to loosen it. It gave with a pop, the resounding movement causing the tea to splash over the rim of the cup, into his wife's lap.

"Damn," he said.

Doctor Soong reached toward a wheeled instrument table, pulling it close. He grabbed a cloth. "Sorry, dear."

Juliana didn't blink. She didn't move.

He eyed the remaining tea in her cup, and her elegant fingers as they grasped its scrolled handle. Her left hand curled, flowerlike, cupping the saucer in her palm, her thumb relaxed, yet purposefully placed along the rim to steady it. She'd been speaking when he switched her off.

He cleaned up the spill, then bunched up the cloth. Wadding it tight, he wedged it into the china cup to soak up the remaining tea, before tossing the rag aside.

"There."

Just one more adjustment. Maybe two.

Soong heard a songbird's rippled melody outside the room's tall windows. He lifted his chin, taking in a breath of the almost-warm air, promise-filled and bright, now that the cool-weather season had ended. His hand stopped, ready to make the final adjustment. Waiting, as he listened.

Juliana had pulled at the draperies this morning, casting away the shadows, letting the natural light come in to cheer and warm and tease. And she'd smiled at him.

But today, her eyes had been different.

As she'd opened the windows, she complained again that he'd worked all night. "Breathe," she'd told him. "Get some fresh air into that body of yours."

But this morning, her voice had been different.

Now, Soong placed his instruments back, arranging them in place with tender precision. Fingers resting on the edge of the table, he stared for a long moment out the windows, blinking at the brightness. He gave a deep sigh.

Coming around to face Juliana, he pulled his ripped chair forward, arranging the black utilitarian monstrosity so he and his wife sat with their knees touching.

He sat there a long time, without speaking.

Her hair was beginning to sport strands of gray. The subroutine he'd designed not only to grow hair on an android, but then to have it turn colors as she aged, had been one of the most intricate. But when Juliana died after the attack on Omicron Theta, he'd been a man possessed.

Unwilling to face life without her, he'd worked relentlessly to create this, his most sophisticated, his most beautiful work.

And now, what?

She wanted to leave him.

Soong gave a short mirthless laugh, twisting his face to fight off the sting in the back of his throat.

She couldn't know that of everything in his life, she had been, and would always be, the most important. He should have told her. He should have told her every day of his life. But he'd kept quiet.

And now it was she who remained quiet.

He reached across to touch her knee. "Juliana?"

No answer.

Soong canted his head, first one way, then the other. "After all we've done together?"

He waited for her to blink in acknowledgment, but of course she did not.

A whip-poor-will. That's what the bird sounded like.

He'd heard a few Terran whip-poor-wills in his day. And perhaps this creature looked just like the dull-looking Earth birds with the whimsical name. He'd never bothered to find out, though he was sure Juliana had.

"What else have I missed?" he asked her.

He imagined that, given the chance, she'd tell him.

"You know," he said to her, "I've been doing this for us. For you. I know how hard it's always been for you to feel as though Data is truly your son. But he is. And with this emotion chip . . . once I get it to work, once I add it to his matrix, then we'll be the family that I know you always wanted us to be."

She didn't shake her head, but she would have.

"You think I'm doing this just for me."

Soong stood up, paced.

"I understand your frustration. And maybe it's true. Maybe I am doing this for myself." He turned. "But don't you see how far I've come?

"We've come," he amended. "We've come."

Moving toward the edge of the long timber counter that lined the tall wall of windows, he leaned toward the brightness, fingertips touching the bare wood, pressing hard.

Maybe keeping his back to her would make this easier.

"You can't leave me," he said. "Really. You can't."

He pictured her giving him "the look."

"We belong together. You've been my reason for being all these years, the reason I've done all I have. The reason I've pushed myself to excel in cybernetics and the reason why you're alive today."

He turned to face her.

"No," he said, anticipating her response, "I can't let it drop. Not now, not when I'm so close to solving the problem of giving my son his emotions."

Seated there, the picture of relaxation, she seemed so very content.

Tenderly, he reached to touch her chin. "Yes, you're happy today," he said. "But you're not the same Juliana, are you?"

She didn't answer.

Whenever he'd cupped her chin like that, she'd smiled. But she couldn't now.

"I'm sorry," he said. "When you told me you were leaving, I couldn't let you go. I had to stop you."

Maybe she would have taken his hand at that point. Or maybe she would have just let him talk.

"You're asking yourself, which is more important to me—you in my life, or solving the riddle of this emotion chip."

He began to pace the room. Stopped.

"The truth is, Juliana, that they're both important. Don't you see what a discovery like this can do for us? I've been able to master so much; you're the testament to that. No one would suspect you're an android. You don't even know."

Resuming a brisk pace between the kitchen area of their compound and the workbench area, he walked along the scuffed tiles. His footsteps and the warbling bird were the only noises, and he felt a jolt of loneliness.

"I . . . I need you."

He walked back and forth, losing all track of time. Taking a look out the window, he tried to spy the little bird, but to no avail. Turning back to look at her, he watched her face, looked into those bright eyes of hers. "But it's not what you want, is it?"

"No," her eyes seemed to say, even though they hadn't changed at all.

"You'd be angry with me if you knew I'd changed your subroutine, wouldn't you?"

He nodded, as though she'd answered.

"I shouldn't have changed you, Juliana," he said, finally.

Sitting again, he arranged himself so that they were very close, and he laid his hand on her knee. "I haven't been fair to you."

He shook his head.

"But it wasn't fair to me that you died."

Doctor Noonien Soong stared at Juliana, memorizing the face, the body, the woman he knew better than he knew himself. A subcircuit attenuation was all it had taken to make her his again. Forever. A small adjustment, really, it effectively eliminated her discontent. "If you were still alive . . ." he said. He spoke the words softly, tracing a finger along her bare arm, but he couldn't finish the thought aloud.

When he looked up again, it was night.

Picking up his tools, he stood and came around behind his wife, returning to the open panel at the back of her head. Examining the changes he'd made, he gave a little frown. He worked quietly for a short while and when he was finished, he closed the access hatch and took up a position in front of her again. Taking her face in his hands, he kissed her, softly. He skimmed her eyebrows with his thumbs, then touched the crow's-feet laugh lines he loved so much. Taking a deep breath, he reactivated her.

She looked down at the empty cup in her hand, then at him, momentarily puzzled. "I've lost my train of thought," she said, with a tilt of her head. She walked to the kitchen and placed the dishware at the sink, glancing out the window. "That's curious. I thought it was going to storm."

"Cleared up," he said.

"I don't remember putting the casserole away."

"I did."

Her smile was sad as she moved toward him. She ran her fingers down the side of his face. "I will miss you," she said, so quietly he wondered if he'd imagined it.

He opened his mouth to speak, but she crossed his lips with her finger. "Go on," she said. "Go on back to work."

Somewhere outside his laboratory window, the whip-poor-will cried one more time. Doctor Soong sat at his work table and stared at the instruments and gadgetry without comprehension. He heard Juliana moving about in the house behind him, cleaning the kitchen, arranging the chairs.

He didn't turn when the door to his laboratory opened. And he didn't turn when he heard her sigh. "Good-bye, Noonien," she said.

Squinting at his pile of circuits, he waited till he heard the door click shut behind her. Soong picked up the prototype of Data's emotions and thought how odd that he held passion in his hand, while his own walked out of his life, forever.

Gripping the chip till his palm stung, he stared out the window, his lips moving in a whisper. "Good-bye, Juliana."

(THIRD PRIZE)

Adventures in Jazz and Time

Kelly Cairo

It was all Wesley Crusher could do to keep himself from grinning as Will Riker rounded the corner, clearly headed for the holodeck. For a very long time, Wesley had considered what he could possibly give Riker. It wasn't that a gift was required. But rather, after all the years of receiving the man's guidance, and many more years being his friend, Wes had the urge to do something special for him. *What to give to a role model? What did the man need or want?* With surprisingly little manipulation, the time and place finally had come together.

"Commander Riker, it's good to see you," Wesley said. He liked Riker with the beard, though he couldn't count how many times Riker had shaved it and grown it out again over the years. After an extended shift, Riker had come directly off the bridge and not bothered to change clothing. He looked tired, but still sharp in the red-and-black uniform.

Riker eyed the older man, trying to hide his disappointment that their guest had picked this moment to use the holodeck. He had been a quiet, polite visitor. However, unlike the other members of the bridge crew, and despite his attempts to be friendly, Riker could not find anything to talk about with him. As a further irritant, the man always looked perfectly content, which did nothing to enhance Riker's mood and his need for uninterrupted relaxation. He desperately hoped one of the other holodecks was still available.

"Professor Jackson," Riker addressed Wesley. "I'm glad to see you've decided to take us up on our hospitality and use the holodeck before you leave the ship." Esteemed professor or not, Riker was always perturbed at the use of the Federation's flagship as a passenger liner.

Wesley smiled at the name. He always thought it was funny to hear them call him by one of his pseudonyms, and Evan Jackson— Jack's son—was such a good one. He knew they would kick themselves if they ever put the information together. It might be a little dangerous to take such liberties with the name, but the temptation was too great to ignore. *And what good is taking the trip without enjoying the journey?* he rationalized.

"Well, I have to admit I was curious. I don't have much experience with these things, though," Wesley said. The lying came so easily now. At first, Wes had great difficulty putting on another persona. But with time and experience—and he had quite a bit of both—he could slip on the Evan Jackson identity at a moment's notice.

As if on cue, Riker approached the panel and began to explain options and settings, how to select a program and what to expect. He had always been a good teacher, whether he was actively trying to offer advice or was simply being himself. The token gift would be quite well suited to the recipient.

"Now this is odd," Riker said. He frowned and stepped back from the panel, though certainly not unhappy.

"What's that?" Wesley replied, knowing Riker had found the bait.

"I have never seen this program before. I can't believe I would have missed it." Riker pressed the button, highlighting the program name for Jackson.

Oh, it's funny, the things people miss, Wesley thought. He considered his reaction to the Traveler revealing his identity over the years. After that first time at Nelvana III, it was easier to accept differing perceptions of reality, and it wasn't quite as surprising to learn that things were not always as they seemed.

"If you have the time, maybe we could go together and you could show me how this thing works," Wesley said. He tried not to sound too eager as he carefully reeled in his catch. "I was just looking for a brief diversion before we reach orbit. To me, any program is as good as the next."

Riker chastised himself for his irritation with Jackson and realized how lucky he was to have bumped into the man. Maybe this was the side of Jackson the others seemed to enjoy. The exercise program he had planned to run now seemed pointless. With a genuine smile, he began pushing buttons. "I'd be happy to show you around."

Wesley knew that someday, he would reminisce with Riker about their adventure, but not until Riker was very old. Perhaps Riker would even allow him to take them other places, but it was unlikely. For now, Wes settled for enjoying this covert plan.

Within a few moments, Riker announced that the program was ready. The pair approached the door, but Jackson hesitated. It was not an uncommon reaction among guests, though Riker was surprised that a professor of engineering would not have much experience with the technology. Riker did his best to ease the man's apprehension, clapping him on the shoulder and announcing, "After you."

Wesley was prepared for that brief moment of contact and executed his plan. He was grateful that Riker initiated the connection—it was easier that way and less awkward. *You can't enjoy the journey if you don't make the trip,* he thought.

Together, Wesley Crusher and Will Riker stepped through the arch and into a cool, fall evening in 1950s Illinois.

The first thing Riker noticed was the smell of the night. Dirt and rain and manure and rotting leaves. It was perfect. Fortunately, the momentary feeling of lightheadedness he had felt as he stepped through the arch faded as quickly as it had developed. He checked out Jackson, who looked fine, and decided it must be stress.

Wesley was unfazed by the transition, and grateful Riker didn't seem to notice anything out of the ordinary. He headed directly for the back door of the auditorium. After all of his planning, it was hard not to lead the way, but he had to get through the maze of people before they got involved in a conversation. He expertly stepped around four men sitting on a log practicing trumpet fingerings in unison, and nodded at two others smoking cigarettes. Riker hurried behind him, catching a whiff of the smoke and thinking it much stronger than he'd expected. Maybe these programs were improving a bit too much.

Wesley graciously held open the gray, rusted door, and he and Riker stepped inside. Two men walked past them carrying black evening jackets and made their way toward an ironing board set up backstage. Beyond the curtain, they could hear platforms rubbing wood flooring as they were eased into their final position, and someone repeatedly saying "test" into a microphone.

It looked like the usual level of activity prior to a performance, and Wes envied the orchestra members. He knew the thrill an audience could give a performer, and counted himself lucky to have played with this group, under the direction and skill of a legendary composer, at this time in their evolution. To come together and create such evocative sounds, something any one of them could not accomplish alone, was more exciting than many of his past travels.

Even in the dim lighting, Wesley was able to spot his friend pointing at lights and motioning. He caught the man's eye and gave him a wink.

The man rushed up to greet them. To Riker, Stan Kenton looked like an advertisement for manners. Like most historical figures, Riker pictured him as the older, white-haired man shown in the biographies. Here and now, the smooth-faced man looked even younger than his years.

Recalling the promise he'd made to his fill-in band member, Kenton played his part as agreed. "Greetings, gentlemen! We're about set up, and we don't go on for a bit, so your timing couldn't be better. Now, which of you is my student?"

"Well, that must be Commander . . . that is, Will Riker here," Wesley said. "I don't play an instrument," he added.

Kenton knew very well that Wes was an excellent conga drum player, and couldn't imagine why he had to pretend not to know him. But he has happy to indulge the musician's eccentricities. It wasn't often you found someone who was able to sit in on short notice when a band member couldn't make a trip. With all the travel and the huge complement of players these days, it was difficult to make every performance. Somehow Wes was able to find the time and seemed to know when to come around—and that solo at the Birdland last summer was more than impressive. Today, he would play under Wes's direction, according to the plan.

Riker quickly recovered and introduced himself. "I'm Will Riker, Mister Kenton, and I must say, I am such a fan. This is a real honor." The thrill was real, even though Riker knew he was in a holodeck. He couldn't help but wonder if Kenton had won the Grammy awards yet. *Adventures in Time* was probably Riker's favorite.

"If you don't mind, I think I'll just take in the sights," Wes said, trying to excuse himself quickly now that the proper events were set in motion. "It is nice to meet you, Mister Kenton."

"Certainly, Mister ah . . . ?" Kenton kept up the part well.

"Jackson." Wes quickly filled in. He shook Kenton's hand and nodded to Riker. "You two take your time, but I might not stay too long, I have some packing to do."

As he watched Professor Evan Jackson turn and wander away, Riker thought that more than ever, the man had that odd look of perfect contentment, as if he knew a secret and had no intention of telling it.

Kenton looked Riker up and down, ignoring the strange red-and-black clothing. "Trombone?"

"Yes, how'd you know?" Riker knew that detail had not been part of the program.

"The tall ones take to trombone—not always—but I have a good feeling for these things. More confidence in making the reach."

The Kenton character was certainly sophisticated. Riker had the sudden urge to check the settings to see who had created the program and how long it had been stored.

Kenton ushered Riker down a corridor with several small storage rooms. He chose one that was nearly empty, flipped on the lights, and unfolded a pair of chairs. There were several saxophone cases, and cups of water with soaking reeds.

"Have a seat."

Although he rarely played seated, Riker accepted the chair offered.

"I myself prefer to play a horn standing. Not enough air in the diaphragm," Kenton explained, patting his slim stomach.

"Actually, sir, so do I." Riker was already grateful to be in this wonderful little room that smelled of molding paper. Actual music paper. Yes, it was wonderful.

Kenton raised an eyebrow in challenge. "Then why'd you sit down?"

Riker stood and looked down at his shoes, smiling. He realized he had already received his first lesson. *How have I missed this program?* he thought again. He eyed the trombone in the stand.

Kenton saw him admiring it.

"I see you didn't bring your own. Well, go ahead and get yourself warmed up, I don't think Fitz will mind. We don't have too much time before we go on, but enough for a short lesson."

Something about this holodeck simulation seemed especially real. Not since his interaction with Minuet had a character seemed so real. Perhaps it was the emphasis on time, or the lack of it, that made Kenton especially believable. Or maybe it was the joy of discovering something so out of the ordinary. Riker wondered if it would feel this genuine the next time he walked through the arch.

He blew air through the horn, pleased to recall that the Bynars were not on board, and mentally reviewed the passenger list for any irregularities. One ensign transferring to Deep Space 9, and Professor Jackson, on his way to Cardassia. Nothing unusual.

Kenton asked, "What do you want to get out of the lesson?"

Riker thought about it and replied, "Well, I can never hit the high note in—"

"Wait right there. I said what do you *want* from this lesson, not tell me what you *can't* do," he reprimanded gently. "Now, I ask you again, what do you want to do?"

That would be lesson number two, Riker thought. He grinned a silly, boyish grin that meant he was embarrassed, though women found it quite charming.

"I want to hit the high note in . . ." He hesitated, knowing the man wouldn't know the title. ". . . in a piece I've been practicing. I want to hit it perfectly, every time."

"Excellent. State what you want. You have to push forward to make progress. That's what it's all about. Always move forward, never look back. Push the frontier."

Wesley listened quietly just outside the door of their makeshift practice room. Stan could always be counted on for the best lessons. He moved farther down the corridor and went inside the next storage room. It was full of empty cartons and pallets, but it would suit his purpose. Regardless of where he was, Wesley could monitor Riker and return him to the holodeck arch at the proper moment. And he really did need to prepare to leave the ship. For form's sake, and in case Riker could hear, he called out, "Arch," and disappeared from the performance hall.

Future Shock

John Coffren

February 24, 2368: I'm writing, yes writing, not dictating to a yeoman or typing on a computer but putting pen to paper because I
was ordered to keep a diary by Starfleet Medical. How I choose to
record my thoughts was left entirely up to my own devising. I requested that the materials be authentic, not replicated. It took them
two weeks to ship the goods in on a rust bucket of a trader from the
Antares group. The craftsmanship was superb, unlike anything
made by human hands. The race are called Inaara and pride themselves on being the best artisans in the sector. I never even knew
they existed until yesterday. I can't write anymore today.

March 3, 2368: More unhappy news. Clark's dead. Dead and
buried for over eighty years. The last conversation I held with him
over subspace I joked about what a garbage scow the *Reliant* was
and he said, "This garbage scow will reduce that flying crate of
yours to so much space dust at the next war games." I told him I'd
see him at Rigel V in two weeks. I lied.

March 10, 2368: The Paris Space and Air Museum has graciously offered to box and crate the *Phoenix* exhibit in exchange for the *Bozeman.* I messaged a Monsieur Henri Boulle, the museum's director, with a private communiqué stating that my crew and I would gladly offer our services as relics of a bygone era. They could store us in cryogenic suspension and thaw us out just long enough to answer questions from patrons and passersby. We would require no sleep and little food, and our only upkeep beyond the proper working order of the suspended animation fields would be a weekly feather dusting by a custodial engineer.

March 17, 2368: The only happy news I've received in this miserable century came today. They're not going to decommission that proud, old lady. Instead, she's going to go through the biggest overhaul and refit since the *Enterprise* back in 2270. Dyno scanners, space matrix restoration coils, and main energizers all state-of-the-art equipment when we left Starbase 10. Now it's so much space junk. All traded in and upgraded to sensor and phaser arrays, EPS power conduits, and a new warp propulsion system. My own integration and that of my crew will follow a parallel course. We're being readmitted to the Academy for "refresher courses." I helped write most of the textbooks through my actions in the field. This isn't a costume I'm wearing. Where I come from we call this a uniform and I for one damn well earned it.

March 24, 2368: I blew my first test in over a hundred years. I hope this was a variant on the old *Kobayashi Maru,* a lose-lose situation, or else I may never graduate. During the simulation, a ship appeared on our main viewer. I didn't recognize the class or registry, but I was sure of one thing: it was Klingon. So I gave the order to fire a full spread of photon torpedoes. My crew followed orders without question, like any good soldiers would, and we vaporized the Klingon ambassador to Earth's diplomatic escort.

*   *   *

March 30, 2368: I've found one friend in this strange new world, Karen. I still call her Number One around the bridge. She told me that lately she'd grown quite fond of older men and since I was the oldest man she knew, would I like to go somewhere for a drink? I agreed. Starfleet Command usually frowns on this kind of fraternization, and rightly so. If I were to develop feelings for a staff member, a subordinate, it could impair my ability to command. But I'm, I mean, we are living in different times and circumstances. She showed me a great little place down by the waterfront with a house band that plays jazz and a chef who serves the freshest seafood in the Bay area. We almost used up all our transporter rations in the first week on dinner dates. Going back to school and out socially made me feel young again, alive. And those jazz tunes are absolutely infectious. The one about tossed salad and scrambled eggs stayed in my head for weeks.

April 6, 2368: I considered taking the *Bozeman* on her scheduled relaunch back into the Typhon Expanse. Somewhere in that inky blue-black distortion of the space-time continuum our rightful time and place await our return. I can't help thinking that we don't belong here. A Mister Dulmer of the Federation's Department of Temporal Investigations disagrees. Even if they could send us back, we might "contaminate the timeline" with our future knowledge. He recommends that the crew of the *Bozeman* be fully integrated into twenty-fourth-century society, and he says that any attempts to slip back into the past would be "prosecuted to the full extent of the temporal laws." The universe I left in the baffles of my ion trail was far less complicated and less violent. We might have reached an accord with the Klingons and a more tenuous agreement with the Romulans, but others have taken their places and pose threats to the Federation unheard of and unimaginable to a twenty-third-century mind. First and foremost among these is a race of cybernetic zombies that roam the galaxy in enormous vessels the size of small moons with enough firepower to cripple fleets of starships and subjugate entire worlds. What kind of a galaxy is this?

*   *   *

April 13, 2368: Teams of psychologists and historians have requested to serve aboard the *Bozeman* the minute she leaves the shipyards of Utopia Planitia. I'm reluctant to grant their requests on the basis that I already feel like we're living under a giant microscope and the watchful eyes of twenty-fourth-century society. Having to worry about our own shipmates scrutinizing our every move is unwarranted and unnecessary. Starfleet Command is pushing me to accept a few of them to nursemaid us through our difficulties. I'm confident that we can feel our way through it, with the old girl's help of course. She's become more than a starship. She's our home. It's the one constant in an ever-changing universe that has swept away all that was familiar and comforting and turned it into the most alien of landscapes. Our mental health and physical well-being are linked to number 1941. She's a survivor, just like us, that carried us down through a century. We crossed the great ocean of time and made landfall here. Maybe if we hadn't chased our own stern all the while, some great tragedy would have befallen us. Most of the crew would be dead or so infirm with old age that our starfaring years would be well behind us. Karen joked that if we can't adapt to life in this period, we can always strike out, lay in a course for the Expanse, and see if the twenty-fifth-century suits us any better.

April 20, 2368: A strange visitor called on me today. Rather, he called on my personal com link. A Captain K'Temoc of the Klingon Empire. His message was angry, terse, and delivered at phaser point, I believe. His ship disappeared a little over a decade after mine and reappeared in this century three years ago. He commanded a sleeper whose mission entailed delivering a payload of Klingon warriors into the future to reignite the Federation/Klingon war. K'Temoc emerged from his deep sleep to discover not a raging battle but a lasting peace between the two governments. The conflict-free era became unbearable and his own kind intolerable. The once proud warrior race had grown weak and soft in his absence. He had made plans for his *Mauk-to'Vor* ceremony as a means of escape when civil war broke out on Qo'noS. He admitted that he much preferred killing humans but would not flinch at an opportunity to kill Klingons. The lesson he learned and imparted to me was that nothing lasts forever, and like a field of grain gone fallow, peace endures until the seeds of war are planted and the deadly harvest reaped. He finished by encouraging me to be of good cheer, there was still a chance that our governments would have a falling out and we could resume our former hostilities.

April 27, 2368: I always knew I had the best crew in Starfleet in any time. Today they proved it. Starfleet Command put an offer on the table to them: Upon their second graduation from the Academy, they could seek a commission with any starship or starbase and that request would be granted. The Federation has grand starships three times the size of a *Soyuz*-class, bristling with new technologies and accommodations fit for an admiral but enjoyed by non-coms and crewmen alike. A courier from the bursar's office arrived with a sealed envelope. Inside it were eighty slips of paper with the same word written on each and every one of them:
Bozeman.

May 3, 2368: Graduation day. We passed. I've had too much Romulan ale.

May 10, 2368: Karen keeps reminding me that I'm supposed to lead, to set the right tone by example. I feel absolutely ridiculous in this child's uniform. I'm practically naked in this garment. You'd think a hundred years would be ample time to design an officer's jacket or shirt that doesn't ride up every two minutes. I'm constantly tugging at the hem of my shell. Somehow I managed to walk out of my cavernous quarters with a grin pasted to my face as I carried out the inspection, all fifteen decks worth. My crew looked like I felt—uncomfortable. This too shall pass.

*   *   *

May 27, 2368: We've been relegated to milk runs along familiar routes, well worn even in the twenty-third century. Karen programmed a re-creation of Old Salts down on Water Street on our new holodeck, standard issue on every Starfleet vessel. The attention to detail, right down to the misses around the dart board and the greasy friendship dollar over the bar, nearly convinced me that I was no longer traveling in space. Nearly. I downed a cup of ale and put on a good show, but Karen saw through it. She never said a word, though, and we both smiled and carried on as if nothing in the universe was amiss.

June 10, 2368: I'm no longer required to keep a journal by Starfleet Medical. No one ever requested to see or review it or have me read excerpts from it. But like my old uniform, I'm reluctant to just give it up. I've placed it in the back of my closet in a box of personal things. I may turn to it again. Whatever purpose it served, the doctors have deemed it obsolete, and I hate that word and the throwing away of something because it is old or old-fashioned. Besides, it would be a terrible waste after all the effort that went into crafting the very tools by which I record my thoughts and feelings. The Inaara believe the disuse of such objects to be sinful. And I happen to agree with them.

January 24, 2369: An outbreak of Rigelian fever struck an outpost near the Mutara sector. Starfleet Command designated it a level-1 biohazard and sent a squad of gunships to prevent anyone or anything from entering or leaving for a radius of 100 parsecs. The disease was previously believed to be extinct and a cure not readily accessible. As hope began to dim and it appeared to all concerned that lives were about to be sacrificed (there was even talk of an executive order of "orbital bombardment" to prevent the plague from spreading), our ship's doctor came up with a brilliant solution. The *Bozeman*'s crew had received their last round of shots before leaving Starbase 10. Even though a great deal of real time had passed, subjectively it was only a year ago. High concentrations of ryetalyn could be found in our bloodstreams, and small amounts could be drawn from everyone, posing little risk to us and saving the lives of the sickened scientists. We produced nearly two liters of the antidote in this fashion and beamed it down to the outpost. I think we've finally proven our worth to them. I wrote a letter of commendation for our chief medic. Good man, that Crane.

November 7, 2371: I made course correction fifteen stardays ago. Captains give these routine orders all the time for reasons as many and varied as respecting a sphere of influence or avoiding an ion storm. As I said before, this is generally regarded as the lowest level of decision making for a command officer. It turned out to be the highest, the most important of my career, my life. A yellow giant went supernova thousands of years ahead of schedule. A man named Soran destroyed it in his mad retreat into the past, chasing a temporal flux phenomenon across the quadrant. We could have joined the hunt and gone back. And all it would have cost was the old girl's life. The energy ribbon takes in biomatter but destroys anything mechanical. Karen held a padd with the last known coordinates of the nexus. She told me it was her job to give me options. And I said we didn't need to head for home because we never left.

Full Circle

Scott Pearson

Admiral John Harriman, along with everyone else in the restaurant, knew something was wrong when several combadges chirped at the same time. A sudden silence followed, except for the sound of moving chairs, as everyone stopped eating and watched about a dozen admirals, captains, and commanders get up and leave the restaurant to respond. Then the clinking of silverware resumed, but the voices of the patrons were now a nervous whisper.

Harriman and his wife, Amina, were celebrating their sixtieth wedding anniversary with some colleagues at Scoma's on Fisherman's Wharf, a popular San Francisco dining spot for over four hundred years. All but one of their guests were among those who had been paged, but Harriman's own combadge hadn't chirped yet. As chief of engineering operations, he was often lower on the priority call list, which was fine with him. Still on active duty at the age of one hundred twelve, he'd earned a break now and then. Besides, everyone knew that he was celebrating tonight.

He looked at Amina, who said nothing. At one hundred eight, she was still beautiful. Her hair was gray—a real gray, not white—and her face was thinner than it used to be, but her personal strength was still evident in the way she carried herself. She had retired from Starfleet as a captain some forty years ago, but she was still held in high regard by officers who hadn't even been born when she left. Their marriage had been easier with only one of them on active duty, but at times like these he knew she wished he had followed suit.

He had never been able to leave, however. He felt an obligation to serve. It had been drilled into him by his father, but he had made it his own decades ago, when he had gotten command of the *Enterprise*-B and had begun to come out from under Admiral Blackjack Harriman's shadow. Now he was a respected member of the admiralty himself, essentially semiretired but often serving as an unofficial advisor in any number of situations. Even though he rarely left San Francisco, he still worked long days away from Amina. It kept him strong, he thought. His shoulders were only slightly stooped under the weight of his many years. His hair, completely white and a little wispy, still covered his head. A deeply lined face served him well as an admiral; he had looked boyish years into his captaincy.

Amina turned now and noticed his reflective look. She smiled, as though indulging him, but he could see the anticipation of disappointment in her dark eyes. He might have to leave tonight, or maybe the next night when their grandchildren were hosting another anniversary party for family and friends. He could only smile back and take her hand. She understood that he could make no promises, having served the Fleet herself. He also knew she would never ask him to retire outright, though it caused a silent sadness in her. But they both knew he served a greater good and had helped protect lives across the Federation. They continued looking at each other, with melancholy dampening their smiles. Their remaining guest decided to fill the awkward silence.

"I've been coming here off and on for a hundred and thirty-one years now," Montgomery Scott said. "Mind you, I was off for quite a stretch there in the transporter buffer aboard the *Jenolen,* so I remember it as though it were only fifty-four years ago." He smiled with a twinkle in his eye as he picked up his glass and took a drink of something green. "I walked down to the Wharf the first week I entered the Academy. That was the fall of 2240. Of course, it was all original in those days—this whole stretch had to be rebuilt back in 2286 after that business with the whale probe. Now that was a storm." He lifted his fork, wrapped with pasta and stabbed through a large shrimp, for emphasis. "Sulu—he was born here in San Francisco—said there'd never been anything like it. Gillian Taylor, the lass we brought back with us with the whales from the twentieth century, had never seen anything like it either. Which brings us back to the beginning, actually." He stuffed the fork in his mouth and chewed quickly to get back to his story. "Gillian had eaten here as a wee lass way back when it first opened in 1965! They've got her picture on the wall here somewhere, you know. Aye, she was something special."

Harriman nodded, directing his gaze over Scott's shoulder and through the restaurant's wide windows. In the dark night over San Francisco Bay the lights of the Golden Gate Bridge struggled to be seen through the fog. He should have been thinking about whatever had called all those officers away, but the mention of Taylor had kept his thoughts moving along a more personal path. He had seen her picture in the restaurant but had generally avoided looking at the autographed photos of various Starfleet officers hanging nearby. Scott's was there, taken just a couple years ago, not long after his rescue from that transporter buffer. A row or two up from there was a line of photos featuring all the *Enterprise* captains. Those of Archer, April, and Pike predated the whale probe incident and showed water damage. It was a minor miracle that all three had been recovered from the wreckage of the original restaurant. As for his own photo, Harriman hadn't looked at it since he'd given it to the owner of the restaurant over fifty years ago. It hung, of course, next to a photo of Captain James T. Kirk on the bridge of the *Enterprise*-A.

Starfleet had arranged the passing of the torch from Kirk to Harriman, but as construction of the *Enterprise*-B had fallen behind schedule, the admiralty rushed other things along to compensate. For her maiden voyage the *Enterprise* had gone out of Spacedock with a skeleton crew and half her major systems off line, ill prepared for the distress call they had soon received. Nevertheless, they had saved forty-seven El-Aurian refugees from the *Lakul* before it was destroyed by a strange energy ribbon, but then the *Enterprise* herself had become trapped. Kirk had performed the deflector relay reconfiguration necessary for the ship to break free of the ribbon's gravimetric field, but as they pulled away a tendril of energy whipped out and breached the hull right where Kirk had been working. In the seconds before automatic containment fields activated, Kirk had been pulled into the vacuum, his body lost to space. It had been a heroic and fitting death for Kirk, giving his life aboard the *Enterprise* to save others, but it had also been a terrible personal blow to Harriman, losing one of his boyhood heroes during his first command.

"This is why I retired, so I wouldn't have to carry the weight of the quadrant," Amina said, mistaking his introspection for concern about whatever incident had interrupted their party. She leaned toward him and gave him a kiss on the cheek. "I may have lured him from the *Enterprise*—"

"A feat in itself," Scott interjected.

"But not from Starfleet. *Il a les défauts de ses qualités*—his faults spring from his qualities." Now she looked over the table toward Scott. "Until he takes off those pips we'll never be able to have a proper party." It was the closest she'd ever come to suggesting he retire.

"You got that right, lass." Scott downed what remained of his green beverage. "They just keep calling and calling, don't they? Aye, even a miracle worker just needs a nap now and then. I tell you, I don't miss the emergencies. Me engines I miss like wee bairns, but not the emergencies."

"You speak the truth, Man from Another Time." Amina and Scott clinked their glasses together.

Harriman rolled his eyes and then looked around the restaurant until he spotted Lieutenant Clarke, his aide-de-camp, walking briskly between the tables. He'd been expecting her since the chorus of combadges.

"Admiral," Clarke began as she sat next to him. Harriman noticed the momentary pause as she glanced around to appraise those within hearing range. Confirming that only Amina and Scott were that close, and considering that they were both retired Starfleet captains, she continued. "There's been a Romulan incursion. Command has issued a general alert."

Harriman exchanged looks with Amina and Scott, then said, "Romulans? Why would they attack us?" Decades ago he had been an expert on the Romulans. There was a time he would have been called immediately about anything involving the Empire, but the Romulans had withdrawn from galactic affairs for many years after the Tomed Incident—which he had been involved with shortly before his marriage—and Starfleet had new experts now.

Clarke's answer matched the foggy view of the Bay. "Details are still sketchy, sir. A lone Romulan ship attacked a research station and ransacked it as though looking for something." She held out a padd in her right hand. "Amargosa Observatory. *Enterprise* responded to the distress call."

Scott piped up. "Still the best ship in the fleet."

"We've only got their preliminary report," Clarke continued, seeming to ignore Scott's comment, but she smiled at the engineer.

Taking the padd, Harriman nodded. He was sure Picard had things under control. Harriman had a momentary flash of longing to be out there, but then he thought about the big, comfortable bed in the "painted lady" Victorian house they had up the hill near Chinatown. They were never thrown around by an unexpected attack, and they could open their windows and breathe in the fresh ocean breeze blowing across the bay. There was much to like about being an old admiral stationed at Starfleet Command.

He looked up from the padd. Among other duties, Harriman oversaw the Starfleet Corps of Engineers, and it was their job to fix whatever was broken. "Looks like the damage to the station was fairly extensive. I think the *da Vinci* is the closest S.C.E. ship to that sector. Get them on their way."

"Aye, sir." She left the table to contact the ship.

"The *da Vinci?*" Scott said. "Is she one of those new *Sabre*-class ships?"

Harriman nodded to Scott as he looked back at the padd and started scrolling through Commander Riker's report. Sadly, it looked like most of the station's complement had been killed in the attack, and they would need to be replaced before the observatory could function at full capacity. He wondered for a moment why Picard hadn't filed a report this serious himself, but forgot about that as he came across the list of survivors. At the sight of one name, he brought up the person's ID photo for confirmation.

Amina placed her hand on his arm when she noticed the look on his face. "John?"

Scott leaned forward. "You look like you've seen a ghost."

"I feel like I have." Harriman slid the padd across to Scott, turning it around to face him.

Scott furrowed his brow as he looked down. Immediately his eyebrows went up his forehead. "Aye, you have: Soran."

"Soran?" Amina looked from her husband to Scott, deducing the connection. "Was he on the *Enterprise*-B all those years ago?"

"Aye," Scott said. "I only remember two of the people we rescued. A lass named Guinan, the kind of person you knew you could trust from the moment you met her. And then there was Soran."

Amina looked confused by her husband's grim look. He shrugged and said, "He was a very angry man."

"Angry? About what?"

"Everything. Angry about losing his family and home—who wouldn't be?—but also about being rescued."

"I don't understand."

Scott said, "None of us did. He wasn't coherent. Chekov had to sedate him soon after he was beamed aboard. On the way back to Earth he tried to steal a shuttlecraft to go after that blasted energy ribbon that killed the captain. He almost came to blows with Chekov in the shuttlebay."

"After we were back at Spacedock I went to see him, where he was under guard for his own good." Harriman frowned at the memory. "He cursed me for ruining what he called his second chance and accused me of detaining him unlawfully, among other alleged violations of his civil liberties. 'Captain Kirk died saving you,' I told him. He just said that he had not asked to be saved. Refugee or not, I wanted to punch him in the nose."

"Did you?" Amina said with a smile.

Harriman sighed. "No, I behaved myself. But I was happy to get him off my ship."

"He's up to something," Scott said. He'd been looking over Soran's file on the padd.

"What?" Harriman and Amina said together.

"Soran's been involved in a lot of research over the last, what is it, seventy-eight years. Some esoteric stuff, across many disciplines. Stellar cartography, gravity wave modulation, space-time continuum distortion, nuclear inhibitors, surface-to-space launching systems, gravimetric topography, temporal phasing fields, stellar probe configurations, portable shield and cloaking technology, stellar fusion . . ."

"He's a scientist with far-ranging interests," said Amina. "That's to be expected when you live as long as El-Aurians do."

"Besides," Harriman said. "The station he was on was just attacked. Sounds like he's a victim."

Scott shrugged. "I just don't trust the man."

Harriman was about to play devil's advocate again but went with his gut feeling instead. "Neither do I, Scotty."

Just then Clarke returned to the table. "The *da Vinci* is on her way to the observatory, sir. They'll be there within three days. And there's been an update from Commander Riker. It seems the Romulans were searching for trilithium."

"What is that?" Harriman said.

"It's a nuclear inhibitor the Romulans have been experimenting with," Scott answered. He held the padd out to Harriman. "Given Soran's studies, the presence of trilithium is no coincidence. I'd guess he's going to implode Amargosa."

Harriman took the padd and looked over the list of Soran's studies before handing it to Clarke. As horrible as Scott's conclusion was, his reasoning seemed logical. "Why would he do that? It would destroy the whole system."

"I don't know. But I'll bet you a bottle of hundred-year-old scotch it has something to do with that energy ribbon."

Harriman had learned seventy-eight years ago to trust whatever Scott said. He tapped his combadge without bothering to take the time to leave the restaurant. "Harriman to Starfleet Command. Patch me through to the *Enterprise.*"

The next person he heard wasn't Picard, but Fleet Admiral Nechayev. "Nechayev here. Why do you need Picard?"

She sounded as brusque as ever, and it was just like her to interrupt him and question his reasons. Didn't she have more to worry about during a general alert?

"I believe that Doctor Soran is planning to destroy Amargosa."

"That seems unlikely on a number of levels."

"Montgomery Scott recognized a pattern in Soran's research over the last several decades that links him to trilithium."

There was a slight pause, but Nechayev didn't explain her thoughts. "We're beaming you to Starfleet Command. Transport will contact you. Nechayev out."

Harriman glanced at Amina. She put on an understanding smile. "Go ahead, Admiral. I'm going to finish my cioppino."

"You know I love you," Harriman said.

"You better," she replied, then gave him a hug.

As Harriman stood up, Scott came around the table to stand between him and Clarke. "I'll be coming with you."

"Nechayev didn't specify that."

"Well, she didn't specify I couldn't come."

Harriman's combadge chirped. He tapped it. "Harriman."

"This is Command Transport, sir."

With a smile at Scott, Harriman said, "Three to beam over."

"Aye, sir."

The situation room was a relatively quiet bustle of activity. Nechayev was sitting at the head of the briefing table, with her aide, Lieutenant Stanley, standing over her right shoulder. Various support staff sat at monitoring stations or moved between them, sharing data on padds. The bleeps and whistles of technology blended with the hushed speech of the staff in the background, creating an almost comforting atmosphere, even given the circumstances.

"Have you contacted the *Enterprise* yet?" Harriman said as he approached the table with Scott and Clarke on either side of him.

Nechayev looked up from a monitor in the briefing table. "We were too late to warn them about Soran." She turned toward Scott. "You were right, Mister Scott. He fired a stellar probe containing trilithium into Amargosa. It imploded with a level-twelve shock wave."

"That must have destroyed everything in the system," Clarke said.

"Luckily the *Enterprise* left at warp with the station's survivors. But the observatory is gone."

Harriman turned toward Clarke. "Inform the *da Vinci*."

"Aye, sir." She moved off to a communications panel.

He turned back to Nechayev. "Now what about this Romulan invasion?"

Nechayev leaned back in her chair. Harriman was a respected admiral, but his old-school approach to the Romulans was a liability to him in the current political climate. "There is no invasion. It was a single scout ship searching for stolen trilithium. Their ambassador acknowledges that the commander of the ship was overzealous in her pursuit of the trilithium, but insists that responsibility for the casualties, which included one of their own officers, must be shared by the unknown Federation national who procured the stolen material."

Harriman frowned. "And you buy that?"

"No. But we are not in a position to protest too loudly if there really was trilithium on the station."

"But what about Soran?" Scott asked. "Does the *Enterprise* have him in custody?"

Nechayev's expression was tense as she turned to look at Scott. "No. He escaped on a Klingon bird-of-prey with Lieutenant La Forge as a hostage."

"Geordi?" Scott said. "Oh, no. That's the lad who got me out of the *Jenolen*. A fine engineer. But what's this about Klingons? I thought we were at peace with them now."

"We are," Nechayev said. "I'm expecting an explanation from their ambassador shortly."

"Explanation?" Scott grimaced. "Klingons don't explain, they growl."

Nechayev took a deep breath. "Mister Scott, that sort of attitude—"

"Ten to one they say it's a rogue ship. They always do." Scott stomped off by himself.

Nechayev turned to Harriman. He shrugged. "He's right, you know."

Nechayev reentered the situation room with Stanley trailing behind her. Harriman motioned to Clarke and Scott to gather around the briefing table. Nechayev didn't bother sitting down before saying, "I've spoken with Ambassador Korrd."

Scott's grim expression softened a bit. "I knew a General Korrd in the old days. He helped pull our bacon out of the fire at the galactic core."

Nechayev nodded. "This is his granddaughter, I believe. She assured me that the Empire is taking no action against the Federation."

Harriman put down the coffee he'd been sipping. "Then how did she explain the bird-of-prey?"

Nechayev hesitated, a look crossing her face that Harriman didn't recognize. Just as he realized it was embarrassment, she said, "Korrd says they suspect Lursa and B'Etor of the House of Duras."

Harriman sighed. "In other words, a rogue ship." Under other circumstances it might have been funny. But the Klingons still had La Forge.

Nechayev turned to her aide and motioned for him to continue the briefing. He activated the monitors in the table. "Lieutenant Commander Data sent us this report." Stellar cartographic information filled the displays. Everyone leaned in closer. Stanley looked at Harriman and Scott. "When Soran destroyed Amargosa, it altered the course of the energy ribbon that you encountered on the *Enterprise*-B. Picard thinks Soran is going to the Veridian system, where the ribbon will be in about forty hours. If Soran implodes Veridian, the energy ribbon will intersect its third planet, and he will be able to return to the nexus, some sort of alternate reality fantasy world that exists within the ribbon."

"Is that what this is all about?" Scotty said. "He's destroying entire star systems for something's that's not even real?"

"It's more than just stars and planets." Clarke tapped at her monitor. "This indicates that Veridian IV is inhabited."

Stanley didn't respond immediately. Finally he said, "There is a preindustrial civilization of approximately two hundred thirty million on the fourth planet. There will be no survivors if the *Enterprise* doesn't stop him."

Nechayev didn't let the silence drag out. "Our three closest ships are the *Bozeman,* the *Farragut,* and the *Columbia.* I've diverted them all to Veridian. Even the closest, the *Farragut,* cannot make it there in under forty-eight hours." She looked around the table. "This all falls on Picard and his crew."

"They'll come through," Scott said. "There's just something about an *Enterprise.*"

Nechayev gave him a long look. "And you are part of why that is true, Captain."

"Now, now, Admiral. Remember, I'm retired."

"Not anymore. You are reinstated until this is over. I want your insights, and I don't like civilians in the situation room."

Harriman smiled. Scott squinted. "I think I must have heard you wrong, Admiral."

"You didn't." Before Scott could say any more, Nechayev turned to Harriman. "And you—go home to your wife. It's your anniversary."

It was Scott's turn to smile. "Now, that's an order that makes sense."

Two days later Harriman was stretched out on the couch at home, still tired from the party the night before. Amina had gone for a walk after lunch, humming some childhood song as she went outside and turned uphill.

"I want coming home to be easy," she had said, as she always did.

There was a knock at the front door. He'd been waiting for something—a knock, a combadge chirp—since leaving the situation room. Harriman got up as fast as he could and hurried to the door. He pulled it open, expecting to see Clarke, but it was Scott on the porch. He was in uniform.

"Scotty. There's news?"

"Aye." His voice seemed heavy.

"What is it? Was Veridian destroyed?"

Scott shook his head. "Picard had to kill Soran, but he saved the system."

"Then what is it?"

"May I come in?"

Harriman stepped aside. "Sorry, of course. Please, sit down. Can I get you something to drink? I think Amina made some fresh lemonade this morning."

Scott came in and sat in a big chair across from the couch. Now Harriman noticed that he carried something in his hands, a bottle, which he placed on the coffee table.

"No, thanks. I brought my own drinks."

"What is that?"

"Hundred-year-old scotch."

"What's going on here, Scotty? I seem to remember you winning that bet."

Scott looked over at him. He hesitated, then seemed to come to a decision about something. "We lost the *Enterprise.*"

Harriman shook his head. "Dammit. How? I thought the Duras sisters only had an old D-twelve."

"Aye. But they compromised the *Enterprise*'s shields somehow. The warp core was damaged. *Enterprise* took out the Klingons, and everybody made it to the saucer before she breached, but the blast blew the saucer out of orbit. They crash-landed on Veridian III."

"Survivors?" Then Harriman remembered the hostage. "La Forge?" He knew Scott had a history with the young engineer.

"La Forge was already back aboard before the breach, thank goodness. He was probably a big part of why there were only seventeen casualties."

Harriman nodded in disbelief. A D-12 taking out a *Galaxy* class? There had to be more to the story. And what a sight that landing must have been. He reached for the bottle. "Then we drink for the seventeen and the *Enterprise.*"

Scott reached out and put a hand on Harriman's arm. "That we will. But there's more."

Harriman drew his arm back slowly. "More?" There was something in Scott's voice . . . something eerie. Harriman felt a shiver start in his neck.

Slumping back in the chair, Scott ran his hands over his face. "Aye. The captain came back. He was in that nexus place and he came out with Picard and helped stop Soran. But he was killed."

"The captain?" Harriman leaned forward to try to see Scott's face. "Who? I thought you said—" And then he stopped. He remembered the bridge of the *Enterprise*-B, and the difficulties Scott had had trying to beam the *Lakul* survivors aboard. They were in temporal flux, phasing in and out of the space-time continuum. The nexus was an alternate reality.

Scott saw the realization in Harriman's eyes and continued. "He came back. And then we lost him again. That bastard, Soran, killed him."

There was a fury in Scott's voice that startled Harriman. He sat back on the couch, trying to take it all in. Kirk hadn't died on the *Enterprise*-B seventy-eight years ago. He hadn't lost a boyhood hero during his first command. Kirk had come back to help save the day again. In fact, if Kirk hadn't been aboard *Enterprise* all those years ago, he couldn't have saved the entire population of Veridian IV now. If Harriman had gone down to the deflector relays instead of letting Kirk go, if he had entered the nexus, would he have come back out and saved Veridian?

Harriman noticed Scott opening the scotch. He got up and went to an antique china cabinet against the far wall for some glasses. He put them down in front of Scott and sat on the couch again.

"You know a lot of people blamed me for Kirk's death," Harriman said.

Scott kept his gaze on his pouring. "Why? We all did our duty that day. Saved some people who would have died without us."

Harriman shrugged as he took the glass Scott held out to him. "I was caught with my pants down. Half the systems weren't installed—until Tuesday. I looked like an idiot on that bridge."

"Anyone can get caught with their pants down. Even the captain. The important part is how you pull them back up." Scott raised his glass in the air. "To James Tiberius Kirk, captain of the *Starship Enterprise*."

Harriman clinked his glass to Scott's. "To Jim." He downed the glass, thinking he had done so quite smoothly, but when he looked across the table Scott's glass was refilled and in the air again already. Harriman quickly poured some more into his own glass.

"To the *Enterprise*," Scott said. "All of them, past and future. Without them . . . well, I don't even want to think about it."

"To the *Enterprise*." They both drank quickly, and Harriman poured for them both this time. He raised his glass first. "And to those who didn't come home—then and now."

"Aye, those who didn't come home."

Harriman finished his glass with a quick toss and put it back on the table with a little more force than necessary. Scott poured again, but neither of them drank. A quiet sadness seeped into the room like a cold fog from the bay. They both let it be for several minutes, as if the silence held some wisdom about the old loss they had been forced to suffer again. Harriman picked up his glass and held it. He swirled the liquid around and watched it run back down the sides of the glass.

"What do you think that is, cognac?" Scott said, his warm brogue chasing the hush away. "This is scotch—it's for drinkin', not swirlin'."

Harriman found himself laughing and replied, even before he had thought it through, "I'm finally going to retire, Scotty." He felt a sense of surprise at having said it out loud.

Scott took a healthy drink. "Funny you should say that. I'm thinking of coming out of retirement."

"Well, sure, you're still a kid practically."

"And I've got a miracle or two up my sleeve yet. After I get used to these new uniforms, I might even be able to get them out."

They laughed together this time, and the silence that followed was less cold, more companionable.

"I should go," Scott said finally, pushing himself up from the chair. "There's going to be a lot of loose ends to wrap up yet."

"Of course." Harriman stood and walked to the door with Scott. "Thanks for bringing the news in person."

Scott just nodded as he opened the door, then hesitated on the threshold. "Are you coming in, Admiral?"

It was only then that Harriman realized he should. But something in the revisiting of Kirk's death had changed his mind. Instead he shook his head. "No, not today. Tell Lieutenant Clarke. She'll coordinate with S.C.E."

"Aye, sir." Scott stepped onto the porch and headed for the sidewalk.

As he reached the sidewalk, Harriman called after him. "You should have my job."

Scott stopped and looked back over his shoulder. "You mean get promoted to admiral?"

"No, I mean overseeing the S.C.E. They only gave it to me to keep an old admiral busy. But an engineer like yourself, you could really do something with it."

Scott shrugged. "I'll have to think it over. Don't really know if I can work outside of an engine room yet." He gave a last wave, then headed down the sidewalk, looking for the nearest streetcar stop.

Harriman watched Scott on his way back to Starfleet Command until he rounded a corner, then went inside. It wasn't long before Amina came in and joined him on the couch.

"I'm home," she said, putting her arms around him.

Harriman grinned. "So am I."

Beginnings

Jeff D. Jacques

Miles O'Brien was sipping a mug of piping hot Jamaican blend coffee in Ten-Forward when his life spiraled off in an unexpected direction.

"Mister O'Brien?"

Lieutenant Commander Data's voice struck O'Brien like a thunderclap. With a start, he looked up from the data padd he'd been reading, his heart fluttering as though he'd been shaken from a dream. The transporter systems analysis hadn't been *that* engrossing, yet O'Brien had been oblivious to Data's approach.

"Commander," he said and tried to mask his surprise with another sip of coffee. Next to Data stood an attractive Asian woman with lovely brown eyes and raven hair that shone in the subdued light of the lounge. The corners of her mouth tweaked slightly as O'Brien glanced her way.

"Are we disturbing you, Chief?" Data asked. The smile on his pale android face looked so phony, it was almost laughable.

O'Brien guessed the two of them were on their way to lunch and just stopped by on the way to their table.

"Ah . . ." O'Brien bit off the obvious response. They *were* disturbing him, and he didn't care for any small talk—particularly not Data's variety, which could be debilitating in heavy doses. "No," he said at last. "No, of course not."

He put the padd on the table and fashioned a cheerful smile. Data was a superior officer, after all, and he couldn't very well brush him off. He doubted the android had a mean streak, but he didn't want to take the chance that he might wind up on sanitation duty for a month.

"What can I do for you, sir?" he asked.

"I was curious as to whether you had ever met Keiko Ishikawa." Data turned in deference and the woman stepped forward.

"I don't believe I have," O'Brien said. He had, however, seen her once or twice before—in a corridor, perhaps, or here in Ten-Forward. As he took in the soft features of her face and her widening smile, O'Brien almost wished he *had* met her before. "Miles O'Brien. How do you do?"

"Very well, thank you," Keiko said, then extended a delicate hand. "It's a pleasure."

O'Brien gazed at the proffered limb for a moment, then accepted it. He was struck by the smoothness and warmth of her skin.

"Likewise," he said, then glanced at Data. What did Data expect him to do? Surely the android hadn't gone and added matchmaker to his endless list of talents.

Keiko seemed to notice his discomfort and jumped into the fray. "Actually, we *have* met before."

Not bloody likely, O'Brien thought. There's no way he would have forgotten *that* meeting. "I think you're mistaken. I'm sure I would have remembered you."

Keiko smiled at his subtle compliment. "Thank you, Miles. But you're wrong."

"I beg your pardon?" O'Brien asked.

"We exchanged hellos before you beamed me down to Calthos

III with an away team," Keiko said. "I was going down to study the flora at the mission site."

Calthos III? O'Brien searched his memory, but it wasn't easy. He'd beamed hundreds of people down to hundreds of different planets over the years. How did she expect him to remember one planet out of them all?

And then it hit him.

"Hold on," he said. "Wasn't that the planet where the away team got some sort of infection that turned their skin yellow?"

"Yes, that's it!" Keiko said. "Although it was closer to orange."

"Hm?"

"Our skin. It turned orange."

"Ah." O'Brien's opinion of this woman began to shift at an alarming rate. She might have the looks, but she was far too persnickety for his tastes. Picking apart everything he said for minor factual discrepancies could get stale very fast. "Anyway, that was a year and a half ago. You can't expect me to remember one passing greeting."

A line furrowed Keiko's otherwise smooth forehead. "Well it wasn't *that* long ago. And *I* remembered it."

"You also turned orange that day. I doubt that's something you'd forget very easily." O'Brien chuckled. She'd walked right into that one.

"You really don't remember me?" she asked. She sounded genuinely disappointed.

"Sorry," O'Brien said. "I guess you just weren't that memorable."

As Keiko's mouth dropped open in a shocked O shape, O'Brien immediately regretted his words. He started to apologize, but Keiko spun around and fled the lounge, leaving him alone with a bewildered Data.

"That exchange did not develop as I had anticipated," Data said, the artificial smile gone from his artificial face.

"I can't believe I said that," O'Brien said. "I did say it, didn't I?"

Data nodded. "I am afraid you did. I can access my audio record of the exchange if you wish to verify—"

"No, thank you, Commander. That won't be necessary." O'Brien shook his head. "Bloody hell, what was I thinking?" But he knew exactly what he had been thinking. He'd wanted to be left alone so he could get back to his padd, and that desire had inadvertently marred his words. It shouldn't have happened, and he was mortified that it had.

"I do not know," Data said. "But an apology would appear to be in order if you have any desire to form a relationship with Keiko and perhaps start a family."

"Whoa, hold on," O'Brien said as warning bells started to ring in his head. "A family?"

"Yes," Data said with a nod. "It was my intention to 'set you up' with Keiko."

"What for?" O'Brien felt the heat of anger creeping through his body and into his tone. He hadn't asked to be set up with a woman. What had Data been thinking?

"I have observed that when you are not in the company of your coworkers, both on duty and off, you are alone," Data said. If he noticed O'Brien's rising ire, he gave no indication. "When Keiko expressed an interest in meeting you, I could not ignore the opportunity to resolve the situation."

O'Brien had to use every ounce of willpower to keep his voice level and in control. "Look, I appreciate the . . . assistance, Commander, but I enjoy my solitude. If I had people around me twenty-four hours a day, I'd probably lose my mind."

"I see," said Data, though O'Brien doubted he did. "Then you do not wish to mate and start a family."

"Well of . . . of course I do, *someday*. I just hadn't counted on it being today." Truth be told, O'Brien hadn't thought about it much at all. It was true that many Starfleet officers didn't have any opportunities to start a family, since they were away from home so often. It was one of the sacrifices that came with the job. Of course, if he were to find someone who served aboard the same ship . . .

"Then perhaps my choice of a potential mate was unsatisfactory," Data said. O'Brien wondered if those perfect android ears of his had even been listening to what he was saying. "Would someone in your field of expertise be more to your liking? Chief Hubble, perhaps."

O'Brien gaped in horror. "Hubble?" An involuntary shiver rippled across the surface of his skin.

"Or perhaps Robin Lefler would be a suitable choice," Data said. "While she is not a transporter operator, she has expressed an interest in the engineering department, with which you are closely affiliated."

O'Brien shook his head at Data's bombardment. He could already feel his brain moving in a slow spin. "Who is Lefler? I've never even heard of her."

"She is a cadet in the midst of Academy field training aboard the *Enterprise,*" Data said.

"A cadet?" O'Brien asked, aghast. "My god, man, what do you think I am?"

"A man in search of female companionship," Data said in all innocence.

O'Brien took a moment to get his frenzied emotions under control. "Did it ever occur to you that the age difference might be an issue?" A cadet on field training! She had to be in her twenties. Data cocked his head, puzzled, but O'Brien had no desire to explain it to him. "Never mind. Look, with all due respect, sir . . . I've got to leave."

He shot to his feet, scooped up his padd, and got the hell out of Ten-Forward as fast as he could.

His head still swimming, O'Brien went down two decks to sickbay. Doctor Crusher was nowhere in sight, but Doctor Selar was treating a young blondhaired woman wearing the uniform of a Starfleet cadet. The girl sat on the central biobed, her legs dangling above the floor. O'Brien wondered if this was the cadet Data had mentioned. She was cute, he had to admit, but he was old enough to be her father.

"You are in perfect health," Selar said, her Vulcan demeanor as warm as a brisk Arctic wind. She closed her tricorder and appeared eager to end the conversation right then.

"But what about the knot in my gut?" asked the girl.

"I would recommend food," Selar said.

"But I just ate an hour ago."

"Eat again."

"But Law Six states that you shouldn't—"

"Your laws are irrelevant, Cadet. Good-bye." Selar held her stone-faced expression until the girl looked away. With a dejected gleam in her eyes, the cadet slipped off the bed and headed straight for the exit—and O'Brien.

"Hello," she said as she passed by. The room seemed brighter when she smiled, but by the time O'Brien managed to get his vocal chords to operate, she was gone.

"Is there something I can do for you, Chief O'Brien, or was it your intention to remain standing there indefinitely?" Selar's severe expression seemed to dare him to bother her with anything less than a medical emergency.

"I'm feeling a little dizzy," O'Brien said, and approached her. "I want to make sure there's nothing wrong."

"Have you been engaging in an activity in which your body has been moving rapidly in a circular motion?" Selar asked.

"No."

"Have you been suspended upside down?"

"Of course not."

"Then I would recommend food," Selar said.

"Food? But that's what you just told *her*," O'Brien said with a glance at the door.

"It is a valid diagnosis," Selar said. "Lack of sustenance often leads to a sense of disorientation."

O'Brien sighed. How this woman ever became a doctor was beyond him. She seemed more interested in getting rid of patients than treating them. "Look, maybe I'll just wait for Doctor Crusher."

"Doctor Crusher will not be in for the rest of the day," Selar said. "I observed that she was overworked and I—"

"Let me guess—you recommended food," O'Brien said, becoming more agitated by the minute.

Selar arched an eyebrow at him. "No, I told her several hours of bed rest were in order." She flipped open her tricorder and tapped at the controls as she aimed it at him. "I am detecting elevated heart rate and blood pressure."

"There's nothing wrong with my heart!" O'Brien snapped. "In fact, I've never felt better." He turned on his heel and left sickbay, almost as quickly as he'd left Ten-Forward.

The rest of the day progressed with little fanfare. At his post in Transporter Room 3, O'Brien performed a level-1 diagnostic, tweaked the Heisenberg compensators to get that point-four-seven percent improvement he'd been looking for, and cleaned away a stubborn smudge on the control console—no doubt a result of Hubble's gorging on sweets while on duty again. He'd have to talk to her about that. Other than the basic busywork, the afternoon was pretty dull.

That provided him with plenty of time to think, and for the most part, his thoughts dwelled on his disastrous encounter with Keiko Ishikawa. The stricken look on her face when he handed down that insult haunted him with a vengeance. And despite Data's questionable idea of setting him up with a total stranger for the purposes of procreation—of all the crazy notions!—there was no question Keiko deserved an apology. In fact, he would tend to that as soon as his shift ended. He might even offer to take her to dinner to help smooth things out.

Lord knew his mother had been on his case about finding a wife, settling down, and making babies. And while he wasn't necessarily looking to do that with this Keiko woman, they *had* gotten off on the wrong foot. At the very least, he wouldn't mind being her friend.

Now all he had to do was find her.

O'Brien stood in the corridor outside Keiko Ishikawa's quarters and stared at the closed door. He tried to send a command from his brain to his hand, which would then prompt him to push the chime, but he was having very little success. As though paralyzed, his arm just would not move. Maybe there *was* something wrong with his head after all. But as long as Selar was on duty, he wasn't going anywhere near sickbay.

His task wasn't that hard. Just push the chime and things would develop on their own. Keiko would either punch him in the throat, causing permanent vocal damage, or she would invite him in and they would talk things through. As he thought about it, more and more he hoped it would be the latter. The Asian culture had a long, textured tradition like the Irish, and he was curious to see what parts of her heritage she had included within her quarters.

He pushed the chime and waited for her response.

And waited.

O'Brien leaned close to the door. "Keiko? Uh, this is Miles O'Brien. We, ah, 'met' earlier today in Ten-Forward. Are you there?" He paused a moment, then continued. "Look, I can understand if you don't want to speak to me. I was an ass and I apologize for that. But Data's ambush flustered me and my behavior reflected that. I'm sorry."

He waited for some sign of acknowledgment from her—a voice through the intercom or even just a sound on the other side of the door—but all was silent.

"Look, if you never want to see me again, I can live with that, but could you at least say something? Even to tell me to get lost?" O'Brien felt his anger bubble up again. She could at least have the courtesy to tell him she never wanted to speak to him again!

"Fine!" He thumped the door with the side of his fist, then stalked up the corridor. "Of all the inconsiderate, lousy—"

"Miles?"

O'Brien broke off and spun around. Keiko was coming around the corner of a branching corridor about five meters away. She hadn't even been at home!

"Keiko!" he gasped, then recovered quickly. "Ah, you didn't hear any of what I just said, did you?"

She stopped in front of her door, folded her arms across her chest and shook her head. "Only the 'inconsiderate, lousy' part."

O'Brien sighed. "Look, that wasn't me."

"It certainly sounded like you."

"Well, it *was* me, but it wasn't—you know?"

"So . . . you're talking about clones now, or alien duplicates of some kind?" she asked, the seriousness of her voice obviously for show.

O'Brien gritted his teeth as he advanced toward her. "Look, I'm trying my best to apologize here, but you're not making it very easy."

"Then why don't you try it again tonight over dinner," Keiko said.

"Tonight?" O'Brien blurted the word like a curse. "I don't see why I have to wait until then if you're standing right—" He broke off as Keiko's words registered. "You mean . . . the two of us . . . at dinner . . . together?"

Keiko smiled. "That is how it's usually done."

O'Brien couldn't have been more astonished if she'd sprouted wings and flown away. "Why in God's name would you want to do that?"

"Because I'm the one who asked Data to introduce us, and I'm not about to give up after a single incident of boorish behavior." Keiko touched the keypad in the entranceway, and her door slid aside with a hiss.

Boorish? O'Brien was about to protest that particular term, but decided she was right. It wasn't the word *he* would have chosen, but he supposed from her perspective it was fitting enough.

O'Brien smiled. "You're far more gracious than I have any right to expect, and I accept your invitation."

"Good," Keiko said. "Eighteen-thirty hours in Ten-Forward. Don't be late." And then she disappeared into her quarters without another word.

Dinner went more smoothly than O'Brien had any right to expect, though Keiko's choice of a simple salad didn't offer any insight into her culture. True, it contained an odd assortment of vegetables and other things he'd never seen before, but for all he knew she could have scraped it from the bottom of a lake she'd visited on some planet. He, on the other hand, had three slices of ham roast, mashed potatoes, corn niblets, and pineapple chunks on his plate. Now *that* was a meal.

O'Brien regarded Keiko's meager serving as he swallowed a helping of gravy-soaked potatoes. "Is that all you're going to eat?" he asked when his mouth was empty again.

Keiko looked at him as though a second head had sprouted from his neck. "Yes. Is there something wrong with what I'm eating?"

"No, no, of course not," O'Brien said. "It's just that . . ."

"What?"

"Well, it doesn't look very filling to me."

Keiko stuffed a forkful of leafy stuff into her mouth. "It suits me just fine."

O'Brien held up his hands in a defensive posture. "All right. I was just asking."

"You don't see me criticizing your dinner choice, do you?" Keiko asked.

O'Brien sighed. *Here we go.* "I wasn't criticizing. I was just making an observation. That's how people generate conversation."

"Do I look like a child to you, Miles?" Keiko asked.

"No . . ."

"Because you're talking to me like I'm a child," she said, then mimicked O'Brien with a whiny exaggeration of his own words: " 'That's how people generate conversation.' " She shook her head and muttered something under her breath.

O'Brien noted that she was even more attractive when she was angry. There was a fire in her eyes that kindled a warmth within himself, and her cheekbones were more defined, giving her an almost feline quality. Appealing as it was, however, that state of mind didn't help him develop any kind of relationship with her.

"I'm sorry if that's how you feel," he said. "It wasn't my intention to talk down to you."

Keiko considered his words for a moment, then smiled. "Apology accepted." The words came so fast, O'Brien wondered if she was intentionally trying to bait him.

They finished the rest of their meal in silence, and when O'Brien offered to walk Keiko home, she suggested they take a detour to the arboretum. He agreed with a cheerful smile.

It was the worst decision he could have made.

The following morning, O'Brien looked up from his coffee in Ten-Forward to see Data standing there, his yellow eyes expectant.

" 'Morning, Commander," O'Brien said.

"Good morning, Chief," Data said. "Might I inquire as to how your evening went with Keiko?"

O'Brien shrugged. "It went fine."

A small smile appeared on the android's lips. "I am pleased to hear you had an enjoyable time." Satisfied, Data turned to go, but O'Brien sighed and called him back.

"Wait," he said, then gestured to the empty seat across the table. Data sat down. "It didn't go well at all—at least, not entirely."

Data frowned. "Then why did you claim otherwise?"

"I don't know," O'Brien said. "I . . . I guess I didn't want to disappoint you. You were the one who introduced us, and I didn't want to feel that your attempt to bring us together had failed."

Data nodded thoughtfully. "Then you have concluded that a relationship with Keiko will not work?"

O'Brien didn't want to admit to that. He wanted to try again with Keiko, but they'd have to work harder to make their divergent personalities more compatible.

"No, I haven't given up on her, but if last night was any indication, it won't be easy," he said.

Data folded his hands atop the table and cocked his head. "Would you like to talk about it?"

O'Brien almost laughed. Was he doing Counselor Troi impressions now? He supposed it wouldn't hurt to tell Data, since the android did have a small stake in the matter.

"Well, it started off all right, but we couldn't get through dinner without having an argument," O'Brien said. "We got past that, but then she decided we should go for a stroll in the arboretum after dinner."

Data nodded. "That is where Keiko works each day. She is a botanist and no doubt felt that bringing you to a place where she is comfortable would help 'smooth the edges' of your relationship."

"Yeah, well, whatever her reasons, it was a disaster," O'Brien said. "I couldn't stop sneezing! Everywhere we went there were strange alien plants and pollen. I thought my head was going to explode from sneezing so much."

"Such an occurrence would be highly improbable," Data said, taking things too literally as usual. He paused a moment, then said, "Perhaps on your next date, you could take her where you feel most comfortable on the ship."

O'Brien shook his head. "Nah, that won't work. The transporter room is no place to take a lady."

Data nodded again. "I am confident you will think of something to solve this dilemma, Chief."

"Thanks," O'Brien said with little enthusiasm.

"Now if you will excuse me," Data said, "I must report for duty." He rose and departed, leaving O'Brien no closer to solving his dilemma than before.

O'Brien's preoccupation with Keiko began to distract him so much, he beamed one of Doctor Crusher's biomedical experiments into Geordi La Forge's office in engineering. O'Brien wasn't aware that anything had gone wrong until La Forge dropped by with the leafy plant in his arms.

"Chief, I like a decorative plant as much as the next guy, but I don't think this is mine." Geordi handed the thing back to him.

O'Brien grinned, his face turning ruddy with embarrassment. "Sorry, Commander. I was . . . uh . . ."

"M-hm," Geordi said, then smiled in understanding. "I'm just glad Data didn't decide to set *me* up." He flashed that bright grin of his as he departed.

The com beeped, accompanied by Doctor Crusher's voice. *"Chief, I'm still waiting for that sample."*

"Sorry, Doc," O'Brien said, "it's on the way." He set the plant on the transporter pad, then felt a small sense of satisfaction as he watched it dematerialize before him.

After his shift, O'Brien set off to find Keiko again. He found her in Ten-Forward, but his heart dropped to his boots as he saw her dining with another man. The guy was making her laugh too!

The intrusive oaf was none other than Ensign Markson, who had a certain reputation as a Casanova. He'd already tried to woo a number of women on the ship, including D'Sora, McKnight, and Felton. O'Brien bet he'd even try his handiwork on Cadet What's-Her-Name—Gelfer? Fefler?—without a second thought.

He watched them for a moment, then decided it simply could not be allowed to continue. He went to the bar as Guinan glided over to him, the folds of her burgundy gown undulating about her.

"What can I get you, Chief?" she asked with that omnipresent barely-there smile.

With his eyes still on Markson, O'Brien said, "Something thick and sticky."

"Now, Chief, you wouldn't be thinking about making a mess in my lounge, would you?" Guinan asked in a playful, chiding tone. It was as though she'd seen right through him.

O'Brien looked at her. "What would give you that idea?"

"Well, you've been staring daggers at Mister Markson over there, who seems to be making quite the impression on your lady friend."

"Really?" O'Brien said. "I hadn't noticed."

"M-hm," Guinan said, then moved off for a moment. When she returned, she handed him a glass of brownish liquid that didn't move at all as she set it down. "Here you go."

O'Brien took a whiff of the stuff and almost lost his lunch. "What in God's name *is* that?"

"It's probably best that you don't know," Guinan said. O'Brien believed her. "Just try to keep it off the carpet, would you?"

The corners of O'Brien's mouth crept up as he saw the gleam in her dark eyes. "I'll do my best."

As he approached Markson and Keiko, O'Brien worried that Guinan's concoction would be too thick to be of any use, but he'd committed himself to his plan and couldn't back out now. As he drew near, he tripped himself and launched the contents of the glass toward Markson. The vile stuff splattered into the side of the ensign's face and oozed onto his uniform. O'Brien couldn't have been more impressed with the results.

Markson let out a cry of alarm and shot to his feet. "You clumsy idiot!"

"Hey, calm down, friend," O'Brien said, trying to stave off the grin that threatened to split his face. "It was an accident."

"It was a pretty precise accident, if you ask me," Markson said as everyone in the room turned to watch the scene unfold. "Look at this!" He tried to brush the stuff off, but it had already started to congeal. "What the hell *is* this?"

O'Brien glanced at Guinan, who leaned forward on the bar as she watched with everyone else. She shrugged her shoulders and continued to smile.

"You probably don't want to know," he said, then added, "but you can't find a pub in Ireland that won't serve it." He looked at Keiko, and to his utter delight, she was covering her mouth with a hand to hide a grin.

"This will take forever to get out," Markson said as he tried to detach his hands from the brown slime that clung to him like warm mozzarella. He started for the door, then came back long enough to say, "Excuse me, Keiko," before resuming his retreat.

"Try not to get any of that stuff on the carpet, would you?" O'Brien called after him. Markson spun around to see if he'd trailed any of the sludge behind him, then as he turned back to the door, he slammed into a young woman who was just coming in. Knocked her clear across the corridor, he did. Before she disappeared from view, O'Brien recognized her from sickbay, one of Doctor Crusher's assistants. Alice, or something, was her name. The two of them picked themselves up and walked off together, Alice (or whatever) with her arm around Markson's gooey shoulder. O'Brien suspected they'd be stuck together for some time.

"Miles."

O'Brien turned to see Keiko shaking her head, but the smile was there and that was what mattered. "Oh, hi," he said with a casual air, as though he hadn't seen her until now.

"That was very sweet of you," Keiko said, "but did you have to destroy the poor man in the process?"

"I'm afraid I did," O'Brien said, and sat down in the chair next to her. "Part of the plan." He gazed into her chocolate eyes and decided he could float within their grasp forever. " 'Sweet,' huh?" he asked and found himself leaning closer to her.

"Very," said Keiko and leaned closer herself. "You know, you're very resourceful when you're jealous."

"Jealous?" He uttered the word as though for the first time. "Is that what that was?"

"M-hm."

O'Brien shrugged. "Well, when I saw the two of you together, I must have gone temporarily insane. I couldn't very well let him—"

"Miles?"

"Yes?"

"Shut up."

O'Brien opened his mouth to respond, but Keiko interrupted him with a deep, lingering kiss that sparked explosive sensations within his body that had long been dormant. His arms swirled as though they were made of liquid, and his chest cavity felt fuller, more alive than ever. And the tingling! Oh, the tingling was heaven.

When Keiko released her spell, O'Brien's mouth was still ajar and she pushed his chin up to fix the malfunction. "And how was that, Mister O'Brien?"

"Miss Ishikawa . . . mere words would not do the experience justice," O'Brien said. "But you know what?"

"What?"

"I think it's safe to say we've got the beginnings of a beautiful friendship here," he said.

"Oh," Keiko said with mock disappointment and a very attractive pouty lip. "So you just want to be friends, is that it?"

O'Brien smiled. He would enjoy showing her how wrong that assessment was.

Solemn Duty

Jim Johnson

Captain Jean-Luc Picard walked through the tall brown grass toward Admiral McCoy's small yet elegant home, tucked into a quiet little corner of land once a part of the old United States of America. Picard recalled from his brief research for this trip that the old-timers who still lived in this area—those who had lived there all their lives—still called it Georgia. *Home is home, no matter what it's called,* he guessed. *That which we call a rose, and all that.*

Thinking of the Bard brought a slight smile to Picard's steady features, though the weight of his mission kept him from taking much pleasure in Shakespeare's timeless words. Like a chorus from one of his plays, perhaps even like Horatio approaching Fortinbras, Picard had a sorrowful message to deliver to two completely unsuspecting people.

As Picard neared the home, he noticed a small shuttlecraft parked on the lawn nearby. The vehicle had seen better days, as evidenced by the occasional scorch mark and spot-weld dotting her hull plates, but overall she looked to be much-loved and well maintained. Her original markings had been either painted over or simply removed, but the simple lines of the craft were unmistakable. It had to be the shuttlecraft *Goddard,* once attached to the shuttle complement of the *Enterprise*-D but on permanent loan to one Captain Montgomery Scott, Starfleet Corps of Engineers, most definitely and much deservedly retired.

Remembering his incredible, nigh-miraculous encounter with the resourceful engineer just a couple of years ago, Picard's slight smile threatened to expand into a wider grin. He couldn't think of anyone else who could have devised a better way to loop a transporter buffer into continual refresh mode and store a person's pattern in that buffer for survival. Scott was truly a marvel for the ages, and . . .

Enough. Picard checked the impulse to lose himself in the memories of that mission around the Dyson Sphere. A more recent mission with much harder memories occupied his mind, and it was time to finish that mission.

Traditionally, it was a captain's solemn duty to personally inform a fallen shipmate's next of kin of the loss to their family and to Starfleet. While Picard had known Captain James T. Kirk on a personal level for just a little while, he felt—no, he *knew*—it was his job to perform that duty on behalf of the fallen legend.

Admiral McCoy and Captain Scott, the two men Picard had come to old Georgia to meet, were the only two people Picard knew of even remotely qualified to be classified as Captain Kirk's relatives. Well, the only two except for one other—the one he hadn't been able to track down. Spock.

Picard had tried to locate the Vulcan ambassador, to invite him to this gathering of his old shipmates, but to no avail. He must still be on Romulus somewhere, working to bring peace and unity to those people. Picard wondered if he would ever see Spock again, and suspected that such a meeting would likely never happen.

Picard reached the front steps of the small house and climbed them with two easy strides. He took a deep breath, mentally reviewing the standard Starfleet protocol for this duty one last time. Realizing he was stalling, Picard gave his uniform tunic a self-conscious tug, then knocked on the door.

There was no answer, nor any to his following pair of knocks. He peered through the curtained window set to the side of the door, but couldn't see anything through the gauzy material. He thought he could hear muffled music, and followed the wide porch around to the back of the house.

A small pine deck was built onto the back of the house, looking out over acres of tall grass. On the deck were several comfortable-looking chairs, each with a matching side table. One of Mozart's quieter compositions, one Picard didn't immediately recognize, wafted out from the open windows set into the back of the house.

One deck chair was fully occupied by the solid bulk of Captain Scott, who looked much the same as Picard remembered, though perhaps a little thinner. Scott was nursing a glass of dark wine, which he idly swirled while watching the grass sway in the breeze.

Seated next to Scott was a white-haired whisper of a man with a calm, ageless face. It had been eight years since Picard had last seen Admiral McCoy, and those years didn't appear to have touched the good doctor. He looked much as he had when he toured the *Enterprise,* just before her first voyage with Picard as captain. A light blanket covered McCoy's legs and lap, even in the warmth of the afternoon. He was sound asleep, snoring quietly.

Scott turned at the sound of Picard's footsteps on the deck. The engineer offered him a wan smile and raised his glass in a toast.

"Top of the day to you, Captain Picard. I'd stand and shake yer hand, but I hope you'll humor an old man intent on drinkin' the day away."

The carefully rehearsed speech Picard had prepared dissipated like smoke in the breeze. He couldn't deliver Starfleet's canned platitudes to these men. He was sure they'd heard the words hundreds of times in their careers, probably had delivered the speech a few times themselves—McCoy especially. Picard had delivered the speech more times than even he could remember, but this one, this time . . . this was different.

Picard forced himself to set a smile on his face and walked over to Scott, shaking the engineer's proffered meaty hand. Scott signaled to a nearby seat. Picard moved the seat closer, careful not to scrape it against the deck and risk waking the sleeping admiral.

As Picard sat down, Scott motioned to an empty glass. "Care for a drink?"

Not now. Not yet. "Thank you, Captain, but I'll have to decline."

Scott shrugged. "Suit yerself. 'Tis a decent merlot, though I don't remember where Len said he got it from."

Scott glanced at his sleeping companion, then turned back. Picard caught the gentle look in Scott's eyes just before they slipped back to casual indifference. "A local vintage, I think. Maybe Virginian. Wines aren't really my thing, y'see."

Picard nodded, though he was distracted, trying to think of the best delivery for his news. After a moment of uncomfortable silence, he decided that working up to it would probably be better than just blurting it all out. Picard knew he didn't have a reputation as a babbler, and didn't intend to start one now.

"Ah, I have heard that the vintners around here offer decent products. Perhaps not at the level of a French varietal, but certainly palatable all the same."

Scott shrugged. "All the same. I prefer my scotch over anything else. This stuff," he waved the glass at Picard, "this is just an appetizer."

Picard clasped his hands together, gathering his resolve to get his message out. *It's now or never, Jean-Luc.* "Captain . . . I need to . . ."

Scott raised a hand. "Ah. Stop right there. Not only am I off duty," he waved the glass again, "but I'm also retired. Very retired. You're welcome to call me Monty, or Scotty if you prefer, but please drop the rank."

Grateful for the delay, Picard nodded. "Of course. Feel free to call me Jean-Luc then, Monty." Picard offered the engineer a smile.

Scott returned the smile and took a small sip from his glass before returning it to the table. "There, that was easy enough. I can tell ye have something important to say, Jean-Luc, but we don't have to let formalities get in the way."

"I agree." Picard looked at McCoy, then back to Scott. "Ah, what I have to say really needs to be heard by both of you."

Scott grinned. "Of course. You didn't ask me to come here just to talk to me. You could have done that any old time."

Scott leaned over to McCoy and gave him a gentle nudge. "Len? Len, wake up, lad."

McCoy shifted in his chair, mumbling something under his breath that sounded to Picard like, "Mrrffing early for this . . ."

Scott gave McCoy another gentle shake. "Len? Captain Picard's here."

McCoy cracked open one eye, squinted against the bright sun. He glared at Scott, then rolled his eye over to Picard with deliberate speed. He gave him a thorough once-over, then turned his one-eyed gaze back to Scott.

"Why in blazes doesn't that man have a drink in his hands?"

Scott shrugged. "The captain's here on official business, Len. I think he thinks he's on *duty*. He's not allowing himself a drink."

"Bullshit. I don't see any Starfleet regulations lyin' around, and unless y'all brought a copy along, we don't have to follow 'em."

"Ah, gentlemen," Picard interjected, "this isn't really official business, but . . ."

McCoy opened his other eye, his still-clear blue stare slicing through Picard. The man had to be, what, 140, 145, and still had eyes as sharp as someone half his age—even a third his age. Possibly even a quarter.

"If this isn't official business, then you're not on duty. And if you're not on duty, you can have a drink with a couple of old warhorses, son."

Picard suppressed a smile at that last comment. McCoy *was* old enough to be his father. Hell, he was old enough to be his *grandfa-*

ther. "My apologies, Admiral. As I mentioned, I'm not here officially, but I . . ."

McCoy leaned toward him, his blanket slipping from his lap. "Don't call me 'admiral,' dammit. I'm too old to be bothered with niceties and ranks and etiquette. Call me Leonard."

Picard took a deep calming breath. "Thank you. Leonard it is. Please call me Jean-Luc."

McCoy gave him a self-satisfied smile and plopped back into his chair. He fished for his blanket and settled it more firmly around his lap. "There, you see, Scotty? The youth of today *can* listen once in a while."

Scott nodded, taking another sip from his merlot. "Indeed they can. I had a similar request for Jean-Luc here just before you woke up."

"Ah? Good." McCoy fixed his gaze on Picard once more. "Your politeness is appreciated, Jean-Luc, especially by this southern gentleman, but let's be honest. It's wasted on the likes of us. We're not for this century. We're a little too . . ." He trailed off, looking for the right word.

". . . rough." Scott chimed in, right in step with his old companion.

McCoy nodded. "Rough. Right to the end. Starfleet doesn't have any old cantankerous hams like us anymore."

Picard could think of a handful of top brass that would fit that bill and then some, but thought it best not to gainsay the doctor. He just smiled in response.

McCoy looked at him, then turned to take in the scene just off the deck. "Now will you look at that? Nothin' better than sittin' and watchin' the grass swing in the breeze, especially with a couple of friends and a little hooch."

Scott offered a wordless grunt of agreement while Picard followed McCoy's gaze out into the grass. It was hypnotic, swaying back and forth, an endless wave of color in motion. Almost hypnotic enough to make him forget why he was here. Realizing he was stalling yet again, Picard cleared his throat.

"Ah, look, Leonard, Scotty. I asked to meet you here for a reason. Something very important and very unfortunate has occurred, and I wanted to bring you the news personally, before the message finally worked its way through official Starfleet channels."

McCoy looked at him with a calculating eye. "This sounds pretty big, boy. I'd better fortify myself." With that he poured himself a glass of merlot and topped off Scott's glass with the remainder left in the bottle.

McCoy took a healthy swig from his glass, then settled deeper into his chair. "All right, Jean-Luc," his easy drawl tinged with curiosity, "what have you got? What earth-shattering news do you have for two old Starfleet officers like us?"

Picard looked at the two of them, seeing that he finally had their attention. "First, let me say that I very much wanted Ambassador Spock to be here as well. This news would interest him."

McCoy blinked, took a sip of wine. "That old green-blooded fool's still alive and kicking? Last I heard he was holed up on Romulus."

Picard nodded, a little annoyed at the tangent. "Yes, that's right. When I met Ambassador Spock a few years ago, he was working toward a unification movement between the Romulans and the Vulcans."

Scott nodded. "I remember reading about that somewhere."

McCoy snorted. "Figures. That Vulcan's just as stubborn as me. He's waiting me out, thinking I'll kick off first, I can guarantee it." He turned to Scott with a mischievous gleam. "His logic failed to remind him that I'm immortal, isn't that right, Scotty?"

Scott gave his old friend a smile. "Perhaps, Len. Perhaps."

McCoy took another sip of wine. "Well, go on, Jean-Luc. You didn't come all the way out here to Georgia to discuss the Romulans with us, Spock or no Spock."

Picard sighed. *Out with it, Jean-Luc. No more delays.* "Quite right. I came here to tell you . . . to tell you . . ." Picard stopped, searching for the words. They weren't there. He struggled to bring his prepared speech to mind, but it was in tatters, victim of the folly of his actions.

Scott must have seen the emotional struggle playing out on his face. "Laddie . . . Jean-Luc . . . it's all right. We can take it, whatever it is." Picard felt Scott's hand touch his hands, felt foolish for being so tongue-tied. He looked at Scott, then turned to McCoy. He saw concern mingled with curiosity in both their faces.

Just let it out. "I came here to tell you that I've just returned from Veridian III. I was there burying Captain James T. Kirk." *Well. There it is.*

The stunned silence that greeted his statement confirmed in his mind that *that* was the last thing either McCoy or Scott would ever have expected him to say.

Scott was the first to recover. "Laddie, I do not know what you mean. Jimmy Kirk died a long, long time ago. I saw him die. I was there, on the *Enterprise*-B."

"And I was at his damn funeral," McCoy said. "I gave his eulogy, for chrissakes."

Picard shook his head and looked at Scott. "No, Scotty. You were on the *Enterprise,* but you didn't see Kirk die."

Scott shook his glass at Picard. "No, Jean-Luc. I *did* see him die. He was sucked out of the bloody ship into bloody space!"

Picard laid a gentle hand on Scott's arm. "Scotty, I know this will be very hard to believe, but Captain Kirk didn't fall into space. He fell into the nexus."

McCoy shifted his gaze from Picard to Scott, then back again. "The what?"

"The nexus. A ribbon of temporal energies that drifts through the galaxy."

McCoy stared. "Like I said, a what?"

"It's an energy field, shaped like a ribbon . . ." Picard began.

Scott interrupted him. "And a damn destructive ribbon at that. It destroyed a pair of transports and put a hole in the *Enterprise* to boot."

Picard pushed forward. "Yes, that too. But the nexus is also a . . . a place. Outside of the regular time stream and galactic continuum."

McCoy waved his hand in a "get on with it" motion. "So it's a place where time is screwed up. Fine. What does that have to do with Kirk?"

"It is my belief," Picard said, "that when the *Enterprise*-B was struck by the nexus, Captain Kirk was thrown into *it* rather than into space."

McCoy stared at him. "How strong's your faith, boy? That belief of yours is pretty hard to swallow."

"It . . . that could explain why we never found his body," Scott said.

Picard nodded. "Exactly. He was thrown into the nexus, and remained there for almost a hundred years."

Scott looked startled. "He was . . . stuck in there?"

"Yes. Just as you were stuck in that transporter buffer on the *Jenolen*."

Scott blew out a sharp breath. "Aye."

McCoy leaned forward, waving his hand. "All right. So Jim was thrown into the nexus for years and years. How did you find him?"

"I was on Veridian III, trying to stop a madman from blowing up that planet's sun," Picard said. "Soran was a very . . . disturbed . . . man trying to get back into the nexus."

McCoy looked confused. "Tryin' to get back in? Why? Doesn't sound like it was anything interesting. You said it was just a . . . sort of energy prison, right?"

Picard sighed. "Not exactly. The nexus suspends a person into whatever time and place they want, but on an unconscious level. I don't know if that makes sense or not. While I was in there, it was Christmas in my mind, and my wife and children were gathered around me."

McCoy shrugged. "That doesn't sound so bad."

Picard gave the doctor a sad smile. "Indeed not. Except that I've never married and I have no children."

"Oh."

"So, the nexus puts you into the time and place you subconsciously want to be in?" asked Scott.

"More or less, yes," said Picard. "It puts you into the most perfect, most ideal place your mind can think of. And then leaves you there."

"How would you get out? How did *you* get out?" asked McCoy.

"I had some help." Picard sighed. "It's my guess there are still people stuck in there who don't know any better. I was fortunate and had an old friend help me. She told me about Kirk, and then I helped Kirk get out."

"But you said you buried him, Jean-Luc," said Scott. "Did you bring him out dying, or was he dead already?"

Picard shook his head. "No to both. He was perfectly fine when we left the nexus. You see, I told him how I had gotten there, and that Soran was still trying to destroy Veridian's sun. He offered to help me, and we left the nexus together."

McCoy grunted. "Leave it to Jim to go out in a blaze of glory. Again."

Scott said, "So the two of you left the nexus and went back to Veridian III . . . ?"

"Right. To stop Soran," said Picard.

"And you were successful, but Kirk . . . died?" asked McCoy.

Picard leaned in close, clenching his hands together. "I'm afraid so. He was on a damaged bridge attempting to get the controls to Soran's weapon. He managed to get them and deactivated the weapon's cloak, but the bridge finally collapsed, with Kirk still on it. He fell some twenty meters with the wreckage, and ended up crushed, pinned beneath it."

Scott and McCoy just listened. Picard could see the wonder in their eyes. "By the time I could reach him, it was too late. I couldn't save him. I . . . I tried to get him out of there, but there wasn't anything I could do."

Scott opened his mouth, then closed it. McCoy looked nonplussed.

"He shared his last words with me, then he was gone. The finest Starfleet captain, gone because of a stupid bridge and because I couldn't . . ."

McCoy reached out and grabbed his hand. "Don't even start with that, boy. You know as well as I do that there was nothin' you could have done. Don't beat yourself up about it."

Scott shook his head. "Listen to Len. Eventually, everyone's time runs out. And when it does, nothing can stop it. Not a Starfleet captain, not even a doctor. Sounds like time finally caught up to Jimmy."

McCoy said, "He gave it a hell of a chase, though."

Scott nodded. "Aye, that he did. That he did."

Picard watched the two, marveling at the depth of their bond of friendship and camaraderie. It was so visible, so palpable, even after all their long decades. And that bond wasn't just between these two; it stretched out to enclose all of Kirk's original crew, all of them. *Amazing.*

Picard took a deep breath and continued. "Once the Federation rescue ships arrived, I had the wreckage cut away and brought him out myself. Kirk didn't have any final requests or any personal burial instructions on file. I mean, he'd been believed dead for decades, so such things wouldn't still be available. And since he had no living relatives, I decided to bury him there."

It was McCoy who spoke first. "That was probably the best thing to do, Jean-Luc. Jim and I never talked about such things, but I'm sure he would have preferred to be laid to rest near his final triumph, if at all possible. If his sacrifice did do some good, he'd want to be near the fruits of it."

Picard nodded. "He helped save the lives of over two hundred million people on Veridian IV. He died a hero." He paused, remembering Kirk's final words. "He made a difference."

Scott drained his glass. Looking at the bottom of it, he grimaced and placed it on the table. Sighing, he said, "Incredible. I dinna have any idea what else to say."

McCoy watched the grass sway for a little while. "I'm not sure what to say either, Jean-Luc. I've lived all these years with the understanding that Jim died that day on the *Enterprise*-B. Now you tell me that he survived that accident, got trapped in a dream, got rescued, then died saving a planet from a madman." He shook his head. "I'm not sure how I should feel about this."

Scott shook his head. "Aye. I made my peace with Jim Kirk decades ago. I don't know that I have anything else to say on his behalf."

"I talked to my counselor before coming here," Picard said. "She thought you might have that reaction."

McCoy snorted. "I bet. What was her suggestion?"

Picard said, "Counselor Troi suggested that you might need some time to sort out your feelings, but that it was all right if you didn't feel much of anything at first. This is, after all, a remarkable circumstance."

McCoy chuckled quietly. "It's not all that hard to accept, really. We've seen some damn strange stuff in our day, right, Scotty?"

Scott smiled. "Aye. That we have."

McCoy nudged Picard on the arm, giving him a serious look. "You did all right, Jean-Luc. Thank you for taking care of our friend. And thank you for coming out here to tell us personally."

Picard gave McCoy's hand a squeeze. "It was the least I could do. He was a remarkable man."

McCoy smiled, then looked out and watched the swaying grass. Picard shared a look with Scott, then joined the doctor in looking out over the deck. They lost themselves in their thoughts, letting them drift and shift and wander, enjoying the companionable silence.

Finally, Scott cleared his throat, bringing them all back to the moment. He nudged McCoy on the arm. "Well, what do you think, Len? Are you up for a little jaunt to Veridian III to say good-bye to an old friend?"

Picard helped the two men pack the few necessities they'd need for the trip, then watched as they loaded the *Goddard*. Scott helped McCoy into the shuttle and strapped him into his seat, enduring mild grumblings from McCoy about his obvious ability to do it himself. Scott exited the shuttle and approached Picard.

"Jean-Luc, I want to thank you again for what you did. Jim was a good man, and you gave him a chance to die the way he wanted to—fighting for something important."

Picard nodded. "It would be nice to be able to pick the time and place of our last moments. I can only hope that I can do as well as Kirk."

"I'm sure you'll do just fine, Jean-Luc." Scott offered his hand, which Picard gladly shook. "Take care of yourself. Maybe we'll pay you a visit after we're done on Veridian III."

Picard nodded. "Any time, Scotty. You and Leonard are always welcome on the *Enterprise.*"

He watched Scott enter the shuttle and cycle the hatch shut. His gaze followed the shuttle as it lifted off from the grass and gracefully arced up into the sky and out of sight. Turning back, Picard allowed himself to indulge in a long walk in the tall grass. He'd return to the *Enterprise* soon enough, but for now, he was on his own time.

Infinite Bureaucracy

Anne E. Clements

Bill of lading in datachip form, attached to a container of 20,735 self-sealing stembolts found floating in the Oort cloud of the Aeolian system:

Consignee Designation:	Quark of Ferenginar
Consignee UAC*:	UFP_.21601.B23.DS9.P26.0000001
Consignor Designation:	Flem of Ferenginar
Consignor UAC:	TZ_.3654.TZ42.KL92.00086540
Order Date:	48601.4
Order Received Date:	48601.4
Order Processed Date:	48601.4

*Universal Address Code

Order Transcription

Image record of a Ferengi, middle-aged, snappy dresser, with wide, pleasant rather than handsome features (by Ferengi stan-

dards), against a backdrop of an empty refreshment/recreation establishment decorated in oranges and browns. He speaks in Ferengi.

"*Flem! Quark here, your uncle Birk's second cousin's mentor's nephew's third partner's older son. I'm in the market for a shipment of self-sealing stembolts, and Goln of Fromaginar II mentioned that a Terellian trader heard that a Tzenkethi manufacturer went bankrupt and sold his entire stock at a discount to one of our people. I did a little digging, and your name came up. I was wondering if you might be interested in unloading, say, a* glerint *or so.*"

The image splits, the right-hand half showing an older, more reptilian-looking Ferengi in a tight gray garment that looks something like mummy wrappings. He tugs thoughtfully at one ear.

"*A* glerint, *you say? I suppose I could spare a* glerint. *If the price is right, of course. Where exactly did you say you were, again?*"

"*Deep Space Nine. It's a Federation space station, near Bajor.*"

"*Never heard of it.*"

"*It's not far from Cardassia. Used to be occupied by the Cardassians, actually, but you know how these things go.*"

"*Oh, yes, now I remember. That's quite a ways off. Your transport costs are going to cut pretty deeply into your profit—I assume you actually do have a buyer? You'd have to be pretty desperate to engage in a venture like this on spec.*"

"*Oh, I have a buyer. I also have a transport connection that can pick up the cargo at Starbase 201 . . .*"

(Haggling ensues, in which Quark, apparently with great reluctance, brings up the rumor he heard about the Tzenkethi factory owner's not having completely filled out the transfer-of-ownership forms, and various creditors working their way through the Tzenkethi legal system to claim the remaining assets. Eventually, a price is agreed upon.)

Price Confirmed Date:	48601.5
Order Confirmed Date:	48601.5

| Contents: | Self-sealing stembolts, quantity 20,736 units. |

Contents: Self-sealing stembolts, quantity 20,736 units.

Composition: 80% mixed duranium, aluminum, and steel alloys, 11% electrically modulated ceramic, 9% thermally stabilized plastic.

Packaging: Bulk-packed in a standard Giffla-37XZ multipurpose interstellar-rated container.

Interior atmosphere: None.

Original Routing

Stage 1
From: Tzenketh Okl!a
To: Starbase 247
Carrier Designation: tz'grtha n!hing ko
Carrier UAC: TZ_.3654.TZ42.KL34.00000141
Transport: !!iikb& a'na 21
Registry: Tzenketh 445693.!!wa29900017&.23
Estimated Departure: 48602.5   Actual: 48602.5
Estimated Arrival: 48604.9   Actual: 48607.0

Stage 2
From: Starbase 247
To: Starbase 201
Carrier Designation: Transgalactic Shipping
Carrier UAC: UFP_.002._C15.NH55.37761321
Transport: Vilossia Twilight
Registry: Alpha Centauri IF34599.100965d
Estimated Departure: 48607.0   Actual:
Estimated Arrival: 48610.5   Actual:

Stage 3
From: Starbase 201
To: Deep Space 9

Carrier Designation: Smith Freightways
Carrier UAC: UFP_.0201.SB201.649.00000001
Transport: Don't Look Back
Registry: UFP IIF2703.807665v
Estimated Departure: 48611.5   Actual:
Estimated Arrival: 48613.5   Actual:

Tzenkethi Customs Validation

Declared Value: 14,203.567 Claws(TZ)
Ferengi equivalent: 22 bars, 10 strips, 75 slips of gold-pressed
                       latinum.
Exchange Rate Date: 48601.5

Image record of a middle-aged male Tzenkethi—a feliform biped with gray-and-black striped fur, including long, stringy whiskers and tall (if slightly bedraggled) pointed ears. He speaks in rather ostentatiously high-caste Tzikaa!n.

"By the Horns of the Great Mother and for the honor of my House, I declare that this container's contents are precisely as specified, with no hazardous, unclean, or treasonous material or intent.

So sealed this 402nd day of the Cycle of the Lemming, by V'kreza O !nragtha Nenzeth, Fourth Claw of the Ministry of Trade, at Tzenketh Okl!a Trade Compound 16."

Received UFP Starbase 247 Temporary Storage Locker 9246b SD 48605.0251
Received Date: 48607.1
Received By: Yeoman Jancy Venkataramani,
               Starfleet, 3rd assistant purser Starbase 247.

Routing Modification

Stage 2

From:	Starbase 247
To:	Aeolia Penta
Carrier Designation:	Aeolia Mercantile
Carrier UAC:	UFP_.0059.Ae01.^~6572.30009445
Transport:	Wings of the Morning
Registry:	Aeolia Prime D@77.800032313.44
Estimated Departure:	48606.2 Actual: 48606.3
Estimated Arrival:	48609.5 Actual: 48609.4

Stage 3

From:	Aeolia Penta
To:	Starbase 201
Carrier Designation:	Zippy Freight
Carrier UAC	UFP_.1223.BZ498.0001.29968731
Transport:	Zippy One
Registry:	Orion IV FIF27031.4445592pzx
Estimated Departure:	48610.0 Actual: 48610.6
Estimated Arrival:	48611.2 Actual:

Stage 4 *(Smith Freightways as per above)*

Routing Modification Notes

Image record of another Tzenkethi, this one with mottled brown fur and wearing a practical arrangement of leather straps holding tools and other small devices. The background shows a dilapidated bridge, with half the consoles dark and at least one of the others sparking intermittently. The crewtzen with his feet up on the adjoining console, filing his claws, does not seem terribly concerned. The captain speaks in a lower-caste dialect, quickly and in as few words as possible, and his slitted yellow eyes dart about as though reluctant to look directly into the camera.

"Warp drive broke down outside of T!chkin'kha Nebula. Took

two and a half cycles to fix him. Scratched our meet with Vilossia Twilight. *Caught a bird ship instead—shifting cargo now."*

The scene abruptly changes to a spacious, immaculate chamber, featuring a tall, pale green feathered biped in the foreground. She has large amber eyes topped by extravagant plumed "eyebrows," and she speaks from a small, opalescent beak in a liquid warble, gesturing expansively with both pairs of pinion-fringed arms.

"Apologies, esteemed gentlebeings, but an unexpected delay in the arrival of the most worthy Tzenkethi transport, caused by a completely unexpected warp drive failure, has necessitated a routing change. We are most honored to convey this cargo to the humble yet proudly efficient space station of Aeolia Penta, which has the privilege of orbiting our homeworld, at a purely nominal rate consistent with the prorated value of the original fee. There we will be met by the excellently trustworthy Captain Li Yuan Fitzsimmons of Zippy One, *who will convey your most precious stembolts to Starbase 201 with only the slightest of scheduling adjustments relative to the original plan, pursuant to receipt of the remainder of the aforementioned fee, plus the extremely minor additional charge of 247 Aeolian plumules, or 36 strips of gold-pressed latinum."*

Again the scene changes, this time back to Flem in his office in Tzenketh Okl!a. *"Thirty-six strips! That's piracy, that's what it is! Pure and simple!"*

The Ferengi fumes for a while longer, then settles down. *"Ah, well, I daresay I can pass it along to Quark. Hold on while I conference him in."*

Again the image splits, but there is no Quark to be seen, only a row of alien faces in the middle distance, across a counter littered with drinks and small bowls of miscellaneous snack foods. After a moment, a big-eared, big-nosed head enters the picture sideways.

"Hello. Rom here. My brother Quark is, um, a little busy right now. Can I help you with something?"

Flem explains the situation. Rom dithers, but eventually agrees to the additional fee.

The view switches back to the Aeolian captain.

"Your generosity is most appreciated, gentlebeings. Please do not experience any concern regarding extraneous inspections or further delays associated with this rerouting. Since we will be transferring this container outside the environs of the Aeolia Penta station itelf, such will not be required. Wings of the Morning, *signing off."*

SPECIAL CUSTOMS NOTICE: DUE TO HEIGHTENED SMUGGLING ACTIVITY IN RECENT DIURNS, ALL TRANSPORTS ENTERING OR LEAVING AEOLIA SYSTEM, REGARDLESS OF ULTIMATE DESTINATION OR TRANSSHIPMENT POINT, *WILL* BE INSPECTED FOR THE PRESENCE OF DAYTONITE (SEE ATTACHED SUPPLEMENTAL FILE FOR DETAILS). NOTE: CARGO SAMPLES MAY BE REQUISITIONED FOR ANALYSIS.

SUPPLEMENTAL FILE:

Image record of a somber-looking elderly male Vulcan, wearing the robes of a high-ranking scientist.

"Official analysis of the Vulcan Science Academy, Academician Sibek recording, Stardate 44021.3, regarding the effects of the mineral compound fallassium literarinate, commonly known as daytonite, on the sentient species inhabiting Aeolia Prime.

"Initial effects include euphoria and a heightened sense of self-importance, resulting in a marked reluctance to perform normal work-related functions. With repeated exposure the subject may lapse into a form of lethargy or torpor, and coma or death has been known to ensue.

"In light of these effects, it is strongly recommended that this material be strictly controlled in Aeolian space. The euphoric effects will, in such an emotionally undisciplined species, undoubtedly entice any lower cultural elements to engage in smuggling and sublegal exchange, and the resulting potential damage to the general populace cannot be overstated."

CERTIFICATE OF INSPECTION

As of Stardate 48610.4, this cargo container is found to be free of daytonite or other contraband. One unit (stembolt) was requisitioned for laboratory analysis.

Verified by Special Guardian Nirrep V'tetsoh, Aeolia Prime Purity Squadron 17.

NOTICE OF INTENT TO JETTISON

Item Description:	One Giffla-37XZ multipurpose interstellar-rated container containing 20,735 self-sealing stembolts.
Jettison Date:	48610.7
Last Retrieval Date:	48620.7
If Salvaged Contact:	Consignee
Reason for Jettison:	

Image record, obviously made from the container's own camera, of a young human male in what might once have been a corporate uniform, leaning over and practically spitting into the vocal pickup. He keeps darting glances back over his shoulder, where half a dozen more crew members are heaving containers out the door of a capacious cargo hold.

"Cap'n Fitz says we have to jettison all the cargo that ain't 'critical,' whatever that means. There's, uh, unidentified raiders on our tail . . ."

Behind him, one of the cargo handlers calls out, *"Hey, did Cap say how the Purity Squad got onto us?"*

The reply is unintelligible at standard humanoid hearing levels.

The human making the recording continues: *" . . . and we have to lose mass to outrun 'em. He says we should be able to lose them and circle back in a day or two."*

A streak of sparks rips across the background, and the young man concludes the report with several terse statements that the bill of lading's rudimentary but thorough cultural relevance filters automatically mute.

*　　*　　*

Rom paused on his way to the back room, balancing three trays full of dishes. It was late in the off-shift on Deep Space 9, and all the employees had gone home. Rom himself was long past ready to crawl onto the pallet in his meager quarters and snatch a few hours of sleep before he had to be back here to open the bar. Quark never seemed to mind—he was always up early and up late, working long hours and making side deals on the run. Rom had to admit that he admired his brother, difficult as he could be to work for.

A howl of outrage arose from the communicator console behind the bar. Rom flinched, but Quark was glaring at the screen, not at him.

"Salvage reclamation form? I'll tell you what you can do with your salvage reclamation form—just bring me my blasted stem-bolts!"

Barclay Program Nine

Russ Crossley

What in the name of eternal destitution is this?

The raven haired hu-man female stood before him with her arms thrown wide, her dusky curls trailing about her milk-white shoulders like a cascade of fine black silk, and her dark uncomprehending eyes gazing into the distant forest surrounding the glade. The artificial breeze that blew across them caused her flowing ground-length robe to billow about her as if she floated on a thunderhead. The only thing she'd said since appearing was, "I am the Goddess of Empathy."

Hu-man females were so ugly when their males allowed them to wear clothes, though with those small lobes they were certainly ugly with or without clothes. And this one gave off a pungent odor that was sickly sweet and reeked of flora. Disgusting.

Balt grimaced. Ever since he'd bought that Federation scrap, he'd not found one thing of use . . . He stopped in mid-thought and regarded the hu-man female warily, his sunken, jet black eyes narrowed. Maybe this was something he could sell to someone or at least offer shares in the potential profits, but to whom? He dismissed the thought with a wave of his hand. An old holoprogram, what use would that be to anyone? Still . . .

Being a galactic trader was a tough business these days. The Dominion War had been an unwelcome disruption to normal trade. How was a hardworking, greedy Ferengi supposed to make his fortune when he didn't have access to his customers? Thank the Gods of the Great Treasure Room the war was finally over. Whoever wrote the 34th Rule of Acquisition, "War is good for business," hadn't been in a war with the Gamma Quadrant. The mindless Jem'Hadar soldiers didn't need to buy weapons, and the Federation wasn't about to buy the used weapons he could offer. For a while he thought he was going to starve. Even though the war was over his usual customers were having difficulty making ends meet, never mind buying his wares. His ship still required desperately needed maintenance to its warp drive, and he hadn't managed to acquire enough funds to pay the Bajoran techs to repair his vessel yet. Maybe he could sell this holoprogram and realize some profit just to get back on his feet. If only there were some suck . . . er . . . customer interested.

Balt shook his head. "Computer off," he said, his voice a low grumble. The image of the hu-man female disappeared, then the pastoral setting faded until he stood alone on the hologrid, the yellow grid lines staring back at him. Hu-mans were such a sentimental lot, he almost felt sorry for them. Almost.

As he approached the exit doors there was a gentle sigh of air pressure as they slid aside to allow him access to the corridor outside. The doors closed behind him, and he went to the control panel for the holosuite. He removed the isolinear chip from the panel, then secreted it inside a hidden compartment inside his waist-length tunic. No sense in taking chances that Quark might see the chip and want to copy the information. He was a cunning adversary and a good Ferengi who knew how to make a profit. Quark's life *was* the 7th Rule of Acquisition, "Keep your ears open." That's probably why he was such a good bartender. After all, bartenders were supposed to be good listeners.

The click and warble of the dabo tables coming from Quark's bar at the bottom of the steel corkscrew-shaped staircase echoed in the silence. *Maybe I should offer him a partnership and sell him the holoprogram? Maybe he might pay enough latinum for his percentage of the profits to get me off the station.*

Balt's thoughts were interrupted by a hu-man male exiting the next holosuite. The man held a plastisteel helmet under one arm and wore a skintight two-toned navy blue–and–yellow body suit. He was smiling as he walked into the corridor. Balt eyed the man with suspicion.

"Oh, hello . . . I'm Doctor Julian Bashir," said the hu-man as he approached, offering his hand in that disgusting way that hu-mans do when they greet each other. Balt wanted no part of this or any other hu-man touching *him.* He frowned, he hoped sufficiently to discourage further conversation, then spun on his heels and headed for the staircase. The salty odors being emitted by this doctor, an unprofitable occupation at the best of times, made his stomach squirm like an Argelian tree snake. He hurried to the bar downstairs, where he was certain the air would be safer to breathe.

He heard the doctor's cry of surprise as he walked away but ignored it and hurried down the stairs. Once inside the noisy bar he marched up to the nearest stool at the bar and set himself on it, his arms resting on its polished surface. A large gray-skinned being with holes where his ears should have been sat two stools down; he eyed Balt for a moment, then went back to fixating on his beverage container. The large gray lump made no attempt to engage him, which the Ferengi trader thought was just fine.

Quark had his back to him as he sat down. The bartender was busy pulling bottles containing a myriad of colorful liquids from the shelves behind the bar, carefully pouring small amounts from each into an ornately gilded and steaming glass. Quark's multicolored tunic was a bit pretentious for Balt's tastes, reminding him of the 47th Rule of Acquisition, "Don't trust a man wearing a better suit than your own." Quark turned to him, cupping a churning glass with both hands in front of him as it boiled and bubbled vigorously, sending up billowing clouds of steam that disappeared near the ceiling. The bartender's dark eyes were filled with the delight reserved for someone who'd just won a lifetime supply of gold-pressed latinum. Balt snorted in disdain. "What have you got to be so happy about?" he asked irately.

Quark ignored him as he carried the glass and placed it in front a tall, thin biped sitting at the end of the bar. The being's face was thin and his skin bore a purplish hue. The biped's ears were small and pointed, so Balt thought the being must be incapable of profitability. Every Ferengi knows the larger the ears, the larger the lobes and the greater the profitability. The Grand Nagus, for example. Now there were some lobes.

"Hello, Balt," said Quark, who stood over him after delivering the drink to his customer. The Ferengi bartender's sunken dark eyes stared at him intently. "Enjoy your time in the holosuite?"

Balt nodded.

"Something special, I hope?" Quark leered at him.

"Yes—special, of course. I'll have a *jepla* berry juice."

"Coming right up," said Quark with an easy grin and a knowing twinkle in his eyes. He turned away and went to a small fridge set into the wall beneath the glass shelves behind the bar. He extracted a glass bottle of mauve liquid with one hand, and in a practiced move pulled a tall, thin glass from the counter where rows of glasses in various sizes and shapes were lined, then poured a measured amount of the juice into the glass he'd selected. He slipped the bottle back into the refrigerator, closed it with his right foot and delivered the glass to Balt. It all happened so quickly that Balt was startled when the full glass appeared in front of him.

"On your account, I presume?"

Balt nodded. "Huh . . . yes, of course." Balt's eyes narrowed as he studied the tangy, bitter juice sitting in the glass, the mauve clouds of pulp boiling and curling as if in a storm. The smell was intoxicating. "I thought you replicated the drinks," he said.

Quark smirked. "I always keep a few special items on hand, but . . ." Quark waved one hand. "Never mind, that's not important. What's more important is why you're on Deep Space Nine."

Balt glanced to either side to ensure no one was looking or listening. The gray lump was staring straight ahead and the purple thing was sipping carefully at its steaming drink, its sky-blue eyes focused on the bottom of the glass.

Balt leaned forward to hunch over the bar and spoke softly. "I have a proposition you might be interested in."

Quark rested on one elbow and leaned toward him. "Why didn't you say so?" The bartender grinned at him.

"Well . . . I . . ."

Quark stood erect and chuckled while shaking his head. "I'm joking, Balt. Really, you mustn't take me so seriously." He again leaned forward and the grin disappeared from his face. "The constable isn't around anymore, so we might be able to do some business . . ."

Balt opened his mouth to speak but abruptly clamped it shut as he saw a worried frown appear on Quark's features, his eyes suddenly looking over Balt's head at someone standing behind him. He heard a female voice inquire, "What're you up to, Quark?"

The bartender smiled, his jagged teeth showing, but his eyes contained more apprehension than joy at the new arrival. "Why, nothing, Colonel, I'm just visiting with an old friend." There was a dismissive snort from behind him.

Balt turned to see a Bajoran female wearing a dark red jumpsuit and an earring that dangled off her right ear, slip into the seat next to him. She appeared about as happy to see Balt as he was to see her. The Bajorans also allowed their females to wear clothes. Disgusting.

"And who are you?" she asked, her intense brown eyes fixed on his. He felt an odd twinge of apprehension as he studied her. No Ferengi female would dare speak to him in this manner, but for some reason he almost enjoyed her aggressive attitude. Almost.

Quark picked up a white towel and began polishing a glass as he studied their interaction. "You better cooperate with her, Balt. She's the station commander."

He felt shock and inner revulsion that this *female* was in charge of this facility. Bajorans were a strange race indeed, even stranger than the hu-mans. Female or not, "It never hurts to suck up to the boss," another Rule that could be applied to this situation came to mind.

He bowed his head slightly to the colonel. "My apologies, Colonel, if I seemed rude. I had no idea you were the commander of the station . . ."

"No problem. Balt, is it?" Balt nodded. "My name is Kira Nerys. I'm the commander of Deep Space Nine and the watchdog over Quark's activities to make sure he stays on the up and up." She eyed Balt with suspicion, her eyes narrowed and slightly crinkled at the corners.

"I can assure you, Colonel—" began Quark, appearing as innocent as a *legarn* bird on Ferenginar.

"All right, for now, but I'm going to keep both eyes on you two," said Kira, interrupting Quark as she stood and quickly disappeared out the front door of the bar.

Quark put down the glass he'd been wiping, then rested his hands flat on the bar. He shook his head and complained," That woman's been impossible ever since Odo left, and she's definitely no Odo."

"Who's Odo?" said Balt.

"Never mind," Quark said with a trace of wistfulness in his voice.

"You wait here. I've got to check something in the back storeroom. Then we can go eat and talk some business."

"Eat?" said Balt.

Quark smiled. "Really, Balt. Have your forgotten the Rules of Acquisition?"

Balt nodded. Quark was right of course. *"Never begin a business negotiation on an empty stomach,"* he recalled. Rule number two hundred fourteen.

Quark hurried off to a door at a corner of the bar. Next to the door, an access security panel was fixed to the wall. Balt watched Quark press a series of buttons on the panel, then the door slid aside. It closed behind him after he'd disappeared inside.

Balt turned his attention back to his drink and took a sip of the cold, tart fruit juice. It tasted surprisingly fresh. He hadn't tasted this kind of quality since leaving Ferenginar all those years ago. The mixture of memories and flavor made him immediately home-sick.

He glanced over at the gray lump of flesh sitting down the bar from him, who by now had turned his massive head to stare at him. Didn't that thing have a neck? It was as if he wore a permanent neck brace. "Can I help you?" he said.

The "thing" shook its head and went back to facing forward.

"That's Morn. A regular customer, so speak nicely to him," said Quark, who suddenly re-appeared over him, startling him. Balt caught himself before he spilled his juice. "Ready to eat?"

Balt nodded.

"C'mon. I know a little place on the Promenade that serves the best replicated spore pie this side of home."

After they'd eaten they sat in the deserted, dimly lit restaurant. It was a Bajoran grill, and since at this hour most Bajorans were in the chapel worshiping the Prophets of the Celestial Temple, it was the perfect place for a Ferengi negotiation.

"What have you got?" said Quark casually as Balt lifted the last of the purple spore pie to his lips. Quark was right: the flavor of the pie exploded in the mouth, tasting as if his beloved Moogie had made it herself.

He put down his fork, reached inside his tunic, and retrieved the isolinear chip hidden there, which he then placed flat on the table. Quark gazed at the blue optical chip, composed of linear memory crystal, and shrugged his narrow shoulders. "So, what's this?"

"A Federation holoprogram," Balt answered, his features split in a wide smile, attempting to sound as if he'd found a back door to the Great Treasury Room. He swiftly dropped the smile to appear nonchalant. He must have done it quickly enough, because Quark didn't seem to notice. *Good,* he thought, *I don't want to scare off a prospective partner.*

"Of what?" said Quark, his voice edged with skepticism.

It suddenly occurred to Balt that he'd forgotten to prepare a pitch line. He'd been so distracted by that meddling Bajoran colonel that he hadn't had the time to prepare properly. "It's a recreational program created by a Starfleet officer," he blurted.

"Who? Someone important, I hope," said Quark, his eyes mildly suspicious.

"A captain named Barclay."

Quark stroked his chin with his fingers and regarded Balt as if he were a mere rodent. "Never heard of him. What's on the program?"

"Oh, a wonderful assortment of things: duels, damsels in distress, and a goddess. Something for every hu-man taste. Perhaps you could offer the program in your holosuites. I've seen a lot of hu-mans while I've been on the station. Surely many of them will enjoy such a diversion."

Quark shook his head. "It doesn't sound like much to me."

Balt felt a twinge of nervousness. He needed this deal if he was ever going to get out of here and back to the Ferengi trade routes. He feared sounding too desperate.

The 57th Rule of Acquisition taught us that "Good customers are as rare as latinum. Treasure them." After all, any true Ferengi knew that. Trying to appeal to Quark's vanity, he replied.

"Now, Quark, you and I go way back. We've had many profitable business dealings over the many years we've known each other. Surely—"

Quark held up one hand to interrupt him and sighed. "You're right, of course, Balt. I must be getting soft, or I've spent too many years among the Bajorans and the hu-mans." The bartender nodded, his eyes focused on the table. "What would my percentage be?"

Balt felt a shiver run down his body as an unwelcome voice drenched in sarcasm interrupted them. "Quark and Balt. My, my. I thought I'd find you two holed up somewhere, plotting some scheme or other." It was Kira Nerys again. She was becoming quite the pest. Balt palmed the isolinear chip in his right hand and dropped his hand below the table. He hoped she hadn't noticed. Since she stood over his left shoulder behind him, there was a good chance she hadn't seen the chip on the table's glossy surface.

She sat down across from him, her intense gaze locked on him. "So tell me, Balt, what have you two pixies been up to?"

Balt didn't know what a pixie was, but her words confirmed his suspicion that she was a xenophobe. A pixie was obviously some kind of slur. He felt his ears grow warm but managed to keep his voice calm. "This is a business negotiation, Colonel, one which I can assure you is perfectly legal."

Her eyes narrowed as she rested her thin arms on the table. Her earring gleamed in the low light of the restaurant. "It better be, Balt, or I'll find out and the two of you will never see the stars again, much less sunlight." She rose and disappeared as quickly as she'd appeared. Was this female everywhere? How could Quark conduct a profitable business in a place like this?

Quark sighed as if he'd started to breathe again. "She makes me nervous," he said.

Balt nodded. "I can understand why." He brought his hand up to the surface of the table, then placed the chip once again between them. "Let's get this deal done," he said, his eyes serious.

Three days later Balt was gone, his ship repaired and headed to Ferengi space with what he thought was a duplicate of the isolinear chip tucked in the hidden compartment of his tunic. Balt's original sat on Colonel Kira's desk in her office, awaiting transport to Earth and its eventual return to its rightful owner, Lieutenant Reginald Barclay.

Quark stood behind the bar, preparing another of the steaming drinks for his customer, when Colonel Kira walked up to the bar and sat on one of the stools, a large grin pasted to her face.

"We did it, Quark."

The Ferengi bartender smirked at her as he delivered the tall, steaming glass to the blue-skinned gentlebeing seated two stools down from Morn, whose focus, as always, was on the mirrored shelves attached to the wall across from him.

"Yes, Colonel, *we* did. I hope that Starfleet engineer is going to be happy. I'm not so sure I am."

Kira's smile faded to a small mischievous grin. "Oh c'mon, Quark, you know you did the right thing. Your friend Balt is certainly going to have a surprise when he sees what's on that copy you switched with him. I'm not so sure he'll appreciate a holosim of an ancient Bajoran wedding ritual. Those things go on for days." She stood, chuckled to herself, then exited the bar. Quark winced as he watched her go.

He glanced at Morn, whose emotionless eyes gazed back at him as his dusky features broke into a wide jagged-toothed grin once Kira was out of view. He knew Balt was very pleased about the females without their clothing in the Betazoid program he'd traded him. He'd lost a good deal of short-term profit on this venture. The latinum he'd paid to obtain the Betazoid wedding program had been considerable, but in the longer term Kira would go a little easier on him now that he'd helped her to retrieve the lieutenant's holoprogram. He might even be able to sell Barclay Program Nine, but somehow he doubted it. He couldn't chance offering it in the holosuites on DS9 because Kira might get wind of it. Of course, she didn't know, nor did she need to, that he had copied everyone's holoprogram when they used the holosuites so he'd probably find something else of use down the road. Those activities of Bashir's were getting tiresome, though. What was the Tour de France anyway?

Perhaps now he'd even become profitable again. Business would be good; after all, there was the higher calling of the 18th Rule of Acquisition: "A Ferengi without profit is no Ferengi at all."

He gazed at his best customer. "You know, Morn, that deal cost me a few bars of latinum, but it was worth it. There should be a new Rule of Acquisition, 'Keep your friends close, but your enemies closer.' " He sighed and moved away to greet a customer taking a seat at the other end of the bar. As he moved away, he muttered, "Some days I really miss Odo. . . ."

Morn rolled his eyes and went back to staring at the mirrored shelves, as he always did.

Redux

Susan S. McCrackin

If only she had turned a second sooner. If only she hadn't ignored that voice calling to her. If only it hadn't been Seven of Nine who had called. Called out to her in that *I-am-Borg-I-am-perfect-you-must-comply* voice. If it had been anyone else, she would have responded immediately. If it had been . . .

But it hadn't been, and she hadn't turned in time and now her life was leaking away from her. With each heartbeat, she felt it leave. The lights around her were blinking red; the alarms were blaring; Janeway was calling her, demanding a response, calling for Vorik, asking for the status of the warp drive, begging for power, begging for warp. She could feel the ship shudder. *Voyager* was dying. Just like her.

Eyes open, she watched the light dim. She felt herself leaving her body, leaving the pain that radiated out from the hole in the middle of her body, the pain pushing the blood out of her, the floor of engineering turning bright red around her.

If only it hadn't been Seven of Nine who had called.

*   *   *

There was light. Bright light. This was not her mother's *Sto-Vo-Kor.* Maybe this was her father's Heaven. There were sounds. Familiar sounds. Comforting sounds. A tricorder. She forced her eyes open, barely able to make out the shape of a hand waving back and forth above her body. She was in the sickbay. The Doctor was caring for her. She had not died after all.

"You should not move, Lieutenant."

She groaned. It was not the Doctor. It was *her.* She tried to sit up, but felt a hand on her shoulder. She tried to rise against it, but could not. Then she heard *that voice* again.

"You were badly damaged. You must lie still so that I can repair you."

"Where's—" She ended in a racking cough that sent pain scurrying through every part of her body. Now she knew she was alive.

"The Doctor is off-line."

B'Elanna Torres squinted into the light, watching as the head of Seven of Nine moved in front of it, blocking the glare. She could see Seven more clearly now, could see the smudges on her face, the strands of hair hanging askew. B'Elanna tried to sit up again, but felt a wave of dizziness overcome her, felt the nausea tear at her gut. She sensed strong hands grab her and slowly lower her back to the biobed; then a hypospray pressed against her neck. She heard the soft swish as medicine was injected into her and felt the immediate relief from the pain, the dizziness, the nausea. B'Elanna gratefully left the bright light behind her.

She was rising slowly toward the surface. The water was warm, and she was reluctant to leave it. She was floating effortlessly, painlessly. She wanted to stay, but something kept pushing at her, kept pushing her up. Finally, she broke the surface and breathed deeply.

"Hello, Lieutenant."

Damn. It was *that voice* again. Where was the Doctor? He should be here caring for her. Not Seven of Nine. Not that insufferable, perfect Borg.

B'Elanna opened her eyes gradually, seeing the figure in front of her. "Hello, Seven." She carefully pushed herself up, surprised when she felt hands helping her.

"You should move slowly, Lieutenant."

"Yeah. Thanks. I'll remember that." She shrugged slightly, freeing herself from the grip. Holding onto the biobed with one hand and raising the other to her head, she looked around the sickbay. "Where's the Doctor?"

"He is off-line."

B'Elanna sighed. "Oh. Right. I remember. You told me that before." She took a couple of deep breaths, then lowered her hand from her head to her stomach, gingerly feeling for her wound.

"I have repaired you."

"Huh?" She glanced in Seven's direction.

"I have repaired you."

"Oh." She continued to feel, noting only soreness where her wound had been. She twisted her body, flexing carefully. "Well, I guess you did a pretty good job. Thanks." She moved to slide off the biobed, but stopped when she felt Seven of Nine position herself directly in front of her.

"It would be advisable for you to remain on the biobed."

B'Elanna leaned back, giving herself some distance from the ex-drone. "I think I can get up. I'm feeling . . ." She looked up into Seven's face, and her words died on her lips. She stared.

Seven's expression changed, going to blank before she turned away from Torres and moved to the center console. "You should continue to rest."

B'Elanna watched Seven's back, then moved her head slowly, taking in the scene around her. She slid off the biobed, giving herself a moment to make certain her legs would support her. She moved to stand in front of Seven of Nine. She opened her mouth to ask her a question, then closed it. She stood waiting for Seven to look at her. It only took a moment.

The head slowly came up. The eyes, guarded, settled on her face. Torres took in everything at once. Seven of Nine, who was usually so perfectly groomed, not a hair out of place, suit always clean, everything neat, was standing in front of her in complete disarray. Her hair was hanging down, her face was smudged, her suit was dirty and torn. There were bags under her eyes; her fingernails were chipped. Blood had dried on her face from a scratch on the side.

B'Elanna backed up and looked around the sickbay again. Wires were hanging from the ceiling. The acrid smell of burnt wiring hung in the air. Consoles along the side were dark and obviously off-line. One biobed was on its side while another was damaged.

"What in the world?" B'Elanna spoke in a whisper. She looked back at Seven. "What happened?"

"We were attacked."

B'Elanna touched her stomach, rubbing at the tender spot. Slowly she nodded her head, looking past Seven. "I . . . I remember. The alien. The alien who shot me." She blinked, trying to get her mind to focus. "There were more."

"Yes. There were many more."

Suddenly, B'Elanna felt her stomach go cold. She jerked her eyes up to Seven's face. "Tom?" She watched as something fleeting passed over Seven's face before it went blank again. B'Elanna moved closer. "Seven, where is everyone? What happened?" Reaching, she grabbed Seven's arm, her voice breaking as she spoke, "Tell me what happened!"

"You should sit down, Lieutenant."

She tightened her grip on Seven's arm and moved even closer. "No. Tell me what happened! Where's Tom?"

Seven of Nine spoke impassively. "Lieutenant Paris is dead."

B'Elanna felt the blood drain from her head. She closed her eyes, barely aware that hands were once again gripping her, helping her to the biobed. She felt a hypospray pressed against her neck but managed to raise her hand in time to push it away.

"No." She shook herself. "No. No more of that stuff." She pushed herself back onto the biobed. Taking a couple of deep breaths, she asked, "Tom . . . is dead?"

"Yes."

B'Elanna looked around the sickbay again, the coldness in her stomach starting to spread. She forced herself to look up at Seven. "The . . . crew?"

"The crew is dead."

"Everyone?"

"Yes."

"Except for you?"

It was an accusatory tone, and she could tell that Seven heard it. Regardless, Seven's response was flat. "Yes."

"And me."

Seven's expression flickered for a moment then went blank again, but Torres saw it. "What?" When there was nothing, B'Elanna demanded, "Tell me!"

"You should rest, Lieutenant. You have received a serious shock. You are alive." Torres watched as Seven looked around the sickbay. "And we have work that needs to be done as soon as you have recovered."

Seven started to pull away, but Torres reached to jerk her arm. "No, Seven. Something is going on here, and you have to tell me. I need to know what happened."

Seven hesitated, then sighed. "What do you remember?"

Torres shook her head. Turning away slightly, she started to pace. "Remember? I . . . don't know. I was working at . . . the main engineering console. Vorik and I were trying to stabilize the warp core. The warp core field was destabilizing, and we were thirty seconds away from having to eject the core. I . . ." She looked at the floor, her head starting to ache. "I moved to the warp core console. I was trying to override the program, to shut down the core. Then . . ." She stopped, trying to remember, forcing herself to concentrate. Suddenly, her head jerked up. "I heard you call me—"

"You heard me?"

Torres looked into Seven's face, surprised at the emotion she had heard in Seven's voice. She saw the eyes widen, their intensity almost frightening. "Yes, I heard you. I—"

"When did you hear me?" Seven stepped closer to her.

B'Elanna reached up and massaged her forehead, trying to rub back the pain. "I think . . . No, I heard you just before I was shot."

"Before." It was a whisper. Seven stepped back. B'Elanna watched as she turned pale, her body wavering slightly.

"Seven?" Torres reached out, grabbing her.

"Are you certain?" Seven's look was now desperate, her voice strained. "Did you hear me before you were shot?"

B'Elanna nodded. "Yes. I heard you call me, just before I was shot. I heard you twice." She snorted slightly. "If I had turned the first time I heard you, I might have seen the alien before it had time to shoot me. Why?"

"Yes." Seven reached out, putting her hand on the biobed to steady herself. "You would have."

"What?" When Seven looked past her, B'Elanna demanded, "Tell me what you are talking about!"

Seven turned back to look at her. The words came slowly. "Lieutenant, you were the first person killed in the attack."

B'Elanna stopped cold, listening.

"The aliens materialized in engineering. You were shot first and died of your wound."

B'Elanna stared at her in disbelief, almost unable to comprehend the words that followed.

"The aliens took over engineering, stole the warp core, and destroyed the main power grid, leaving *Voyager* defenseless. Within a matter of hours, the crew was killed." Seven turned slightly and took a deep breath before continuing. "Captain Janeway, Commander Chakotay, and Lieutenant Paris were killed in a battle on the bridge. Commander Tuvok and Ensign Kim were killed trying to take back the bridge. Once the senior crew was killed, the rest of the crew fell quickly. I was in a Jefferies tube when the attack started. I tried to gain access to engineering, but could not. I backtracked to sickbay. The Doctor and I . . ." For the first time her voice broke. She took a moment, then continued. "The Doctor and

I tried to fight the aliens. The Doctor's program was decompiled. I was undamaged."

"You were undamaged," B'Elanna whispered, echoing Seven's words. "What happened next?"

"The aliens left."

"They left?" When there was no response, she said, "They left, and you were undamaged?" Again, there was nothing. Torres felt her anger spike. She reached out, jerking Seven around to face her. "Everyone's dead, and you're undamaged?"

"Yes."

"And how is it that everyone's dead, and they just go and leave you alive?" She stopped. "Wait. You said I was the first to die. But I'm alive." She pushed Seven's arm away and scrambled away, putting the biobed between the two of them. Eyes searching for a weapon, she demanded, "Who are you?"

Seven's expression was calm, almost bored. "I am Seven of Nine. And you are Lieutenant B'Elanna Torres. And yes, you were killed."

"That makes no sense! If I was killed, how can I be alive now?"

She watched as Seven straightened, putting her hands behind her back. "We are caught in a temporal loop."

"A temporal loop?"

"Yes. When you were shot, you fell into the warp core field and were caught in the temporal backsurge caused by the alien's weapon. A temporal anomaly occurred. Your body reappeared in engineering approximately seventy-two hours after the aliens left."

"I reappeared?"

"Yes. I was able to recover your body and revive you."

B'Elanna stood, uncertain. This was too much. She hunted for something to say. "I guess I should be glad you found me in time."

The shoulders shrugged. "I did not the first two times."

"The first two times?"

"Yes.

"Two times?"

"Yes." Seven sighed. "This is the fifth time you have reappeared."

B'Elanna Torres looked blankly at the woman standing in front of her. She opened and closed her mouth a number of times, words and thought failing her. Finally, she said, "I need to sit down."

"Five times?" There was only the slightest of nods in return. "So I di— I've come back five times."

"Yes." Seven turned from her slightly. "Five times *Voyager* has been attacked and you and the rest of the crew killed, and five times you have reappeared in engineering."

B'Elanna closed her eyes, the pounding in her head intensifying. This had to be a dream. Soon, she would wake up from this nightmare. This was not real. She opened her eyes, allowing them to wander around the sickbay. She raised her hand to rub at her forehead, then lowered it to rest against her stomach. Did one feel pain in a dream? She pressed at the place where her wound had been, wincing as she did. No. This was real. It had to be real.

Tom. Janeway. Chakotay. Tuvok. Harry. Dead. The Doctor decompiled. This was not possible. How could everyone be dead? Except for Seven of Nine. How could everyone be dead except for the ex-drone? She looked back at Seven, feeling her anger spark again.

"And how is it that you weren't killed?" She slid off the biobed and moved to the only working console, suddenly feeling the need to put distance between herself and Seven. "Huh, Seven? How do you explain that? Tell me!"

Seven did not look at her. She turned her head slightly, and B'Elanna was surprised to see emotions playing across her face. As she watched, Seven took a deep breath and spoke.

"Approximately thirty-five seconds before that attack, *Voyager* was hit by temporal disruptors. The disruptors temporarily altered *Voyager*'s position in the time continuum, causing it to go slightly out of temporal phase and allowing the aliens to transport through our shields."

When her voice trailed off, B'Elanna said, "But that doesn't explain you, Seven."

The corner of Seven's mouth tightened, then she continued. "I am . . . not certain. I have, however, developed a theory."

A theory. Of course Seven of Nine has developed a theory. She forced herself to concentrate. *Hold on, B'Elanna. You can deal with this.*

"Okay. Let's hear your theory."

"I believe . . ."

She said "believe." Seven of Nine said "believe." No, concentrate, Torres. Concentrate.

". . . that my implants make me impervious to the aliens' weapons."

B'Elanna pulled in her chin. "Impervious?"

"Yes."

Damn. She wished her head would quit hurting. "You believe you are impervious." She turned away from the ex-drone. "I don't understand."

"The temporal disruptors did not throw *Voyager* completely out of its time continuum. It is only slightly out of phase. The aliens had to use temporal sensors to identify members of the crew." Seven paused, almost seeming to gather her thoughts. "I continue to exist on *Voyager,* but am out of phase with the aliens' sensors. Therefore, to them, I do not exist."

B'Elanna's mind was working furiously, trying to comprehend Seven's words. It was plausible. She laughed to herself. When it came to the time continuum, anything was plausible. "And you think that's why you weren't killed?"

"That is correct."

B'Elanna laughed ironically. "While I've been killed five times."

"Yes. You and the rest of the crew."

She shook her head. "How have you figured all of this out? If we're caught in a temporal loop, wouldn't you simply relive the experience and not realize you were . . . reliving the experience?" *Kahless, this is confusing.* Before Seven could respond, B'Elanna answered her own question. "Oh, right. Your implants." She put her hand down on the console, feeling the need to touch something solid, to give herself something to hold on to, to ground herself. Looking at Seven of Nine, she saw how empty her eyes were, how weary she looked. Suddenly, she felt the coldness start to gnaw at her stomach again. Her eyes moved around the sickbay, noting for the first time the dimness of the lighting and the coolness caused by the low-level environmental setting. The fear building inside her, she looked at Seven and struggled to ask her question. "Seven, how . . . long since the attack . . . the first attack?"

The words came back flat and emotionless. "One year, six months, twenty-one days."

B'Elanna stared at her open-mouthed. Finally, she said, "I need to sit down again."

B'Elanna was flat on her back on the biobed, her knees up in the air, her hands covering her eyes, thumbs pressing tightly against her temples. Her head was killing her.

"It is the temporal loop."

She lifted her palm to peer out at Seven. Not for the first time in the last two hours, she noticed that Seven was standing close to her. "Excuse me?"

"You are suffering from sensory aphasia due to the temporal loop. It is most likely causing your headache." When she gave Seven a puzzled look, the ex-drone continued. "Each time you loop . . . die and return, your molecules grow more out of phase. That is what is causing your headache."

B'Elanna stared at her, silent for a moment. Then she asked, "Exactly how is it that you've figured this out?"

Seven turned and moved to the console, reached for something, then returned to stand beside the biobed. "After the second loop, I realized I was reliving the attack. I started recording everything that happened during the loops and downloading the data into my cortical implants. As soon as the loop is completed, I transfer the information into *Voyager*'s system for a complete analysis. Then, before the loop can repeat, I download them into my systems again."

"That makes sense." B'Elanna rested her head back on the biobed. "I guess." She stayed quiet, trying to process everything. "How do you know when the loop is about to end?"

"You will grow fuzzy and disappear."

"Then the loop starts again?"

"Eventually."

"What?"

"The loop does not start immediately. There is a lapse."

"How long?"

"It varies."

"Seven," B'Elanna sat up, watching as Seven's face started to take on that blank expression, "how long since it happened the last time?"

Seven's eyes cut away from her and her mouth worked. For a second, B'Elanna thought she was going to break down and cry. When Seven finally spoke, her voice was barely above a whisper. "Six months."

"Six months?"

Seven nodded.

For the first time, B'Elanna realized what she was seeing in Seven's face. Isolation. Fear. Loneliness. Seven had been on this ship alone for six months. Six months to live with knowing that seeing people again would only mean she would watch them die, then be alone again. Swinging her legs over the side of the biobed, B'Elanna shook her head. "But you said this was the fifth time I've reappeared."

Seven nodded, understanding what the lieutenant was asking. "The time between the loops is lasting longer each time. The second loop occurred only days after the first. The third was a couple of weeks later. Now, they are months apart."

Dropping her head into her hands, B'Elanna pressed her thumbs into her eye sockets. Then she looked up at Seven. "Can't you just leave?"

"No. The ship is trapped in this place in time. Besides"—Seven picked a padd off a nearby tray and activated it—"I am working to find a way to break the loop."

B'Elanna grabbed at the padd Seven offered. "How?"

"Each time, I am able to affect small changes immediately before the attack. The last time, you heard me warn you."

B'Elanna raised her head, remembering. "Yes, I did."

"That was the first time in three efforts to warn you that you heard me."

B'Elanna studied the padd. "How did you do that?"

"I have been adjusting the frequency of my implants, trying to adapt to that of the temporal loop."

B'Elanna frowned slightly. "But if you do, won't that make you vulnerable to their weapons?"

"Yes, but I believe that if I can disrupt the sequence of events, it might be possible to change what happened."

"But," B'Elanna was trying to follow her words and study the screen in front of her, "you could be killed just like the rest of the crew . . . us . . . me."

"Whether I live or die is irrelevant."

B'Elanna's head jerked up, and she saw the look in Seven's eyes before they became blank and distant again. She sucked in her cheeks. "Okay." She deactivated the padd, took a deep breath, and rubbed at her forehead. "Do you have a plan?"

There was light. Bright light. This was not her mother's *Sto-Vo-Kor.* Maybe this was her father's Heaven. There were sounds. Familiar sounds. Comforting sounds. A tricorder. She forced her eyes open, barely able to make out the shape of a hand waving back and forth above her body. She was in the sickbay. The Doctor was caring for her. She had not died after all.

"You should not move, Lieutenant."

She groaned. It was not the Doctor. It was *her.* She tried to sit up, but felt a hand on her shoulder. She tried to rise against it, but could not. Then she heard *that voice* again.

"You were badly injured. You must lie still so I can repair you."

"Where's—" She ended in a racking cough that sent pain scurrying through every part of her body. Now she knew she was alive.

Wait. This is familiar.

Jerking her eyes toward the ex-drone, B'Elanna immediately grabbed her head with both hands. Groaning, she said, "It didn't work."

Seven's eyes widened at her words, but her reply was terse, her voice controlled. "No. Hold still. I have to repair you."

B'Elanna tried to lie still to give Seven time to tend to her. The pain in her head was excruciating.

"You are repaired. Be careful sitting up."

B'Elanna accepted Seven's assistance as she struggled to pull herself into a sitting position. Focusing all of her attention on Seven, she shook her head. "The eighth time?"

"Yes."

"How long this time?"

"A year."

"Ohhh." B'Elanna groaned again, sinking back down on the biobed. She felt Seven move closer to the biobed.

"You remember."

"What?" She blinked a couple of times. Then whispered, "Yes." Her eyes widened, and she sat up quickly. "Yes! I remember. That's different. How can I remember?"

Seven was scanning her, adjusting the tricorder, then scanning again. "Your body seems to be adjusting to the temporal loop."

"Is that good news?"

Seven's mouth tightened, and she sighed. "It is possible it means we are running out of opportunities." She turned to scan the ship, frowning as she did. "It seems the frequency of the ship is also changing."

"What does that mean?"

"I am not certain. It could mean you will remember more and more of the attack each time."

"Or?"

"Or it could mean you will simply . . . phase out of this time continuum."

They stayed silent, neither quite knowing what to say. Finally, B'Elanna asked, "And you?"

Seven scanned herself. "I am not changing."

She hesitated. "And that means?"

Seven shook her head. "I . . . am not certain."

B'Elanna looked at her, seeing that the eyes looked even emptier than the last time. "How much time, now, total?"

"Three years, nine months, fifteen days."

"Ugh." B'Elanna grunted. She covered her eyes with her hand, rubbing at her forehead, fighting the fierce headache. She watched as Seven of Nine moved toward the center console, injecting it with her assimilation tubules to download information. B'Elanna studied her, noting the stooped shoulders, the haggard look. Even though Seven was not technically aging in this loop, she looked older, worn. B'Elanna wondered what it would be like to live this time over and over and yet remember each moment. To see friends die eight times over and to know you would watch them die eight more, then eight more, and so on. For time not to move and yet to be able to track its movement through a continuum in which one did not technically exist.

She gritted her teeth. This was only making her headache worse. She tried to think of something else. What could she remember?

She had been in engineering. She had heard the call. She had fought against responding, but this time, only for a second. She had turned. She had seen the alien. She had moved; then she had been hit.

"Seven!" She slid off the biobed, noting how empty eyes turned in her direction. "I moved first this time!"

The eyes widened. B'Elanna watched as Seven disconnected with the console, then quickly activated it, watching the screen. "Yes. There is a change in the continuum." The eyes turned toward her, brighter this time. "That must be why you remembered." They turned back to the console. "Can you remember anything else?"

B'Elanna closed her eyes, struggling to recall. After a long moment, she caught her breath. "You!"

"Explain."

"I saw you there!"

Seven of Nine stared at her. Then her eyes cut away. "The adjustments."

B'Elanna stepped forward. "Adjustments? What adjustments?"

"The adjustments we made before the loop started the last time. I had been making adjustments to enable me to be in engineering. As a result, each time, I was able to get closer to the alien. The last time, you assisted me in making the adjustments. You suggested I attempt to adjust my implants to a modulating frequency that would adapt to that of the temporal disruptors. You believed that doing so would allow me to insert myself in engineering at a critical moment of the attack."

"I don't remember that." B'Elanna frowned, her hands kneading her temples.

The eyes started to glint with anticipation. "We must have been close if you were able to see me. What else do you remember?"

"I remember . . . you moving. I remember seeing you . . . in front of me!" She ended yelling the words. "Seven, you had gotten between me and the alien. When it shot me . . ." She stopped, then finished in a whisper. "The shot came through you, Seven."

B'Elanna watched Seven's head nod, the face a mask of defeat.

"The shot came through your body and hit me. I fell backwards, into the field surrounding the warp core." Her hand went to her stomach. "I was bleeding. I . . . died." Her voice choked off. She felt tears starting to rise to the surface. She remembered the pain. She remembered the fear of dying. She remembered her hand burning from the contact with the field. She remembered. . . .

She stopped. Closing her eyes, she concentrated. *Damn this headache.* Something was there. Something. What was it?

Her breath caught in her throat. She remembered. The alien had not been shooting at her. It had been shooting at the warp core console. The alien had actually been closer to Vorik and had purposely shot away from him. In her mind, she saw the angle the shot had taken.

It was as though the alien had not known she was there.

Turning back to face Seven, she said, "Seven, you said your implants made you invisible to the alien's sensors."

"Yes."

B'Elanna spoke her next words slowly. "When the Doctor removed my implants after my assimilation, he couldn't remove all of them. I still have Borg implants."

Seven's eyes opened wide. Quickly, she worked at the console, her jaw tightening as she concentrated. Finally, she looked up, and B'Elanna saw her nod. "I . . . think . . . you are correct. You were not shot with the same weapon as the others."

"They were trying to destroy the warp core console, not kill me."

She watched Seven's face as she studied her data. "I believe you are correct." Seven keyed in more commands, and B'Elanna watched the eyes move back and forth as they read the screen. "It is possible that your implants masked your presence so that the alien's sensors could not identify you. However, you obviously do not have enough implants to protect you from being damaged."

"I deflected their beam and then the temporal phase of the ship when I fell into the warp core field." When Seven nodded, B'Elanna continued. "When that happened, the aliens were probably trapped on *Voyager.*"

"That is a plausible theory."

"They had to fight their way off the ship, killing the crew in the process." B'Elanna started pacing back and forth, kicking debris out of her way. "So, do you think all we have to do is figure out how to get me out of the way of that shot?"

She turned back to see Seven give a weary shrug. "Possibly."

Possibly. Did Seven of Nine really just say "possibly"?

"So, this time, I simply fall instead of turning?"

B'Elanna watched the indecision in Seven's face, watched her lips tighten as she considered what had been said. She saw the answer form in her eyes before the words were spoken.

"It would be a prudent action."

B'Elanna Torres was yelling orders in engineering. The warp core field was destabilizing, and she was doing everything she could think of to shut the warp core down. If she could not shut it down soon, she would have to eject the core.

Remember. You must remember.

The thought flicked through her mind, and she pushed it back. Remember? Remember what? She didn't have time to remember right now. She had to get the core to shut down or remembering anything would not be an issue anymore.

Remodulate the shields.

Why would remodulating the shields do anything to correct this problem? The thought buzzed in her mind. She reached out, putting her hand on Vorik's shoulder, pushing him away. "You need to remodulate the shields."

He gave her the strange look she deserved. "I do not understand, Lieutenant."

She gripped his uniform, pulling him back, growling her response, "Never mind. Continue."

Get Vorik out of the way.

"Vorik!"

"Yes, Lieutenant."

She gave him a stunned look.

Get Vorik out of the way.

Recovering, she said, "Try the secondary console. See if you can reroute power to the program."

"Yes, Lieutenant." He quickly moved away.

Why did she just do that? She shook her head. She couldn't afford to worry about it now. Concentrate. Concentrate. They had less than a minute.

Remodulate the shields.

Damn it. Why did she keep thinking that? No. Think through the shut-down program. Why wasn't it working? What was destabilizing the warp core field? Think, Torres. Think. You can do this. One step at a time. Thirty-five seconds.

She moved to the center warp core console.

No. Do not move here.

What was wrong with her?

"Lieutenant!"

That voice! It was that damn Borg!

"Drop, Lieutenant!"

"Drop! Fall!"

She didn't have time to listen to that know-it-all perfect Borg. She . . .

Suddenly, she turned. As soon as she did, she saw the alien. She was supposed to do something. What was she supposed to do? She stood, now desperately working to remember what it was she was supposed to do. It was important. Lives depended on it.

Before she could act, she saw a weapon swing up and point in her direction. She saw the alien's face, saw the decisiveness of action in its eyes, saw it fire the weapon. She started to move. Then she felt something slam into her stomach, felt the air forced from her body. She felt herself falling. As she slammed into the deck, she felt something warm, wet, and sticky around her.

If only she had turned a second sooner. If only she hadn't ignored that voice calling to her. If only it hadn't been Seven of Nine who had called. Called out to her in that *I-am-Borg-I-am-perfect-you-must-comply* voice. If it had been anyone else, she would have responded immediately. If it had been. . . .

The lights around her were blinking red; the alarms were blaring; Janeway was calling her, demanding a response, calling for Vorik, asking for the status of the warp drive, begging for power, begging for warp. She could feel the ship shudder.

If only it hadn't been Seven of Nine who had called.

She was rising slowly toward the surface. The water was warm, and she was reluctant to leave it. She was floating effortlessly, painlessly. She wanted to stay, but something kept pushing at her, kept pushing her up. Finally, she broke the surface and breathed deeply.

She started choking. She couldn't breathe. She fought her way up, arms flailing.

"Whoa, B'Elanna." She felt hands pulling at her arms, arms wrapping themselves around her. "Take it easy. It's okay. It's only a dream."

She stopped fighting and turned to see her husband's face. "Tom!" Her voice cracked as she spoke his name. Putting her hand to his face, she said, "You're alive!"

"Yes." He was whispering to her, pulling her head to his. "You were only having that dream again." He kissed her softly on the cheek. "I'm okay; you're okay. Nobody died."

"Nobody died?"

"Nobody died. We're okay. You're in your bed, the warp core is running at peak efficiency, and those weird aliens are far behind us." He hugged her tightly to him.

She pressed herself against him, trying to stop her trembling. She looked up, seeing the line of his jaw as the muscles in his face tightened. She could see how concerned he was for her. She allowed herself to rest in her husband's arms, her mind whirling. It had seemed so real. She was so certain they had all died. That she had died. But that she had kept coming back. That she had died and had come back eight times. That each time Seven of Nine had . . .

Seven of Nine.

She jerked away from Tom. "Seven?"

He gave her a sad look. "B'Elanna, you know the Doctor is doing everything he can."

Oh, no.

She remembered now. She pressed her hand to her stomach, feeling the soreness that still existed, even a week later. A week. It had been a week. She pulled out of her husband's embrace, sliding toward the edge of the bed.

"B'Elanna, no. You need to sleep. There isn't anything you can do."

She ignored him, grabbing for her robe.

"B'Elanna, please."

"I'll be back later, Tom." She turned, quickly leaving their quarters. She wrapped the sash of her robe around her, pulling it taut as she entered the turbolift. "Level five." Waiting impatiently, she adjusted the sash again, suddenly nervous. She was already in midstride as the doors opened, quickening her pace as she walked down the corridor toward the opening doors. As soon as she entered, she saw the smile on his face.

"Ah, Lieutenant Torres." The Doctor turned aside. "I have a surprise for you."

She saw past him, saw the figure lying still on the biobed, eyes weak but open. Eyes looking back at her.

"I was just about to call you." The Doctor crossed to stand beside the biobed, obviously pleased with himself. "As you can see, our patient has regained consciousness."

He kept talking, but she did not hear him. It took her a few moments to be able to move toward the biobed. She noted the eyes stayed on her as she made her way across the sickbay.

She managed to find her voice, having to work to keep it calm. "It's good to see you awake."

The eyes blinked, but there was no answer.

"She's still very weak. Don't expect her to be able to talk much." The Doctor moved around the biobed to stand opposite her. "Seven?" B'Elanna watched as Seven's eyes moved slowly toward the Doctor's face. "You have Lieutenant Torres to thank for your recovery." The eyes moved toward her as the Doctor continued to talk. "She's the one who suggested adjusting my program to match the frequency of your body so I could care for you. It took a bit of doing, but between us, we managed to pull you through. You should be fine, Seven." He patted her arm and smiled at B'Elanna. Seeing the expression on her face, he backed up. "Why don't I give the two of you a few minutes alone?" He started to leave, then said, "Lieutenant, please don't tire her out."

B'Elanna nodded. Once she knew the Doctor was out of earshot, she leaned forward and spoke softly, "It really happened?"

Seven dipped her head in confirmation. B'Elanna watched as Seven ran her tongue over her dry lips. "You saved my life."

B'Elanna snorted. "Only after you saved me." B'Elanna looked away, her eyes becoming moist. "I couldn't remember everything. I kept getting flashes of things I was supposed to do, the messages you had downloaded into my implants, but I couldn't connect them in time." She raised her hand to rub her forehead, aware that she still had a lingering headache. "I blew it, Seven. If it hadn't been for you, if you hadn't knocked me out of the way of that weapon. . . ." She stopped, wiping the tears from her cheeks as she remembered.

She had started to turn. She had not remembered to drop out of the way. She had straightened, putting herself between the alien and the warp core console. Their plan had been for her to drop, to let the aliens take the warp core if necessary, anything to make certain that the crew survived and the loop was broken. But she had not been able to remember.

From nowhere, Seven had come at her. She remembered seeing her out of the corner of her eye, her mind immediately wondering what the Ice Queen was doing in engineering, had turned, not realizing that Seven was hurtling toward her at full speed. Arms out, Seven had collided with her, Seven's head hitting her squarely in the stomach, knocking the air out of her. They had crashed to the deck, but not before Seven had taken the shot that B'Elanna had taken eight times before. Once again, B'Elanna found herself lying in a pool of blood, but this time, it was Seven whose life was spilling out on *Voyager*'s deck.

But they had not fallen into the warp drive field. Seven, who had finally adjusted her implants to match the frequency of the temporal disruptor, had taken the full shot meant for the warp core console. It was Seven whose momentum had sent them both away from the warp core. Seven's sudden appearance had rattled the aliens. Vorik, who was now away from the warp core console, at the secondary console, had fired at the aliens. A brief phaser fight had ensued, and as quickly as the aliens had come, they had left.

Vorik had rerouted the power and stabilized the warp core, allowing *Voyager* to leave the area at maximum warp. While he worked, B'Elanna had transported with Seven to the sickbay.

She looked at Seven, seeing her through a haze of tears. Suddenly, she was exhausted. Well, she should be, she decided. She had just lived and died eight times and relived almost four years in about a week. It took her a second to realize Seven was talking to her. "I'm sorry, Seven. What did you say?"

The voice cracked, weak and airless. "Have you told anyone?"

B'Elanna shook her head slowly. "No, not really. Everyone thinks it's just a nightmare I keep having."

It took a second for Seven to respond. "It was a nightmare."

B'Elanna started, her eyes cutting away. She nodded. "Yeah."

Seven licked her lips again. "The aliens?"

"Gone. No real trace of them. And," B'Elanna grinned at her, "they didn't get the warp core." When Seven's eyes widened, B'Elanna continued, "You took the shot. It wasn't a disrupted shot like mine had been. You absorbed it completely." B'Elanna's eyes wandered down toward the middle of Seven's body. "It was bad, Seven. You were bleeding, and you were phasing in and out. I thought we were going to lose you." She gave a sharp laugh. "I couldn't decide if you were going to bleed to death or disappear on us first. But," she reached out and hesitantly, awkwardly patted Seven on the arm, "we managed."

Seven glanced down at B'Elanna's hand on her arm. "I am glad."

B'Elanna shrugged. "So am I." She watched as Seven's eyelids drooped. "You need to rest. I don't want the Doctor yelling at me for wearing you out." Seven nodded, but B'Elanna saw it in her eyes. She recognized the look. It was the same empty, lonely look she had seen before. She glanced away, aware of the days, months, and years that Seven had spent alone on this ship, in this sickbay, living the same time over and over, living inside and outside of that time, living the nightmare again and again.

B'Elanna was still looking away from Seven. "Uh, if you don't mind, I'd like to . . . stay here." She patted Seven's arm again and looked back at her. "I won't bother you. I'll just . . . sit here."

She watched as Seven blinked, a hint of relief appearing behind the almost expressionless look now in her eyes, her tongue running slowly over her lips again. Finally, the words came. "It . . . would be acceptable."

"Good. Thanks. I appreciate it." She reached out, pulled up a chair, and sat down. "Rest. I'll be here when you wake up."

She saw Seven's eyes close, watched the muscles in her face relax, listened as her breathing gained a long, slow rhythm. B'Elanna looked around at the sickbay, pristine and ordered. So unlike what she remembered, so unlike the sickbay in her dreams.

Her eyes moved to the chronometer, and she watched as the seconds ticked away, suddenly grateful. Time was moving forward; it would not be yesterday again.

She remembered. The warp core. That voice. That voice yelling at her. She remembered the pain in her stomach, the fall, the warm, wet stickiness around her. She remembered dying. She remembered. . . .

If only it hadn't been Seven of Nine who had called. If it had been . . . .

She looked at the figure now sleeping on the biobed and laughed ironically.

Adjusting her position in the chair, she pulled her robe around her, rested her head against the biobed, and slept a dreamless sleep.

The Little Captain

Catherine E. Pike

Naomi Wildman squinted as she stepped from the cave's opening. They'd been exploring the grotto for three hours, and her eyes had grown used to darkness broken only by their wrist lamps. The sky, though dark and cloudy, seemed bright compared to the inky blackness of the tunnels they'd left behind.

Beside her, Seven of Nine cast a critical glance skyward. "There appears to be a storm coming in." Glancing down at Naomi, she added, "We had best go."

"Do we have to?" Naomi asked, admiring the view of the valley floor, filled with wildflowers and lavender-colored grass. "It's not every day we get to explore a planet no one's ever seen before! Wouldn't it be fun to camp here overnight?"

"I doubt camping would be 'fun' at all. Haven't you noticed those clouds? We'll be fortunate to reach our shuttle before it rains." Seven, ever practical, retorted.

"We could stay in the cave . . . build a fire . . . eat those berries we found." Naomi used her most winning tones.

Seven shouldered the rope they'd used inside the cave. *"You're* the one that spotted the animal droppings along that passageway. Would you care to share our fire with an animal large enough to leave those behind?"

"You have a point." Naomi said. "But can I come back with you and Lieutenant Torres tomorrow?"

Seven began descending the slope leading from the cave to the valley floor. "Why? Now that we've located the dilithium, we need only mine it and transport it aboard *Voyager.*"

Naomi shrugged, but Seven was keeping a watchful eye on the rocky path and didn't spot the gesture. "Shouldn't I know how to mine and transport dilithium safely?"

"Only if you wish to be chief engineer. I thought you wanted to be a starship captain."

"I do, but won't I have to learn all I can about the jobs in between?"

The logic was too true to ignore, and the Borg nodded. "Very well. If your mother grants permission, you may return with us tomorrow." Taking another glance at the sky as a smattering of rain struck the ground, she added, "For now I suggest we hurry. I don't want to get wet."

Her wish would not be granted. By the time they'd taken a dozen steps the rain had become a downpour and the day so dark they were forced to turn on their wrist lamps to light the way ahead. Naomi slid her hand into Seven's, and they walked quickly across the uneven ground.

They'd covered a quarter of the distance to their shuttlecraft when Naomi noticed a change in the clouds on the horizon. She stopped suddenly, pulling on their joined hands to stop Seven as well.

A funnel of dirt that looked like a giant inverted V dropped from the clouds. Narrow at the bottom, wider on top, it whirled and roared in rage as it stretched toward the ground.

"Look!" Naomi pointed toward the sky. "What is that?"

Impatiently Seven followed Naomi's point. Her impatience quickly changed to concern, and Seven took a step backward. "I've heard about such phenomena. Storm-produced funnel clouds that create winds over one hundred sixty kilometers per hour and destroy almost everything in their path. We have to find shelter before that funnel touches the ground."

"If we run we can reach the shuttle," Naomi suggested.

"No, it is too far away. We have to return to the cave." Seven turned to retrace their steps, guiding Naomi ahead of her. "Run, Naomi, as fast as you can. Don't look back!"

Sensing the urgency in Seven's command, Naomi obeyed without a word. Together they raced back over the ground, grown slippery now from the rain. As they reached the base of the hill and started climbing, Naomi stumbled and fell, tumbling down to the bottom of the slope she'd just ascended. Struggling to her feet, she risked a glance behind her.

The funnel cloud had touched down and was racing toward them! Mud and rock became airborne, sucked up into the wind's wake, creating a cloud of debris that added to the funnel's width. As Naomi watched, captivated despite the danger, the funnel changed course, following a random path only it knew the rhyme or reason to. It was still bearing down on them, but now it appeared the heart of the tornado would miss them. Not by much, but hopefully enough to save their lives.

Unless it changed course again.

"Naomi!" Seven's call snapped the girl out of her fascinated stare.

"It's on the ground!" Naomi had to shout to be heard.

"I know. We'll never make it to the cave! Come on!"

Half carrying, half guiding Naomi back up the hill, Seven headed for a tree ten meters away. It's thick trunk, though stunted, clung stubbornly to the hillside. It had obviously survived there many years, through all sorts of weather. Hopefully it would make it through one more storm.

"Hold on to the trunk of the tree!" Seven ordered. As Naomi wrapped both hands around the trunk, Seven unshouldered the rope and tied it first around the girl's waist, then around the tree. "This will keep you safe!"

"What about you?" There was not enough rope to secure them both.

"I will be right behind you." Seven reached around Naomi to grasp the tree, sheltering the girl from the worst of the oncoming wind with her own body. "Don't let go, no matter what happens!"

The temperature plummeted. The rain gave way to hail. Naomi closed her eyes and buried her face against her arm, seeking protection. Together, they waited.

It was the sound Naomi became aware of first: a roaring louder than a warp core on the brink of explosion, a thunder more deafening than the silence had been deep inside the cave.

Then the wind itself slammed against them, so hard Seven was thrown against Naomi, pinning her against the unyielding tree. It took every ounce of strength, every sliding inch of purchase Seven could achieve by digging her heels into the quagmire of mud on which they stood, but she managed to push back into the force of the wind. Not far—only a half inch or so—but enough to allow Naomi room to breathe.

There was no shielding either of them from the debris the storm had picked up on its way across the valley floor. The smallest clumps of mud, the tiniest stone, were transformed into shrapnel that pelted them with more ferocity than the worst of the hail. A stone gouged Naomi's cheek. Every muscle ached with the strain of fighting the whirlwind.

It might have been a minute. It might have been an hour. As suddenly as it had started, the wind died away, taking the hail with it but leaving the cold, steady rain. Shivering, Naomi opened her eyes. Everywhere she looked was destruction. It was a wonder the tree to which she was still tied had withstood the maelstrom. Her ribs ached from when Seven had been thrown against her, and her cheek stung where the stone had hit it, but otherwise she seemed uninjured.

Wait a minute! Why was she so cold? The rain pelting so hard against her back?

"Seven?"

Naomi looked behind her. Seven was gone! She'd been taken by the storm!

"Seven!" Naomi fought with the knots on the rope with numb fingers. It seemed to take hours to free herself, but as soon as she had she stumbled down the slope, searching frantically for Seven of Nine.

It was the halogen lamp that finally alerted Naomi to Seven's whereabouts. Somehow it had remained on—and strapped to Seven's wrist. Now it shone feebly in the darkness, almost fifty meters away.

"Seven!" Naomi cried as she reached her friend. The Borg lay in a heap on the ground, right leg at an awkward angle, bent back on itself at the knee. A gash on Seven's forehead streamed blood, and one cheek was swelling. She was paler than Naomi had ever seen her. Her eyes opened at the girl's cry, looking momentarily confused. She tried to raise her head. Gasping, one hand went to the gash on her temple. She lowered her head again gingerly and surveyed her young friend.

"Naomi. Are you all right?"

"Yes." Naomi dropped to her knees in the mud. "Your leg! Is it broken?"

"Yes. I think I have also suffered a head injury." Spotting the frightened tears shining in the girl's eyes, Seven hardened her voice accordingly. "You must be brave, Naomi!"

"But you're hurt! And I don't know what to do! Please don't die!"

"I do not intend to die." Seven said. "And fear will not achieve our rescue." She tapped her combadge. "Seven of Nine to *Voyager!*"

There was no response to her hail.

"My com link must not be strong enough to penetrate the storm!"

"The shuttle's com link might work!" Naomi suggested. "It has a stronger signal."

"The shuttle is too far away. I could not reach it." Answered Seven.

"*I* could! I bet I could get there and back in no time!"

"No. It's best if we are not separated. *Voyager* will dispatch a search party when we fail to report in."

"But that could take hours! You need help now! At least let me try!" Naomi pleaded. "If I go back to the shuttle I can get blankets and water! If I can reach *Voyager,* they'll know you're hurt and can send the Doctor down to help you! Please, Seven! Let me try."

The Borg considered, then, finally, nodded. "Very well."

"You rest. I'll be back before you know it!" Naomi rose and disappeared into the darkness.

By the time she reached the shuttle, Naomi was shivering with exhaustion and caked with mud. It had taken her almost an hour to cross the distance they'd traversed in ten minutes that morning. The muddy ground sucked at her feet, forcing her to use all her strength to pull each foot free and take another step forward. The shuttle seemed to have survived the windstorm intact, although the front windshield had splintered into a spider web of cracks and the door had come off its hinges. It felt wonderful to be out of the rain! It was warm inside the cabin. She hadn't realized how thirsty she was until she caught sight of the emergency rations in a cupboard. Grasping a canteen, she drank her full, feeling the water refresh her. How easy it would be for Naomi to curl up on the floor and doze, just for a short while, until she stopped shivering and the aches in her legs from fighting the mud eased.

Suddenly she remembered what Captain Janeway had told her when Seven had been kidnapped by the Borg. That a captain had to remember three things: always keep your shirt tucked in, always go down with the ship . . . and never abandon a member of your crew. She could not leave Seven out there alone. No matter how tired she was, she had to help her friend. Muscles screaming in protest, Naomi approached the pilot control panel.

Activating the computer was no problem. Seven had shown her how the last time she'd gone on an away mission. If only its sensitive circuitry hadn't been damaged in the storm!

"Voyager, this is Shuttlecraft One. Mayday!"

Only static hissed from the speakers. Naomi waited a moment, then tried again.

"Voyager, come in, please! This is Shuttlecraft One!"

There! Was that Captain Janeway's voice calling Naomi's name? There was too much static to tell for sure.

"Captain?"

There was no answer at all now. Nothing but the rain pelting the sides of the shuttle. Desperately, Naomi tried one more time. *"Voyager!* If you can hear me, our shuttle is damaged and Seven of Nine's hurt! I'm okay, but Seven needs help!"* It was the best she could do.

Naomi pushed herself out of her chair. She began to gather blankets and water. Her gaze fell on the row of phasers in the gun locker. A weapon might come in handy. Wouldn't it? Why was it so hard to decide? She shook herself resolutely.

"If you want to be a starship captain some day, start thinking like one!" she admonished herself. A fellow crewman was injured and it was up to her to help!

She moved about the cabin, rapidly deciding what else she could carry that would help them.

She'd drawn close to where she'd left her friend. The lamp on her wrist could pick out the rocks and Seven of Nine's form . . . and something else in the shadows at the edge of Naomi's circle of light.

Something that moved. Something slow, stealthy, either very short or purposely low to the ground.

With a start Naomi realized this must be the animal that had left the droppings in the cave. It was much bigger than she had imagined. It appeared to be a cross between a wolf and a boar, standing perhaps three feet at the shoulder, every ounce hardened muscle. Its eyes gleamed redly in the light from her lamp, and two tusks framed a snout from which fangs protruded, dripping saliva. Its black fur was matted, except for a curving scar along one shoulder. Even this far away she could hear it growling, and she stood, transfixed by the sight.

It took a step forward, inching along low to the ground toward Seven in a hunter's stealthy crouch. Seven grabbed a rock and threw it at the animal, striking him a stunning blow. With a howl of outrage, it charged.

"No!" Naomi screamed, running forward before realizing she'd even moved, rucksack of supplies banging against her hip. "Leave her alone!"

The animal paid her no mind. Naomi reached for the phaser at her waist, aimed, and pulled the trigger with a trembling hand. The energy beam went wild, but it succeeded in turning the animal's attention toward her. Terrified, Naomi fired again. Her shot missed, but only because the animal had turned in her direction.

"Naomi! Look out!" Seven called, but the beast was already charging toward her.

Naomi started to back up. Her feet slid in the mud and she fell hard onto the ground. A startled scream escaped her. In the light of her wrist lamp, the beast leapt. Hot spittle flew from his mouth and splattered against her cheek. She scrabbled backward, clawing at the mud with her hands, the rucksack slicing a path in the ground. The beast landed short, just so, snapping at her foot, and fangs sliced a tear in her boot. She kicked at it as hard as she could, her foot connecting with its snout, and blood joined the spittle flying everywhere. She didn't dare pause for breath, but kept scrambling backward.

More angered than hurt, the beast leapt after her. There was no way it would miss her this time.

From the darkness came Seven's voice.

"Naomi! Shoot! Shoot again *now!*"

She'd forgotten she still held the phaser. She obeyed the command instantly, pointing the phaser in the beast's direction. There was no time to aim. She squeezed the trigger and closed her eyes at the same time. The beast fell heavily at her feet, its last foul-smelling breath washing over her. She'd killed it!

"Naomi!" Seven called frantically, searchingly. Naomi realized Seven could not see her in the darkness.

"I'm here!" Naomi ran to Seven's side. "Did it bite you?"

"No. You arrived just in time."

Naomi glanced from the dead animal into the darkness. "Do you think there's any more out there?"

"Unknown. But if we keep the phaser ready, we'll be all right."

"You take it!" Naomi extended the weapon in a shaking hand.

Seven grasped both the weapon and the hand that held it. "What made you think to bring it along?"

"I thought we could use it to light a fire. If we could find any fuel, that is." Naomi answered.

"You did well."

Trembling, the girl could only nod.

"Did you reach *Voyager?*"

"I don't know. I transmitted a mayday, and thought I heard the captain answer, but there was so much static I couldn't tell for sure."

"You tried, that's the important thing. We'll just have to wait for the search party."

"Maybe this will help them find us." Naomi said, pulling a cylindrical object from the sack.

"A locating beacon!"

"You showed it to me the first time you let me go on an away mission with you. Remember?"

"That was eight months ago! How did you remember that?"

"I try and remember everything you teach me." Naomi shrugged. "You said it was used to help rescue parties locate downed shuttles when the shuttle's own built-in locator was damaged." Naomi recited. "Couldn't it lead a rescue party to us here?"

"Yes, it can." Seven nodded. "Good thinking, Naomi!"

The girl visibly swelled at the praise. "How do I set it up?"

Seven indicated a spot on the ground a few steps away. "Stand it up over there and turn its base counterclockwise."

Naomi did as instructed. Once activated, the beacon produced an intermittent pulse of blue light.

"That light indicates the subsonic pulsar is working." Seven explained. "They'll be able to follow it with both their tricorders and shipboard computers."

"What do we do now?"

"Wait." Seven grimaced. "Did you bring any water?"

"Yes. Here."

Naomi held the canteen to Seven's lips. The Borg drank, coughed, then drank again, finishing the canteen.

"I brought blankets, too, but I could only carry three of them. You can use one for a pillow." Naomi folded it and placed it behind Seven's head. "I'll put the other two on top of you."

"We will share them." Seven answered. "We'll both stay warmer that way."

Naomi draped the blankets over Seven. Careful not to touch the Borg's broken leg, she curled up beside the injured woman, settling her head against Seven's shoulder.

"Seven?" She inquired drowsily. "Do you get scared?"

"Why? Are you frightened now?"

"No. But I was when I saw that animal attacking you. And after that windstorm, when I realized you'd been pulled away from me." Naomi paused. "And I started thinking that if I get scared over stuff like that then maybe I shouldn't be a starship captain after all."

"Don't you think Captain Janeway gets scared?" countered Seven.

"If she does, she never shows it."

"That doesn't mean she doesn't get frightened. She wouldn't be a good captain if she didn't. The trick is in not letting your crew—and especially your enemies—know when you're scared."

"But she's the bravest person I know! Besides you, that is."

"I've been scared, too, Naomi." Seven answered. "When the Borg assimilated me. I was also frightened when I was left behind on *Voyager.*"

"Why?" Naomi was surprised.

"I didn't know what would happen to me. I thought Captain Janeway would kill me. I was her enemy. Had our positions been reversed, I would have destroyed her without a second thought. Of course, I didn't know the captain then. I wasn't aware of her tenacity for seeing the good in people."

"Do you remember your parents?" Naomi asked after a while.

"Not well. The Borg suppressed such memories, finding them damaging to the collective mindset. I do remember my mother singing lullabies as she tucked me into bed and my father reading to me. Then he'd kiss me, say, 'Good night, Annika, sweet dreams' . . ."

"Annika. That was your name?"

"Yes."

"I like it." Naomi decided.

"Thank you. Perhaps I will use it again someday."

"Aren't you mad at your father for taking you to the Delta Quadrant to study the Borg?"

"Mad?"

"If you hadn't gone you wouldn't've been assimilated. Your parents would still be here. You'd still be Annika—not Seven of Nine, Tertiary Adjunct of Unimatrix Zero One."

"And I would never have known *Voyager.* I would not have made the first friendships of my life. People like Neelix and the captain." Seven glanced at the girl beside her. "And you."

"My mother says everything happens for a reason."

"I think your mother is right. My father took us to the Delta Quadrant in pursuit of a dream. He'd study the Borg—unlock their mystery—and for three years he did just that. The research he left behind is invaluable to Starfleet. I sometimes wish we'd never gone . . . but my life would have been poorer if I had not met all of you."

"I wonder what my father is like." Naomi whispered. "I look at his picture on Mom's dresser and try to imagine how his voice sounds. Do you think he'll be there to meet us when we get back to Earth?"

"I'm sure he will."

"Do you think he'll like me? He's never met me, you know. Mom had me on *Voyager*. I heard her tell Neelix once that he'd wished for a boy." Naomi paused, then added softly, "I hope he won't be disappointed in me."

"He will love you, Naomi. I am sure of it."

Suddenly the girl reached an arm across Seven's waist to hug her.

"You'll visit us when we get back to Earth, won't you?" Naomi asked, sounding close to tears.

"Of course I will!" Seven answered.

"I almost wish we wouldn't get there at all!"

"Explain."

"*Voyager*'s the only home I've had. What will I do on Earth?"

"You'll go to school. Make new friends. Attend Starfleet Academy, if you wish."

"It won't be the same as having you around!"

"If you want to be a starship captain, you'll need an advisor for Starfleet's Command School. I'm sure Captain Janeway would be honored to be asked. Neelix will want to give you a hot meal now and then, to make sure you're eating right."

"But what about you?"

"Do you honestly think I would not want to know how you're doing? Now rest, Naomi. The rain is lessening. The storm must be over. That means they'll come looking for us soon."

"I love you, Seven." The girl yawned, settling deeper into the meager warmth of the blankets.

"I love you, too, Naomi."

Someone was shaking her awake. Naomi smelled lavender soap—her mother's lavender soap. Surely it wasn't time to get up for school yet!

"Come on, sleepyhead! Wake up! We've come to take you home!" Her mother's voice, sounding as if she'd been crying.

What did she mean, they were going home? Why was Naomi so cold, her clothes so wet? Why was her bed so hard?

Yawning, Naomi woke. This wasn't *Voyager!* Where was she? She glanced around, saw only darkness beyond the light cast by several halogen lamps. She remembered where she was—and what had happened—a moment later.

"Mom!" She gasped, looking up into Samantha's worried face.

Samantha gathered her into a hug. "Are you all right?"

"I'm fine—" Naomi was interrupted by the sound of Seven crying out sharply.

In her sleep, the girl had rolled onto her side, away from Seven of Nine, taking the blankets with her. Naomi kicked at the soaked cloth that entangled her legs and squirmed out of her mother's arms.

"Seven!"

She heard her friend cry out again and someone murmuring to her.

"Naomi, it's all right!" It was Captain Janeway. Turning around, the captain squatted in the mire beside the girl.

"Seven's going to be fine, Naomi!" She said. "In order to get her ready for transport back to *Voyager,* the Doctor had to splint her broken leg. That hurt, as you might imagine."

"But she'll be all right?" Demanded Naomi.

The captain's gaze never wavered, never moved from Naomi's own. "She'll be fine. I give you my word." The captain paused. "That was a brave thing you did, walking all that way back to your shuttle to use the com link."

"You heard me?"

"Yes. I tried to answer, but there was too much interference. Did you bring that locating beacon back with you?"

"I thought it would help you find us quicker."

"Good thing. Seven might not have survived much longer." The captain glanced at the fallen beast beyond them. "Looks like you had some unwanted company, too."

Would Naomi get in trouble for killing it? Was that a violation of the Prime Directive? If she would—if it was—so be it. "I had to, Captain! It was attacking Seven of Nine! It would have killed her if I hadn't shot."

"Sounds to me like you did exactly what you had to do," the captain replied. "You did what I would have done. Without a second thought."

"Captain?" The Doctor called. "I'm ready to move Seven. I'm going to need your help over here."

"Be right there." The captain turned back to Naomi. "Go with your mother to our shuttle, Naomi. There are dry clothes and warm blankets for you there."

"No! I want to stay with Seven!"

"We'll be right behind you. Go on, now." When Naomi started to protest further, the captain lifted a warning hand. "That's an order, crewman."

Naomi sighed. "Yes, ma'am."

The short walk to the shuttle seemed to take forever. Naomi barely had the strength to put one foot in front of the other, despite her mother's support. She stood in the back of the shuttle, shivering, as Samantha quickly substituted dry clothes for her wet ones and wrapped a blanket around her shoulders. She didn't protest when Samantha sat down in one of the seats and pulled Naomi onto her lap. She thought for a moment that sitting on your mother's lap was not something a future starship captain should do, then dismissed the thought with a sigh as Samantha pulled Naomi's head onto her shoulder. Eyes closed, she listened to the captain and the Doctor securing Seven's stretcher in the cargo area, felt the captain's fingertips lightly brush her shoulder as Janeway moved forward to the pilot's spot, and sighed again as the engines powered up beneath her and her mother's arms tightened their hold.

She was asleep before the shuttle had lifted from the ground.

I Have Broken the
Prime Directive

G. Wood

I have broken the Prime Directive. This is a statement of my crime and my defense.

I am the Emergency Medical Hologram (EMH) aboard the *Starship Voyager.* I am a self-aware entity who has been allowed to exceed his original programming. I have adapted myself to new situations during the five years that we have been stranded in the Delta Quadrant, so far from home. I have grown. I have also become an integral part of this crew and this family, serving as their doctor and friend.

My crime came about as a result of my away mission to a planet where time was different, or as one of our crew has taken to calling it, the Weird Planet.

This planet had a time differential where one of our seconds was equal to almost one of their days. As the only noncorporeal lifeform aboard, and therefore the only one able to survive the transition, I was chosen for the mission. I was to be down there for three seconds, or just over two of their days. However, due to a transporter difficulty, I was trapped on the planet for eighteen minutes, or nearly three of their years.

I was to gather information to help *Voyager* break out of orbit and to minimize contact with the native people during my stay.

This was in accordance with the Prime Directive, which states that we do not interfere with a pre-warp culture, and that we do not introduce advanced technology to that culture.

My programming was designed to allow both my Hippocratic Oath and the Prime Directive to coexist. For example, I never think about beaming down to a planet with a host of medicines to stop a virulent plague. My ethics subroutines would not permit it.

However, my programming did not cover the situation that I found myself in.

When *Voyager* was not able to retrieve me from the surface, I realized that my time among the natives would be extended. Although I always knew I would be rescued, I did not know how long it would take.

For purposes of camouflage, I sought employment. I did not wish to display my superior medical skills, so I took a position as a backup singer in a popular musical.

It was then that I met Mareza, a young widow whose husband had died in a recent spate of bombings by the country we were at war with.

Mareza was kind, compassionate, and beautiful. She had once been a nurse, but she had been unable to inure herself to the daily agonies of the dead and the dying. This is not unheard of in our professions, so I was greatly sympathetic.

Mareza was also an understudy. She was the Juliet to my Romeo. While we rarely had the opportunity to play against each other, we still became good friends. We had much in common.

During my three years, I helped her develop her talents in singing, in opera writing, and in child rearing, as well.

You see, Mareza's late husband had left her with child.

Our close relationship contributed to my crime.

Six months after we met, she and I were trapped in an elevator during a bombing attack. The city's main power plant had been destroyed, so we were trapped in the dark and between floors until the backup units compensated.

It was at that moment that Mareza went into labor.

I had purposely distanced myself from the planet's medical branch. However, we were the only two in the elevator. I did not think that my oath as a doctor would conflict with the Prime Directive in this instance.

The birth was difficult in the cramped circumstances. I delivered Mareza's little boy.

Unfortunately, I was not aware that one of the techniques that I used during the birth had not yet come into use by the planet's medical profession.

This is how I broke the Prime Directive. I used a piece of advanced knowledge to save a small life that would have otherwise died, although no one but I knew.

Mareza asked me to name the boy. I called him Jason—Jason Tabrieze.

For the following three years, we were a family. I became Jason's father, and he became my son.

I knew my time was limited, so I prepared my *yu-mat* (to use the planetary term for family) for my eventual departure.

I had told them that I had great responsibilities elsewhere, and I might someday be called to fulfill them. I would have to leave without saying good-bye.

Mareza was confused, but understanding, and Jason was too young to know.

The day of my retrieval came. I could feel the transporter effects beginning. Due to the time differential, I knew that I had a moment, but it was all too brief. I whispered good-bye to my lady, and left her sight before I was taken.

All those on the planet that I had known were gone shortly after I left. Time passed too swiftly for them.

My mission had been successful, and soon we were able to escape.

However, I knew that I must still face the consequences of my crime.

Captain Janeway has told me that in this situation, the Prime Directive had been badly "bent" when we were unwillingly dragged into orbit.

I can verify that. The "skyship" as *Voyager* became known, had led the people to reach for the stars much sooner than they otherwise would have.

The captain also said that, since they became a warp-capable civilization before we left, the Prime Directive would not have been in force at the time of our escape. She said that I had done nothing in the larger context of our predicament. She thinks no charges are warranted because of the gray areas involved.

I understand her point, and part of me agrees with her.

Unfortunately, I am also left alone with my conscience, and it is not so easily satisfied.

If I had known the true facts, if I had thought the matter through beforehand, if cultural contamination did not already exist, I am not certain that I would have acted differently.

I believe I would have been obedient to my oath as a doctor and I still would have delivered that baby with the advanced knowledge that I possess.

When we return to Earth, I am not sure whether anyone will ever read my statement, or whether they will care about it if they do, but two things I know.

First, I have lived in accordance with the Prime Directive since that time, and I intend to continue to do so.

Second, I am glad that I saved the life of my son. He was the apple of his father's eye, and a joy and comfort to his mother's heart.

END STATEMENT OF EMERGENCY MEDICAL HOLOGRAM

Don't Cry

Annie Reed

The smallest thing, the tiniest, most inconsequential thing—a word uttered without a second thought, as so many words had been uttered over the years—this one simple thing would change the future and erase her past.

All of her life up to this point—gone, simply gone. All with the one word "yes."

Miral sat alone at her desk, the collar of her uniform loosened, and waited for the signal from Admiral Janeway. The lights in her quarters were set at nighttime minimum. A Starfleet mug with half-forgotten coffee cooled near the terminal. Miral had drunk only a little of the coffee before it had soured her stomach and she had pushed it away.

She had learned to drink coffee from her father. Tom Paris drank coffee whenever he could, which on the *Voyager* of her childhood wasn't often. Miral associated the rich, slightly bitter coffee smell with her father as much as his sandy hair, his blue eyes, or his easy smile. Her best memories were of being wrapped in his arms in a hug, the smell of coffee on his breath, as he stroked her hair and told her stories that sprang from his imagination. The aroma of coffee was her childhood memory of safety, of love.

Tom Paris, famous author. That's who he was now. Who Tom Paris would be in the reshaped now . . . Miral didn't know. Would he understand what she was doing? Why she said yes to the admiral?

If he knew what Miral had planned, would he forgive her?

Miral ordered the computer to dim the lights even lower. She felt comfortable in the dark. She remembered *Voyager* as a dark ship. Even after all these years, when Miral thought of home, it was *Voyager* she pictured.

Comfort. Tonight was all about comfort. And paying respect to her honored dead. Soon her past would be among the dead.

Miral wondered how best to pay respect to her own life.

She touched a small scar just beneath her collarbone. Faded almost completely, the scar was the physical manifestation of a memory. Miral wondered if it would still be there. After.

"Don't cry, baby," her father had comforted. "Don't cry."

But tears ran down his own face as he held the knife over her. Miral closed her eyes. She could still see the glint of sunlight on the blade of the knife, hear the whine of phaser fire and smell the sharp odor of charred vegetation. The ground had been hard under her back, and she had been so scared. So very, very scared.

Eight years old, she sneaked on board the *Delta Flyer* with her father and Neelix. It sounded so simple. Hide in an empty storage locker—at eight Miral was still small enough to fit—and tag along with her father while he went planetside to help Neelix restock *Voyager*'s food stores. Her father wouldn't be mad at her for long—he never stayed mad at her long—and it would be fun. Like a real picnic.

Her father told her stories about picnics, and he wrote a holodeck program to simulate one. But holodeck picnics weren't the same as being outside. Even in the holodeck Miral could always smell the metallic, stale odor of *Voyager*'s recycled air, no matter what the program made the holodeck look like. Miral wanted to have her own picnic outside, where there was fresh air and trees and grass and maybe even birds singing, and she could feel the sun warm on her face. They could spread the food they found on a red-and-white checked tablecloth just like in her father's program, this time for real.

Only there were no trees or grass, just carnivorous plants with wildly colorful flowers and sharply barbed vines that tangled Miral's feet and tripped her as she ran after her father and Neelix, so excited about surprising them that she didn't watch where she was going. She would never forget the look of absolute shock on her father's face as he ran to her side after she screamed.

Pain . . . she remembered the pain in a vague way, more a memory of having suffered intense pain rather than the actual feel of the white-hot agony she experienced at the time. One vine tripped her up, and as she fell, another barbed vine snaked around her neck and pulled tight. Her father cut the vines with his phaser and pulled them off her, but one of the barbs broke off and burrowed into her flesh just below her collarbone. She screamed at the pain, so much pain for such a little thing. She could feel the barb burrow deeper into her, almost as if it was a living thing on its own.

Her father carried her away from the vined plants and laid her down on a bare patch of ground.

"Miral, what are you doing here?" His hands shaking as he ran a tricorder over her wound. "Oh, god . . . Neelix, it's poisoned. And it's *moving*."

"Daddy?"

She remembered being so frightened. As much by the fear on her father's face as by her own fear and pain.

"Don't you worry," Neelix said. He smiled at Miral. "We're going to take good care of you."

Her father grabbed her arm and hit his combadge. "Emergency beam-out," he said.

Nothing happened.

"Dammit!"

Neelix peered at her and his smile faltered. "We need to get her back to the *Flyer*. I think I cleared a wide enough path through the vines—we can run for it."

"No time," her father said. "We don't have time."

He smoothed Miral's hair away from the shallow ridges on her forehead. His hand still trembled.

"I need your knife, Neelix," her father said. "The one the captain pretends she doesn't know you take off *Voyager* when you go planetside."

Her father heated Neelix's knife with a phaser set on the lowest setting possible.

"I need you to be brave for me," her father said, and he cut away the neckline of Miral's tunic. "This is going to hurt, sweetheart. I can't give you anything for the pain. I don't know how the poison would react."

"Daddy, please don't hurt me!" She could still remember her terror.

Her father wiped his face with the back of his hand. "Neelix, I don't think I can do this."

"You can, because you have to."

Movement along the ground. Neelix turned and fired his phaser as vines reached blindly toward them.

"Don't cry, baby," her father said. His own face was wet, but his hand holding the knife no longer trembled. "Be brave for me. Please don't cry."

She hadn't, not then. Miral touched her faded scar and wondered if the memory of all that caused it would be lost. If it was, would she even know? Would she become a new person with memories of different experiences? Or would she start over from the moment of the change, the adult Miral sacrificed in place of the child.

Miral shifted in her seat, her back stiff from sitting so long in one position. She stretched and rolled her shoulders, twisted her torso from side to side. Her gaze fell on a miniature holoprojector sitting on her bookshelf.

Seven.

Miral hadn't cried when her father cut the poisonous barb from her chest with Neelix's kitchen knife. She had cried when Seven of Nine died.

"Don't cry, baby," her father said, rocking her. "It will be all right."

But it wasn't. Seven was gone.

At four years old, Miral didn't understand death. She didn't understand the finality of it. All she knew was that Seven was her friend, and now her father said Seven was gone and never coming back.

"That's not true!" Miral yelled at him with all the anger a four-year-old could muster. "Seven's my friend!"

Her father sat down on Miral's bed and she crawled into his lap.

"Seven was your friend," he said. "She was my friend too, and Mommy's."

He stroked Miral's hair and held her close. She smelled the aroma of coffee on his breath, felt his comforting warmth through the thin fabric of her nightdress, and heard his heartbeat, a steady rhythm in his chest.

"But sometimes," he said, "even if people are our friends, something happens to them they can't prevent—or change—and they die. That happened to Seven."

His voice almost seemed to give out on him, and he was silent for a moment, just sat on Miral's bed holding her tight and rocking both of them back and forth a little.

"I know she loved you," her father said. "We can't change what happened, Miral. Seven's not coming back."

She cried then, the loud sobs of a bereft child who can't understand forever but only understands immediate loss and sorrow.

"Don't cry, baby," her father said. His voice betrayed his own sorrow. "Please don't cry."

At four she'd learned to accept the finality of death. Only now had she learned to question it.

Miral got up and retrieved the holoprojector from her bookshelf.

The heavy black base was a smooth, comforting weight in her hand. It reassured her that what she was doing was right. Miral put the holoprojector on her desk next to her coffee cup. She didn't turn the projector on. She had one more honor to pay.

He answered her call almost immediately. Miral knew he would still be awake, even at such a late hour. He said he wrote his best late at night.

"Miral?" her father asked. His brows creased in concern. "Is everything all right?"

His hair was no longer the sandy brown of her childhood memories. Now it was salted with gray, and lines creased the skin around his eyes and mouth. His eyes were as sharp and blue as ever. Miral wished she could hold him, hug him. She moved the coffee cup closer to her so she could smell the aroma.

"I'm fine, Dad." She smiled at him. "Are you working on something new?"

"As a matter of fact, I just started a new novel." He tilted his head. "You called me in the middle of the night to ask me about my work?"

"I just wanted to talk to you." She took a sip of her cold coffee. "So tell me all about it."

In the bottom corner of her terminal, a small symbol began to blink, a steady pulse. The signal from Admiral Janeway. The "yes" that corresponded to Miral's own.

Miral sat back in her chair, sipped the cold coffee, and listened to her father as he spun another one of his tales of adventure. Miral wondered if any of this would be the same, the second time around. Would her father be the same? Would they have this conversation again someday, or would this be all the time they had?

Miral glanced at the holoprojector on her desk, and then back at her father.

Don't cry, she told herself. *Don't cry.*

—STAR TREK®—
ENTERPRISE

Earthquake Weather

Louisa M. Swann

Trip peered over Doctor Phlox's shoulder as the doctor examined a slide under the new microscope. There was no one else in sickbay, yet Trip had this funny feeling in his stomach. He glanced at the exam rooms curtained off along the walls.

Sickbay was impeccably clean and white as usual. Not an instrument out of place.

Something smelled funny, though.

Trip wrinkled his nose at the vinegary scent that seemed to be coming from somewhere over by the stasis chambers.

"What can I do for you, Commander?" Phlox's smiling face was too cheery to suit Trip's mood.

"I'm telling you, Doc. You gotta do something for me. I'm still not sleeping and I keep forgetting things. Nothing seems to help. It's kinda scary, you know, when I find myself riding the lift and then can't remember where I'm going."

He backed up as Phlox pulled the slide free and set another in its place.

"You've been getting the massages from T'Pol I prescribed?"

Trip heaved a sigh. "The massages are great. But I'm still not sleeping. You think there's something, you know, *wrong* with me?"

Phlox looked at Trip, a bemused expression on his face. "I don't belief grief can be considered abnormal pathology."

Why did everyone insist all Trip's problems had something to do with his sister's death? He bit his lip in an effort to tamp down his anger. "This is not about my sister, Doc. Things just don't *feel* right, you know what I mean?"

"I'm not sure that I do." Phlox waved Trip over to one of the biobeds.

"You know how animals can sense an earthquake coming?" Trip scooted his seat onto a biobed and stared across the room. He yawned and tried to force his eyes to stay open. How do you explain a gut feeling to someone who didn't even have the same kind of guts as you?

Trip started again. "I stayed with my cousins in California one summer when I was thirteen. They had an earthquake that summer. Not a big one, according to them. But it was enough to make me sit up and take notice."

"Lie down," Phlox said. He twisted a few knobs on the biobed as Trip scooted his feet down and stretched out on the bed.

"Did you know there's ways of telling an earthquake's coming?" Trip continued. "Just before the last big earthquake hit the Los Angeles basin, the pond above Lawson's Creek near where my cousins live ran dry. Cows went dry too."

The smell was getting worse, but Trip tried to ignore it. "Horses ran into barbed wire fences, and my uncle's favorite mare wrapped her pretty legs in wire so tight she near sliced one hoof free of the bone. Skunks were running all over the place right in broad daylight, scaring themselves and everything else in the process."

"Go on." Phlox poked and prodded at Trip's stomach.

"Earthquake weather. That's what they called it. Even the air smells different—like something's gonna happen." Now he could taste that vinegar. It clung in the air like bad sauerkraut.

"What *is* that smell?"

Phlox stopped poking and stepped back. "You can sit up now." He stepped over and pushed a button on the control panel as Trip let his feet drop back over the edge of the bed.

"I'm working on something that should help you sleep a little better," Phlox said. "Nothing to be worried about."

Right. Trip's eyes started to burn, but he decided not to push the point. "I feel kinda like those animals right now—all antsy inside. My stomach's tied up in knots; I haven't been able to eat much the past two days. I got this gut feeling that *something's* gonna happen."

"Maybe your stomach is telling you to cut back on the grits," Phlox said. "Open up." Phlox stuck a tongue depressor in Trip's mouth and peered down his throat.

"Er's aw . . . eh . . ."

"Hold still."

Trip studied the Denobulan's ridged face impatiently and tried to ignore the stick tickling the back of his throat. Finally, Phlox pulled the depressor free.

"There's nothing wrong with the grits," Trip said. "And even if there was, that's not how my stomach feels. It's more like a sense of nervous anticipation."

"Considering the circumstances the ship is now in, I don't find that too surprising."

"I guess you could be right." Trip thought about it a moment, then threw up his hands and shook his head. "It's not the same, Doc. I know all kinds of weird stuff's been happening since we've been in this Delphic Expanse, but what I'm feeling now's different from wanting to kick some Xindi butt."

It all seemed a bit ridiculous, Trip knew. But all he could picture was how scared his aunt's face had looked when she talked about earthquake weather.

"Are you suggesting that *Enterprise* is about to experience an earthquake?"

Trip shook his head. " 'Course not. You're making fun of me now."

"No, no. I'm simply interested in how easily humans can turn perfectly normal phenomena into signs of portent."

Something in one of the cages squawked—an unearthly mix that sounded like a cross between a parrot and a barking dog. Trip nodded toward the stasis cages. "I think you're being paged."

Phlox just smiled. "Maybe it's the earthquake weather."

"You *are* making fun of me."

"Perhaps just a little," Phlox said. He settled back down on the stool in front of the telescope. "I think it's entirely possible your sense of foreboding stems, in part, from the sleep deprivation you're currently suffering."

Trip opened his mouth to protest, then closed it again. "So if I got some sleep, these feelings would go away?"

Phlox nodded. "It's possible."

"It's a vicious circle then, isn't it? I'm drinking coffee and soda—anything with caffeine to stay awake during my shift—then it comes time to sleep . . ."

"Bridge to Captain Archer." Hoshi Sato's voice came over the intercom, startling them both.

Trip and Phlox both glanced at the com unit on the wall. "Is it just me or did Hoshi sound a bit perturbed?"

Before Phlox could reply, another message came through. "Captain Archer, would you please get up here? This is an emergency."

"Hoshi must be sick or something," Trip said. "She'd never talk to the captain that way. Guess I'd better go see what's going on."

He slid off the biobed and headed to the bridge.

Trip drummed his fingers against his thigh as he waited for the turbolift to reach the bridge. All he wanted to do was lie down and sleep—finally, sleep—and now this had to happen.

And to top it all off the darn lift moved slow as a seven-year itch. With all their advanced technology—phase pistols, laser canons, transporters even—you'd think Starfleet would come up with a faster way to get to the bridge.

"About time," he muttered when the door finally hissed open. He stepped over the threshold, and an odd rasping sound brought him up short.

Trip took a quick glance around to see where the noise was coming from and suddenly felt like he'd been gut-punched. The captain was nowhere in sight, and what was left of the bridge crew appeared to be unconscious.

"T'Pol to *Enterprise*. Come in, *Enterprise*."

Enterprise wasn't responding.

Trip hurried over to where Hoshi lay hunched over her communications console. He placed two fingers over her carotid artery and let loose a relieved sigh when he felt her pulse thump against his fingertips.

"T'Pol to *Enterprise*." T'Pol's voice held what Trip might have called a note of exasperation if the science officer had been another species besides Vulcan. But everyone knew Vulcans didn't get exasperated. Trip leaned over Hoshi and pushed the com button.

"This is Commander Tucker. We've got a bit of an emergency up here. Is there something I can help you with?"

"Does Captain Archer require my assistance?" T'Pol's voice held that emotionless I-am-a-Vulcan-and-you-are-an-idiot tone that always managed to set his teeth on edge.

Trip glanced at Ensign Mayweather slumped in his chair. The navigator's head was tilted to one side, and the rasping noise Trip heard a few moments ago seemed to be coming from him.

"I haven't spoken to the captain, Sub-commander. Look, I don't know if we're going through another Delphic thing or what, but the situation isn't exactly normal up here. Maybe you guys better come on back."

"Very well. Tell Captain Archer we should be back on *Enterprise* in approximately fifteen minutes."

Hoshi sighed and rolled her head so it rested against Trip's forearm. He tried to move her head away, but she just pressed closer. "Will do. Tucker out."

There wasn't much he could do by himself. Trip carefully slid his arm out from beneath Hoshi's head and called down to sickbay.

"Doctor Phlox. I think you'd better come up here."

No answer. Trip tried again on the shipwide channel. "Doctor?"

The com unit stayed silent. "Of all the times to wander around the ship, he has to pick now."

Trip tried calling engineering, but it seemed as deserted as the rest of the ship.

"What in the world is going on?" Trip took one last look at the sleeping ensigns as the monitors hummed quietly in the background. He buried a yawn in his hand. There didn't seem to be anything life threatening, so maybe he'd better find the captain first.

"Bridge to Captain Archer."

Silence.

Was everyone sleeping on this ship except him? Trip tried the captain's quarters. Tried the shipwide channel one more time.

It looked like he was going to have to do a lot of footwork.

Finding the captain wasn't difficult—he was in his quarters. Sleeping.

"Come on now, Cap'n." Trip's gut clenched tight as he shook the captain's shoulder for what must have been the tenth time. "I can't run the ship by myself. Only got ten fingers and ten toes. I'm gonna need some help here . . ."

The door hissed open. Trip glanced up to see who had overridden the captain's security codes. Doctor Phlox stood in the doorway, a perplexed look on his face.

Trip sagged against the desk, wishing he could lie down and join the captain for a nap. "About time someone showed up."

"It appears the crew is suffering from some sort of narcolepsy," Phlox said as he shuffled inside and slumped onto the couch.

Trip wasn't sure he liked how the doctor was looking. "Stay with me, Doc."

Phlox looked at Trip as if trying to remember who he was. "I seem to be rather tired." The Denobulan's eyes slid closed.

"Doctor Phlox? Doc?"

The doctor's mouth sagged open. Trip dropped his hands in exasperation. He took a deep breath and tried to relax. Just because he was the only officer awake on the ship was no reason to get all panicky. He glanced down at Porthos. The little beagle wagged his tail.

At least he wasn't totally alone.

For some reason it helped having Porthos along as Trip wove his way through the corridors to the galley. He'd checked the systems monitor on the bridge—both the ventilation and water systems seemed to be in order. That left only one alternative: the food.

It seemed people were sleeping everywhere they weren't supposed to be sleeping. Trip gave up after trying to wake up half a dozen crewmen and just concentrated on getting to the galley. If not for Porthos, he'd definitely be alone. Even though the crew was just sleeping, Trip felt abandoned.

Everyone had left him, just like his sister had left him.

He tried to ignore the tantalizing aroma teasing his nose as they passed through the mess hall, but his stomach kept reminding him he hadn't had his dinner yet. In fact, he hadn't had much to eat all day.

"You hungry, boy?" Trip ruffled Porthos's ears as the little beagle wagged his tail enthusiastically.

"Chef has a new stew recipe that's supposed to be the next best thing to Gram's apple pie. Maybe if we're lucky, he'll give us a taste."

He'd make another cup of Gram's coffee while he was here. His stash was getting a bit low, though, he'd been using so much of it to stay awake during the day. Maybe that's what was keeping him up at night.

Porthos's toenails clicked loudly on the decking as they made their way through the deserted mess hall. That uneasy feeling was back in Trip's stomach—the unnerving sense that something was wrong. He poked his head through the galley doorway and received immediate confirmation that his gut sense was right on track.

Again.

"Hello?" Trip called.

Porthos looked up and gave a quiet bark, but his was the only reply.

"This is kinda spooky, you know?" Trip gazed around at all the food left scattered across the prep counter. "Like one of them movies where aliens've abducted everyone except the hero and his sidekick."

He glanced down at Porthos. "So, hero. What's next?"

Porthos didn't answer this time. He trotted around the galley, sniffing here and there. "Guess you are a bit hungry."

Trip went over to the stew bubbling on the stove. He raised the spoon and sniffed the stew, trying to decide just what might have been different from the chef's usual recipe.

"You know, it just doesn't make sense that there'd be something in the food. The crew eats at different times and not everyone eats the same thing." He yawned, his cheeks stretching so wide it made his skin hurt. "There. You see? And I haven't had anything to eat since breakfast."

Trip looked down at the little beagle's eager face. "No way. The cap'n would kill me if I gave you this stuff."

There had to be some way of testing it, though. He just had to figure out how. Trip dished up a bowl and set it aside, then grabbed an abandoned pan from the counter.

"Guess I do it the old-fashioned way," Trip said as he filled the pan with water.

He pulled out his stash of Gram's finest, measured a portion into the pot, and turned the burner on before leaning back against the counter. Half-chopped potatoes, onions, and mushrooms littered the cutting board.

Stew ingredients.

Porthos's tail wagged back and forth like an antenna in the wind as he watched Trip move around. The beagle finally gave up and disappeared toward the back of the galley.

Trip smothered another yawn and stared at his improvised coffeepot. "Come on."

His eyelids started to slide closed . . .

Porthos started barking, loud and insistent, jolting Trip awake. "What's up?"

The little beagle stood outside the storage locker door. He barked again, looked at Trip, then back at the door.

"You find something, boy?" Trip walked over and opened the locker door. Porthos ran inside as Trip switched on the light.

The chef was curled up on what looked like a flour sack. Loud, ratcheting snores filled the storage room as Porthos licked the chef's broad face.

So much for asking Chef any pertinent questions. Trip glanced at his chronometer.

"Let the man sleep, Porthos. We'd better check and make sure the sub-commander has a safe landing." Trip turned out the stock-room light and headed for the launchbay, gulping a cup of strong, bitter coffee as he ran.

"What?" The incredulity in Malcolm Reed's voice almost made Trip smile. The pair stood in the launchbay just outside the shuttle, waiting for T'Pol.

"Everyone's asleep. The captain, Hoshi, Mayweather. Doctor Phlox. There's only Porthos and me."

"Have you figured out why?"

"No, I haven't figured out why." Trip gave Reed a cranky glare. "I've checked the ventilation system, the food, and the water."

Reed didn't back down. "That's a start, I should think. What else have you done?"

"Done? I don't fix people, I fix machines!" Sometimes this Brit could be so darn irritating. "What about you. You got any ideas?"

"Me? My specialty's blowing things to bloody hell, and that's a long way from anything having to do with medicine. Can't you wake anyone up?" Reed said with an angry edge in his voice.

T'Pol climbed from the shuttle's open hatch. "I suggest our time would be better spent determining what caused this outbreak."

"Outbreak?" Trip snorted. "Sleep break's what I'd call it."

"Have you run a bioscan yet?"

Trip shook his head and frowned. "Hadn't gotten that far."

"I'll be on the bridge. Maybe the bioscanner will come up with additional data." T'Pol stepped confidently to the launchbay door, Trip and Reed close behind. They filed into the corridor as the door hissed closed. T'Pol turned, smothering what looked like a yawn behind her hand.

"I would suggest you try to wake up the doctor, Commander."

"Are you all right?" Trip asked.

"I'm fine." T'Pol widened her eyes, then turned on her heel and left.

Trip looked at Reed. "Why don't you go with her."

Reed nodded and followed after the sub-commander.

"Back to the drawing board." Trip sighed and headed back to sickbay. He'd stop along the way for another cup of his Gram's coffee.

Sickbay was still empty when Trip walked through the doorway. He set the stew he'd brought from the galley on the doctor's desk along with a fresh cup of coffee.

"What we need here is a volunteer." Porthos stretched out on the floor and put his head down. Trip chuckled. "Don't tell me you're getting tired now."

He had to find some way to test the food, just to be on the safe side. Trip scratched his chin and looked around the room at the empty biobeds, the diagnostic bed looking stern and official beneath its colorful monitor, shelves upon shelves of medical tools and paraphernalia, jars of liquid in which alien life forms drifted and swam.

The cages containing Phlox's bloodthirsty bat and other sundry zoological specimens.

Trip had watched Phlox feed his critters more than once. He didn't want to end up losing a finger. There had to be some way to feed some of the stew to the creatures without risking life and limb.

He took the spoon from the bowl, fished out a spoonful of

stew, and shook it free inside the bat cage. Nothing. Not even a peep.

Another try. This time inside the marsupial's cage.

Still nothing.

Trip grabbed the spoon tightly, took a deep breath, and poked at the tiny ball of fur curled up in the corner. Gently at first, then a bit harder. Jerked his hand back as the creature moved.

But it just curled into a tighter ball.

Trip put down the spoon with a sigh. "Looks like they're already asleep."

Porthos answered with a snore.

Just then the sickbay door hissed open. Lieutenant Reed stood in the doorway, cradling T'Pol's body in his arms.

"What the hell happened?" Trip hurried over and helped Reed get T'Pol onto a biobed.

Reed laid T'Pol down gently, then leaned against the edge of the bed and put his head in his hands. "I don't know. We were heading for the bridge and she collapsed. Standing there one moment, on the floor the next."

"Well, that's great. Just great."

Reed looked around. "Where's the doctor?"

Trip sighed. "Where everyone else is—sleeping."

"Haven't you woken him up yet?" Reed glared at Trip. Maybe that gut feeling of Trip's was also affecting his imagination, but it sure seemed like Reed was trying to blame this whole incident on him.

"I've tried. You got any brilliant suggestions?" Trip asked defensively.

Reed glanced at T'Pol and shook his head. "She doesn't look good, does she?"

"I'm sure she'll be fine," Trip said. But he wasn't so sure about Reed. "How are you doing?"

The weapons officer rubbed his eyes. "I'm fine, though I feel like I could polish off a pot of tea."

Bingo. Trip hated it when the answer to a problem was right in front of his eyes and he couldn't see it. "You're brilliant, Malcolm. Come on."

Reed looked at T'Pol. "Don't you think—"

"I don't think staring at her's gonna help. We gotta get the doctor back on his feet, and I think I know just the thing."

Doctor Phlox stared at the cup in Trip's hands. His eyes still looked a bit bleary, but at least he was sitting up. It had taken three cups of Gram's coffee to keep Reed awake. Together Reed and Trip had taken turns pouring coffee down the doctor's throat with a straw.

"What did you say this was again?" Phlox reached out an unsteady hand and took the cup from Trip. He slurped noisily and then set the cup back down.

"It's an old family remedy."

"Oh, really? Remedy for what?"

"Hangovers." Trip watched Phlox with satisfaction as the Denobulan looked around the captain's quarters. Captain Archer was still snoring at his desk.

"Doc, everyone on the ship's asleep, except you, me, and Malcolm. We gotta do something."

Phlox shook his head, then nodded. "I'm not quite sure that I have a hangover, but your remedy seems to be working. I feel quite fit." Phlox swayed as he stood, but he held out a hand as Reed and Trip both reached for him. "I'm perfectly fine, gentlemen. Perfectly fine."

With that the good doctor turned and walked into the doorjamb. He held out his hand again, a cheerful smile on his round face. "Perfectly fine."

This time he made it through the doorway.

Reed stared at Trip. "I thought you were just making coffee."

"Coffee and a little something extra my grandmother always used to add for those mornings when nothing seemed worth getting up for—you know what I mean?" Trip headed out the door after Phlox.

"Knowing you, that coffee probably contains a half pint of whiskey," Reed said as he followed behind.

"Tabasco sauce. That was Gram's cure for what she called the morning-after blues. Good strong southern coffee and a hefty dose of homemade tabasco."

Reed's face was blank as a sheet of unmarked paper.

"Hot sauce, you know."

"You put hot sauce in coffee?" Now Reed looked a little on the green side.

"Helped keep me awake. You, too."

"How'd you know it wouldn't make things worse?"

"It worked, didn't it?"

They both squeezed through the sickbay door at the same time, anxious to see how Phlox was doing. He stood by T'Pol's bed, his usual cheerful smile spread across his face.

"She should be coming around in a minute," Phlox said.

"What'd you give her?" Trip felt his shoulders relax slightly as T'Pol's eyes fluttered open.

"I injected her with a dose of straight caffeine," Phlox answered.

"What? No tobasco?" Reed said. Trip decided to ignore the Brit's sarcasm.

"What am I doing here?" T'Pol asked as she sat up. Her eyes still looked a bit out of focus, but otherwise, she appeared fine.

"You fell asleep," Reed said.

T'Pol stood up, one hand on the biobed. She straightened her shoulders. "I believe we still have a scan to complete?"

Reed nodded. "We've been rather busy since you decided to nap."

T'Pol raised an eyebrow and headed for the door.

"I'll go with her," Reed said. He followed the sub-commander through the doorway before it hissed shut.

"It appears your grandmother's remedy is working," Phlox said.

Trip walked over to the desk, picked up the bowl of stew, and tried not to yawn. "I still don't get it, Doc. I checked the food, the water, the air-conditioning . . ."

241

Phlox came over and took the stew from Trip's hand. "Did you run a scan on this?"

"No. I tried to feed it to your critters."

Phlox's smile disappeared and his eyes widened. "You fed that stuff to my Altarian marsupial?"

"Well, I tried feeding it to your bat, but it wouldn't touch the stuff."

Phlox looked at his desk monitor and adjusted something on the controls. "Pyrethian bats only eat live food. I am a bit surprised to see you have all of your fingers."

Trip glanced down at his hands and shuddered. He set down the stew. "Look, Doc. I know you're miffed I fed stew to your animals, but I was only trying to figure out what was going on."

"I'm sure you did the best you could under the circumstances."

"You gotta admit you weren't being very cooperative."

"Bridge to sickbay."

Phlox turned away from Trip and answered the com. "Yes, Subcommander."

"Doctor, the bioscan shows an abnormality in the ventilation system."

"I checked the ventilation system." Trip frowned. He'd checked everything twice, as a matter of fact.

"It's not something that would show up on the system scan," T'Pol said. "Whatever has entered the system is of a biological nature, much like perfume or the odor of cooking food."

"You mean our problem could come from something that stinks?" Trip asked.

"That is correct, Commander."

Phlox had a thoughtful look on his face. "Did your scan indicate where the source of this odor might be?"

"It seems to be emanating from sickbay."

"I see." Phlox and Trip both looked at the container steaming away in the corner of Phlox's lab—directly under the air vent.

Trip had gotten so used to the noxious vinegar smell he'd forgotten about that pot until now. He followed Phlox over to the simmering pot.

"I should have realized the fumes might have an effect."

"This is the stuff you thought would help me sleep?" Trip asked.

Phlox nodded. "A combination of herbs I picked up while we were on Earth. I was hoping to find a natural alternative that would give you the desired soporific effect without all the side effects drugs often carry."

Trip was heading back to engineering to check on his crew when Doctor Phlox showed up, syringe in hand.

"I wanted to stop by and let you know things will be back to normal soon. I've administered the antidote to almost half the crew, and everyone seems to be fine." Phlox held up a bottle. "It also appears my experiment was a success. Take a teaspoon of this before bedtime and see if it helps."

Trip took the bottle. "Thanks, Doc."

Phlox nodded and headed down the corridor, stepping aside to let Ensign Sato pass.

"Hello, Hoshi." Trip smiled.

"Hi, Commander." Hoshi looked at him curiously. "You sure seem happy."

"Just nice to see a friendly face."

SPECULATIONS

Guardians

Brett Hudgins

The Present

Soon the dead world would again teem with life.

Lonely and weary, the mother of the next generation laid her last egg and nestled the fragile, iridescent silicon sphere safely among thousands of others filling the vast cavern called the Vault of Forever. Hers was the greatest duty and highest honor her species could bestow. So it had always been; so it would always be. Even now, after all they had seen and done.

Her contemporaries were gone, the penultimate Horta having passed away mere hours ago. Only a very few, confused or distracted, had failed to fulfill the noble mission that had seen the Horta leave behind Janus VI so many millennia ago to adopt this strange new homeworld. They had served when called, fought when necessary, and yielded to nothing but the inevitable. Some had died along the way, rarely of natural causes, but that was a risk they'd understood from the beginning. Just as they'd understood that each beginning had an end, and that each end was a new beginning. This was the essence of Horta generations. All but one must die before the renewal of the species.

The mother of the next generation didn't mourn. Regretting the natural order of being was a waste of emotion better devoted to the celebration of lives that had been. She left her eggs, unafraid for their safety, and shimmied through a tunnel to the dusty, ancient surface. The vanished humans had christened this world the Rock of Ages, never bothering to explain the reference or the odd delight they'd taken in their wordplay.

She sometimes missed them, for she wouldn't be here now without their instigation. She wouldn't be poised to see her offspring inherit a legacy inextricably connected to the safekeeping of existence.

But such thoughts, while rare, were not modest. Her job wasn't finished. She emerged into the thin, dry atmosphere, easily maneuvering through the perpetual twilight. There was time to check the unblinking eye once more before the next generation hatched and the cycle began anew.

49,970 Years Ago—2297

The elderly human looked across the Vault of Tomorrow and smiled. Turning the cavern into a memorial had seemed only natural to Chief Engineer Vanderberg, considering the misunderstanding that nearly led his people to unknowingly commit genocide. Even he had believed the Horta eggs to be attractive curiosities and nothing more. So what if they were damaged or destroyed? Only the bravery and resourcefulness of Captain James T. Kirk and his *Enterprise* crew had averted tragedy and led to a wonderful, and wonderfully unexpected, alliance.

Now the cavern was full again, not with eggs but with living, maturing Horta, the fascinating silicon-based sentients who had given Vanderberg's life so much meaning. Thousands strong, they waited patiently for him to speak, respecting that mere words could never adequately express his feelings.

Despite a lump in his throat, his voice carried easily. "My friends. I've spent my entire career on Janus VI. I've been privileged to forge unbreakable bonds of fellowship between the United Federation of Planets and the Horta. However, the pergium you've helped my people mine for the decades since your births is no longer necessary, thanks to advances in life support technology. Many of us have moved on already to seek our fickle fortunes elsewhere. The rest of us will depart following the disassembly of our offices and processing stations. I assure you I'll be the last person to board the transport. I was here at the beginning, and I have enough Horta in me to want to see my work through to its conclusion."

Members of his audience produced sounds of appreciation by digesting small amounts of stone.

Vanderberg held up his hands for silence. "I gathered you here because of how much you mean to me, and to thank you for indulging an old man. Though my family hasn't always appreciated my devotion to your world, the Horta changed my life for the better. This farewell *isn't* permanent. After I've enjoyed a month or a year of retirement on Earth—or however long it takes me to miss being entombed in millions of tons of rock," he added with a laugh, "I'll be back to visit Janus VI. That's a promise. And any of you who want to leave with us to seek new opportunities and adventures throughout the Federation are certainly welcome. We're part of each other's lives now."

Though not many Horta accepted his offer for reasons of tradition and cultural preference, relations with the Federation remained amicable.

Former Chief Engineer Vanderberg kept his word, visiting several times before dying peacefully of old age. According to his wishes, and with Horta permission, he was buried in the Vault of Tomorrow—the only human ever granted such an honor.

Time passed.

49,805 Years Ago—2462

High-level officers called the siege "the atrocity on the edge of forever."

Fleet Admiral Ian Kyle Riker found the phrase glib, vaguely insensitive. He didn't like it and he didn't use it. Making his distaste known to his colleagues and subordinates hadn't been hard, either. Gathered in his office to stare at the blank wallscreen and wait for word, they spoke among themselves in whispers and left the admiral to his thoughts.

Gazing out a transparisteel window at the vivid Boothby Gardens, he didn't see beauty. He wanted to—indeed, hardly a pessimist, he expected to . . . someday—but there was no beauty in recovery. Recovery was raw and painful, like the stitches or scab that closed a wound. Rebuilding Starfleet Headquarters and turning the tide of the Second Romulan War was only the start of a long, grueling process. Beauty would come with peace, lasting peace.

That everything could change in an instant without his ever knowing was Riker's paramount concern. Events of the preceding years had taken so much from him already. His parents, his sister . . . his youngest child. He hadn't lived, and often struggled, for eighty years just to see everyone and everything he cared about wiped from existence, without even an afterimage by which to remember them.

But he wasn't a captain anymore. He couldn't insert himself into the thick of crucial situations, grab hold with his teeth and both hands, and *force* the desired outcome. Flying a desk and making decisions for the good of Starfleet as a whole meant being patient and trusting the capabilities of others.

The wallscreen beeped and the standard UFP placeholder appeared.

Grateful to the steady beat of his artificial heart—an upgraded version of the model Uncle Jean-Luc had used—Riker turned from the window and resumed his place at the table. Expectant silence filled the room.

"Incoming communication from the *Enterprise*," Admiral T'Min reported. The venerable Vulcan had assumed comm duties with Riker's consent. "Descrambling."

The wall filled with encryption symbols dissipating like digital bubbles to reveal the welcome image of Captain Edward Sherwood. The veteran Starfleet commander sat on the edge of his chair, burned and bloodied, one of his eyes swollen shut. A plasma fire blazed behind him, illuminating far too many unmoving bodies in its shimmering green light.

"They're gone," he said simply, forgoing protocol for the sake of relief. *"Fleshing out intelligence that's been sketchy at best, I can confirm that the Romulans seized our military and research installations on the Rock of Ages. They mined the surrounding space, towed in their own orbital warbase, and—"* He shook his head, a hitch in his husky voice. *"Their obsession unleashed their basest instincts—and damn the Romulans if they didn't revel in their perverse liberation. Shedding any last pretense of nobility, they eradicated our personnel down to the last xenohistorian. Innocent people, devoted to knowledge—lost to the worst carnage I've seen during this whole bloody struggle.*

"The few Romulans we managed to capture killed themselves rather than submitting to interrogation, meaning we still don't know how those sadistic bastards found out about the Guardian—"

"Yet," Riker added darkly, taking no issue with the captain's editorializing. A familiar anger welled in him as he imagined the cruel fate of people he was sworn to protect.

"But possession catalyzed them. Gave them something tangible to dig in and fight for, and incentive to take chances. Blitzkrieg, kamikaze, every brand of assault they could muster. They even mobilized forces from other sectors, substantially weakening their remaining presence in Federation territory."

"And . . . ?" Just because he'd said they were "gone"—

Sherwood smiled grimly, as if reading the admiral's mind. *"We didn't give a motherloving inch. Reinforced by the* Hood *and the* Exeter, *we took it to the Romulans with everything we had left and then some. Uprooted them like weeds, one pointy ear at a time. They finally tried to retreat, and we goosed them from behind with our last nova torpedo.*" He allowed a satisfied pause. *"No survivors."*

Riker let out the breath he'd been holding as his fellow officials broke into excited chatter. "Excellent, Captain. On behalf of Starfleet and the Federation, thank you, and well done. You've likely saved the universe as we know it."

"That's the only acceptable compensation for the losses we endured."

"I know," Riker said softly. To his eternal regret, he knew. "We'll reassign whatever battleships we can now spare to the Rock of Ages. The *Enterprise,* the *Hood* and the *Exeter* are hereby ordered to return to Utopia Planitia for leave and repairs. You're coming home."

Sherwood nodded but didn't break the connection. He might have been addressing the admiral from six inches away, so intense was his demeanor. *"This isn't over, Ian. We won a single battle in a war we can't fully envision. They'll come again. If not the Romulans, then someone else. The Guardian of Forever is too valuable— we might never be able to protect it sufficiently. Think about that."* He coughed and glanced at his devastated bridge. *"Sherwood out."*

The wallscreen went dark again.

Steepling his fingers, Riker looked at his colleagues seated around the table. "The unthinkable happened and we survived. I couldn't begin to quantify our good fortune. Yet the captain raises a point we've all considered recently. Everything becomes public knowledge sooner or later. The spectacular collapse of Section 31 proved that beyond a doubt. Our enemies—even our less scrupulous allies—will stop at nothing to tear away the artfully plain shroud we've thrown over the Rock of Ages if they ever uncover the pertinent facts. Battleships, undeniably necessary, will catch someone's eye. The truth will out.

"Thanks to Jean-Luc Picard's interest in the classics, I'm put in mind of something the Roman satirist Juvenal wrote: *Quis cus-*

todiet ipsos custodes? 'Who guards the guardsmen?' His context was more cynical, concerning abuse of authority, but, to secure our way of life at the most basic temporal level, it's vitally important that we ask: who guards the Guardian?"

"Actually, sir, I have an idea about that. I wasn't quite sure how to broach it."

Riker gestured for the speaker to continue. "Go ahead, Vice-Admiral Vanderberg."

"I've been remembering family stories about an ancestor who ran a mining colony on Janus VI . . ."

49,803 Years Ago—2464

The two years after the humans made their startling revelation and proposition passed quickly.

First came debate, then refusal. Then curiosity, followed by questions, more questions, and more debate. The whole process was unfamiliar to the Horta, but they adapted well and made sure that, in their way, they understood precisely what their carbon-based allies were asking of them.

When they eventually agreed to be transferred en masse from Janus VI to a world known merely as the Rock of Ages, they did so wholeheartedly. Their days of mining pergium were long gone; even dilithium was being phased out. Horta were happiest when they had a purpose, and with nearly fifty thousand years before the next generation, there was no greater responsibility they could assume than becoming the last line of defense in the preservation of space-time.

Besides, no world was dead to them—not once they got below the surface.

Starfleet successfully disguised the population transfer as military maneuvers, then left the Horta to acquaint themselves with their new home.

None of them ever forgot the first time they looked into the unblinking eye.

49,571 Years Ago—2696

Energy became matter as three Romulan Tal Shiar agents materialized among the gray, desolate ruins. Wind blew through crumbled pillars and arches with a spectral moan and called fluttering eddies of dust to dance like ghosts.

"Status?" said the leader, Sotar, not budging from the protective triangle formation.

The science technician, T'Lior, paused while confirming readings on her sensorband. "Personal cloaks operating at peak efficiency. Optical links active, allowing us to see each other and share instrumentation. No indication the humans are aware of our presence. I estimate we'll be safe from their progressive smartscans for just under an hour."

"And our ship?" Leaving the stealth-shielded vessel in orbit was the riskiest part of the plan.

"Less than half an hour."

"Not good enough. There'll be no experimentation. Timidity and cautiousness are what cost us our hold on this planet the last time our people were here. We may never get another chance. We must use the time portal to cripple human expansion into space."

"Understood."

They'd tried other means of eradicating humanity, of course; losing a war hadn't deadened their ambition. Sending squadrons of warbirds back through time using the slingshot effect had been a promising gambit. Unfortunately, the humans undid each incident of temporal sabotage with relative ease by manipulating the mysterious portal their Romulan foes had coveted for over two centuries.

Now the Romulans were here again, to capture it—or destroy it.

"Advance."

Sotar took the point position, picking his way across the broken landscape and ancient formations. Behind him followed T'Lior and Trivik, the demolitionist. Moving with great care, the latter carried the time bomb. Doubly accurate, the name referred to the Bajoran Orb of Time, stolen from the Terrestrial Temple and, as a last resort, rigged to detonate on passage through the portal. Romulan theoretical scientists predicted the resulting temporal holocaust would erase most of the Alpha Quadrant from space-time, leaving the Romulans the supreme power in their new Beta Quadrant home.

T'Lior hesitated. "Did you hear something?"

"Just the cursed wind," said Sotar. "Hurry. The longer we tarry, the better the chance of this dust fouling our cloaks and exposing us."

The portal was visible now, a weathered, irregular hole in the horizon. Nearby stood the modest Federation outpost dedicated to studying and protecting the temporal phenomenon.

Sotar paused then, holding out a palm to arrest his comrades. This time he'd heard it too, a strange rustling shuffle that was oddly omnipresent, yet distinct from the keening wind. "Life signs?" he whispered. At worst they were leaving footprints. There was no way the humans could have detected them so quickly.

"Nothing." T'Lior held up her sensorband, holoexpanding the readings.

"Being on the brink of our redemption and triumph as a species is no excuse for nervous floundering," said Sotar. "I include myself in the condemnation. Fitting, then, that this is a suicide mission. We press on."

Not two steps later he heard a sound like acid washing across gravel and turned to see a mottled orange and brown shape burst from the ground and land on T'Lior. Hissing strangely, it shambled off her an instant later, leaving no remains but an ashen smear.

Sotar drew his pulse pistol and leapt between the creature and Trivik. "Go!" he cried at the stocky Romulan with the time bomb. "Complete our mission! I'll hold—"

To his utter horror, three more creatures tunneled to the surface as easily as moving through air and converged on the demolitionist, disintegrating him in their corrosive embrace. Amazingly, the Orb of Time rolled free, unharmed.

Sotar lunged. There was still a chance—

More creatures rose from the ruins, inhuman and unstoppable. Sotar fired on them, succeeding only in chipping their rocky hides. He wondered what they were, why they exhibited no biological characteristics—and how they could see him. And then they were on him, eating him alive, a burning wave sweeping him into oblivion.

None of which was as agonizing as the pain of failure.

49,400 Years Ago—2867

Largely planetbound but for rare individual offworld ventures, the Horta often weren't abreast of the latest developments in the Federation. Truthfully, most so-called developments didn't matter to them—though at least the Vulcan-Romulan reunification meant one less potential enemy of the unblinking eye. Other events, such as the Metron Psycho-Plague and the rescission of Starfleet General Order 7 on Talos IV, passed virtually unnoticed.

Then time travel underwent a renaissance with the invention of timeships and the creation of the Temporal Integrity Commission. Suddenly, though it retained its enigmatic allure, the Guardian of Forever was more a failsafe than a vital tool.

But no matter how intently the Federation tried to understand and utilize time, time didn't change. Even the stolid and reliable Horta weren't sure they could make such a claim in perpetuity.

46,960 Years Ago—5307

The solo Horta didn't have a name as most biological sentients understood such designations. He knew who he was, though, and the other Horta knew him. That was enough.

The others also knew he wasn't content guarding the unblinking eye on this dreary little mote of a world. They waited patiently for him to decide on a more pleasing course and pursue it, for that was his right. They didn't judge or unduly influence him in any way. Each individual bore the responsibility for finding his proper place in the universe.

That responsibility concerned this particular Horta. He knew he was different, and even minor differences were obvious among his people, without necessarily being an issue. With the Guardian receiving less attention than ever from friend and foe alike, there had never been a better time to break with tradition and do something new.

What, though? He tunneled to the surface and found an isolated spot, determined to stare at the sky until inspiration struck.

Only a few years later he heard the voice.

Startled, he returned to the unblinking eye, circling it suspiciously. But the portal wasn't the source of the voice. Nor was the language or means of communication familiar, based on his knowledge of Federation life-forms.

As if sensing his confusion—though he hadn't explicitly expressed it—the voice told him a story. It called itself the Crystalline Entity. It had been destroyed thousands of years earlier by a vengeful human named Kila Marr and had struggled to reconstitute its delicate spaceborne form. Upon succeeding, it tried to find a former ally, an android named Lore. The closest it came was a similar, but much less interesting, android named B-4. B-4 didn't approve of the entity's primary means of sustenance, absorbing biological life energy, and the entity had no choice but to destroy the synthetic life-form. Now the Crystalline Entity freely traveled space once more, feeding and exploring. Blind chance had brought it to the remote Rock of Ages, where it was thrilled to discover the existence of a completely different variety of silicon-based life. It wondered if it could stay awhile.

The Horta had a better idea. Maybe he could join the Crystalline Entity on its journey.

They struck their bargain. The Crystalline Entity appeared in the sky like a giant, glittering snowflake—or so the biological sentients from the Federation described it in frantic distress calls before it fed on them, scientists and military personnel alike. It gathered the willing, unashamed Horta in a crystal cocoon to protect him from the harshness of space and then hurtled away through the stars.

Upset at this surprising evidence of deviance among their kind, the remaining Horta vowed to provide even more thorough protection of the biological sentients who depended on them.

They owed the unblinking eye no less.

42,126 Years Ago—10,141

The sentient cube felt the fierce heat of atmospheric entry as it descended toward the surface of the Rock of Ages. It compensated with ablative cryoshielding. Heat was irrelevant. Pain was irrelevant. The ship was Borg. It would add the technological distinctiveness of the anomalous time portal to its own. Resistance was futile.

Young and ambitious, not yet having attained its mature growth, the cube left behind in orbit the wreckage of three Starfleet mindships, their biological overseers no doubt dead or comatose in distant psionic command modules.

Emerging from a bank of leaden clouds, the cube released a swarm of nanopredators. They dropped like a hazy blanket toward the Federation base, eager to consume its inhabitants and component materials.

One by one, each voracious microscopic machine vanished in a pinpoint of light as a dislocator shield shredded it at the subatomic level. What effect such a shield might have on a Borg the size of the cube was difficult to estimate. The technology was intriguing, however, and would be a useful acquisition if it could be reverse-engineered.

Hovering, the cube cycled its sonic cannons and pummeled the base and surrounding area with concentrated sound waves. The troublesome energy barrier soon flared and died as the equipment that maintained it rattled, collapsed, and liquefied. The base, not the first of its kind and possibly not the last, succumbed moments later. Only the time portal and the strangely ageless ruins remained standing at a safe distance.

Engaging antigrav landing beams, the cube settled to the planet's surface directly in front of the portal. It immediately initiated deepscans, but the readings that bounced back were gibberish.

It tried again on revolving frequencies, including a number of dimensional phase variances. The results were the same.

I am Borg, the cube transmitted in mounting frustration, trying to batter through the time portal's awareness with brute force. *Resistance is futile. You will be—*

The cube paused. Self-awareness meant knowing when something was wrong. The Borg ship could sense an unusual flurry of activity directly underneath its body where there should have been nothing but flattened antediluvian dust. It began a fresh sequence of deepscans, only to discover with some alarm that the planet was riddled with tunnels through which moved thousands of creatures possessing mass and velocity but no life signs.

Unless . . .

The cube quickly recalibrated sensors to detect silicon-based—

Intelligence-gathering subroutines shut down in favor of self-defense imperatives as the strange creatures tore into the cube from below, invading with significant numbers and savagery. Internal shields proved useless as the creatures simply ate around them, churning without pause through ceilings, walls, and floors. They spread like a computer virus, bypassing and engulfing, burning and destroying. The cube deployed its relentless biodrones to no avail; each was quickly reduced to cinders upon encountering the enemy.

With a last, longing pass of its scanners over the time portal, the cube initiated its launch sequence, hoping to incinerate as many creatures as possible during a violent retreat. Its commands went unheeded. Backups were off-line. Diagnostics faltered and crashed. Weapons died, fizzling and sputtering. Engines went cold. Cascade failures raced through the cube's systems as it cannibalized itself in the hopes of self-preservation. Nonessential systems were shutting down as quickly as vital ones were malfunctioning.

Gutted, the cube would never fly or think or feel again.

It had been Borg—and it had been wrong about resistance.

34,665 Years Ago—17,602

Another benchmark in sentient existence theory came with the realization that the *space* part of space-time might be as important as the *time* part.

The races of the Federation marshaled their quantum resources behind this new way of thinking and in short order learned how to bend the universe into a multidimensional shape called, of all possible names, a *pretzel*. Of what interest was mere time travel when concentrated multispecies effort could compress entire galaxies, bind them with superstrings, and move them to strange new locations in the furthest corners of infinity, where accepted physical and mental laws were entirely different?

The Omnipax took hold, embraced by all.

Peace and prosperity flourished. No one wanted for stimulation or satisfaction of any sort. Life in the Federation became an ongoing celebration of curiosity, discovery, and joy. The Borg had become extinct after trying to assimilate the shape-shifting allasomorphs of Daled IV. Even the Klingons were happy—in their own surly fashion.

Perhaps the most telling vote of confidence and prosperity was the decision to dismantle the permanent Federation presence on the Rock of Ages. The humans didn't make a big production of it; they just quietly returned the world to the condition in which they'd found it, saying they'd come back whenever they needed the time portal. And they did. They could have terraformed the planet to be entirely habitable but refrained out of respect for the current occupants.

The Horta accepted these new developments as they had every other, preferring to appreciate them from afar while concentrating on more important matters.

Namely: trying to fathom the nature of a regular visitor to the Rock of Ages. He, if indeed that was the appropriate pronoun, had started dropping by every few decades and seemed benign. Yet he shouldn't have been able to exist. He looked human but didn't eat or sleep or age, and only breathed to facilitate speech. He wore a Starfleet uniform thousands of years out of date. And he was, by his own admission, the only person in the whole universe, "plus a bunch of alternate realities," who was "bored stiff."

He called himself Q, whatever that meant.

". . . So then I said to him, 'Eat any good books lately?' He laughed. At least, I *think* he laughed. It might have been a grunt. Or constipation—sometimes he neglected his prune juice, and he'd go entire days without unclenching a single body part from his jaw on down. But the point is, Worf and I were always needling each other. It was our thing." Q leaned against the unblinking eye, absently rapping his pale knuckles against the portal's shell and completely ignoring the audience of wary Horta. "Any of this sinking in, Guardian? Are the lights on in there? If you don't make with a little feedback I might be tempted to reinvent the wheel, if you know what I mean. If there's one thing I hate, it's talking to myself." He glanced at the Horta and waved. "No offense, Flintstones."

He waited, apparently desiring some sort of reaction. "Sheesh. Tough room. I thought a real-life 'modern Stone Age family' would be more fun than this. Anyone want to see a baby mastodon vacuum cleaner? No? You don't know what you're missing. You should have named this planet Oa, you know. But I guess good in-jokes have gone out of style—along with everything else, come to think of it."

He sighed. "All my old friends are dead. I could probably resurrect them, though I doubt they'd appreciate it. Most of them had real attitude problems. And I don't really have any *new* friends—see 'attitude problems' above. I should be out there"—he waved his hand at space, and a glorious rain of shooting stars dazzled the otherwise stark sky—"shepherding the primitive corporeal beings through their new discoveries, testing them, making sure they're worthy of their endless stream of staggering advances. And *they*—they should need *me* to show them the way. Why else would I still be marking time in the rear end of the multiverse? But they *don't* need me, not as badly as they ought to, and all I feel like doing is reminiscing. Beats going home to the wife, anyway." He nudged the unblinking eye. "You're a good listener, I'll give you that."

The portal glowed and for the first time since the Horta had colonized its world, the unblinking eye spoke in their presence. *"All is as it should be."*

Q sighed again. "Tell me about it. On second thought . . ."

And still the Horta kept watch.

29,405 Years Ago—22,862

Using precise command of an array of tiny personal force fields to work the controls, the malevolent entity known as Armus piloted his vessel toward the surface of the barren world. *Another barren world*, he fumed in his boundless fury, *much like Vagra II*. The ship he had flown such a distance, with such tenacity, was actually an amalgam of an ancient Starfleet shuttlecraft—or what little he'd been able to salvage after its destruction from orbit—and a much newer, more bizarre automated explorer with a rudimentary mechanical consciousness but no life aboard. Both vessels had crashed thousands of years apart on desolate Vagra II, the world whose former residents had cast Armus off as their "skin of evil" so they could exist as beings of perfect beauty.

He *hated* them for their selfishness and narcissism. Hated them with a black passion that had kept his oil-slick body seething with rage for countless millennia. But he was about to satisfy his eternal grudge, provided that the records from the explorer were accurate and that this little planet dubbed the Rock of Ages was home to a time portal one could use to alter the past.

Oh, the delicious horrors Armus intended to visit upon the callous Titans of Vagra II . . .

And in taking his vile revenge, he'd make it impossible for the Vagrans to abandon him in the first place, thus ending his blighted existence in a paradox.

He craved oblivion—for himself . . . and for any beings he could make suffer along the way.

The ship touched down roughly. Rather than savoring his successful arrival, Armus deactivated all power, opened the hatch, and oozed toward his destiny. He could already hear the sweet screams, the cries for mercy, and the begging, oh yes the endless precious begging, that would satiate every dark impulse he'd ever had. It had been *so long* since he'd killed, for pleasure or sport or any other reason—or no reason at all. He suspected the imminent release of aggressive ire would be virtually orgasmic.

He oozed faster.

Ahead, an artifact stood out among the ruins, somehow noble despite its surroundings. He hated it on sight; it could only be the time portal he sought. He assumed its operation would be straightforward. If for some reason it didn't work, he'd simply crack its shell and flow through the innards until he understood how to effect repairs.

Suddenly a creature seemingly made of stone rose from the dust ahead of Armus, blocking his path. Rather than changing course, the evil entity flowed over the unexpected obstacle, engulfing it in his black, gooey mass. Its struggles felt wonderful—the fear and confusion, the mounting panic as it failed to burst free. Armus twisted with a violent internal squeeze, ripping the rock creature in half and spitting out the remains like so much waste.

Divine . . .

He hoped the Vagrans tasted half so delicious.

More of the tunnelers came, plowing through the ground, toppling columns and arches in their haste. Their melodious anger was a symphony and Armus spread himself wide, eager to annihilate them all at once.

They circled him instead, continuing to devour dust and underlying strata at an incredible rate. They were trying to strand him on a little island, surrounded by an empty moat. How quaint. He'd kill them extra slowly for such a ridiculous affront.

A few of them disappeared as the moat deepened. Then all of them disappeared. The island wobbled and Armus had a single moment to consider flowing across the channel before his pedestal of rock collapsed, spilling him into a tunnel that went straight down. The walls were not only too slick for him to stick and stabilize himself, they were also red-hot from acid and friction.

This was too much. He tried shooting tendrils back to the surface, only to see the shaft caving in above him as more of the creatures went to work. Falling dirt and stone mixed with his mass, increasing his physical discomfort.

Apoplectic with anger and frustration, knowing the time portal was so close, Armus used his force fields to protect himself from the shower of grit. This only increased the speed of his descent, and he welcomed it. If he could catch and destroy the creatures forming this slide into the bowels of the planet, then he could climb back out at his leisure.

Yet accelerating didn't help. Still he was pounded from above as his escape route filled itself in, and still the creatures below outdistanced him.

Armus lost track of how fast and far he fell, knowing only that the heat and pressure within the planet's mantle were becoming intense. It didn't take much analysis to understand what was happening: the creatures were sacrificing themselves to these brutal conditions to prevent him from using the time portal. They believed they had power over him.

Never. He *couldn't* falter. He *couldn't* die without taking his revenge on the Vagrans.

Yet he couldn't do a damned thing to save himself.

His liquid body began to bubble with heat rather than rage, each little blister-burst compounding his agony. Far below him, near the world's core, the creatures that had sealed his fate erupted into flame and melted into puddles of molten rock.

In his final moments, Armus lost his mind to his animosity—and discovered there was no hatred stronger than that which he bore himself.

23,870 Years Ago—28,397

Several Horta watched from hiding as the holoship landed not far from the unblinking eye. Holoships, flying mobile emitters capable of opening and closing their own wormholes, had been all the rage after their invention by the holopeople of Yadera II. That had been thousands of years ago, though, and the Horta hadn't seen one in almost as long.

A door blinked open in the light-plated hull, revealing a silver-haired human. A mobile emitter shone on his jacket lapel. "Here we are, pally," he said in a smooth voice. "The Rock of Ages. Home to the Horta, the Guardian of Forever, and some pretty poor acoustics. There could be a musical here, though. How does this grab ya? 'Singin' in the ruins, I'm just singin' in the ruins . . .' " He grinned. "Not impressed, huh? That's 'cause you haven't seen the *dancing*." In a gentler, less frivolous tone, he added, "I'll noodle with it. You take care of business. Good luck, pally." And the holographic man stepped aside so a pool of liquid gold could flow from the ship onto the ground.

The Horta charged, remembering the struggle they'd fought against a similar being that had cost a number of their lives.

This liquid didn't attack, though. Instead, it rose in a narrow wave to stand vertical, shimmering as it assumed a humanoid form with rounded, unfinished features. The evil black one hadn't done this.

Taken aback, the Horta drew up short. They recognized the newcomer as a changeling of the Gamma Quadrant species called the Founders, who'd once been inimical toward the Federation before retreating permanently to their Great Link. But there had been one who—

"My name is Odo," the changeling said gruffly. "I mean you no harm or trouble. I—I probably shouldn't have come, shouldn't have asked an old acquaintance for transportation. But I had to see her one more time. Every second she slips a bit further away. I—I understand your purpose. You may watch me every moment I'm here, and block my direct path to the Guardian. I don't care. Just . . . please . . . don't obstruct my view."

That said, the changeling walked slowly toward the unblinking eye. The Horta accepted his word and blocked his path, not his view. They remembered Odo and the role he'd played in ending the Dominion War.

Odo stopped a respectful distance from the time portal and said, "Guardian, please show me the life of Kira Nerys. It's been so long. I want to remember." He trembled as he spoke, as if not daring to hope.

The portal instantly filled with images of a vibrant Bajoran woman.

The changeling, who likely could have vaulted the Horta at any moment and plunged into history to be with his one true love, simply watched.

And when he smiled, his face became beautiful.

15,565 Years Ago—36,702

Representatives of the various Federation races gathered at the Rock of Ages to mourn not only the destruction of two sentient peoples but also the weakening of an ideal.

After generations of allied peace marred by occasional flare-ups of hostility, the Elasians and the Troyians had finally lost the war against their ancient enmity and wiped each other out in a mutual apocalypse. Mediation, arranged marriages, outright bribery by allies who didn't want to lose Elas and Troyius to the futility of what had started so long ago as a minor feud—none of it mattered. The Elasians and Troyians had even tried living in separate galaxies, but they always let themselves be drawn back to their traditional conflict, and their weakness was their downfall.

The Horta couldn't imagine surrendering their potential as a species and a culture to pointless warfare, and though they didn't understand how others could succumb, they joined in the mourning. They believed all races should contribute to a better universe, as they were by protecting the unblinking eye.

A human spoke to the assembly about her people's checkered past and about how they had learned from their own frightening brushes with suicidal stubbornness, foolishness, and blindness. "If we had known of the Guardian then, we might have willingly made mistakes on the assumption we could correct them afterwards. That simply isn't true. We cannot use the portal to resurrect the Elasians and Troyians, only to remember them. They acted of their own free will, and we have to accept the consequences, however painful. We must never stop learning that there are better ways."

She wasn't alone in her tears when she finished her speech.

8020 Years Ago—44,247

Humans were still obsessed with demolishing boundaries.

The Horta had first noticed this trait among the pergium miners of Janus VI, who'd been determined to explore and exploit the interior of that world to a degree never before achieved, and nothing had changed in the forty-two millennia since then. Every human was, at heart, a pioneer—and every challenge was another final frontier.

The manipulation of time and space—gaudy talents that they were—didn't prevent the humans and their cousins from working to unlock the full potential of their outwardly unassuming carbon-based forms. When they finally succeeded, they were astounded at the great gift they'd been given by the unnamed humanoid race that had seeded their respective species throughout the galaxy billions of years before. The boon, very simply, was the ability to abandon their bodies to mortality—to become, and accomplish, whatever they could imagine.

That was when the biological sentients grew up and put away their toys. They unplugged the intergalactic beam grid, mothballed the Dyson transwarpspheres, let loose their self-aware metatech, bequeathed new endowments to the far-flung offspring of V'Ger, swept some excess dark matter under the rug, and told Q in no un-certain terms to spruce up the Continuum because company was coming.

In short, they did everything but say good-bye to the Horta.

"Bothersome humans," Q complained, scuffing his toe in the Rock of Ages' plentiful regolith. "We weren't expecting them for another million years at least. They're always throwing off the curve with their exponential evolutionary and technological leaps." His ageless face registered a strange expression. "Oh no . . . what if they evolve through the Continuum faster than we Q do? Wouldn't that be just perfect? Somewhere, somehow, Jean-Luc Picard is laughing. Hmm, I wonder if he knows I'm the one who made him bald . . ."

Q looked at his now-regular audience of Horta and smiled with rare sincerity. "So long, folks. It's been real—or as real as reality gets. You're good eggs. Keep looking out for the unrolling stone, here. It deserves the attention. My work on this plane might be finished, but the Guardian's older than us all—its job won't be done until even you and I are distant memories."

The enigmatic being disappeared in a flash of light, leaving the Horta to regard the unblinking eye with newfound awe.

One Year Ago—52,266

Though their overall method of perception was fairly complex, the Horta didn't consider any one sense more important than others. Their sight included the infrared spectrum, allowing them to navigate by heat within pitch-black planetary bodies; not many tunnels were as well lit as those in a mining colony. Their hearing was acute enough to pick up physical signals transmitted through solid rock, such as tapped codes. By smell they could detect changes in atmosphere, particularly useful in the event of dangerous gas accumulations. Horta also had a form of sonar with which they could gauge the depth and density of mineral formations before burrowing through. Having been born with these senses, having used them all their lives, the Horta were usually completely at ease with the world around them.

Until the day a new sensation overtook the males.

At first it was subtle, a tickle in the back of the mind and minor discomfort at the extremities, like excess nerve stimulation. The Horta tried to dismiss it, to focus on the necessities of their duties and daily lives, but the unfamiliar feeling wouldn't go away. Fearing that a strange new force was attacking the Rock of Ages, they hurried in the direction of the surface.

They didn't make it.

Powerful urges seized them, jolting their bodies like an ion storm. Their subterranean world took on undreamed-of crispness and clarity, and the very air itself became an intoxicating perfume. It wafted through the tunnels, calling the males, filling an inner emptiness that briefly threatened to swallow them. Helpless to resist and eager for more, they followed.

She awaited them in the Vault of Forever.

A single female exuding waves of desire, she was a starburst of stimulation to the hyperactive senses of the male Horta. Vigor suffused them. They realized it was time.

They shuffled forward, letting her heat become theirs—soon to ensure the future of their species . . .

The Present

The mother of the next generation shuffled across the Rock of Ages, following a path worn glass-smooth by thousands of years of repetition. The unblinking eye saw her as clearly as it ever had. All was well.

To her amazement, the edges of the time portal lit up like a sun's corona and images appeared in the eye. She needed but a moment to realize she was seeing the complete history of the Horta species, every single generation. The intimacy and honesty of the presentation was the second most moving experience she'd ever known. She would have wept had she been able.

And there was the Vault of Forever, filled with her eggs. Filled with *promise.*

Then the light leapt from the portal to the sky as the fabric of space itself opened to reveal a force so pure and joyous that the mother of the next generation thought she might burst. Loving voices filled her mind and soothed her soul as the once-biological sentients returned in their new configuration to celebrate the hatching of her eggs. The Horta hadn't been forgotten and never would be.

Thanks to the Guardian.

The Future

The Rock of Ages revolved through space, an incomparable jewel to the precious few who understood, and the Guardian of Forever watched existence with an unblinking eye.

"All is as it should be."

The Law of Averages

Amy Sisson

My name is Dax. Technically, of course, I have a longer name, one that identifies my current host. But since he is dead, for the first time in centuries I am the symbiont alone. If only for the short time between my host's death and mine, I am simply Dax.

I don't fear death—I've died too many times to be frightened of it now. Over the course of my lifetimes—so many!—I've died of old age, I've died in accidents, I've been killed in battle. I've even been murdered twice. Every time I died, I had the comfort of knowing I would not really be dead. I would be joined to a new host, would start yet another life and live on.

But not this time.

"Doctor Dax, sir. Lieutenant Sheffield reporting for duty." The redheaded young human stood at rigid attention.

"Just Dax, Lieutenant," Dax said. "I'm a diplomat, not a doctor. Not this time around, anyway. It's easier to stick to 'Dax'—one of the few constants in my lives." His eyes twinkled as he spoke, making him look younger than his host's sixty or seventy years. Younger, yet ancient.

"Yes, Doc . . . yes, Dax, sir."

"At ease, Lieutenant. Technically I don't outrank you anyway, since I'm a civilian."

"Yes, sir."

"Is this your first first-contact?" Dax asked.

"Yes, sir."

"Well, relax, son, they don't usually bite. Although I do remember this one time . . . oh never mind, that was a long time ago. The first time I was a diplomat, in fact. Curzon Dax."

"Of course, sir. We read about Curzon Dax in our first-contact seminar at the Academy."

"First-contact situations are a little harder to come by these days," Dax said. "Space seems to be getting smaller all the time. But they're damn exciting when they do happen."

"Sir, is it true you witnessed the signing of the Borg-Federation Treaty?" Sheffield asked eagerly. "That was so long ago. I mean . . . sometimes it's hard for me to remember the Borg were ever our enemies. Did you know we have two on board for this mission? A Cardassian-Borg and a Human-Borg. If I hadn't gotten into the Academy, I probably would have thought about joining myself."

"Yes, the Borg have come a long way. A great many unjoined Trill have joined the Cooperative—our species simply can't get away from that joining instinct! Of course, it helps knowing you can turn off your link whenever you want. It was a little different in the old days of the Collective."

"So you were there?" Sheffield asked again.

"Yes, I was there. Not as a diplomat, though. Now *there's* a story. Tell you what, I'll tell you all about it if you join me for a drink. We've got some time before we get where we're going." Dax draped his arm over Sheffield's shoulder and steered the younger man gently, but firmly, toward the crew lounge.

*   *   *

Even though there won't be a new host this time, still I'm not afraid. It's been a long series of lives, perhaps more than I've deserved.

Eventually, the law of averages catches up with all of us, even joined Trill. Symbionts don't generally die of old age, of course. Most can go on and on indefinitely, because the youth of their hosts rejuvenates them mentally and physically. But accidents do happen, even though the Trill Symbiosis Commission—they do worry so—tries to see to it that any joined Trill traveling far from the homeworld are accompanied by at least one or two unjoined Trill. We had two other Trill on this trip, as a matter of fact. Cretia and Janra, both lovely young women, initiates who were cleared to serve as hosts in emergencies. It is of great sadness to me that now they will never be joined.

But sometimes there is simply no escaping the law of averages. I picture chance as a fussy little person, an accountant perhaps, making sure all the books are eventually balanced. After all, what were the odds that the diplomatic contingent would be taking a tour of engineering just when the accident—I assume it was an accident—happened? What were the odds that both Cretia and Janra would be accompanying us, even though they're scientists rather than diplomats?

One moment I was telling the ladies the same joke that had made poor Sheffield turn redder than his hair, and the next moment was utter chaos. There was a blinding flash, then shouts and alarms. Terrible pain. I was dimly aware that Sheffield, himself injured, was shouting casualty reports to the bridge. Cretia and Janra were dead. The chief engineer, a Jem'Hadar named Kans'let, also dead. They had all been standing closer to the transwarp core than I was, which is likely the only reason I wasn't killed immediately along with them.

As Sheffield cradled me, urging me to hang on, I felt my host's body cease functioning, relieving the pain yet thrusting me into a silent darkness that seemed far worse. Instinctively, I cast out electrical discharges in a panic, trying to communicate with my fellow symbionts. But I was not in the pools. I was on a ship very far from the homeworld, with no surviving Trill on board.

"Bridge to engineering, report!"

Sheffield, kneeling on the floor with Dax half-lying in his arms, mentally activated his communicator implant. "Captain, it's Sheffield. I think Kans'let is dead. There was some sort of explosion. . . ."

"Emergency medical transport protocol," the captain ordered. Sheffield and everybody around him were immediately enveloped by the familiar grip of the transport beam.

When Sheffield materialized in sickbay, however, Dax was nowhere to be seen. Belatedly Sheffield remembered that the computer automatically assessed each patient and assigned triage status while still in transport, directing each of them to materialize at the appropriate station in sickbay.

"Where's Dax?" Sheffield asked the nurse who was already preparing to inject him with a hypospray. "I need to talk to the doctor!"

Now that the initial panic has passed, I feel calm. After all, I'm not suffering. I'm alone, but at least I have the memories of my hosts to keep me company, and time to prepare myself for death. There's no chance we'll be able to reach the Trill homeworld in time. Even if the ship wasn't badly damaged by whatever happened, we were already more than a day's travel away from the Gamma Quadrant end of the wormhole. And the Trill homeworld is yet some distance from the wormhole's other end near Bajor in the Alpha Quadrant.

I suppose it's possible there could be an unjoined Trill on Deep Space 9. No, not Deep Space 9—I keep forgetting that DS9 was retired and replaced by FP-1, or Federation Portal 1, back when the wormhole was permanently opened between the two quadrants. I have a lot of memories of DS9 . . . two great wars fought from that base. A wedding that almost didn't happen but finally did. Two weddings, actually. And an old, dear friend.

But a Trill on FP-1? Even if I can hold on that long, the chances of finding a suitable host there are remote. Even after all these centuries, most Trill, whether joined or not, remain homebound. I've never understood that inclination, but our sociologists believe it comes from a deep-seated instinct to protect the symbionts.

And the doctors on FP-1 . . . no doubt they would do their best, but they wouldn't have the expertise necessary to join a severely injured symbiont to a hastily prepared host. No, it has to be the homeworld, but there's simply no way to reach it in time.

"I'm sorry, Lieutenant, that's the best we can do for now."

"But, Doctor," Sheffield said. "The symbiont . . . we've got to—"

"I know, Lieutenant. But we have several other critical cases as well, and there aren't any Trill on board who can serve as host. I don't think the symbiont would survive even a temporary transplant to a non-Trill. We're going to have to keep it in stasis and hope for the best."

Sheffield looked resigned. "All right, Doctor. But I'd like to stay with him, I mean, um, it. Should I talk to it? Can it hear anything?"

The doctor's expression softened to one of sympathy. "It's unlikely, Lieutenant. The symbiont doesn't have any external auditory organs, and it's in stasis—synaptic activity levels are too low to register on our equipment. But you can stay if you want to. It can't hurt."

Time is passing, although I have no way of knowing how much. As my control over my memories weakens, the images come and go more quickly—friends made and lost, husbands and wives and children. My first trip to the Delta Quadrant. My final opera performance on Vulcan. Was that before or after the Delta Quadrant? Brief joinings with twisted minds—Joran and Verad. Giving birth to Neema. The heft of a *bat'leth* in my hands.

All these memories will soon be gone, but still I do not feel regret. If the accountant has found me, so be it—I still have my one small secret from him. He doesn't know, the old miser, that even a dead symbiont is not really lost as long as its remains are eventually returned to the pools, no matter how many years or decades later. The specific memories will be gone, yes, but the symbiont's essence fills the pools as its body gently dissolves, awakening in the as-yet-unjoined symbionts the desire to experience life beyond the caverns.

If I concentrate, I can almost remember existence before the first joining, remember that faint taste in the pools. It was wisdom, maybe, or age. Experience. Joy. It was so long ago, well over a millennium, but I can remember how that taste made me yearn to be joined.

Then, even as I slip further toward unconsciousness, I feel something change. We must be entering the wormhole. Ridiculous, of course—I'm completely without sight or sound. But ever since Ezri I've been peculiarly sensitive to the currents of space. Her children used to tease her, tell her there was no physiological proof that she could sense these things, but we knew better.

We've made it as far as the wormhole, then. Our ship will undoubtedly stop at FP-1, but it's almost over.

And then, as I sense the wormhole's ebb and flow, I feel something else. A deep rumble passes gently through my symbiont body like a wave, before resolving into a voice that I feel rather than hear. Deep and rich, a voice from the past.

Or from the future, old man?

Old man. . . . I've been an old man many times before, and I am one again, it seems. But only one person has ever called me that.

An instant passes, stretching into eternity.

"Lieutenant Kelly, report," said Captain Grayson, tense but calm.

"Sir, we've emerged from the wormhole, but the coordinates are all wrong. We're nowhere near FP-1 or Bajor."

"Get a fix on our location, Lieutenant."

"Aye, sir." There was a pause while Kelly manipulated her holoscreen with rapid eye movements, a frown of concentration on her face.

"We're at the edge of the Trill system, sir. I don't understand— we were traversing the wormhole normally and then we were just . . . here. It doesn't make any sense."

"We'll worry about that later. LaMoigne, raise the Symbiosis Commission and tell them we'll be there in a few minutes." The captain's face remained impassive, but the bridge crew heard the smile in his voice.

The instant is gone, fading into a ghost of an echo, the wave receding from my symbiont body. I still don't know what is happening on the ship around me—-explanations will come later. But somehow I know that it will be all right. We'll make it in time. The accountant will have to wait.

And then another, gentler afterwave, coalescing and dispersing even more quickly than the first. My symbiont body has no shoulders, of course, but still I feel an arm around them, a presence filled with affection and amusement.

Try to stay out of trouble, old man, it tells me.

I'll try, Benjamin, I answer in my thoughts. Not likely, but I'll try.

Forgotten Light

Frederick Kim

Vorlkai watched the sun rise, and marveled as the gold rays fell upon the land, there to stir colors into full brilliance. The old Renewer needed a way to inspire the people again, even if his voice in the Session was not what it once had been. Surely, if he could capture this dawn's essence, it would be enough. He brought up the spectrographic display, linked it to the molecular modeling interface, and began to create.

Picard suppressed a grimace. On the viewscreen before him was Havarrnus, a black, shriveled world blasted by the light of a red giant star. The planet looked like a lump of coal going into a furnace, and the captain perceived from the first glance that there was no possibility for life of any sort here, not anymore. How appropriate it was that this hellish place had once incubated the Borg.

The *V'ruc,* a deep space explorer, had stumbled upon Havarrnus four months ago while charting the Neghari star cluster. Her crew had detected the ruins of ancient cities on its surface, and later ascertained that these were the remains of a colony whose inhabitants had emigrated from the Delta Quadrant. When analysis of the ruins uncovered notable similarities to Borg architectonics, the explorers realized they had made an astounding discovery: Havarrnus had been a part of the precursor civilization that became the Collective.

Picard had gone to see Admiral Nechayev shortly after the *V'ruc* had returned home. Havarrnus was the best opportunity the Federation had ever had to understand the origins of one of its worst adversaries, and he had been determined to lead the return mission to it. In arguing his case, he cited his background in xenoarcheology and his experience in combating the Borg. Neither he nor Nechayev mentioned his unique intimacy with the Collective, but in the end she gave him the mission anyway.

Now that he was here, though, Picard realized he had underestimated how difficult this would be for him. Over the past few nights the dreams had returned, and he could feel the weight of the Borg's history in this place. It was enough to make him dread what they might unearth during the expedition, but he told himself that his unease was overridden by his duty. If there was anything on Havarrnus that could be used against the Borg, he would find it. If he succeeded, maybe it would finally, finally be enough to make up for . . .

He turned away from the viewscreen and glanced in Riker's direction. "I'll be in my ready room, Number One," he said. "Begin scanning the surface, full sensor sweep. I want away teams down on the surface as soon as possible." Riker responded in the affirmative, and Picard departed the bridge of the *Enterprise*-E. As he left, he sensed Counselor Troi's eyes on him. She had surreptitiously been paying a great deal of attention to him lately, but he did his best to ignore it.

"The upper levels of the planet exhibit the most conspicuous similarities to Borg construction and design." Data was reporting the initial sensor findings to the assembled officer staff in the observation lounge.

Picard nodded. A part of his mind kept searching, reaching out to voices that had once been there. "That's consistent with the reports from the *V'ruc,*" he said. "They found evidence of what almost looked like Borg distribution nodes scattered across the surface."

"That is correct, sir. Those remains date back to a time period just prior to my estimate of when the Borg first appeared on Havarrnus. By then Havarrnan society had already adopted a very decentralized structure, one highly reliant on technology.

"Unfortunately, there is not much more that will be available for useful study from this period. On closer inspection it appears most of the interesting structures of this level have been deliberately stripped from the surface. That is why the initial findings of the *V'ruc* were not more substantive. The evidence would indicate this occurred shortly after the Borg's evolution: in essence, the Borg 'assimilated' their own precedent culture."

"Don't tell me we've come all this way for nothing," Doctor Crusher complained.

Data shook his head. "Our efforts are not in vain, Doctor. While the upper levels of the surface have been removed almost in entirety, the same is not true for the lower ones, which come from an era approximately two centuries prior to assimilation. Here the removal of artifacts occurred in a much more haphazard fashion. Apparently, the Borg did not find it as necessary to absorb the remnants of their more distant past."

Picard frowned. "What can we expect to find?"

La Forge spoke up. "Captain, it looks as if the Borg assimilated these layers almost as an afterthought, maybe in order to obtain raw materials. They probably used an early form of their nanotechnology to do it. These 'protonanites' appear to have operated on a fractal algorithm, with the level of deconstruction being dictated by a bifurcation cascade protocol. In any given location the damage to features and artifacts ranges from complete destruction down to flaws only visible at the microscopic level."

"Security risks?"

"As the system's sun is now a red giant, the planet is no longer able to support life," replied Data. "There are no automated orbital defense systems, and no systemic technologies appear to be functional on the surface. Nevertheless, I do recommend caution while exploring this world. Havarrnus' atmosphere has long since dissipated, and daytime temperatures on the surface exceed 170 degrees Celsius. Away teams will need to be outfitted with environmental pressure suits, at least until environmental control fields are erected around the dig sites. There may also be less obvious dangers of which we are unaware."

"Very well," said Picard. The throbbing in his temples was growing worse. "Mister Data, I would like you to run the scan results through the main computer core. See if you can better localize fruitful areas for excavation. In the meantime, we'll begin sending away teams to the surface at once."

"I assume you'll want to visit the excavation sites for yourself, sir?" asked Riker.

"Not this time," Picard replied. That raised a few eyebrows around the table, while Troi frowned. "Given the size of this dig, the best place to coordinate it from will be here. I'll be able to review the data as it comes in from the different teams, as well. For once, Number One, you won't have to worry about my gallivanting off on some away mission."

Sunlight streamed in through the high apertures of the Primary Chamber, onto the teeming Renewers assembled for the Session. The members of the polity were seated in tiers arranged to face the back of the great hall, and listened as Renewer Sivdar, leader of the Technologist faction, spoke to them from the rostrum.

Vorlkai shifted impatiently in his chair and resisted the impulse to shout down Sivdar's words by telling himself his turn would come soon enough. He noted that Sivdar, usually an atonal public speaker, now employed a voice that was cold but seductive.

"Havarrnus has long been stricken by pessimism and disarray," she declared. "The news of our sun's impending death has only compounded the problem. Anarchy is inevitable now, unless we can find a new solution, one that will bind each of us to one another and bring order to chaos. Fortunately, that solution exists. If we have the vision to pass it, the Interlinkage Act will provide the restoration our people so desperately need.

"This won't be the first time the Technology has come to our salvation. We all remember when the Outbreaks crippled our bodies and threatened to destroy our way of life. How then did we overcome our disabilities?"

Vorlkai looked down at his right hand and arm. The cybernetic appendage looked entirely natural, a mirror image of his left upper extremity.

"The difference, Sivdar," he whispered in a voice too low for anyone else to hear, "is that my arm serves merely as an extension of myself. It does not substitute *for* myself." He turned his attention to the graphics display he held on his lap, which portrayed the outlines of his planned sculpture in three dimensions. He adjusted one of its curves, and then recalculated how the new shape would affect the crystal's refractive qualities.

The next two days were marked by disappointment for Picard. He sent the initial expeditions to the planet's surface with orders to gather any material that might be of strategic significance. They came back with evidence of what had been a very technologically oriented society, superior in some respects to the Federation. Specific details, however, were lacking. Information storage from even the earlier time periods had been on highly advanced lithographic data crystals, most of which had been destroyed by nanites or deteriorated over the intervening millennia. The process of reconstructing these records was going slowly, and Picard spent most of his waking hours sifting through the few fragments of data that were

available. He was in his ready room going over the latest transla-
tions when Troi came to visit him.

"Yes, Counselor," he said, without looking up from his padd.

Troi settled into her chair and assessed the situation. "How is the
excavation going?" she asked.

Picard sighed and pushed away the report. "It's been frustrating," he said. "At any excavation site you expect much to be destroyed or missing due to time, but there nevertheless usually
remains a pattern you can draw upon to fill in the blanks. Here, the
damage is intentional and virtually random, making it that much
harder to relate any one thing to another."

"I'd have thought you'd be thrilled. Normally this is exactly the
kind of challenge you seek for yourself."

Picard shook his head. "This mission is far too important for me
to treat as the focus of a hobby. There *are* tantalizing clues here and
there. This report, for instance, mentions a plague that was sweeping Havarrnus approximately two hundred eighty years prior to assimilation. But so far, I haven't found anything that would be of
benefit to Starfleet."

Troi nodded. "Even the limited data we've acquired could take
years to fully analyze. Perhaps you shouldn't limit yourself to
purely tactical information. Why not look at what you have from a
different perspective? I hear the fourth away team found an almost
intact library of lithographic cubes, records of government officials, from the sounds of it. Have you looked at them?"

"No, I haven't. The records came from fairly unimportant legis-
lators, and were concerned with personal matters."

"Captain," Troi said, a reproachful tone in her voice. "An arche-
ologist as knowledgeable as yourself knows that much of great significance can be gleaned from the seemingly trivial." She paused,
and chose her next words carefully. "I can't help but wonder if your
history as Locutus is preventing you from fully engaging this culture."

Picard slowly straightened in his chair. How dare she strike at
his deepest wound in order to accuse him in this manner . . .

But Troi kept her eyes fixed on him, without any hint of cruelty or malice.

And Picard realized then that Troi was only speaking the truth.

"You're right," he said softly. "I have been keeping my distance from the people who lived here."

Troi felt encouraged. Not everyone would have gotten through that difficult moment. "What exactly is it that's been troubling you?"

Picard collected his thoughts before answering. "Given my . . . 'experience' with the Borg, I know far more than I wish to about how the Collective views the universe, and what it conceives of as its own predominant position within it. What I know will never leave me, never cease to horrify me.

"I've always valued archaeology as a means of enhancing my own appreciation for uniqueness and diversity. But here on Havar-rnus I am applying its tools and methodology to a society that stood as the antithesis to those very qualities. I have no desire to better comprehend the malevolent nature of such beings—I'm much too familiar with it as it is."

Troi looked at Picard with sadness and understanding. The wounds that had been inflicted by the Borg had never truly healed, had they?

"I know this has been difficult for you," she said. "And I don't know what there is to be discovered here. But you've come this far because you wanted to help. How will you feel if you don't make the most of this opportunity?"

The room was silent for a time while Picard considered this. He realized anew how fortunate he was to have Deanna for a friend.

"Point taken, Counselor," he said.

Renewer Ciparxa scowled from the gallery. "You can't be serious."

There was only a scattering of people within the Tertiary Chamber. Once, the Forum on Aesthetics had been attended by practically all the Renewers and had been at the center of the most heated debates, but now the younger members chose not to attend, uninterested in a subcommittee they thought lacked any real power.

Vorlkai knew better.

He turned to face Ciparxa from the dais. "The precedent in this matter is clear," he said.

"Precedent! That antiquated custom fell by the wayside over a century ago. All proposed legislation is now debated directly in the Primary Chamber, without any creative nonsense."

"Then the debate there must cease until the error has been corrected."

"You're *trying* to stop deliberation on the Interlinkage Act," said Ciparxa, comprehending. "Vorlkai, this forum only lingers on at the whim of the Session, as a place for you and the other senile Renewers to prattle about your fatuous artworks. The fact that you head the committee means nothing!"

"I disagree, Ciparxa. And my decision stands: all deliberation on the Interlinkage Act must cease until the optimal framework for the debate has been chosen, here in this forum."

Ciparxa rose from his chair. "You doddering fool," he snarled. "They will not stand for this transgression in the Primary Chamber. Sivdar least of all." He turned and stormed out of the chamber.

Vorlkai watched him go. *So,* he thought, *it begins.*

Picard awoke with a start. Disoriented and unable to see, he touched the side of his face and felt only his own smooth skin. He was not on the Borg cube after all.

"Lights," he called out. The reassuring surroundings of his quarters became visible. He got to his feet and walked over to the replicator, where he ordered some water. Taking the glass from the terminal, he moved toward the table, but then stopped when he noticed the padd lying on its surface: it contained the journal documents Troi had mentioned.

Picard sat down reluctantly, his eyes never leaving the padd. He hadn't been able to bring himself to read it yet. Did he really need to know more? Wasn't it enough that these people haunted him, even in his dreams?

But he still hadn't accomplished his mission here, and Troi's words came back to him. If he didn't find something soon, he would have to end the expedition. Surrender to the Borg. Again. He picked up the padd. According to the index, the largest portion of the journals had been written by someone named Vorlkai. Picard selected the first of his entries and began to read.

Vorlkai was in his workshop, modeling the effects of different molecular bond lengths on his easel, when Renewer Tulos paid him a visit.

"We met in the Primary Chamber today," Tulos said without preamble from the doorway. Vorlkai's longtime friend looked unhappy.

"I'm sure Sivdar and her crowd missed my presence," said Vorlkai. "Besides, I had more important work here."

Tulos moved closer for a better view of the easel. "For your new sculpture?"

"Some of us still honor the old ways. I've come to realize that art offers the only true hope we have of ever understanding one another."

Tulos sighed loudly before sitting down. "I wish more of us were as devoted to the core disciplines as you, Vorlkai. We would serve Havarrnus better for it. Lately, however, your conduct worries me. You're still planning to go through with these hearings?"

"Of course. Did you know that in the debate over the Iconology Act, arguments were presented as opposing musical compositions? I'm tempted to try something similar, just so I can watch Sivdar bang a drum."

"Vorlkai, you have no idea how angry you have made the Session. Stalling the Interlinkage Act in Tertiary Committee has incensed many of your colleagues. You have made enemies."

"My enemies are fools."

"Still, it makes no sense to provoke others unduly. Tell me, what do you hope to gain from this maneuver?"

"Time," replied Vorlkai. "Time for Havarrnus to realize the danger. Time for the people so they can see the true source of their salvation."

Tulos shook his head. "The Interlinkage Act is tremendously popular. Sivdar makes a compelling case, and the Technology she brings is impressive."

"Don't tell me you've been swayed in favor of this nonsense."

"I haven't made a decision yet. But there are times I wonder if the Technology is all we have left."

"We have other resources to draw upon, Tulos. This Interlinkage Act is a false hope, a glorified lie. It's a betrayal of everything our ancestors dreamed of achieving, when they left the homeworld."

"In retrospect, our ancestors could have done better, than to colonize a world whose sun will become a red giant in the next few hundred years," said Tulos. "Vorlkai, before things become worse, meet with the Technologists. Talk to Sivdar."

Vorlkai bristled. "You expect me to compromise? How could you even—"

"Not compromise, Vorlkai. I know you would never do that. But emotions are running high in the Session right now. Anything could happen in this toxic atmosphere. Just listen to what Sivdar has to say, and in turn inform her of your views. Find some way to at least defuse these tensions, if not end the debate. Restore civility to the polity now, before something drastic occurs."

Vorlkai's brow furrowed in thought. It wasn't such a bad idea, just to talk, was it?

"Very well."

"So once I work with Geordi on the biofilters, I think we'll be able to kiss our problems with the protonanites good-bye." Doctor Crusher sipped her tea, satisfied with the outcome of her efforts against this unexpected nuisance.

"Good," said Picard. "The away team members will be relieved not to go through those lengthy decontamination procedures anymore." They were in his quarters, and had just finished an excellent course of *mignonette de poulet petit duc* Picard had elected to cook himself, as a change from the replicator.

"I'm glad you offered to make dinner tonight. Lately, you've been so preoccupied."

Picard smiled ruefully. "Well. There's been a lot to think about."

Crusher understood. "Any progress at all on the excavation?"

"I wish I could claim to understand early Borg society the way you understand protonanites," he replied. "At least the work doesn't seem like so much drudgery anymore. On Deanna's recommendation, I've been studying some of the personal journals of midlevel government officials, from about two hundred years prior to the planet's assimilation. Some of them were remarkable individuals."

"How so?"

"Well, Havarrnus' leaders from this period were far more than just political figures. Members of the legislature were called Renewers. They bore the charge of reaffirming Havarrnus' morals and ideals, of revitalizing its culture. To accomplish this, Renewers were expected to be knowledgeable in numerous disciplines: aesthetics, philosophy, and scientific theory, to name just a few.

"There's one Renewer I find particularly fascinating—his name was Vorlkai. His journal entries record his progress on a new art project. For Renewers, there was often no point of distinction between art and politics, and they frequently used art to substantiate their political ideas. Vorlkai was creating a sculpture meant to underscore his arguments regarding a piece of legislation called the Interlinkage Act. I'm still deciphering the significance of that measure, but Vorlkai's descriptions of his own creative process provide some intriguing insights into Havarrnan cultural values."

"Sounds like an enlightened man."

"An enlightened society," said Picard. He frowned. "And for that reason, I cannot see how they became the Borg."

*   *   *

"It's . . . interesting." Sivdar regarded the tall slab of uncut crystal. "But I would have thought you'd be much farther along by now." Vorlkai had brought her, Ciparxa, and Tulos to the workshop to show them the product of his labors.

"Before I could synthesize it I had to develop the appropriate molecular structure for the material, one that exhibited the correct excitation properties," he responded.

"Why does your sculpture need such precise molecular modeling?" asked Tulos.

"Let me show you," said Vorlkai. He rummaged through the workshop until he found the photon collector. When he activated the emitter, the room was flooded with a warm, golden light.

"This is light I've collected from our sun," said Vorlkai. "It is the light that has sustained and nourished us ever since we came to this world. When properly energized, my sculpture will fluoresce with the same light, in exactly the same spectrographic pattern."

Ciparxa had shielded his eyes from the light with his hand. "What purpose will that serve?" he asked, annoyed.

Vorlkai shut down the emitter. "Our people are agitated into social unrest because they have lost hope. They despair over Havarrnus' eventual death. My sculpture will serve as a beacon to them, to remind them that in truth Havarrnus exists within us. No matter what happens to our sun or this planet, we can preserve all that we are. We can start over."

Sivdar shook her head. "If you wish to preserve our world, Vorlkai, you should support the Technologists. We offer a way for our people to evolve into a stronger race."

"I have seen your interlinked volunteers, Sivdar. The ones already plugged into this vaunted cybernetic network. Havarrnus will not find salvation by adopting their choice."

"They are far more harmonious than the general population," said Tulos. "The ability to communicate in such a pure, unimpeded manner eliminates the discord and cynicism you and I both deplore."

"It also eliminates plurality. These volunteers are so similar to one another in thought and deed I can scarcely tell one apart from the whole."

"Ridiculous," said Ciparxa. "At any rate, implantation of the neuroprocessor will be a voluntary action. No one will be coerced into joining."

"Not at first, perhaps," said Vorlkai. "But by disposing of heterogeneity of thought, your interlinked drones will come to believe they embody perfection, thus giving rise to megalomania. Havarrnus cannot endure such madness and survive."

"You will continue to stall the Interlinkage Act in Tertiary, then?" asked Ciparxa.

"Indeed. This measure was brought up in haste; it gained support without consideration. The people need more time, but they will come to see through this doomed scheme."

"I can see there will be no persuading you, Vorlkai," said Sivdar. She had a distant look in her eyes, and Vorlkai realized she was consulting her own neuroprocessor. "But it doesn't matter now. I have just been informed we have the necessary votes in the Primary Session to abolish the Forum on Aesthetics." She turned to look again at the crystalline slab. "It appears, in fact, to be your own actions that are doomed."

Closing time was near, and only a few people were left in Ten-Forward. Guinan looked up from the bar. Picard was still standing by one of the large windows, contemplating the blood-tinged planet beyond the transparent aluminum. He had been like that for some time, and Guinan had felt it best to leave him alone. Now, however, she decided to approach him.

"It's not my first choice for a vacation spot," she said, drawing up behind Picard. "But maybe I've been quick to judge. I'm thinking of going down with the next away team. I have a hunch the sunsets are spectacular."

Picard looked up, and smiled. "We're not really seeing the planet at its best. The tourist season ended hundreds of thousands of years ago." He returned his gaze to the window. "At

any rate, we'll be leaving soon. I've received word from
Starfleet Command: there's been another incident within the
Neutral Zone, and tensions are mounting. We're needed to re-
lieve the *Archer.*"

"It must be frustrating, to leave before you've finished your
work here."

"No," said Picard, shaking his head. "I've failed in that effort. I
haven't been able to find anything that would help the Federation."

"Yet you sound reluctant to leave."

Picard stared at his reflection in the window. "I thought I knew
these people, Guinan. I believed cruelty and single-mindedness
was all there was to them. It's only now that I can perceive how
wrong I was. Only now do I understand the full scope of the
tragedy that occurred here."

"Your friend from the journals."

"Yes. Vorlkai was one of the last of his people who tried to hold
on to everything his civilization had stood for and accomplished."

"He wasn't able to convince anyone of his cause?"

"The later journal entries are too damaged for us to determine
what eventually happened to him. But in the end we know what became of Havarrnus."

They both stood there, looking at the stricken orb below.

"The only thing more tragic than a dead world," said Guinan, "is
the legacy of a people who've forgotten who they are."

Vorlkai lifted the cutter and pondered where the laser should
make the next incision into the crystal. His gaze kept returning to the
viewplate—the Interlinkage Act was being passed by an over-
whelming margin. Sivdar was already down on the floor of the Primary Chamber, proudly declaring a new age of community and
understanding.

Vorlkai set the cutter down and left the workshop. He climbed
the building's stairs until he came to the roof, and then stepped out
onto the viewing promontory. He looked out upon a landscape he
had contemplated a thousand times, and as his eyes welled with

tears, the mountains, cities, and forests of his world blurred and dissolved.

Picard and Troi entered through the central archway. Here, about fifty meters below the planet's surface, the searing heat from Havarrnus' sun was more tolerable, at least to the point it caused the environmental suits' life-support controls no difficulty. The two used their spotlights to pass between looming columns, and make their way to the center of the dark and crumbling hall.

"This was the Tertiary Chamber, where the Forum on Aesthetics was held," said Picard. "It was also a museum of sorts, where they could display their greatest artworks. There were once sculptures, friezes, and paintings all throughout here."

"Do you think Vorlkai's sculpture was ever displayed here?" asked Troi.

"He was a tenacious and hopeful being. I'd like to think he did eventually finish his sculpture, and display it, hoping that one day his people would understand what he had been trying to tell them."

"It's still hard to believe, that a society so accomplished could have forsaken everything it valued."

Picard nodded. "Passage of the Interlinkage Act was only the first step in creating the Borg. But while we may never be able to fully reconstruct the events that generated the Collective, I nevertheless think I understand now why they occurred. These people forgot that the greatest resource they had, the solution to whatever problems beset them as a society, laid within themselves. Their downfall was inevitable."

Picard climbed a few short steps to the dais. "Speakers would address the forum from here," he said. "Vorlkai must have stood in this place countless times."

He removed an item that had been found with Vorlkai's journals from one of the suit pockets. He knelt and placed the photon collector on the floor. In a moment, the chamber was suffused with light. The rays of Havarrnus' sun as Vorlkai had known it.

"It's fortunate we came here when we did," said Troi. "Data tells me that the sun is about to enter another period of expansion. In a few decades the surface layers of Havarrnus will melt, erasing every trace of this civilization."

"Yes," said Picard. "At least now that we have come, we can remember them. For their true selves." He looked around the chamber once more, then stood and called for the transporter. The two witnesses sparkled and faded away, leaving the room bathed in the light of its former glory for one last time.

Contest Rules

1) ENTRY REQUIREMENTS:
No purchase necessary to enter. Enter by submitting your story as specified below.

2) CONTEST ELIGIBILITY:
This contest is open to nonprofessional writers who are legal residents of the United States and Canada (excluding Quebec) over the age of 18. Entrant must not have published any more than two short stories on a professional basis or in paid professional venues. Employees (or relatives of employees living in the same household) of Simon & Schuster, VIACOM, or any of their affiliates are not eligible. This contest is void in Puerto Rico and wherever prohibited by law.

3) FORMAT:
Entries should be no more than 7,500 words long and must not have been previously published. They must be typed or printed by

word processor, double spaced, on one side of noncorrasable paper. Do not justify right-side margins. The author's name, address, e-mail address, and phone number must appear on the first page of the entry. The author's name, the story title, and the page number should appear on every page. No electronic or disk submissions will be accepted. All entries must be original and the sole work of the Entrant and the sole property of the Entrant.

4) ADDRESS:

Each entry must be mailed to:

STRANGE NEW WORLDS VIII
Star Trek Department
Pocket Books
1230 Sixth Avenue
New York, NY 10020

Each entry must be submitted only once. Please retain a copy of your submission. You may submit more than one story, but each submission must be mailed separately. Enclose a self-addressed, stamped envelope if you wish your entry returned. Entries must be received by October 1, 2004. Not responsible for lost, late, stolen, postage due, or misdirected mail.

5) PRIZES:

One Grand Prize Winner will receive:

Simon & Schuster's *Star Trek: Strange New Worlds VIII* Publishing Contract for Publication of Winning Entry in our *Strange New Worlds VIII* Anthology with a bonus advance of One Thousand Dollars ($1,000.00) above the Anthology word rate of 10 cents a word.

One Second Prize winner will receive:

Simon & Schuster's *Star Trek: Strange New Worlds VIII* Publishing Contract for Publication of Winning Entry in our *Strange New Worlds VIII* Anthology with a bonus advance of Six Hundred Dollars ($600.00) above the Anthology word rate of 10 cents a word.

One Third Prize winner will receive:

Simon & Schuster's *Star Trek: Strange New Worlds VIII* Publishing Contract for Publication of Winning Entry in our *Strange New Worlds VIII* Anthology with a bonus advance of Four Hundred Dollars ($400.00) above the Anthology word rate of 10 cents a word.

All Honorable Mention winners will receive:

Simon & Schuster's *Star Trek: Strange New Worlds VIII* Publishing Contract for Publication of Winning Entry in the *Strange New Worlds VIII* Anthology and payment at the Anthology word rate of 10 cents a word.

There will be no more than twenty (20) Honorable Mention winners. No contestant can win more than one prize.

Each Prize Winner will also be entitled to a share of royalties on the *Strange New Worlds VIII* Anthology as specified in Simon & Schuster's *Star Trek: Strange New Worlds VIII* Publishing Contract.

6) JUDGING:

Submissions will be judged on the basis of writing ability and the originality of the story, which can be set in any of the *Star Trek* time frames and may feature any one or more of the *Star Trek* characters. The judges shall include the editor of the Anthology, one employee of Pocket Books, and one employee of VIACOM Consumer Products. The decisions of the judges shall be final. All prizes will be awarded provided a sufficient number of entries are received that meet the minimum criteria established by the judges.

7) NOTIFICATION:

The winners will be notified by mail or phone. The winners who win a publishing contract must sign the publishing contract in order to be awarded the prize. All federal, local, and state taxes are the responsibility of the winner. A list of the winners will be available after January 1, 2005 on the Pocket Books *Star Trek* Books Web site,

> http: www.simonsays.com/startrek

or the names of the winners can be obtained after January 1, 2005 by sending a self-addressed, stamped envelope and a request for the list of winners to

WINNERS' LIST
STRANGE NEW WORLDS VIII
Star Trek Department
Pocket Books
1230 Sixth Avenue
New York, NY 10020

8) STORY DISQUALIFICATIONS:

Certain types of stories will be disqualified from consideration:

a) Any story focusing on explicit sexual activity or graphic depictions of violence or sadism.

b) Any story that focuses on characters that are not past or present *Star Trek* regulars or familiar *Star Trek* guest characters.

c) Stories that deal with the previously unestablished death of a *Star Trek* character, or that establish major facts about or make major changes in the life of a major character, for instance a story that establishes a long-lost sibling or reveals the hidden passion two characters feel for each other.

d) Stories that are based around common clichés, such as "hurt/comfort" where a character is injured and lovingly cared for, or "Mary Sue" stories where a new character comes on the ship and outdoes the crew.

9) PUBLICITY:

Each Winner grants to Pocket Books the right to use his or her name, likeness, and entry for any advertising, promotion, and publicity purposes without further compensation to or permission from such winner, except where prohibited by law.

10) LEGAL STUFF:

All entries and any copyrights therein become the property of Pocket Books and of Paramount Pictures, the sole and exclusive owner of the *Star Trek* property and elements thereof. Entries will be returned only if they are accompanied by a self-addressed, stamped envelope. Contest void where prohibited by law.

About the Contributors

Kelly Cairo ("Adventures in Jazz and Time") is proud to return to *SNW* following her previous contribution to *SNWII*. She lives in the Phoenix area with her husband, Jeff, and children, Alex and Michael. Kelly is a communications consultant specializing in writing and publication design. She is also an avid knitter and quilter, and fancies herself a decent conga drum player.

Anne E. Clements ("Infinite Bureaucracy") lives in central Illinois, where she has a surprisingly congenial day job as a programmer/analyst. Last spring, certain (temporary) developments had her wandering around muttering "infinite bureaucracy in infinite combination," and since very few people there would get the joke, she decided to use the idea for one of this year's *SNW* submissions. It ended up being her first sale. She is also finishing up (honest!) a novel in her own universe, as well as some short stories in the same setting, but will continue sending in *SNW* stories as long as she is

qualified. She has a son who tolerates her strangeness (having inherited his own brand of it), most excellent parents from whom she
inherited same, and two cats.

John Coffren ("Future Shock") has published nonfiction with the
Washington Post and the *Baltimore Sun*. He calls Reisterstown,
Maryland, home with wife Joanie, sons Jack and Evan, and dogs
Maggie and Pierre. Still in a state of shock, he would like to thank
those responsible: Dean, John, Elisa, and Paula.

Russ Crossley ("Barclay Program Nine") lives in Vancouver, B.C.,
with his wife Rita, son Glenn, dog Simon, and cat Sultan. He's been
writing for many years and is thrilled to be in *SNW* again. He's a
graduate of the Oregon Coast Professional Fiction Writers Master
Class and is currently working on his seventh novel.

Pat Detmer ("A Sucker Born") is older than Martian dirt and lives in
the Seattle area with her understanding and patient non-fan husband, and she proudly admits that she has in her possession every
one of the original series novelizations written by James Blish, first
printing: 1967. She thanks Dean, John, Elisa, and Paula for the obvious reasons, and also thanks Gene Roddenberry for dreaming up
a great universe and great characters that made writing about them
a joy.

Christian Grainger ("Project Blue Book") lives in Massachusetts
with the hope of becoming a full-time writer. He works as an assistant manager at a video game store. This is his first professional
short story sale. His success here is due to the support of his mother
and his friends, Joe, Jane, Jennifer, Kim, and Annie.

Brett Hudgins ("Guardians"), after having stories published in both
Cat Crimes Through Time and *SNW VI* anthologies, earns *SNW* in-
eligibility with this, his third professional sale. Thanks to his
friends and supporters for their encouragement, and to Rush for

music to work by. Brett hopes his many other short story and novel projects will prove as fulfilling as his *SNW* experiences. He lives in Richmond, B.C.

Julie A. Hyzy ("Life's Work") marks her final appearance in *SNW VII* with "Life's Work." Having happened upon the message boards dedicated to *SNW* about five years ago, she's learned much from Dean's online commentary. She writes every day and has recently expanded her horizons into mystery writing. Her first novel, *Artistic License,* a romantic suspense, will debut in 2004. She's very grateful to everyone who supports *SNW*. It's been a wonderful experience.

Jeff D. Jacques ("Beginnings") toils away as a self-employed desktop publisher in Ottawa, Canada, where he has lived all his life. Jeff previously co-wrote "Kristin's Conundrum" for *SNW V* and is thrilled to be returning to the *Trek* fold with this solo effort. Go Queue!

Jim Johnson ("Solemn Duty") lives in northern Virginia with his beautiful (and patient and understanding!) wife Andi, four cats, and two horses. When he's not writing fiction, he's tending to any number of other writing endeavors, including stage plays, screenplays, comic book scripts, freelance work for Decipher, Inc.'s *The Lord of the Rings Roleplaying Game,* and a novel series that's impatiently waiting to be written. Jim would like to offer heartfelt thanks to his family for their love and unconditional support. Thanks also go out to all the members of his Yahoo! *SNW* Writers group (http://groups.yahoo.com/group/SNW_Writers) and the Queue Continuum on AOL for their inspiration, advice, and conversation. "Solemn Duty" is his first professional fiction sale.

Paul J. Kaplan ("The Trouble with Tribals") remains an unrepentant tool of the Man, practicing evil big-firm law in Atlanta. This is his second appearance in *SNW*. He's as surprised as you are.

About the Contributors

Kevin Killiany ("Indomitable") is a minister and community college instructor who years ago told his wife Valerie that he wanted to be a writer. She replied: "It's your dream; make it work." This year his third story in *SNW,* his first *Trek* e-book ("Orphans") and his first non-*Trek* stories are being released. Thank you, Valerie, Alethea, Anson, and Daya, for sticking with me. Thanks also to Dean and the entire *Trek* writing community for freely sharing how it's done.

Frederick Kim ("Forgotten Light") lives in Los Angeles, California. He recently wrote a teleplay for the TV series *The Dead Zone* that won Third Prize in the Scriptapalooza writing competition. Currently he is working on original fiction while waiting to hear if the editors at Marvel Comics will publish a story he wrote for them. "Forgotten Light" is his first professional sale. He'd like to thank his brother, Walter, for being willing to read all of its various drafts.

Kevin Lauderdale ("A Test of Character") has published a wide variety of nonfiction, ranging from newspaper articles to encyclopedia entries, but this is his first fiction sale. He lives in northern Virginia with his wife, two daughters, and one dog. He is hard at work on more *SNW* stories and a murder mystery set in an alternate-universe version of his alma mater, UCLA.

Gerri Leen ("Obligations Discharged") was once a Seattle native but now lives in northern Virginia. She grew up watching classic *Star Trek* and is thrilled that her first professional sale is an original series story. She thanks Lisa and Kathryn for all their input and support. This is for her mom, who always encouraged her to write but didn't live to see her do it.

Muri McCage ("All Fall Down") discovered *Star Trek* by picking up one of the novels on a whim. The whim unleashed a dormant writing bug, to the point that she is currently working on an original novel, a screenplay, and a poetry collection. In her spare time, she enjoys reading everything from Virginia Woolf to *Star Trek*, though not in the original Klingon. Yet.

Susan S. McCrackin ("Redux") lives and works in northern Virginia. This is her first professional sale. Susan is grateful for the help and support of friends who have cajoled, cheered, and beta-read her stories throughout the years. She is currently editing her novel and hoping that someone besides her loyal friends will like it.

Scott Pearson ("Full Circle") lives in St. Paul, Minnesota, with his wife, Sandra, and six-year-old daughter, Ella. A raving *Star Trek* fan for more than thirty years, he swears it was only by chance that he married Sandra on September 8, 1995, the twenty-ninth anniversary of the broadcast of the first episode.

Catherine E. Pike ("The Little Captain") This is Catherine's second appearance in the *SNW* anthologies. Her short story "Fragment" was in *SNW V*. Catherine lives in Signal Hill, California, with a poodle and three cats, and works as a dispatch supervisor for a large police department. Thanks to Anita, Annette, Kathy, Li, and Rich for their encouragement.

Annie Reed ("Don't Cry") lives in northern Nevada with her extremely patient and understanding husband and daughter. This is her second appearance in *SNW*. She wants to thank: Dean, Elisa, Paula, and John for the opportunity; her family for giving her time, space, and encouragement to write; the incredible Oregon Coast Writers (you guys rock!); the incomparable Melissa for her faith (and insightful story analysis); and especially road trip buddy Louisa Swann, who also appears in this volume.

Amy Sisson ("The Law of Averages") a recently minted librarian, currently lives in Houston with her NASA husband, Paul Abell, and a collection of ex-stray cats. She wishes to thank Rob Cho, who took her to her first SF convention and got her hooked on *Star Trek*. Amy is a graduate of the Clarion West class of 2000.

Louisa M. Swann ("Earthquake Weather") lives on eighty acres in northern California with her husband and son, along with an assortment of critters and no electricity. This is Louisa's third and final appearance in the *SNW* anthologies, and she wants to thank the powers that be (Dean, John, Elisa, and Paula) for the opportunity to be part of the wonderful *SNW* family. Thanks also go out to all her OCPFWW and WAM cohorts as well as Jim and Brandon for hanging in there, Annie Reed for being a faithful road buddy, AlphaDoc for mental support, and all the readers who help make *SNW* successful. See you among the stars!

G. Wood ("I Have Broken the Prime Directive") also contributed to *SNW III* ("Dorian's Diary") and *SNW VI* ("A Piece of the Pie"). Guy is a computer programmer who lives in Windsor, Ontario, Canada. He is greatly blessed by this third and final appearance in these pages.